H.P. LOVECRAFT

THE MASTERWORKS

VOL. 1

H.P. LOVECRAFT

THE MASTERWORKS

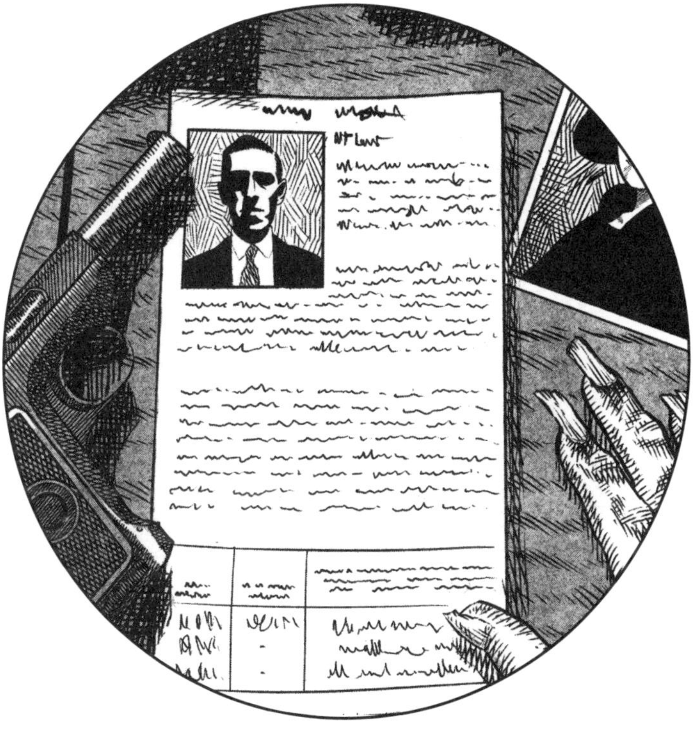

VOL. 1

Published 2024 by Passage Classics, an imprint of Passage Publishing

Cover art by Wide Dog

Story illustrations and key cover art by Alex Wisner

Printed in the United States of America

For information, contact support@passage.press

ISBN: 978-1-959403-27-2

Passage Publishing
www.passage.press

CONTENTS

Publisher's Note

Howard Phillips Lovecraft was born to a wealthy family on August 20, 1890 in Providence, Rhode Island. At a young age, his father was institutionalized for dementia, likely caused by syphilis. His grandfather, whose business supported the entire Lovecraft family, died soon thereafter, and the family fortune vanished with him. Lovecraft lived with his mother until she suffered her own mental breakdown and had to be institutionalized. Sickly, both physically and mentally, and reduced to poverty, Lovecraft turned to writing as an escape from his increasingly bleak reality.

Though Lovecraft's formal education was sporadic due to his family's circumstances, his maternal grandfather, Whipple Van Buren Phillips, encouraged him at a young age to explore the classics, along with modern astronomy and science. Lovecraft was a quick study. He was a voracious reader and soon turned his attention to more contemporary writers like Edgar Allen Poe, whose influence persisted throughout Lovecraft's career.

Lovecraft began writing as an amateur journalist while also experimenting in fiction and poetry during World War I. After the war, he became a fixture in East Coast literary circles, first as a critic and commenter, and eventually writing his own full-length stories. Lovecraft grew to modest prominence after moving to New York in 1924 where he started the intellectual salon, the Kalem Club, and began publishing in *Weird Tales*, a fantasy and horror magazine that would be home to the bulk of Lovecraft's mid-period work.

Lovecraft was a master of mood and illusion. His stories, which nearly all take place in New England, are uniquely haunting. They combine elements of horror, pulp detective stories, and allusions to the classic texts and thinkers Lovecraft studied as a young man. Perhaps no other American writer could draw so completely from the high, the low, and the utterly alien.

Although his work was well received during his lifetime, Lovecraft was never able to financially support himself through his writing. He died in relative obscurity on March 15, 1937 at the age of 46, succumbing to intestinal cancer he was too poor to have properly treated.

Despite muted enthusiasm for his later works, including his novel *The Shadow over Innsmouth* which sold just 200 copies of its initial print run, Lovecraft's stature steadily rose in the decades after his death. Friends and admirers dedicated themselves to disseminating Lovecraft's writing. Scholars and literary critics began to recognize the vast literary genius layered beneath the works' pulpy façade. By the 1960s, Lovecraft was generally recognized as one of America's greatest writers, the godfather of pulp, and on par with his hero Edgar Allen Poe as the standard bearer of American horror.

His growing critical reputation has since been helped along by a series of legal idiosyncrasies that allowed his entire catalog to fall into public domain decades before it otherwise would have. Since the mid-20th century, countless movies, radio programs, and television shows have adapted his stories, or have cribbed so heavily from them that they're functionally indistinguishable. The pervasiveness of Lovecraft's influence cannot be overstated. Perhaps no other writer casts such a large shadow over American culture.

Despite Lovecraft's outsized impact, starting in the 1990s, he began to fall out of favor in certain quarters of American life due to his views on race and religion. Once a mainstay on college curriculums, Lovecraft was quietly removed from reading lists and English department coursework. Cynical "reevaluations" of his legacy soon followed, accompanied by petty personal attacks and attempts to shame people for uncritically promoting his work. Such politically-motivated responses to Lovecraft continue to this day, but are little more than a whimper in relation to the enormous ongoing admiration he inspires.

Our hope with this collection is to carry on Lovecraft's legacy and (re)introduce his work to another generation of readers. His work is timeless, in the most literal sense. It reaches back into the ancient past and forward into the infinite future. These stories are as potent now as they have ever been, and will terrify, thrill, and transform readers for as long as they stay in print.

Thank you for reading.

The Music of Erich Zann

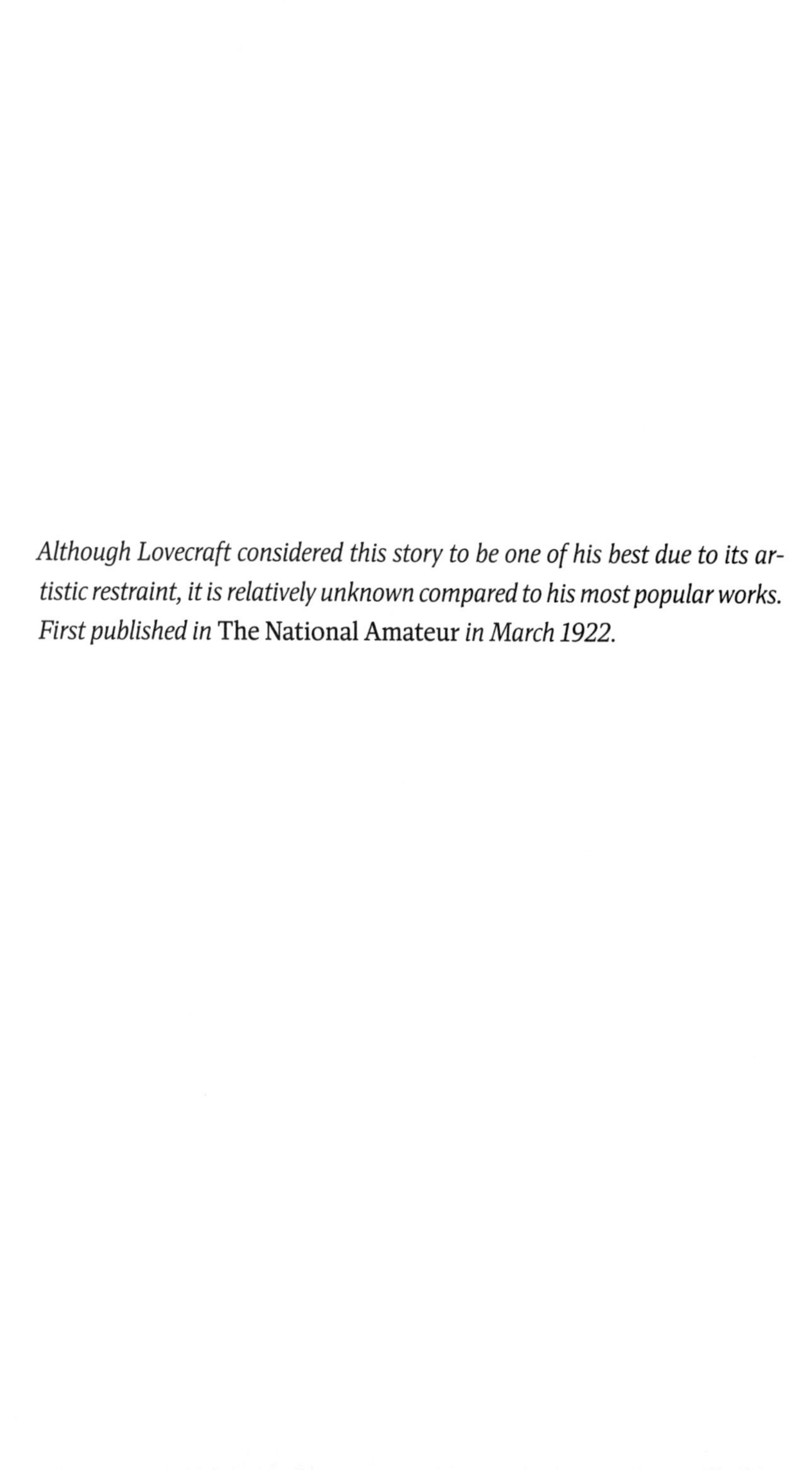

Although Lovecraft considered this story to be one of his best due to its artistic restraint, it is relatively unknown compared to his most popular works. First published in The National Amateur *in March 1922.*

I have examined maps of the city with the greatest care, yet have never again found the Rue d'Auseil. These maps have not been modern maps alone, for I know that names change. I have, on the contrary, delved deeply into all the antiquities of the place; and have personally explored every region, of whatever name, which could possibly answer to the street I knew as the Rue d'Auseil. But despite all I have done it remains an humiliating fact that I cannot find the house, the street, or even the locality, where, during the last months of my impoverished life as a student of metaphysics at the university, I heard the music of Erich Zann.

That my memory is broken, I do not wonder; for my health, physical and mental, was gravely disturbed throughout the period of my residence in the Rue d'Auseil, and I recall that I took none of my few acquaintances there. But that I cannot find the place again is both singular and perplexing; for it was within a half-hour's walk of the university and was distinguished by peculiarities which could hardly be forgotten by anyone who had been there. I have never met a person who has seen the Rue d'Auseil.

The Rue d'Auseil lay across a dark river bordered by precipitous brick blear-windowed warehouses and spanned by a ponderous bridge of dark stone. It was always shadowy along that river, as if the smoke of neighbouring factories shut out the sun perpetually. The river was also odorous with evil stenches which I have never smelled elsewhere, and which may some day help me to find it, since I should recognise them at once. Beyond the bridge were narrow cobbled streets with rails; and then came the ascent, at first gradual, but incredibly steep as the Rue d'Auseil was reached.

I have never seen another street as narrow and steep as the Rue d'Auseil. It was almost a cliff, closed to all vehicles, consisting in several places of flights of steps, and ending at the top in a lofty ivied wall. Its paving was irregular, sometimes stone slabs, sometimes cobblestones, and sometimes bare earth with struggling greenish-grey vegetation. The houses were tall, peaked-roofed, incredibly old, and crazily leaning backward, forward, and sidewise. Occasionally an opposite pair, both leaning forward, almost met across the street like an arch; and certainly they kept most of the light from the ground below. There were a few overhead bridges from house to house across the street.

The inhabitants of that street impressed me peculiarly. At first I thought it was because they were all silent and reticent; but later decided it was because they were all very old. I do not know how I came to live on such a street, but I was not myself when I moved there. I had been living in many poor places, always evicted for want of money; until at last I came upon that tottering house in the Rue d'Auseil, kept by the paralytic Blandot. It was the third house from the top of the street, and by far the tallest of them all.

My room was on the fifth story; the only inhabited room there, since the house was almost empty. On the night I arrived I heard strange music from the peaked garret overhead, and the next day asked old Blandot about it. He told me it was an old German viol-player, a strange dumb man who signed his name as Erich Zann, and who played evenings in a cheap theatre orchestra; adding that Zann's desire to play in the night after his return from the theatre was the reason he had chosen this lofty and isolated garret room, whose single gable window was the only point on the street from which one could look over the terminating wall at the declivity and panorama beyond.

Thereafter I heard Zann every night, and although he kept me awake, I was haunted by the weirdness of his music. Knowing little of the art myself, I was yet certain that none of his harmonies had any relation to music I had heard before; and concluded that he was a composer of highly original genius. The longer I listened, the more I was fascinated, until after a week I resolved to make the old man's acquaintance.

One night, as he was returning from his work, I intercepted Zann in the hallway and told him that I would like to know him and be with him when he played. He was a small, lean, bent person, with shabby clothes, blue eyes, grotesque, satyr-like face, and nearly bald head; and at my first words seemed both angered and frightened. My obvious friendliness, however, finally melted him; and he grudgingly motioned to me to follow him up the dark, creaking, and rickety attic stairs. His room, one of only two in the steeply pitched garret, was on the west side, toward the high wall that formed the upper end of the street. Its size was very great, and seemed the greater because of its extraordinary bareness and neglect. Of furniture there was only a narrow iron bedstead, a dingy washstand, a small table, a large bookcase, an iron music-rack, and three old-fashioned chairs. Sheets of music were piled in disorder about the floor. The walls were of bare boards, and had probably never known plaster; whilst the abundance of dust and cobwebs made the place seem more deserted than inhabited. Evidently Erich Zann's world of beauty lay in some far cosmos of the imagination.

Motioning me to sit down, the dumb man closed the door, turned the large wooden bolt, and lighted a candle to augment the one he had brought with him. He now removed his viol from its moth-eaten covering, and taking it, seated himself in the least uncomfortable of the chairs. He did not employ the music-rack, but offering no choice and playing from memory, enchanted me for over an hour with strains I had never heard before; strains which must have been of his own devising. To describe their exact nature is impossible for one unversed in music. They were a kind of fugue, with recurrent passages of the most captivating quality, but to me were notable for the absence of any of the weird notes I had overheard from my room below on other occasions.

Those haunting notes I had remembered, and had often hummed and whistled inaccurately to myself; so when the player at length laid down his bow I asked him if he would render some of them. As I began my request the wrinkled satyr-like face lost the bored placidity it had possessed during the playing, and seemed to shew the same curious mixture of anger and fright which I had noticed when first I accosted the old man. For a moment I was inclined to use persuasion, regarding rather lightly the whims of senility; and even tried to awaken my host's weirder mood by whistling a few of the strains to which I had listened the night before. But I did not pursue this course for more than a moment; for when the dumb musician recognised the whistled air his face grew suddenly distorted with an expression wholly beyond analysis, and his long, cold, bony right hand reached out to stop my mouth and silence the crude imitation. As he did this he further demonstrated his eccentricity by casting a startled glance toward the lone curtained window, as if fearful of some intruder—a glance doubly absurd, since the garret stood high and inaccessible above all the adjacent roofs, this window being the only point on the steep street, as the concierge had told me, from which one could see over the wall at the summit.

The old man's glance brought Blandot's remark to my mind, and with a certain capriciousness I felt a wish to look out over the wide and dizzying panorama of moonlit roofs and city lights beyond the hill-top, which of all the dwellers in the Rue d'Auseil only this crabbed musician could see. I moved toward the window and would have drawn aside the nondescript curtains, when with a frightened rage even greater than before the dumb lodger was upon me again; this time motioning with his head toward the door as he nervously strove to drag me thither with both hands. Now thoroughly disgusted with my host, I ordered him to release me, and told him I would go at once. His clutch relaxed, and as he saw my disgust and offence his own anger seemed to subside. He tightened his relaxing grip, but this time in a friendly manner; forcing me into a chair, then with an appearance of wistfulness crossing to the littered table, where he wrote many words with a pencil in the laboured French of a foreigner.

The note which he finally handed me was an appeal for tolerance and forgiveness. Zann said that he was old, lonely, and afflicted with strange fears and nervous disorders connected with his music and with other things. He had enjoyed my listening to his music, and wished I would come again and not mind his eccentricities. But he could not play to another his weird harmonies, and could not bear hearing them from another; nor could he bear having anything in his room touched by another. He had not known until our hallway conversation that I could overhear his playing in my room, and now asked me if I would arrange with Blandot to take a lower room where I could not hear him in the night. He would, he wrote, defray the difference in rent.

As I sat deciphering the execrable French I felt more lenient toward the old man. He was a victim of physical and nervous suffering, as was I; and my metaphysical studies had taught me kindness. In the silence there came a slight sound from the window—the shutter must have rattled in the night-wind—and for some reason I started almost as violently as did Erich Zann. So when I had finished reading I shook my host by the hand, and departed as a friend. The next day Blandot gave me a more expensive room on the third floor, between the apartments of an aged money-lender and the room of a respectable upholsterer. There was no one on the fourth floor.

It was not long before I found that Zann's eagerness for my company was not as great as it had seemed while he was persuading me to move down from the fifth story. He did not ask me to call on him, and when I did call he appeared uneasy and played listlessly. This was always at night—in the day he slept and would admit no one. My liking for him did not grow, though the attic room and the weird music seemed to hold an odd fascination for me. I had a curious desire to look out of that window, over the wall and down the unseen slope at the glittering roofs and spires which must lie outspread there. Once I went up to the garret during theatre hours, when Zann was away, but the door was locked.

What I did succeed in doing was to overhear the nocturnal playing of the dumb old man. At first I would tiptoe up to my old fifth floor, then I grew bold enough to climb the last creaking staircase to the peaked garret. There in the narrow hall, outside the bolted door with the covered keyhole, I often heard sounds which filled me with an indefinable dread—the dread of vague wonder and brooding mystery. It was not that the sounds were hideous, for they were not; but that they held vibrations suggesting nothing on this globe of earth, and that at certain intervals they assumed a symphonic quality which I could hardly conceive as produced by one player. Certainly, Erich Zann was a genius of wild power. As the weeks passed, the playing grew wilder, whilst the old musician acquired an increasing haggardness and furtiveness pitiful to behold. He now refused to admit me at any time, and shunned me whenever we met on the stairs.

Then one night as I listened at the door I heard the shrieking viol swell into a chaotic babel of sound; a pandemonium which would have led me to doubt my own shaking sanity had there not come from behind that barred portal a piteous proof that the horror was real—the awful, inarticulate cry which only a mute can utter, and which rises only in moments of the most terrible fear or anguish. I knocked repeatedly at the door, but received no response. Afterward I waited in the black hallway, shivering with cold and fear, till I heard the poor musician's feeble effort to rise from the floor by the aid of a chair. Believing him just conscious after a fainting fit, I renewed my rapping, at the same time calling out my name reassuringly. I heard Zann stumble to the window and close both shutter and sash, then stumble to the door, which he falteringly unfastened to admit me. This time his delight at having me present was real; for his distorted face gleamed with relief while he clutched at my coat as a child clutches at its mother's skirts.

Shaking pathetically, the old man forced me into a chair whilst he sank into another, beside which his viol and bow lay carelessly on the floor. He sat for some time inactive, nodding oddly, but having a paradoxical suggestion of intense and frightened listening. Subsequently he seemed to be satisfied, and crossing to a chair by the table wrote a brief note, handed it to me, and returned to the table, where he began to write rapidly and incessantly. The note implored me in the name of mercy, and for the sake of my own curiosity, to wait where I was while he prepared a full account in German of all the marvels and terrors which beset him. I waited, and the dumb man's pencil flew.

It was perhaps an hour later, while I still waited and while the old musician's feverishly written sheets still continued to pile up, that I saw Zann start as from the hint of a horrible shock. Unmistakably he was looking at the curtained window and listening shudderingly. Then I half fancied I heard a sound myself; though it was not a horrible sound, but rather an exquisitely low and infinitely distant musical note, suggesting a player in one of the neighbouring houses, or in some abode beyond the lofty wall over which I had never been able to look. Upon Zann the effect was terrible, for dropping his pencil suddenly he rose, seized his viol, and commenced to rend the night with the wildest playing I had ever heard from his bow save when listening at the barred door.

It would be useless to describe the playing of Erich Zann on that dreadful night. It was more horrible than anything I had ever overheard, because I could now see the expression of his face, and could realise that this time the motive was stark fear. He was trying to make a noise; to ward something off or drown something out—what, I could not imagine, awesome though I felt it must be. The playing grew fantastic, delirious, and hysterical, yet kept to the last the qualities of supreme genius which I knew this strange old man possessed. I recognised the air—it was a wild Hungarian dance popular in the theatres, and I reflected for a moment that this was the first time I had ever heard Zann play the work of another composer.

Louder and louder, wilder and wilder, mounted the shrieking and whining of that desperate viol. The player was dripping with an uncanny perspiration and twisted like a monkey, always looking frantically at the curtained window. In his frenzied strains I could almost see shadowy satyrs and Bacchanals dancing and whirling insanely through seething abysses of clouds and smoke and lightning. And then I thought I heard a shriller, steadier note that was not from the viol; a calm, deliberate, purposeful, mocking note from far away in the west.

At this juncture the shutter began to rattle in a howling night-wind which had sprung up outside as if in answer to the mad playing within. Zann's screaming viol now outdid itself, emitting sounds I had never thought a viol could emit. The shutter rattled more loudly, unfastened, and commenced slamming against the window. Then the glass broke shiveringly under the persistent impacts, and the chill wind rushed in, making the candles sputter and rustling the sheets of paper on the table where Zann had begun to write out his horrible secret. I looked at Zann, and saw that he was past conscious observation. His blue eyes were bulging, glassy, and sightless, and the frantic playing had become a blind, mechanical, unrecognisable orgy that no pen could even suggest.

A sudden gust, stronger than the others, caught up the manuscript and bore it toward the window. I followed the flying sheets in desperation, but they were gone before I reached the demolished panes. Then I remembered my old wish to gaze from this window, the only window in the Rue d'Auseil from which one might see the slope beyond the wall, and the city outspread beneath. It was very dark, but the city's lights always burned, and I expected to see them there amidst the rain and wind. Yet when I looked from that highest of all gable windows, looked while the candles sputtered and the insane viol howled with the night-wind, I saw no city spread below, and no friendly lights gleaming from remembered streets, but only the blackness of space illimitable; unimagined space alive with motion and music, and having no semblance to anything on earth. And as I stood there looking in terror, the wind blew out both the candles in that ancient peaked garret, leaving me in savage and impenetrable darkness with chaos and pandemonium before me, and the daemon madness of that night-baying viol behind me.

I staggered back in the dark, without the means of striking a light, crashing against the table, overturning a chair, and finally groping my way to the place where the blackness screamed with shocking music. To save myself and Erich Zann I could at least try, whatever the powers opposed to me. Once I thought some chill thing brushed me, and I screamed, but my scream could not be heard above that hideous viol. Suddenly out of the blackness the madly sawing bow struck me, and I knew I was close to the player. I felt ahead, touched the back of Zann's chair, and then found and shook his shoulder in an effort to bring him to his senses.

He did not respond, and still the viol shrieked on without slackening. I moved my hand to his head, whose mechanical nodding I was able to stop, and shouted in his ear that we must both flee from the unknown things of the night. But he neither answered me nor abated the frenzy of his unutterable music, while all through the garret strange currents of wind seemed to dance in the darkness and babel. When my hand touched his ear I shuddered, though I knew not why—knew not why till I felt of the still face; the ice-cold, stiffened, unbreathing face whose glassy eyes bulged uselessly into the void. And then, by some miracle finding the door and the large wooden bolt, I plunged wildly away from that glassy-eyed thing in the dark, and from the ghoulish howling of that accursed viol whose fury increased even as I plunged.

Leaping, floating, flying down those endless stairs through the dark house; racing mindlessly out into the narrow, steep, and ancient street of steps and tottering houses; clattering down steps and over cobbles to the lower streets and the putrid canyon-walled river; panting across the great dark bridge to the broader, healthier streets and boulevards we know; all these are terrible impressions that linger with me. And I recall that there was no wind, and that the moon was out, and that all the lights of the city twinkled. Despite my most careful searches and investigations, I have never since been able to find the Rue d'Auseil. But I am not wholly sorry; either for this or for the loss in undreamable abysses of the closely written sheets which alone could have explained the music of Erich Zann.

Pickman's Model

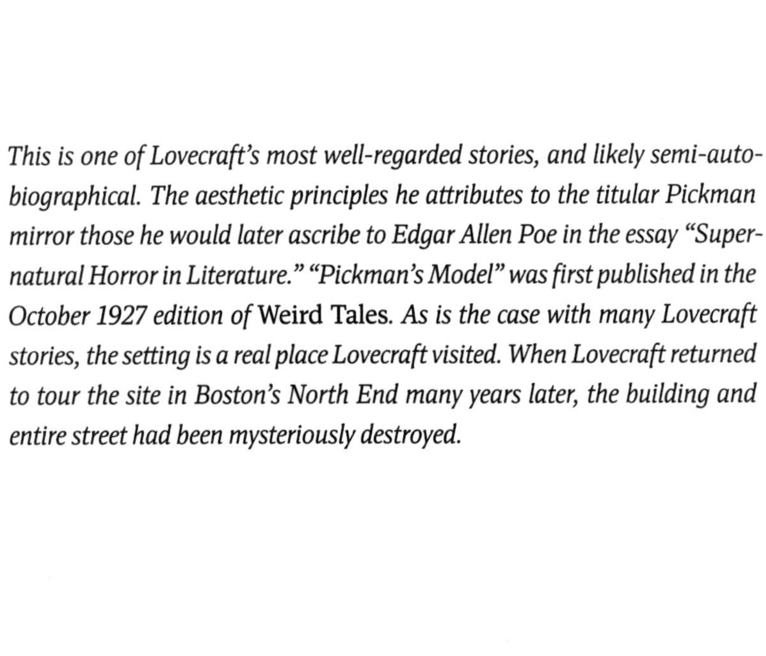

This is one of Lovecraft's most well-regarded stories, and likely semi-autobiographical. The aesthetic principles he attributes to the titular Pickman mirror those he would later ascribe to Edgar Allen Poe in the essay "Supernatural Horror in Literature." "Pickman's Model" was first published in the October 1927 edition of Weird Tales. *As is the case with many Lovecraft stories, the setting is a real place Lovecraft visited. When Lovecraft returned to tour the site in Boston's North End many years later, the building and entire street had been mysteriously destroyed.*

You needn't think I'm crazy, Eliot—plenty of others have queerer prejudices than this. Why don't you laugh at Oliver's grandfather, who won't ride in a motor? If I don't like that damned subway, it's my own business; and we got here more quickly anyhow in the taxi. We'd have had to walk up the hill from Park Street if we'd taken the car.

I know I'm more nervous than I was when you saw me last year, but you don't need to hold a clinic over it. There's plenty of reason, God knows, and I fancy I'm lucky to be sane at all. Why the third degree? You didn't use to be so inquisitive.

Well, if you must hear it, I don't know why you shouldn't. Maybe you ought to, anyhow, for you kept writing me like a grieved parent when you heard I'd begun to cut the Art Club and keep away from Pickman. Now that he's disappeared I go around to the club once in a while, but my nerves aren't what they were.

No, I don't know what's become of Pickman, and I don't like to guess. You might have surmised I had some inside information when I dropped him—and that's why I don't want to think where he's gone. Let the police find what they can—it won't be much, judging from the fact that they don't know yet of the old North End place he hired under the name of Peters. I'm not sure that I could find it again myself—not that I'd ever try, even in broad daylight! Yes, I do know, or am afraid I know, why he maintained it. I'm coming to that. And I think you'll understand before I'm through why I don't tell the police. They would ask me to guide them, but I couldn't go back there even if I knew the way. There was something there—and now I can't use the subway or (and you may as well have your laugh at this, too) go down into cellars any more.

I should think you'd have known I didn't drop Pickman for the same silly reasons that fussy old women like Dr. Reid or Joe Minot or Bosworth did. Morbid art doesn't shock me, and when a man has the genius Pickman had I feel it an honour to know him, no matter what direction his work takes. Boston never had a greater painter than Richard Upton Pickman. I said it at first and I say it still, and I never swerved an inch, either, when he shewed that "Ghoul Feeding." That, you remember, was when Minot cut him.

You know, it takes profound art and profound insight into Nature to turn out stuff like Pickman's. Any magazine-cover hack can splash paint around wildly and call it a nightmare or a Witches' Sabbath or a portrait of the devil, but only a great painter can make such a thing really scare or ring true. That's because only a real artist knows the actual anatomy of the terrible or the physiology of fear—the exact sort of lines and proportions that connect up with latent instincts or hereditary memories of fright, and the proper colour contrasts and lighting effects to stir the dormant sense of strangeness. I don't have to tell you why a Fuseli really brings a shiver while a cheap ghost-story frontispiece merely makes us laugh. There's something those fellows catch—beyond life—that they're able to make us catch for a second. Doré had it. Sime has it. Angarola of Chicago has it. And Pickman had it as no man ever had it before or—I hope to heaven—ever will again.

Don't ask me what it is they see. You know, in ordinary art, there's all the difference in the world between the vital, breathing things drawn from Nature or models and the artificial truck that commercial small fry reel off in a bare studio by rule. Well, I should say that the really weird artist has a kind of vision which makes models, or summons up what amounts to actual scenes from the spectral world he lives in. Anyhow, he manages to turn out results that differ from the pretender's mince-pie dreams in just about the same way that the life painter's results differ from the concoctions of a correspondence-school cartoonist. If I had ever seen what Pickman saw—but no! Here, let's have a drink before we get any deeper. Gad, I wouldn't be alive if I'd ever seen what that man—if he was a man—saw!

You recall that Pickman's forte was faces. I don't believe anybody since Goya could put so much of sheer hell into a set of features or a twist of expression. And before Goya you have to go back to the mediaeval chaps who did the gargoyles and chimaeras on Notre Dame and Mont Saint-Michel. They believed all sorts of things—and maybe they saw all sorts of things, too, for the Middle Ages had some curious phases. I remember your asking Pickman yourself once, the year before you went away, wherever in thunder he got such ideas and visions. Wasn't that a nasty laugh he gave you? It was partly because of that laugh that Reid dropped him. Reid, you know, had just taken up comparative pathology, and was full of pompous "inside stuff" about the biological or evolutionary significance of this or that mental or physical symptom. He said Pickman repelled him more and more every day, and almost frightened him toward the last—that the fellow's features and expression were slowly developing in a way he didn't like; in a way that wasn't human. He had a lot of talk about diet, and said Pickman must be abnormal and eccentric to the last degree. I suppose you told Reid, if you and he had any correspondence over it, that he'd let Pickman's paintings get on his nerves or harrow up his imagination. I know I told him that myself—then.

But keep in mind that I didn't drop Pickman for anything like this. On the contrary, my admiration for him kept growing; for that "Ghoul Feeding" was a tremendous achievement. As you know, the club wouldn't exhibit it, and the Museum of Fine Arts wouldn't accept it as a gift; and I can add that nobody would buy it, so Pickman had it right in his house till he went. Now his father has it in Salem—you know Pickman comes of old Salem stock, and had a witch ancestor hanged in 1692.

I got into the habit of calling on Pickman quite often, especially after I began making notes for a monograph on weird art. Probably it was his work which put the idea into my head, and anyhow, I found him a mine of data and suggestions when I came to develop it. He shewed me all the paintings and drawings he had about; including some pen-and-ink sketches that would, I verily believe, have got him kicked out of the club if many of the members had seen them. Before long I was pretty nearly a devotee, and would listen for hours like a schoolboy to art theories and philosophic speculations wild enough to qualify him for the Danvers asylum. My hero-worship, coupled with the fact that people generally were commencing to have less and less to do with him, made him get very confidential with me; and one evening he hinted that if I were fairly close-mouthed and none too squeamish, he might shew me something rather unusual—something a bit stronger than anything he had in the house.

"You know," he said, "there are things that won't do for Newbury Street—things that are out of place here, and that can't be conceived here, anyhow. It's my business to catch the overtones of the soul, and you won't find those in a parvenu set of artificial streets on made land. Back Bay isn't Boston—it isn't anything yet, because it's had no time to pick up memories and attract local spirits. If there are any ghosts here, they're the tame ghosts of a salt marsh and a shallow cove; and I want human ghosts—the ghosts of beings highly organised enough to have looked on hell and known the meaning of what they saw.

"The place for an artist to live is the North End. If any aesthete were sincere, he'd put up with the slums for the sake of the massed traditions. God, man! Don't you realise that places like that weren't merely made, but actually *grew*? Generation after generation lived and felt and died there, and in days when people weren't afraid to live and feel and die. Don't you know there was a mill on Copp's Hill in 1632, and that half the present streets were laid out by 1650? I can shew you houses that have stood two centuries and a half and more; houses that have witnessed what would make a modern house crumble into powder. What do moderns know of life and the forces behind it? You call the Salem witchcraft a delusion, but I'll wage my four-times-great-grandmother could have told you things. They hanged her on Gallows Hill, with Cotton Mather looking sanctimoniously on. Mather, damn him, was afraid somebody might succeed in kicking free of this accursed cage of monotony—I wish someone had laid a spell on him or sucked his blood in the night!

"I can shew you a house he lived in, and I can shew you another one he was afraid to enter in spite of all his fine bold talk. He knew things he didn't dare put into that stupid *Magnalia* or that puerile *Wonders of the Invisible World*. Look here, do you know the whole North End once had a set of tunnels that kept certain people in touch with each other's houses, and the burying-ground, and the sea? Let them prosecute and persecute above ground—things went on every day that they couldn't reach, and voices laughed at night that they couldn't place!

"Why, man, out of ten surviving houses built before 1700 and not moved since I'll wager that in eight I can shew you something queer in the cellar. There's hardly a month that you don't read of workmen finding bricked-up arches and wells leading nowhere in this or that old place as it comes down—you could see one near Henchman Street from the elevated last year. There were witches and what their spells summoned; pirates and what they brought in from the sea; smugglers; privateers—and I tell you, people knew how to live, and how to enlarge the bounds of life, in the old times! This wasn't the only world a bold and wise man could know—faugh! And to think of today in contrast, with such pale-pink brains that even a club of supposed artists gets shudders and convulsions if a picture goes beyond the feelings of a Beacon Street tea-table!

"The only saving grace of the present is that it's too damned stupid to question the past very closely. What do maps and records and guide-books really tell of the North End? Bah! At a guess I'll guarantee to lead you to thirty or forty alleys and networks of alleys north of Prince Street that aren't suspected by ten living beings outside of the foreigners that swarm them. And what do those Dagoes know of their meaning? No, Thurber, these ancient places are dreaming gorgeously and overflowing with wonder and terror and escapes from the commonplace, and yet there's not a living soul to understand or profit by them. Or rather, there's only one living soul—for I haven't been digging around in the past for nothing!

"See here, you're interested in this sort of thing. What if I told you that I've got another studio up there, where I can catch the night-spirit of antique horror and paint things that I couldn't even think of in Newbury Street? Naturally I don't tell those cursed old maids at the club—with Reid, damn him, whispering even as it is that I'm a sort of monster bound down the toboggan of reverse evolution. Yes, Thurber, I decided long ago that one must paint terror as well as beauty from life, so I did some exploring in places where I had reason to know terror lives.

"I've got a place that I don't believe three living Nordic men besides myself have ever seen. It isn't so very far from the elevated as distance goes, but it's centuries away as the soul goes. I took it because of the queer old brick well in the cellar—one of the sort I told you about. The shack's almost tumbling down, so that nobody else would live there, and I'd hate to tell you how little I pay for it. The windows are boarded up, but I like that all the better, since I don't want daylight for what I do. I paint in the cellar, where the inspiration is thickest, but I've other rooms furnished on the ground floor. A Sicilian owns it, and I've hired it under the name of Peters.

"Now if you're game, I'll take you there tonight. I think you'd enjoy the pictures, for as I said, I've let myself go a bit there. It's no vast tour—I sometimes do it on foot, for I don't want to attract attention with a taxi in such a place. We can take the shuttle at the South Station for Battery Street, and after that the walk isn't much."

Well, Eliot, there wasn't much for me to do after that harangue but to keep myself from running instead of walking for the first vacant cab we could sight. We changed to the elevated at the South Station, and at about twelve o'clock had climbed down the steps at Battery Street and struck along the old waterfront past Constitution Wharf. I didn't keep track of the cross streets, and can't tell you yet which it was we turned up, but I know it wasn't Greenough Lane.

When we did turn, it was to climb through the deserted length of the oldest and dirtiest alley I ever saw in my life, with crumbling-looking gables, broken small-paned windows, and archaic chimneys that stood out half-disintegrated against the moonlit sky. I don't believe there were three houses in sight that hadn't been standing in Cotton Mather's time—certainly I glimpsed at least two with an overhang, and once I thought I saw a peaked roof-line of the almost forgotten pre-gambrel type, though antiquarians tell us there are none left in Boston.

From that alley, which had a dim light, we turned to the left into an equally silent and still narrower alley with no light at all; and in a minute made what I think was an obtuse-angled bend toward the right in the dark. Not long after this Pickman produced a flashlight and revealed an antediluvian ten-panelled door that looked damnably worm-eaten. Unlocking it, he ushered me into a barren hallway with what was once splendid dark-oak panelling—simple, of course, but thrillingly suggestive of the times of Andros and Phipps and the Witchcraft. Then he took me through a door on the left, lighted an oil lamp, and told me to make myself at home.

Now, Eliot, I'm what the man in the street would call fairly "hard-boiled," but I'll confess that what I saw on the walls of that room gave me a bad turn. They were his pictures, you know—the ones he couldn't paint or even shew in Newbury Street—and he was right when he said he had "let himself go." Here—have another drink—I need one anyhow!

There's no use in my trying to tell you what they were like, because the awful, the blasphemous horror, and the unbelievable loathsomeness and moral foetor came from simple touches quite beyond the power of words to classify. There was none of the exotic technique you see in Sidney Sime, none of the trans-Saturnian landscapes and lunar fungi that Clark Ashton Smith uses to freeze the blood. The backgrounds were mostly old churchyards, deep woods, cliffs by the sea, brick tunnels, ancient panelled rooms, or simple vaults of masonry. Copp's Hill Burying Ground, which could not be many blocks away from this very house, was a favourite scene.

The madness and monstrosity lay in the figures in the foreground—for Pickman's morbid art was preëminently one of daemoniac portraiture. These figures were seldom completely human, but often approached humanity in varying degree. Most of the bodies, while roughly bipedal, had a forward slumping, and a vaguely canine cast. The texture of the majority was a kind of unpleasant rubberiness. Ugh! I can see them now! Their occupations—well, don't ask me to be too precise. They were usually feeding—I won't say on what. They were sometimes shewn in groups in cemeteries or underground passages, and often appeared to be in battle over their prey—or rather, their treasure-trove. And what damnable expressiveness Pickman sometimes gave the sightless faces of this charnel booty! Occasionally the things were shewn leaping through open windows at night, or squatting on the chests of sleepers, worrying at their throats. One canvas shewed a ring of them baying about a hanged witch on Gallows Hill, whose dead face held a close kinship to theirs.

But don't get the idea that it was all this hideous business of theme and setting which struck me faint. I'm not a three-year-old kid, and I'd seen much like this before. It was the *faces*, Eliot, those accursed *faces*, that leered and slavered out of the canvas with the very breath of life! By God, man, I verily believe they were alive! That nauseous wizard had waked the fires of hell in pigment, and his brush had been a nightmare-spawning wand. Give me that decanter, Eliot!

There was one thing called "The Lesson"—heaven pity me, that I ever saw it! Listen—can you fancy a squatting circle of nameless dog-like things in a churchyard teaching a small child how to feed like themselves? The price of a changeling, I suppose—you know the old myth about how the weird people leave their spawn in cradles in exchange for the human babes they steal. Pickman was shewing what happens to those stolen babes—how they grow up—and then I began to see a hideous relationship in the faces of the human and non-human figures. He was, in all his gradations of morbidity between the frankly non-human and the degradedly human, establishing a sardonic linkage and evolution. The dog-things were developed from mortals!

And no sooner had I wondered what he made of their own young as left with mankind in the form of changelings, than my eye caught a picture embodying that very thought. It was that of an ancient Puritan interior—a heavily beamed room with lattice windows, a settle, and clumsy seventeenth-century furniture, with the family sitting about while the father read from the Scriptures. Every face but one shewed nobility and reverence, but that one reflected the mockery of the pit. It was that of a young man in years, and no doubt belonged to a supposed son of that pious father, but in essence it was the kin of the unclean things. It was their changeling—and in a spirit of supreme irony Pickman had given the features a very perceptible resemblance to his own.

By this time Pickman had lighted a lamp in an adjoining room and was politely holding open the door for me; asking me if I would care to see his "modern studies." I hadn't been able to give him much of my opinions—I was too speechless with fright and loathing—but I think he fully understood and felt highly complimented. And now I want to assure you again, Eliot, that I'm no mollycoddle to scream at anything which shews a bit of departure from the usual. I'm middle-aged and decently sophisticated, and I guess you saw enough of me in France to know I'm not easily knocked out. Remember, too, that I'd just about recovered my wind and gotten used to those frightful pictures which turned colonial New England into a kind of annex of hell. Well, in spite of all this, that next room forced a real scream out of me, and I had to clutch at the doorway to keep from keeling over. The other chamber had shewn a pack of ghouls and witches overrunning the world of our forefathers, but this one brought the horror right into our own daily life!

Gad, how that man could paint! There was a study called "Subway Accident," in which a flock of the vile things were clambering up from some unknown catacomb through a crack in the floor of the Boylston Street subway and attacking a crowd of people on the platform. Another shewed a dance on Copp's Hill among the tombs with the background of today. Then there were any number of cellar views, with monsters creeping in through holes and rifts in the masonry and grinning as they squatted behind barrels or furnaces and waited for their first victim to descend the stairs.

One disgusting canvas seemed to depict a vast cross-section of Beacon Hill, with ant-like armies of the mephitic monsters squeezing themselves through burrows that honeycombed the ground. Dances in the modern cemeteries were freely pictured, and another conception somehow shocked me more than all the rest—a scene in an unknown vault, where scores of the beasts crowded about one who held a well-known Boston guide-book and was evidently reading aloud. All were pointing to a certain passage, and every face seemed so distorted with epileptic and reverberant laughter that I almost thought I heard the fiendish echoes. The title of the picture was, "Holmes, Lowell, and Longfellow Lie Buried in Mount Auburn."

As I gradually steadied myself and got readjusted to this second room of deviltry and morbidity, I began to analyse some of the points in my sickening loathing. In the first place, I said to myself, these things repelled because of the utter inhumanity and callous cruelty they shewed in Pickman. The fellow must be a relentless enemy of all mankind to take such glee in the torture of brain and flesh and the degradation of the mortal tenement. In the second place, they terrified because of their very greatness. Their art was the art that convinced—when we saw the pictures we saw the daemons themselves and were afraid of them. And the queer part was, that Pickman got none of his power from the use of selectiveness or bizarrerie. Nothing was blurred, distorted, or conventionalised; outlines were sharp and life-like, and details were almost painfully defined. And the faces!

It was not any mere artist's interpretation that we saw; it was pandemonium itself, crystal clear in stark objectivity.

That was it, by heaven! The man was not a fantaisiste or romanticist at all—he did not even try to give us the churning, prismatic ephemera of dreams, but coldly and sardonically reflected some stable, mechanistic, and well-established horror-world which he saw fully, brilliantly, squarely, and unfalteringly. God knows what that world can have been, or where he ever glimpsed the blasphemous shapes that loped and trotted and crawled through it; but whatever the baffling source of his images, one thing was plain. Pickman was in every sense—in conception and in execution—a thorough, painstaking, and almost scientific *realist.*

My host was now leading the way down cellar to his actual studio, and I braced myself for some hellish effects among the unfinished canvases. As we reached the bottom of the damp stairs he turned his flashlight to a corner of the large open space at hand, revealing the circular brick curb of what was evidently a great well in the earthen floor. We walked nearer, and I saw that it must be five feet across, with walls a good foot thick and some six inches above the ground level—solid work of the seventeenth century, or I was much mistaken. That, Pickman said, was the kind of thing he had been talking about—an aperture of the network of tunnels that used to undermine the hill. I noticed idly that it did not seem to be bricked up, and that a heavy disc of wood formed the apparent cover. Thinking of the things this well must have been connected with if Pickman's wild hints had not been mere rhetoric, I shivered slightly; then turned to follow him up a step and through a narrow door into a room of fair size, provided with a wooden floor and furnished as a studio. An acetylene gas outfit gave the light necessary for work.

The unfinished pictures on easels or propped against the walls were as ghastly as the finished ones upstairs, and shewed the painstaking methods of the artist. Scenes were blocked out with extreme care, and pencilled guide lines told of the minute exactitude which Pickman used in getting the right perspective and proportions. The man was great—I say it even now, knowing as much as I do. A large camera on a table excited my notice, and Pickman told me that he used it in taking scenes for backgrounds, so that he might paint them from photographs in the studio instead of carting his outfit around the town for this or that view. He thought a photograph quite as good as an actual scene or model for sustained work, and declared he employed them regularly.

There was something very disturbing about the nauseous sketches and half-finished monstrosities that leered around from every side of the room, and when Pickman suddenly unveiled a huge canvas on the side away from the light I could not for my life keep back a loud scream—the second I had emitted that night. It echoed and echoed through the dim vaultings of that ancient and nitrous cellar, and I had to choke back a flood of reaction that threatened to burst out as hysterical laughter. Merciful Creator! Eliot, but I don't know how much was real and how much was feverish fancy. It doesn't seem to me that earth can hold a dream like that!

It was a colossal and nameless blasphemy with glaring red eyes, and it held in bony claws a thing that had been a man, gnawing at the head as a child nibbles at a stick of candy. Its position was a kind of crouch, and as one looked one felt that at any moment it might drop its present prey and seek a juicier morsel. But damn it all, it wasn't even the fiendish subject that made it such an immortal fountain-head of all panic—not that, nor the dog face with its pointed ears, bloodshot eyes, flat nose, and drooling lips. It wasn't the scaly claws nor the mould-caked body nor the half-hooved feet—none of these, though any one of them might well have driven an excitable man to madness.

It was the technique, Eliot—the cursed, the impious, the unnatural technique! As I am a living being, I never elsewhere saw the actual breath of life so fused into a canvas. The monster was there—it glared and gnawed and gnawed and glared—and I knew that only a suspension of Nature's laws could ever let a man paint a thing like that without a model—without some glimpse of the nether world which no mortal unsold to the Fiend has ever had.

Pinned with a thumb-tack to a vacant part of the canvas was a piece of paper now badly curled up—probably, I thought, a photograph from which Pickman meant to paint a background as hideous as the nightmare it was to enhance. I reached out to uncurl and look at it, when suddenly I saw Pickman start as if shot. He had been listening with peculiar intensity ever since my shocked scream had waked unaccustomed echoes in the dark cellar, and now he seemed struck with a fright which, though not comparable to my own, had in it more of the physical than of the spiritual. He drew a revolver and motioned me to silence, then stepped out into the main cellar and closed the door behind him.

I think I was paralysed for an instant. Imitating Pickman's listening, I fancied I heard a faint scurrying sound somewhere, and a series of squeals or bleats in a direction I couldn't determine. I thought of huge rats and shuddered. Then there came a subdued sort of clatter which somehow set me all in gooseflesh—a furtive, groping kind of clatter, though I can't attempt to convey what I mean in words. It was like heavy wood falling on stone or brick–wood on brick–what did that make me think of?

It came again, and louder. There was a vibration as if the wood had fallen farther than it had fallen before. After that followed a sharp grating noise, a shouted gibberish from Pickman, and the deafening discharge of all six chambers of a revolver, fired spectacularly as a lion-tamer might fire in the air for effect. A muffled squeal or squawk, and a thud. Then more wood and brick grating, a pause, and the opening of the door–at which I'll confess I started violently. Pickman reappeared with his smoking weapon, cursing the bloated rats that infested the ancient well.

"The deuce knows what they eat, Thurber," he grinned, "for those archaic tunnels touched graveyard and witch-den and sea-coast. But whatever it is, they must have run short, for they were devilish anxious to get out. Your yelling stirred them up, I fancy. Better be cautious in these old places–our rodent friends are the one drawback, though I sometimes think they're a positive asset by way of atmosphere and colour."

Well, Eliot, that was the end of the night's adventure. Pickman had promised to shew me the place, and heaven knows he had done it. He led me out of that tangle of alleys in another direction, it seems, for when we sighted a lamp post we were in a half-familiar street with monotonous rows of mingled tenement blocks and old houses. Charter Street, it turned out to be, but I was too flustered to notice just where we hit it. We were too late for the elevated, and walked back downtown through Hanover Street. I remember that walk. We switched from Tremont up Beacon, and Pickman left me at the corner of Joy, where I turned off. I never spoke to him again.

Why did I drop him? Don't be impatient. Wait till I ring for coffee. We've had enough of the other stuff, but I for one need something. No–it wasn't the paintings I saw in that place; though I'll swear they were enough to get him ostracised in nine-tenths of the homes and clubs of Boston, and I guess you won't wonder now why I have to steer clear of subways and cellars. It was–something I found in my coat the next morning. You know, the curled-up paper tacked to that frightful canvas in the cellar; the thing I thought was a photograph of some scene he meant to use as a background for that monster. That last scare had come while I was reaching to uncurl it, and it seems I had vacantly crumpled it into my pocket. But here's the coffee–take it black, Eliot, if you're wise.

Yes, that paper was the reason I dropped Pickman; Richard Upton Pickman, the greatest artist I have ever known–and the foulest being that ever leaped the bounds of life into the pits of myth and madness. Eliot–old Reid was right. He wasn't strictly human. Either he was born in strange shadow, or he'd found a way to unlock the forbidden gate. It's all the same now, for he's gone–back into the fabulous darkness he loved to haunt. Here, let's have the chandelier going.

Don't ask me to explain or even conjecture about what I burned. Don't ask me, either, what lay behind that mole-like scrambling Pickman was so keen to pass off as rats. There are secrets, you know, which might have come down from old Salem times, and Cotton Mather tells even stranger things. You know how damned life-like Pickman's paintings were–how we all wondered where he got those faces.

Well–that paper wasn't a photograph of any background, after all. What it shewed was simply the monstrous being he was painting on that awful canvas. It was the model he was using—and its background was merely the wall of the cellar studio in minute detail. But by God, Eliot, *it was a photograph from life.*

Houdini Under the Pyramids

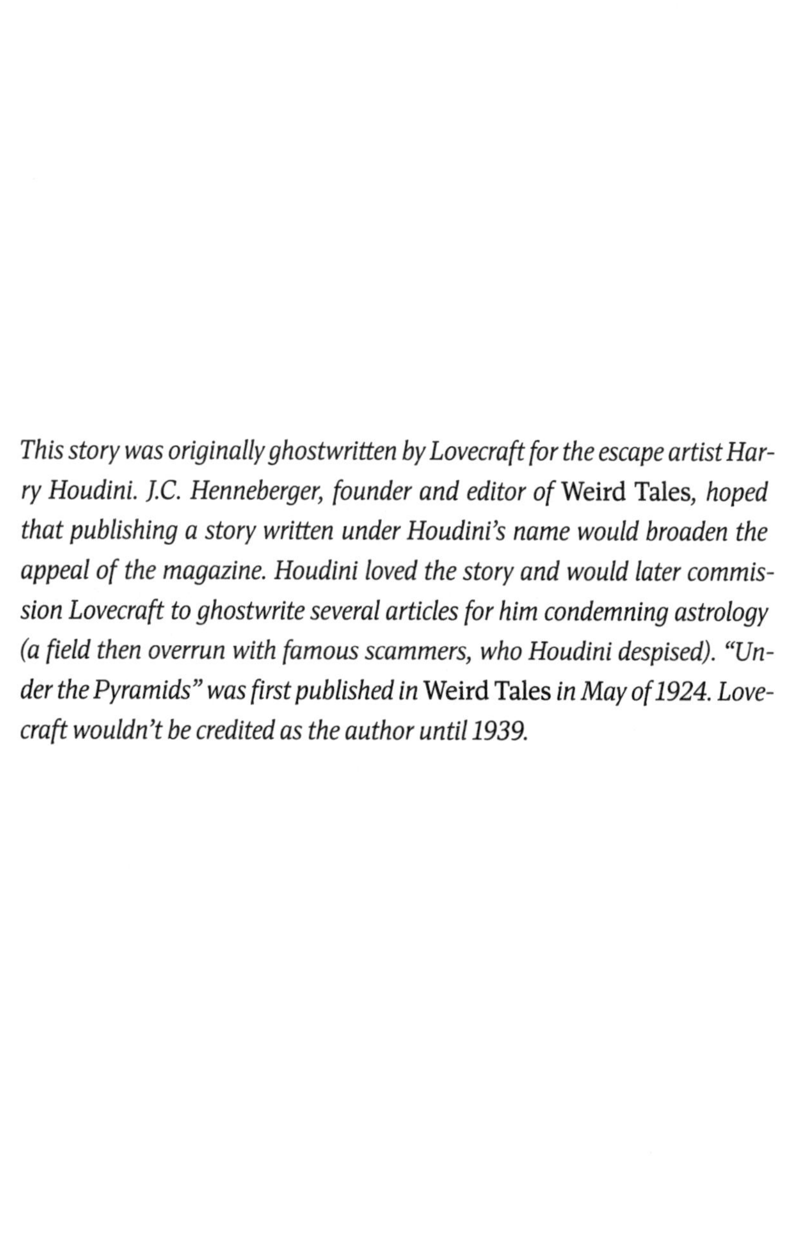

This story was originally ghostwritten by Lovecraft for the escape artist Harry Houdini. J.C. Henneberger, founder and editor of Weird Tales, *hoped that publishing a story written under Houdini's name would broaden the appeal of the magazine. Houdini loved the story and would later commission Lovecraft to ghostwrite several articles for him condemning astrology (a field then overrun with famous scammers, who Houdini despised). "Under the Pyramids" was first published in* Weird Tales *in May of 1924. Lovecraft wouldn't be credited as the author until 1939.*

Mystery attracts mystery. Ever since the wide appearance of my name as a performer of unexplained feats, I have encountered strange narratives and events which my calling has led people to link with my interests and activities. Some of these have been trivial and irrelevant, some deeply dramatic and absorbing, some productive of weird and perilous experiences, and some involving me in extensive scientific and historical research. Many of these matters I have told and shall continue to tell freely; but there is one of which I speak with great reluctance, and which I am now relating only after a session of grilling persuasion from the publishers of this magazine, who had heard vague rumours of it from other members of my family.

The hitherto guarded subject pertains to my non-professional visit to Egypt fourteen years ago, and has been avoided by me for several reasons. For one thing, I am averse to exploiting certain unmistakably actual facts and conditions obviously unknown to the myriad tourists who throng about the pyramids and apparently secreted with much diligence by the authorities at Cairo, who cannot be wholly ignorant of them. For another thing, I dislike to recount an incident in which my own fantastic imagination must have played so great a part. What I saw—or thought I saw—certainly did not take place; but is rather to be viewed as a result of my then recent readings in Egyptology, and of the speculations anent this theme which my environment naturally prompted. These imaginative stimuli, magnified by the excitement of an actual event terrible enough in itself, undoubtedly gave rise to the culminating horror of that grotesque night so long past.

In January, 1910, I had finished a professional engagement in England and signed a contract for a tour of Australian theatres. A liberal time being allowed for the trip, I determined to make the most of it in the sort of travel which chiefly interests me; so accompanied by my wife I drifted pleasantly down the Continent and embarked at Marseilles on the P. & O. Steamer Malwa, bound for Port Said. From that point I proposed to visit the principal historical localities of lower Egypt before leaving finally for Australia.

The voyage was an agreeable one, and enlivened by many of the amusing incidents which befall a magical performer apart from his work. I had intended, for the sake of quiet travel, to keep my name a secret; but was goaded into betraying myself by a fellow-magician whose anxiety to astound the passengers with ordinary tricks tempted me to duplicate and exceed his feats in a manner quite destructive of my incognito. I mention this because of its ultimate effect—an effect I should have foreseen before unmasking to a shipload of tourists about to scatter throughout the Nile Valley. What it did was to herald my identity wherever I subsequently went, and deprive my wife and me of all the placid inconspicuousness we had sought. Travelling to seek curiosities, I was often forced to stand inspection as a sort of curiosity myself!

We had come to Egypt in search of the picturesque and the mystically impressive, but found little enough when the ship edged up to Port Said and discharged its passengers in small boats. Low dunes of sand, bobbing buoys in shallow water, and a drearily European small town with nothing of interest save the great De Lesseps statue, made us anxious to get on to something more worth our while. After some discussion we decided to proceed at once to Cairo and the Pyramids, later going to Alexandria for the Australian boat and for whatever Graeco-Roman sights that ancient metropolis might present.

The railway journey was tolerable enough, and consumed only four hours and a half. We saw much of the Suez Canal, whose route we followed as far as Ismailiya, and later had a taste of Old Egypt in our glimpse of the restored fresh-water canal of the Middle Empire. Then at last we saw Cairo glimmering through the growing dusk; a twinkling constellation which became a blaze as we halted at the great Gare Centrale.

But once more disappointment awaited us, for all that we beheld was European save the costumes and the crowds. A prosaic subway led to a square teeming with carriages, taxicabs, and trolley-cars, and gorgeous with electric lights shining on tall buildings; whilst the very theatre where I was vainly requested to play, and which I later attended as a spectator, had recently been renamed the "American Cosmograph." We stopped at Shepherd's Hotel, reached in a taxi that sped along broad, smartly built-up streets; and amidst the perfect service of its restaurant, elevators, and generally Anglo-American luxuries the mysterious East and immemorial past seemed very far away.

The next day, however, precipitated us delightfully into the heart of the Arabian Nights atmosphere; and in the winding ways and exotic skyline of Cairo, the Bagdad of Haroun-al-Raschid seemed to live again. Guided by our Baedeker, we had struck east past the Ezbekiyeh Gardens along the Mouski in quest of the native quarter, and were soon in the hands of a clamorous cicerone who—notwithstanding later developments—was assuredly a master at his trade. Not until afterward did I see that I should have applied at the hotel for a licenced guide. This man, a shaven, peculiarly hollow-voiced, and relatively cleanly fellow who looked like a Pharaoh and called himself "Abdul Reis el Drogman," appeared to have much power over others of his kind; though subsequently the police professed not to know him, and to suggest that reis is merely a name for any person in authority, whilst "Drogman" is obviously no more than a clumsy modification of the word for a leader of tourist parties—*dragoman.*

Abdul led us among such wonders as we had before only read and dreamed of. Old Cairo is itself a story-book and a dream—labyrinths of narrow alleys redolent of aromatic secrets; Arabesque balconies and oriels nearly meeting above the cobbled streets; maelstroms of Oriental traffic with strange cries, cracking whips, rattling carts, jingling money, and braying donkeys; kaleidoscopes of polychrome robes, veils, turbans, and tarbushes; water-carriers and dervishes, dogs and cats, soothsayers and barbers; and over all the whining of blind beggars crouched in alcoves, and the sonorous chanting of muezzins from minarets limned delicately against a sky of deep, unchanging blue.

The roofed, quieter bazaars were hardly less alluring. Spice, perfume, incense, beads, rugs, silks, and brass—old Mahmoud Suleiman squats cross-legged amidst his gummy bottles while chattering youths pulverise mustard in the hollowed-out capital of an ancient classic column—a Roman Corinthian, perhaps from neighbouring Heliopolis, where Augustus stationed one of his three Egyptian legions. Antiquity begins to mingle with exoticism. And then the mosques and the museum—we saw them all, and tried not to let our Arabian revel succumb to the darker charm of Pharaonic Egypt which the museum's priceless treasures offered. That was to be our climax, and for the present we concentrated on the mediaeval Saracenic glories of the Caliphs whose magnificent tomb-mosques form a glittering faery necropolis on the edge of the Arabian Desert.

At length Abdul took us along the Sharia Mohammed Ali to the ancient mosque of Sultan Hassan, and the tower-flanked Bab-el-Azab, beyond which climbs the steep-walled pass to the mighty citadel that Saladin himself built with the stones of forgotten pyramids. It was sunset when we scaled that cliff, circled the modern mosque of Mohammed Ali, and looked down from the dizzying parapet over mystic Cairo—mystic Cairo all golden with its carven domes, its ethereal minarets, and its flaming gardens. Far over the city towered the great Roman dome of the new museum; and beyond it—across the cryptic yellow Nile that is the mother of aeons and dynasties—lurked the menacing sands of the Libyan Desert, undulant and iridescent and evil with older arcana. The red sun sank low, bringing the relentless chill of Egyptian dusk; and as it stood poised on the world's rim like that ancient god of Heliopolis—Re-Harakhte, the Horizon-Sun—we saw silhouetted against its vermeil holocaust the black outlines of the Pyramids of Gizeh—the palaeogean tombs there were hoary with a thousand years when Tut-Ankh-Amen mounted his golden throne in distant Thebes. Then we knew that we were done with Saracen Cairo, and that we must taste the deeper mysteries of primal Egypt—the black Khem of Re and Amen, Isis and Osiris.

The next morning we visited the pyramids, riding out in a Victoria across the great Nile bridge with its bronze lions, the island of Ghizereh with its massive lebbakh trees, and the smaller English bridge to the western shore. Down the shore road we drove, between great rows of lebbakhs and past the vast Zoölogical Gardens to the suburb of Gizeh, where a new bridge to Cairo proper has since been built. Then, turning inland along the Sharia-el-Haram, we crossed a region of glassy canals and shabby native villages till before us loomed the objects of our quest, cleaving the mists of dawn and forming inverted replicas in the roadside pools. Forty centuries, as Napoleon had told his campaigners there, indeed looked down upon us.

The road now rose abruptly, till we finally reached our place of transfer between the trolley station and the Mena House Hotel. Abdul Reis, who capably purchased our pyramid tickets, seemed to have an understanding with the crowding, yelling, and offensive Bedouins who inhabited a squalid mud village some distance away and pestiferously assailed every traveller; for he kept them very decently at bay and secured an excellent pair of camels for us, himself mounting a donkey and assigning the leadership of our animals to a group of men and boys more expensive than useful. The area to be traversed was so small that camels were hardly needed, but we did not regret adding to our experience this troublesome form of desert navigation.

The pyramids stand on a high rock plateau, this group forming next to the northernmost of the series of regal and aristocratic cemeteries built in the neighbourhood of the extinct capital Memphis, which lay on the same side of the Nile, somewhat south of Gizeh, and which flourished between 3400 and 2000 B.C.. The greatest pyramid, which lies nearest the modern road, was built by King Cheops or Khufu about 2800 B.C., and stands more than 450 feet in perpendicular height. In a line southwest from this are successively the Second Pyramid, built a generation later by King Khephren, and though slightly smaller, looking even larger because set on higher ground, and the radically smaller Third Pyramid of King Mycerinus, built about 2700 B.C.. Near the edge of the plateau and due east of the Second Pyramid, with a face probably altered to form a colossal portrait of Khephren, its royal restorer, stands the monstrous Sphinx—mute, sardonic, and wise beyond mankind and memory.

Minor pyramids and the traces of ruined minor pyramids are found in several places, and the whole plateau is pitted with the tombs of dignitaries of less than royal rank. These latter were originally marked by *mastabas*, or stone bench-like structures about the deep burial shafts, as found in other Memphian cemeteries and exemplified by Perneb's Tomb in the Metropolitan Museum of New York. At Gizeh, however, all such visible things have been swept away by time and pillage; and only the rock-hewn shafts, either sand-filled or cleared out by archaeologists, remain to attest their former existence. Connected with each tomb was a chapel in which priests and relatives offered food and prayer to the hovering ka or vital principle of the deceased. The small tombs have their chapels contained in their stone *mastabas* or superstructures, but the mortuary chapels of the pyramids, where regal Pharaohs lay, were separate temples, each to the east of its corresponding pyramid, and connected by a causeway to a massive gate-chapel or propylon at the edge of the rock plateau.

The gate-chapel leading to the Second Pyramid, nearly buried in the drifting sands, yawns subterraneously southeast of the Sphinx. Persistent tradition dubs it the "Temple of the Sphinx;" and it may perhaps be rightly called such if the Sphinx indeed represents the Second Pyramid's builder Khephren. There are unpleasant tales of the Sphinx before Khephren—but whatever its elder features were, the monarch replaced them with his own that men might look at the colossus without fear. It was in the great gateway-temple that the life-size diorite statue of Khephren now in the Cairo Museum was found; a statue before which I stood in awe when I beheld it. Whether the whole edifice is now excavated I am not certain, but in 1910 most of it was below ground, with the entrance heavily barred at night. Germans were in charge of the work, and the war or other things may have stopped them. I would give much, in view of my experience and of certain Bedouin whisperings discredited or unknown in Cairo, to know what has developed in connexion with a certain well in a transverse gallery where statues of the Pharaoh were found in curious juxtaposition to the statues of baboons.

The road, as we traversed it on our camels that morning, curved sharply past the wooden police quarters, post-office, drug-store, and shops on the left, and plunged south and east in a complete bend that scaled the rock plateau and brought us face to face with the desert under the lee of the Great Pyramid. Past Cyclopean masonry we rode, rounding the eastern face and looking down ahead into a valley of minor pyramids beyond which the eternal Nile glistened to the east, and the eternal desert shimmered to the west. Very close loomed the three major pyramids, the greatest devoid of outer casing and shewing its bulk of great stones, but the others retaining here and there the neatly fitted covering which had made them smooth and finished in their day.

Presently we descended toward the Sphinx, and sat silent beneath the spell of those terrible unseeing eyes. On the vast stone breast we faintly discerned the emblem of Re-Harakhte, for whose image the Sphinx was mistaken in a late dynasty; and though sand covered the tablet between the great paws, we recalled what Thutmosis IV inscribed thereon, and the dream he had when a prince. It was then that the smile of the Sphinx vaguely displeased us, and made us wonder about the legends of subterranean passages beneath the monstrous creature, leading down, down, to depths none might dare hint at—depths connected with mysteries older than the dynastic Egypt we excavate, and having a sinister relation to the persistence of abnormal, animal-headed gods in the ancient Nilotic pantheon. Then, too, it was I asked myself an idle question whose hideous significance was not to appear for many an hour.

Other tourists now began to overtake us, and we moved on to the sand-choked Temple of the Sphinx, fifty yards to the southeast, which I have previously mentioned as the great gate of the causeway to the Second Pyramid's mortuary chapel on the plateau. Most of it was still underground, and although we dismounted and descended through a modern passageway to its alabaster corridor and pillared hall, I felt that Abdul and the local German attendant had not shown us all there was to see. After this we made the conventional circuit of the pyramid plateau, examining the Second Pyramid and the peculiar ruins of its mortuary chapel to the east, the Third Pyramid and its miniature southern satellites and ruined eastern chapel, the rock tombs and the honeycombings of the Fourth and Fifth Dynasties, and the famous Campell's Tomb whose shadowy shaft sinks precipitously for 53 feet to a sinister sarcophagus which one of our camel-drivers divested of the cumbering sand after a vertiginous descent by rope.

Cries now assailed us from the Great Pyramid, where Bedouins were besieging a party of tourists with offers of guidance to the top, or of displays of speed in the performance of solitary trips up and down. Seven minutes is said to be the record for such an ascent and descent, but many lusty sheiks and sons of sheiks assured us they could cut it to five if given the requisite impetus of liberal baksheesh. They did not get this impetus, though we did let Abdul take us up, thus obtaining a view of unprecedented magnificence which included not only remote and glittering Cairo with its crowned citadel and background of gold-violet hills, but all the pyramids of the Memphian district as well, from Abu Roash on the north to the Dashur on the south. The Sakkara step-pyramid, which marks the evolution of the low *mastaba* into the true pyramid, shewed clearly and alluringly in the sandy distance. It is close to this transition-monument that the famed Tomb of Perneb was found—more than 400 miles north of the Theban rock valley where Tut-Ankh-Amen sleeps. Again I was forced to silence through sheer awe. The prospect of such antiquity, and the secrets each hoary monument seemed to hold and brood over, filled me with a reverence and sense of immensity nothing else ever gave me.

Fatigued by our climb, and disgusted with the importunate Bedouins whose actions seemed to defy every rule of taste, we omitted the arduous detail of entering the cramped interior passages of any of the pyramids, though we saw several of the hardiest tourists preparing for the suffocating crawl through Cheops' mightiest memorial. As we dismissed and overpaid our local bodyguard and drove back to Cairo with Abdul Reis under the afternoon sun, we half regretted the omission we had made. Such fascinating things were whispered about lower pyramid passages not in the guide-books; passages whose entrances had been hastily blocked up and concealed by certain uncommunicative archaeologists who had found and begun to explore them. Of course, this whispering was largely baseless on the face of it; but it was curious to reflect how persistently visitors were forbidden to enter the pyramids at night, or to visit the lowest burrows and crypt of the Great Pyramid. Perhaps in the latter case it was the psychological effect which was feared—the effect on the visitor of feeling himself huddled down beneath a gigantic world of solid masonry; joined to the life he has known by the merest tube, in which he may only crawl, and which any accident or evil design might block. The whole subject seemed so weird and alluring that we resolved to pay the pyramid plateau another visit at the earliest possible opportunity. For me this opportunity came much earlier than I expected.

That evening, the members of our party feeling somewhat tired after the strenuous programme of the day, I went alone with Abdul Reis for a walk through the picturesque Arab quarter. Though I had seen it by day, I wished to study the alleys and bazaars in the dusk, when rich shadows and mellow gleams of light would add to their glamour and fantastic illusion. The native crowds were thinning, but were still very noisy and numerous when we came upon a knot of revelling Bedouins in the Suken-Nahhasin, or bazaar of the coppersmiths. Their apparent leader, an insolent youth with heavy features and saucily cocked tarbush, took some notice of us; and evidently recognised with no great friendliness my competent but admittedly supercilious and sneeringly disposed guide. Perhaps, I thought, he resented that odd reproduction of the Sphinx's half-smile which I had often remarked with amused irritation; or perhaps he did not like the hollow and sepulchral resonance of Abdul's voice. At any rate, the exchange of ancestrally opprobrious language became very brisk; and before long Ali Ziz, as I heard the stranger called when called by no worse name, began to pull violently at Abdul's robe, an action quickly reciprocated, and leading to a spirited scuffle in which both combatants lost their sacredly cherished headgear and would have reached an even direr condition had I not intervened and separated them by main force.

My interference, at first seemingly unwelcome on both sides, succeeded at last in effecting a truce. Sullenly each belligerent composed his wrath and his attire; and with an assumption of dignity as profound as it was sudden, the two formed a curious pact of honour which I soon learned is a custom of great antiquity in Cairo—a pact for the settlement of their difference by means of a nocturnal fist fight atop the Great Pyramid, long after the departure of the last moonlight sightseer. Each duellist was to assemble a party of seconds, and the affair was to begin at midnight, proceeding by rounds in the most civilised possible fashion. In all this planning there was much which excited my interest. The fight itself promised to be unique and spectacular, while the thought of the scene on that hoary pile overlooking the antediluvian plateau of Gizeh under the wan moon of the pallid small hours appealed to every fibre of imagination in me. A request found Abdul exceedingly willing to admit me to his party of seconds; so that all the rest of the early evening I accompanied him to various dens in the most lawless regions of the town—mostly northeast of the Ezbekiyeh—where he gathered one by one a select and formidable band of congenial cutthroats as his pugilistic background.

Shortly after nine our party, mounted on donkeys bearing such royal or tourist-reminiscent names as "Rameses," "Mark Twain," "J.P. Morgan," and "Minnehaha," edged through street labyrinths both Oriental and Occidental, crossed the muddy and mast-forested Nile by the bridge of the bronze lions, and cantered philosophically between the lebbakhs on the road to Gizeh. Slightly over two hours were consumed by the trip, toward the end of which we passed the last of the returning tourists, saluted the last in-bound trolley-car, and were alone with the night and the past and the spectral moon.

Then we saw the vast pyramids at the end of the avenue, ghoulish with a dim atavistical menace which I had not seemed to notice in the daytime. Even the smallest of them held a hint of the ghastly—for was it not in this that they had buried Queen Nitokris alive in the Sixth Dynasty; subtle Queen Nitokris, who once invited all her enemies to a feast in a temple below the Nile, and drowned them by opening the water-gates? I recalled that the Arabs whisper things about Nitokris, and shun the Third Pyramid at certain phases of the moon. It must have been over her that Thomas Moore was brooding when he wrote a thing muttered about by Memphian boatmen—

"The subterranean nymph that dwells
'Mid sunless gems and glories hid—
The lady of the Pyramid!"

Early as we were, Ali Ziz and his party were ahead of us; for we saw their donkeys outlined against the desert plateau at Kafr-el-Haram; toward which squalid Arab settlement, close to the Sphinx, we had diverged instead of following the regular road to the Mena House, where some of the sleepy, inefficient police might have observed and halted us. Here, where filthy Bedouins stabled camels and donkeys in the rock tombs of Khephren's courtiers, we were led up the rocks and over the sand to the Great Pyramid, up whose time-worn sides the Arabs swarmed eagerly, Abdul Reis offering me the assistance I did not need.

As most travellers know, the actual apex of this structure has long been worn away, leaving a reasonably flat platform twelve yards square. On this eerie pinnacle a squared circle was formed, and in a few moments the sardonic desert moon leered down upon a battle which, but for the quality of the ringside cries, might well have occurred at some minor athletic club in America. As I watched it, I felt that some of our less desirable institutions were not lacking; for every blow, feint, and defence bespoke "stalling" to my not inexperienced eye. It was quickly over, and despite my misgivings as to methods I felt a sort of proprietary pride when Abdul Reis was adjudged the winner.

Reconciliation was phenomenally rapid, and amidst the singing, fraternising, and drinking which followed, I found it difficult to realise that a quarrel had ever occurred. Oddly enough, I myself seemed to be more of a centre of notice than the antagonists; and from my smattering of Arabic I judged that they were discussing my professional performances and escapes from every sort of manacle and confinement, in a manner which indicated not only a surprising knowledge of me, but a distinct hostility and scepticism concerning my feats of escape. It gradually dawned on me that the elder magic of Egypt did not depart without leaving traces, and that fragments of a strange secret lore and priestly cult-practices have survived surreptitiously amongst the fellaheen to such an extent that the prowess of a strange "hahwi" or magician is resented and disputed. I thought of how much my hollow-voiced guide Abdul Reis looked like an old Egyptian priest or Pharaoh or smiling Sphinx...and wondered.

Suddenly something happened which in a flash proved the correctness of my reflections and made me curse the denseness whereby I had accepted this night's events as other than the empty and malicious "frameup" they now shewed themselves to be. Without warning, and doubtless in answer to some subtle sign from Abdul, the entire band of Bedouins precipitated itself upon me; and having produced heavy ropes, soon had me bound as securely as I was ever bound in the course of my life, either on the stage or off. I struggled at first, but soon saw that one man could make no headway against a band of over twenty sinewy barbarians. My hands were tied behind my back, my knees bent to their fullest extent, and my wrists and ankles stoutly linked together with unyielding cords. A stifling gag was forced into my mouth, and a blindfold fastened tightly over my eyes. Then, as the Arabs bore me aloft on their shoulders and began a jouncing descent of the pyramid, I heard the taunts of my late guide Abdul, who mocked and jeered delightedly in his hollow voice, and assured me that I was soon to have my "magic powers" put to a supreme test which would quickly remove any egotism I might have gained through triumphing over all the tests offered by America and Europe. Egypt, he reminded me, is very old; and full of inner mysteries and antique powers not even conceivable to the experts of today, whose devices had so uniformly failed to entrap me.

How far or in what direction I was carried, I cannot tell; for the circumstances were all against the formation of any accurate judgment. I know, however, that it could not have been a great distance; since my bearers at no point hastened beyond a walk, yet kept me aloft a surprisingly short time. It is this perplexing brevity which makes me feel almost like shuddering whenever I think of Gizeh and its plateau—for one is oppressed by hints of the closeness to every-day tourist routes of what existed then and must exist still.

The evil abnormality I speak of did not become manifest at first. Setting me down on a surface which I recognised as sand rather than rock, my captors passed a rope around my chest and dragged me a few feet to a ragged opening in the ground, into which they presently lowered me with much rough handling. For apparent aeons I bumped against the stony irregular sides of a narrow hewn well which I took to be one of the numerous burial shafts of the plateau until the prodigious, almost incredible depth of it robbed me of all bases of conjecture.

The horror of the experience deepened with every dragging second. That any descent through the sheer solid rock could be so vast without reaching the core of the planet itself, or that any rope made by man could be so long as to dangle me in these unholy and seemingly fathomless profundities of nether earth, were beliefs of such grotesqueness that it was easier to doubt my agitated senses than to accept them. Even now I am uncertain, for I know how deceitful the sense of time becomes when one or more of the usual perceptions or conditions of life is removed or distorted. But I am quite sure that I preserved a logical consciousness that far; that at least I did not add any full-grown phantoms of imagination to a picture hideous enough in its reality, and explicable by a type of cerebral illusion vastly short of actual hallucination.

All this was not the cause of my first bit of fainting. The shocking ordeal was cumulative, and the beginning of the later terrors was a very perceptible increase in my rate of descent. They were paying out that infinitely long rope very swiftly now, and I scraped cruelly against the rough and constricted sides of the shaft as I shot madly downward. My clothing was in tatters, and I felt the trickle of blood all over, even above the mounting and excruciating pain. My nostrils, too, were assailed by a scarcely definable menace; a creeping odour of damp and staleness curiously unlike anything I had ever smelt before, and having faint overtones of spice and incense that lent an element of mockery.

Then the mental cataclysm came. It was horrible—hideous beyond all articulate description because it was all of the soul, with nothing of detail to describe. It was the ecstasy of nightmare and the summation of the fiendish. The suddenness of it was apocalyptic and daemoniac—one moment I was plunging agonisingly down that narrow well of million-toothed torture, yet the next moment I was soaring on bat-wings in the gulfs of hell; swinging free and swoopingly through illimitable miles of boundless, musty space; rising dizzily to measureless pinnacles of chilling ether, then diving gaspingly to sucking nadirs of ravenous, nauseous lower vacua...Thank God for the mercy that shut out in oblivion those clawing Furies of consciousness which half unhinged my faculties, and tore Harpy-like at my spirit! That one respite, short as it was, gave me the strength and sanity to endure those still greater sublimations of cosmic panic that lurked and gibbered on the road ahead.

II.

It was very gradually that I regained my senses after that eldritch flight through Stygian space. The process was infinitely painful, and coloured by fantastic dreams in which my bound and gagged condition found singular embodiment. The precise nature of these dreams was very clear while I was experiencing them, but became blurred in my recollection almost immediately afterward, and was soon reduced to the merest outline by the terrible events—real or imaginary—which followed. I dreamed that I was in the grasp of a great and horrible paw; a yellow, hairy, five-clawed paw which had reached out of the earth to crush and engulf me. And when I stopped to reflect what the paw was, it seemed to me that it was Egypt. In the dream I looked back at the events of the preceding weeks, and saw myself lured and enmeshed little by little, subtly and insidiously, by some hellish ghoul-spirit of the elder Nile sorcery; some spirit that was in Egypt before ever man was, and that will be when man is no more.

I saw the horror and unwholesome antiquity of Egypt, and the grisly alliance it has always had with the tombs and temples of the dead. I saw phantom processions of priests with the heads of bulls, falcons, cats, and ibises; phantom processions marching interminably through subterraneous labyrinths and avenues of titanic propylaea beside which a man is as a fly, and offering unnamable sacrifices to indescribable gods. Stone colossi marched in endless night and drove herds of grinning androsphinxes down to the shores of illimitable stagnant rivers of pitch. And behind it all I saw the ineffable malignity of primordial necromancy, black and amorphous, and fumbling greedily after me in the darkness to choke out the spirit that had dared to mock it by emulation. In my sleeping brain there took shape a melodrama of sinister hatred and pursuit, and I saw the black soul of Egypt singling me out and calling me in inaudible whispers; calling and luring me, leading me on with the glitter and glamour of a Saracenic surface, but ever pulling me down to the age-mad catacombs and horrors of its dead and abysmal pharaonic heart.

Then the dream-faces took on human resemblances, and I saw my guide Abdul Reis in the robes of a king, with the sneer of the Sphinx on his features. And I knew that those features were the features of Khephren the Great, who raised the Second Pyramid, carved over the Sphinx's face in the likeness of his own, and built that titanic gateway temple whose myriad corridors the archaeologists think they have dug out of the cryptical sand and the uninformative rock. And I looked at the long, lean, rigid hand of Khephren; the long, lean, rigid hand as I had seen it on the diorite statue in the Cairo Museum—the statue they had found in the terrible gateway temple—and wondered that I had not shrieked when I saw it on Abdul Reis... That hand! It was hideously cold, and it was crushing me; it was the cold and cramping of the sarcophagus...the chill and constriction of unrememberable Egypt...It was nighted, necropolitan Egypt itself...that yellow paw...and they whisper such things of Khephren...

But at this juncture I began to awake—or at least, to assume a condition less completely that of sleep than the one just preceding. I recalled the fight atop the pyramid, the treacherous Bedouins and their attack, my frightful descent by rope through endless rock depths, and my mad swinging and plunging in a chill void redolent of aromatic putrescence. I perceived that I now lay on a damp rock floor, and that my bonds were still biting into me with unloosened force. It was very cold, and I seemed to detect a faint current of noisome air sweeping across me. The cuts and bruises I had received from the jagged sides of the rock shaft were paining me woefully, their soreness enhanced to a stinging or burning acuteness by some pungent quality in the faint draught, and the mere act of rolling over was enough to set my whole frame throbbing with untold agony. As I turned I felt a tug from above, and concluded that the rope whereby I was lowered still reached to the surface. Whether or not the Arabs still held it, I had no idea; nor had I any idea how far within the earth I was. I knew that the darkness around me was wholly or nearly total, since no ray of moonlight penetrated my blindfold; but I did not trust my senses enough to accept as evidence of extreme depth the sensation of vast duration which had characterised my descent.

Knowing at least that I was in a space of considerable extent reached from the surface directly above by an opening in the rock, I doubtfully conjectured that my prison was perhaps the buried gateway chapel of old Khephren—the Temple of the Sphinx—perhaps some inner corridor which the guides had not shewn me during my morning visit, and from which I might easily escape if I could find my way to the barred entrance. It would be a labyrinthine wandering, but no worse than others out of which I had in the past found my way. The first step was to get free of my bonds, gag, and blindfold; and this I knew would be no great task, since subtler experts than these Arabs had tried every known species of fetter upon me during my long and varied career as an exponent of escape, yet had never succeeded in defeating my methods.

Then it occurred to me that the Arabs might be ready to meet and attack me at the entrance upon any evidence of my probable escape from the binding cords, as would be furnished by any decided agitation of the rope which they probably held. This, of course, was taking for granted that my place of confinement was indeed Khephren's Temple of the Sphinx. The direct opening in the roof, wherever it might lurk, could not be beyond easy reach of the ordinary modern entrance near the Sphinx; if in truth it were any great distance at all on the surface, since the total area known to visitors is not at all enormous. I had not noticed any such opening during my daytime pilgrimage, but knew that these things are easily overlooked amidst the drifting sands. Thinking these matters over as I lay bent and bound on the rock floor, I nearly forgot the horrors of the abysmal descent and cavernous swinging which had so lately reduced me to a coma. My present thought was only to outwit the Arabs, and I accordingly determined to work myself free as quickly as possible, avoiding any tug on the descending line which might betray an effective or even problematical attempt at freedom.

This, however, was more easily determined than effected. A few preliminary trials made it clear that little could be accomplished without considerable motion; and it did not surprise me when, after one especially energetic struggle, I began to feel the coils of falling rope as they piled up about me and upon me. Obviously, I thought, the Bedouins had felt my movements and released their end of the rope; hastening no doubt to the temple's true entrance to lie murderously in wait for me. The prospect was not pleasing—but I had faced worse in my time without flinching, and would not flinch now. At present I must first of all free myself of bonds, then trust to ingenuity to escape from the temple unharmed. It is curious how implicitly

I had come to believe myself in the old temple of Khephren beside the Sphinx, only a short distance below the ground.

That belief was shattered, and every pristine apprehension of preternatural depth and daemoniac mystery revived, by a circumstance which grew in horror and significance even as I formulated my philosophical plan. I have said that the falling rope was piling up about and upon me. Now I saw that it was *continuing to pile*, as no rope of normal length could possibly do. It gained in momentum and became an avalanche of hemp, accumulating mountainously on the floor, and half burying me beneath its swiftly multiplying coils. Soon I was completely engulfed and gasping for breath as the increasing convolutions submerged and stifled me. My senses tottered again, and I vainly tried to fight off a menace desperate and ineluctable. It was not merely that I was tortured beyond human endurance—not merely that life and breath seemed to be crushed slowly out of me—it was the knowledge of *what those unnatural lengths of rope implied*, and the consciousness of what unknown and incalculable gulfs of inner earth must at this moment be surrounding me. My endless descent and swinging flight through goblin space, then, must have been real; and even now I must be lying helpless in some nameless cavern world toward the core of the planet. Such a sudden confirmation of ultimate horror was insupportable, and a second time I lapsed into merciful oblivion.

When I say oblivion, I do not imply that I was free from dreams. On the contrary, my absence from the conscious world was marked by visions of the most unutterable hideousness. God!...If only I had not read so much Egyptology before coming to this land which is the fountain of all darkness and terror! This second spell of fainting filled my sleeping mind anew with shivering realisation of the country and its archaic secrets, and through some damnable chance my dreams turned to the ancient notions of the dead and their sojournings in soul *and body* beyond those mysterious tombs which were more houses than graves. I recalled, in dream-shapes which it is well that I do not remember, the peculiar and elaborate construction of Egyptian sepulchres; and the exceedingly singular and terrific doctrines which determined this construction.

All these people thought of was death and the dead. They conceived of a literal resurrection of the body which made them mummify it with desperate care, and preserve all the vital organs in canopic jars near the corpse; whilst besides the body they believed in two other elements, the soul, which after its weighing and approval by Osiris dwelt in the land of the blest, and the obscure and portentous *ka* or life-principle which wandered about the upper and lower worlds in a horrible way, demanding occasional access to the preserved body, consuming the food offerings brought by priests and pious relatives to the mortuary chapel, and sometimes—as men whispered—taking its body or the wooden double always buried beside it and stalking noxiously abroad on errands peculiarly repellent.

For thousands of years those bodies rested gorgeously encased and staring glassily upward when not visited by the *ka*, awaiting the day when Osiris should restore both *ka* and soul, and lead forth the stiff legions of the dead from the sunken houses of sleep. It was to have been a glorious rebirth—but not all souls were approved, nor were all tombs inviolate, so that certain grotesque *mistakes* and fiendish *abnormalities* were to be looked for. Even today the Arabs murmur of unsanctified convocations and unwholesome worship in forgotten nether abysses, which only winged invisible kas and soulless mummies may visit and return unscathed.

Perhaps the most leeringly blood-congealing legends are those which relate to certain perverse products of decadent priestcraft—*composite mummies* made by the artificial union of human trunks and limbs with the heads of animals in imitation of the elder gods. At all stages of history the sacred animals were mummified, so that consecrated bulls, cats, ibises, crocodiles, and the like might return some day to greater glory. But only in the decadence did they mix the human and animal in the same mummy—only in the decadence, when they did not understand the rights and prerogatives of the ka and the soul. What happened to those composite mummies is not told of—at least publicly—and it is certain that no Egyptologist ever found one. The whispers of Arabs are very wild, and cannot be relied upon. They even hint that old Khephren—he of the Sphinx, the Second Pyramid, and the yawning gateway temple—lives far underground wedded to the ghoul-queen Nitokris and ruling over the mummies that are neither of man nor of beast.

It was of these—of Khephren and his consort and his strange armies of the hybrid dead—that I dreamed, and that is why I am glad the exact dream-shapes have faded from my memory. My most horrible vision was connected with an idle question I had asked myself the day before when looking at the great carven riddle of the desert and wondering with what unknown depths the temple so close to it might be secretly connected. That question, so innocent and whimsical then, assumed in my dream a meaning of frenetic and hysterical madness...*what huge and loathsome abnormality was the Sphinx originally carven to represent?*

My second awakening–if awakening it was–is a memory of stark hideousness which nothing else in my life–save one thing which came after–can parallel; and that life has been full and adventurous beyond most men's. Remember that I had lost consciousness whilst buried beneath a cascade of falling rope whose immensity revealed the cataclysmic depth of my present position. Now, as perception returned, I felt the entire weight gone; and realised upon rolling over that although I was still tied, gagged, and blindfolded, *some agency had removed completely the suffocating hempen landslide which had overwhelmed me.* The significance of this condition, of course, came to me only gradually; but even so I think it would have brought unconsciousness again had I not by this time reached such a state of emotional exhaustion that no new horror could make much difference. I was alone...with *what?*

Before I could torture myself with any new reflection, or make any fresh effort to escape from my bonds, an additional circumstance became manifest. Pains not formerly felt were racking my arms and legs, and I seemed coated with a profusion of dried blood beyond anything my former cuts and abrasions could furnish. My chest, too, seemed pierced by a hundred wounds, as though some malign, titanic ibis had been pecking at it. Assuredly the agency which had removed the rope was a hostile one, and had begun to wreak terrible injuries upon me when somehow impelled to desist. Yet at the time my sensations were distinctly the reverse of what one might expect. Instead of sinking into a bottomless pit of despair, I was stirred to a new courage and action; for now I felt that the evil forces were physical things which a fearless man might encounter on an even basis.

On the strength of this thought I tugged again at my bonds, and used all the art of a lifetime to free myself as I had so often done amidst the glare of lights and the applause of vast crowds. The familiar details of my escaping process commenced to engross me, and now that the long rope was gone I half regained my belief that the supreme horrors were hallucinations after all, and that there had never been any terrible shaft, measureless abyss, or interminable rope. Was I after all in the gateway temple of Khephren beside the Sphinx, and had the sneaking Arabs stolen in to torture me as I lay helpless there? At any rate, I must be free. Let me stand up unbound, ungagged, and with eyes open to catch any glimmer of light which might come trickling from any source, and I could actually delight in the combat against evil and treacherous foes!

How long I took in shaking off my encumbrances I cannot tell. It must have been longer than in my exhibition performances, because I was wounded, exhausted, and enervated by the experiences I had passed through. When I was finally free, and taking deep breaths of a chill, damp, evilly spiced air all the more horrible when encountered without the screen of gag and blindfold edges, I found that I was too cramped and fatigued to move at once. There I lay, trying to stretch a frame bent and mangled, for an indefinite period, and straining my eyes to catch a glimpse of some ray of light which would give a hint as to my position.

By degrees my strength and flexibility returned, but my eyes beheld nothing. As I staggered to my feet I peered diligently in every direction, yet met only an ebony blackness as great as that I had known when blindfolded. I tried my legs, blood-encrusted beneath my shredded trousers, and found that I could walk; yet could not decide in what direction to go.

Obviously I ought not to walk at random, and perhaps retreat directly from the entrance I sought; so I paused to note the direction of the cold, foetid, natron-scented air-current which I had never ceased to feel. Accepting the point of its source as the possible entrance to the abyss, I strove to keep track of this landmark and to walk consistently toward it.

I had had a match box with me, and even a small electric flashlight; but of course the pockets of my tossed and tattered clothing were long since emptied of all heavy articles. As I walked cautiously in the blackness, the draught grew stronger and more offensive, till at length I could regard it as nothing less than a tangible stream of detestable vapour pouring out of some aperture like the smoke of the genie from the fisherman's jar in the Eastern tale. The East...Egypt...truly, this dark cradle of civilisation was ever the well-spring of horrors and marvels unspeakable! The more I reflected on the nature of this cavern wind, the greater my sense of disquiet became; for although despite its odour I had sought its source as at least an indirect clue to the outer world, I now saw plainly that this foul emanation could have no admixture or connexion whatsoever with the clean air of the Libyan Desert, but must be essentially a thing vomited from sinister gulfs still lower down. I had, then, been walking in the wrong direction!

After a moment's reflection I decided not to retrace my steps. Away from the draught I would have no landmarks, for the roughly level rock floor was devoid of distinctive configurations. If, however, I followed up the strange current, I would undoubtedly arrive at an aperture of some sort, from whose gate I could perhaps work round the walls to the opposite side of this Cyclopean and otherwise unnavigable hall. That I might fail, I well realised. I saw that this was no part of Khephren's gateway temple which tourists know, and it struck me that this particular hall might be unknown even to archaeologists, and merely stumbled upon by the inquisitive and malignant Arabs who had imprisoned me. If so, was there any present gate of escape to the known parts or to the outer air?

What evidence, indeed, did I now possess that this was the gateway temple at all? For a moment all my wildest speculations rushed back upon me, and I thought of that vivid mélange of impressions–descent, suspension in space, the rope, my wounds, and the dreams that were frankly dreams. Was this the end of life for me? Or indeed, would it be merciful if this moment were the end? I could answer none of my own questions, but merely kept on till Fate for a third time reduced me to oblivion. This time there were no dreams, for the suddenness of the incident shocked me out of all thought either conscious or subconscious. Tripping on an unexpected descending step at a point where the offensive draught became strong enough to offer an actual physical resistance, I was precipitated headlong down a black flight of huge stone stairs into a gulf of hideousness unrelieved.

That I ever breathed again is a tribute to the inherent vitality of the healthy human organism. Often I look back to that night and feel a touch of actual *humour* in those repeated lapses of consciousness; lapses whose succession reminded me at the time of nothing more than the crude cinema melodramas of that period. Of course, it is possible that the repeated lapses never occurred; and that all the features of that underground nightmare were merely the dreams of one long coma which began with the shock of my descent into that abyss and ended with the healing balm of the outer air and of the rising sun which found me stretched on the sands of Gizeh before the sardonic and dawn-flushed face of the Great Sphinx.

I prefer to believe this latter explanation as much as I can, hence was glad when the police told me that the barrier to Khephren's gateway temple had been found unfastened, and that a sizeable rift to the surface did actually exist in one corner of the still buried part. I was glad, too, when the doctors pronounced my wounds only those to be expected from my seizure, blindfolding, lowering, struggling with bonds, falling some distance—perhaps into a depression in the temple's inner gallery—dragging myself to the outer barrier and escaping from it, and experiences like that...a very soothing diagnosis. And yet I know that there must be more than appears on the surface. That extreme descent is too vivid a memory to be dismissed—and it is odd that no one has ever been able to find a man answering the description of my guide Abdul Reis el Drogman—the tomb-throated guide who looked and smiled like King Khephren.

I have digressed from my connected narrative—perhaps in the vain hope of evading the telling of that final incident; that incident which of all is most certainly an hallucination. But I promised to relate it, and do not break promises. When I recovered—or seemed to recover—my senses after that fall down the black stone stairs, I was quite as alone and in darkness as before. The windy stench, bad enough before, was now fiendish; yet I had acquired enough familiarity by this time to bear it stoically. Dazedly I began to crawl away from the place whence the putrid wind came, and with my bleeding hands felt the colossal blocks of a mighty pavement. Once my head struck against a hard object, and when I felt of it I learned that it was the base of a column—a column of unbelievable immensity—

whose surface was covered with gigantic chiselled hieroglyphics very perceptible to my touch. Crawling on, I encountered other titan columns at incomprehensible distances apart; when suddenly my attention was captured by the realisation of something which must have been impinging on my subconscious hearing long before the conscious sense was aware of it.

From some still lower chasm in earth's bowels were proceeding certain sounds, measured and definite, and like nothing I had ever heard before. That they were very ancient and distinctly ceremonial, I felt almost intuitively; and much reading in Egyptology led me to associate them with the flute, the sambuke, the sistrum, and the tympanum. In their rhythmic piping, droning, rattling, and beating I felt an element of terror beyond all the known terrors of earth–a terror peculiarly dissociated from personal fear, and taking the form of a sort of objective pity for our planet, that it should hold within its depths such horrors as must lie beyond these aegipanic cacophonies. The sounds increased in volume, and I felt that they were approaching. Then–and may all the gods of all pantheons unite to keep the like from my ears again–I began to hear, faintly and afar off, *the morbid and millennial tramping of the marching things.*

It was hideous that footfalls so *dissimilar* should move in such perfect rhythm. The training of unhallowed thousands of years must lie behind that march of earth's inmost monstrosities...padding, clicking, walking, stalking, rumbling, lumbering, crawling...and all to the abhorrent discords of those mocking instruments. And then...God keep the memory of those Arab legends out of my head! The mummies without souls...the meeting-place of the wandering *kas*...the hordes of the devil-cursed pharaonic dead of forty centuries...the *com-*

posite mummies led through the uttermost onyx voids by King Khephren and his ghoul-queen Nitokris...

The tramping drew nearer—heaven save me from the sound of those feet and paws and hooves and pads and talons as it commenced to acquire detail! Down limitless reaches of sunless pavement a spark of light flickered in the malodorous wind, and I drew behind the enormous circumference of a Cyclopic column that I might escape for a while the horror that was stalking million-footed toward me through gigantic hypostyles of inhuman dread and phobic antiquity. The flickers increased, and the tramping and dissonant rhythm grew sickeningly loud. In the quivering orange light there stood faintly forth a scene of such stony awe that I gasped from a sheer wonder that conquered even fear and repulsion. Bases of columns whose middles were higher than human sight...mere bases of things that must each dwarf the Eiffel Tower to insignificance...hieroglyphics carved by unthinkable hands in caverns where daylight can be only a remote legend...

I *would not* look at the marching things. That I desperately resolved as I heard their creaking joints and nitrous wheezing above the dead music and the dead tramping. It was merciful that they did not speak...but God! *their crazy torches began to cast shadows on the surface of those stupendous columns. Heaven take it away! Hippopotami should not have human hands and carry torches...men should not have the heads of crocodiles...*

I tried to turn away, but the shadows and the sounds and the stench were everywhere. Then I remembered something I used to do in half-conscious nightmares as a boy, and began to repeat to myself, "This is a dream! This is a dream!" But it was of no use, and I could only shut my eyes and pray...at least, that is what I think I did, for one is never sure in visions—and I know this can have been nothing more. I wondered whether I should ever reach the world again, and at times would furtively open my eyes to see if I could discern any feature of the place other than the wind of spiced putrefaction, the topless columns, and the thaumatropically grotesque shadows of abnormal horror. The sputtering glare of multiplying torches now shone, and unless this hellish place were wholly without walls, I could not fail to see some boundary or fixed landmark soon. But I had to shut my eyes again when I realised how many of the things were assembling–and when I glimpsed a certain object walking solemnly and steadily *without any body above the waist.*

A fiendish and ululant corpse-gurgle or death-rattle now split the very atmosphere–the charnel atmosphere poisonous with naphtha and bitumen blasts–in one concerted chorus from the ghoulish legion of hybrid blasphemies. My eyes, perversely shaken open, gazed for an instant upon a sight which no human creature could even imagine without panic fear and physical exhaustion. The things had filed ceremonially in one direction, the direction of the noisome wind, where the light of their torches shewed their bended heads...or the bended heads of such as had heads...They were worshipping before a great black foetor-belching aperture which reached up almost out of sight, and which I could see was flanked at right angles by two giant staircases whose ends were far away in shadow. One of these was indubitably the staircase I had fallen down.

The dimensions of the hole were fully in proportion with those of the columns–an ordinary house would have been lost in it, and any average public building could easily have been moved in and out. It was so vast a surface that only by moving the eye could one trace its boundaries...so vast, so hideously black, and so aromatically stinking...Directly in front of this yawning Polyphemus-door the things were throwing objects—evidently sacrifices or religious offerings, to judge by their gestures. Khephren was their leader; sneering King Khephren or the guide Abdul Reis, crowned with a golden pshent and intoning endless formulae with the hollow voice of the dead. By his side knelt beautiful Queen Nitokris, whom I saw in profile for a moment, noting that the right half of her face was eaten away by rats or other ghouls. And I shut my eyes again when I saw what objects were being thrown as offerings to the foetid aperture or its possible local deity.

It occurred to me that judging from the elaborateness of this worship, the concealed deity must be one of considerable importance. Was it Osiris or Isis, Horus or Anubis, or some vast unknown God of the Dead still more central and supreme? There is a legend that terrible altars and colossi were reared to an Unknown One before ever the known gods were worshipped...

And now, as I steeled myself to watch the rapt and sepulchral adorations of those nameless things, a thought of escape flashed upon me. The hall was dim, and the columns heavy with shadow. With every creature of that nightmare throng absorbed in shocking raptures, it might be barely possible for me to creep past to the faraway end of one of the staircases and ascend unseen; trusting to Fate and skill to deliver me from the upper reaches. Where I was, I neither knew nor seriously reflected upon—and for a moment it struck me as amusing to plan a serious escape from that which I knew to be a dream. Was I in some hidden and unsuspected lower realm of Khephren's gateway temple—that temple which generations have persistently called the Temple of the Sphinx? I could not conjecture, but I resolved to ascend to life and consciousness if wit and muscle could carry me.

Wriggling flat on my stomach, I began the anxious journey toward the foot of the left-hand staircase, which seemed the more accessible of the two. I cannot describe the incidents and sensations of that crawl, but they may be guessed when one reflects on *what I had to watch steadily in that malign, wind-blown torchlight* in order to avoid detection. The bottom of the staircase was, as I have said, far away in shadow; as it had to be to rise without a bend to the dizzy parapeted landing above the titanic aperture. This placed the last stages of my crawl at some distance from the noisome herd, though the spectacle chilled me even when quite remote at my right.

At length I succeeded in reaching the steps and began to climb; keeping close to the wall, on which I observed decorations of the most hideous sort, and relying for safety on the absorbed, ecstatic interest with which the monstrosities watched the foul-breezed aperture and the impious objects of nourishment they had flung on the pavement before it. Though the staircase was huge and steep, fashioned of vast porphyry blocks as if for the feet of a giant, the ascent seemed virtually interminable. Dread of discovery and the pain which renewed exercise had brought to my wounds combined to make that upward crawl a thing of agonising memory. I had intended, on reaching the landing, to climb immediately onward along whatever upper staircase might mount from there; stopping for no last look at the carrion abominations that pawed and genuflected some seventy or eighty feet below—yet a sudden repetition of that thunderous corpse-gurgle and death-rattle chorus, coming as I had nearly gained the top of the flight and shewing by its ceremonial rhythm that it was not an alarm of my discovery, caused me to pause and peer cautiously over the parapet.

The monstrosities were hailing something which had poked itself out of the nauseous aperture to seize the hellish fare proffered it. It was something quite ponderous, even as seen from my height; something yellowish and hairy, and endowed with a sort of nervous motion. It was as large, perhaps, as a good-sized hippopotamus, but very curiously shaped. It seemed to have no neck, but five separate shaggy heads springing in a row from a roughly cylindrical trunk; the first very small, the second good-sized, the third and fourth equal and largest of all, and the fifth rather small, though not so small as the first. Out of these heads darted curious rigid tentacles which seized ravenously on the *excessively great* quantities of unmentionable food placed before the aperture. Once in a while the thing would leap up, and occasionally it would retreat into its den in a very odd manner. Its locomotion was so inexplicable that I stared in fascination, wishing it would emerge further from the cavernous lair beneath me.

Then it *did* emerge...it *did* emerge, and at the sight I turned and fled into the darkness up the higher staircase that rose behind me; fled unknowingly up incredible steps and ladders and inclined planes to which no human sight or logic guided me, and which I must ever relegate to the world of dreams for want of any confirmation. It must have been a dream, or the dawn would never have found me breathing on the sands of Gizeh before the sardonic dawn-flushed face of the Great Sphinx.

The Great Sphinx! God!—that *idle question* I asked myself on that sun-blest morning before...*what huge and loathsome abnormality was the Sphinx originally carven to represent?* Accursed is the sight, be it in dream or not, that revealed to me the supreme horror—the Unknown God of the Dead, which licks its colossal chops in the unsuspected abyss, fed hideous morsels by soulless absurdities that should not exist. The five-headed monster that emerged...that five-headed monster as large as a hippopotamus...the five-headed monster—*and that of which it is the merest fore paw...*

But I survived, and I know it was only a dream.

The Picture in the House

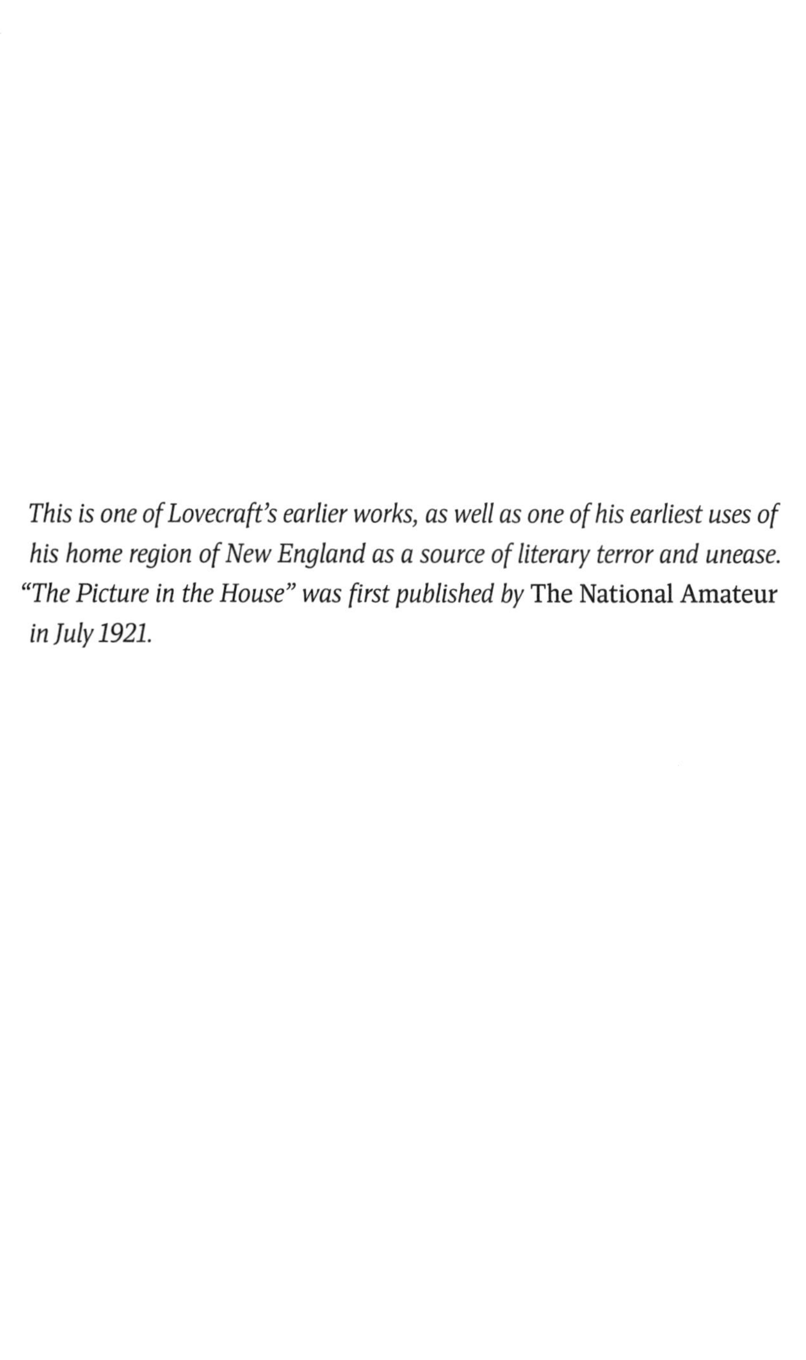

This is one of Lovecraft's earlier works, as well as one of his earliest uses of his home region of New England as a source of literary terror and unease. "The Picture in the House" was first published by The National Amateur *in July 1921.*

Searchers after horror haunt strange, far places. For them are the catacombs of Ptolemais, and the carven mausolea of the nightmare countries. They climb to the moonlit towers of ruined Rhine castles, and falter down black cobwebbed steps beneath the scattered stones of forgotten cities in Asia. The haunted wood and the desolate mountain are their shrines, and they linger around the sinister monoliths on uninhabited islands. But the true epicure in the terrible, to whom a new thrill of unutterable ghastliness is the chief end and justification of existence, esteems most of all the ancient, lonely farmhouses of backwoods New England; for there the dark elements of strength, solitude, grotesqueness, and ignorance combine to form the perfection of the hideous.

Most horrible of all sights are the little unpainted wooden houses remote from travelled ways, usually squatted upon some damp, grassy slope or leaning against some gigantic outcropping of rock. Two hundred years and more they have leaned or squatted there, while the vines have crawled and the trees have swelled and spread. They are almost hidden now in lawless luxuriances of green and guardian shrouds of shadow; but the small-paned windows still stare shockingly, as if blinking through a lethal stupor which wards off madness by dulling the memory of unutterable things.

In such houses have dwelt generations of strange people, whose like the world has never seen. Seized with a gloomy and fanatical belief which exiled them from their kind, their ancestors sought the wilderness for freedom. There the scions of a conquering race indeed flourished free from the restrictions of their fellows, but cowered in an appalling slavery to the dismal phantasms of their own minds. Divorced from the enlightenment of civilisation, the strength of these Puritans turned into singular channels; and in their isolation, morbid self-repression, and struggle for life with relentless Nature, there came to them dark furtive traits from the prehistoric depths of their cold Northern heritage. By necessity practical and by philosophy stern, these folk were not beautiful in their sins. Erring as all mortals must, they were forced by their rigid code to seek concealment above all else; so that they came to use less and less taste in what they concealed. Only the silent, sleepy, staring houses in the backwoods can tell all that has lain hidden since the early days; and they are not communicative, being loath to shake off the drowsiness which helps them forget. Sometimes one feels that it would be merciful to tear down these houses, for they must often dream.

It was to a time-battered edifice of this description that I was driven one afternoon in November, 1896, by a rain of such chilling copiousness that any shelter was preferable to exposure. I had been travelling for some time amongst the people of the Miskatonic Valley in quest of certain genealogical data; and from the remote, devious, and problematical nature of my course, had deemed it convenient to employ a bicycle despite the lateness of the season. Now I found myself upon an apparently abandoned road which I had chosen as the shortest cut to Arkham; overtaken by the storm at a point far from any town, and confronted with no refuge save the antique and repellent wooden building which blinked with bleared windows from between two huge leafless elms near the foot of a rocky hill. Distant though it was from the remnant of a road, the house none the less impressed me unfavourably the very moment I espied it. Honest, wholesome structures do not stare at travellers so slyly and hauntingly, and in my genealogical researches I had encountered legends of a century before which biassed me against places of this kind. Yet the force of the elements was such as to overcome my scruples, and I did not hesitate to wheel my machine up the weedy rise to the closed door which seemed at once so suggestive and secretive.

I had somehow taken it for granted that the house was abandoned, yet as I approached it I was not so sure; for though the walks were indeed overgrown with weeds, they seemed to retain their nature a little too well to argue complete desertion. Therefore instead of trying the door I knocked, feeling as I did so a trepidation I could scarcely explain. As I waited on the rough, mossy rock which served as a doorstep, I glanced at the neighbouring windows and the panes of the transom above me, and noticed that although old, rattling, and almost opaque with dirt, they were not broken. The building, then, must still be inhabited, despite its isolation and general neglect. However, my rapping evoked no response, so after repeating the summons I tried the rusty latch and found the door unfastened. Inside was a little vestibule with walls from which the plaster was falling, and through the doorway came a faint but peculiarly hateful odour. I entered, carrying my bicycle, and closed the door behind me. Ahead rose a narrow staircase, flanked by a small door probably leading to the cellar, while to the left and right were closed doors leading to rooms on the ground floor.

Leaning my cycle against the wall I opened the door at the left, and crossed into a small low-ceiled chamber but dimly lighted by its two dusty windows and furnished in the barest and most primitive possible way. It appeared to be a kind of sitting-room, for it had a table and several chairs, and an immense fireplace above which ticked an antique clock on a mantel. Books and papers were very few, and in the prevailing gloom I could not readily discern the titles. What interested me was the uniform air of archaism as displayed in every visible detail. Most of the houses in this region I had found rich in relics of the past, but here the antiquity was curiously complete; for in all the room I could not discover a single article of definitely post-revolutionary date. Had the furnishings been less humble, the place would have been a collector's paradise.

As I surveyed this quaint apartment, I felt an increase in that aversion first excited by the bleak exterior of the house. Just what it was that I feared or loathed, I could by no means define; but something in the whole atmosphere seemed redolent of unhallowed age, of unpleasant crudeness, and of secrets which should be forgotten. I felt disinclined to sit down, and wandered about examining the various articles which I had noticed. The first object of my curiosity was a book of medium size lying upon the table and presenting such an antediluvian aspect that I marvelled at beholding it outside a museum or library. It was bound in leather with metal fittings, and was in an excellent state of preservation; being altogether an unusual sort of volume to encounter in an abode so lowly. When I opened it to the title page my wonder grew even greater, for it proved to be nothing less rare than Pigafetta's account of the Congo region, written in Latin from the notes of the sailor Lopez and printed at Frankfort in 1598. I had often heard of this work, with its curious illustrations by the brothers De Bry, hence for a moment forgot my uneasiness in my desire to turn the pages before me. The engravings were indeed interesting, drawn wholly from imagination and careless descriptions, and represented negroes with white skins and Caucasian features; nor would I soon have closed the book had not an exceedingly trivial circumstance upset my tired nerves and revived my sensation of disquiet. What annoyed me was merely the persistent way in which the volume tended to fall open of itself at Plate XII, which represented in gruesome detail a butcher's shop of the cannibal Anziques. I experienced some shame at my susceptibility to so slight a thing, but the drawing nevertheless disturbed me, especially in connexion with some adjacent passages descriptive of Anzique gastronomy.

I had turned to a neighbouring shelf and was examining its meagre literary contents—an eighteenth-century Bible, a *Pilgrim's Progress* of like period, illustrated with grotesque woodcuts and printed by the almanack-maker Isaiah Thomas, the rotting bulk of Cotton Mather's *Magnalia Christi Americana*, and a few other books of evidently equal age—when my attention was aroused by the unmistakable sound of walking in the room overhead. At first astonished and startled, considering the lack of response to my recent knocking at the door, I immediately afterward concluded that the walker had just awakened from a sound sleep; and listened with less surprise as the footsteps sounded on the creaking stairs. The tread was heavy, yet seemed to contain a curious quality of cautiousness; a quality which I disliked the more because the tread was heavy. When I had entered the room I had shut the door behind me.

Now, after a moment of silence during which the walker may have been inspecting my bicycle in the hall, I heard a fumbling at the latch and saw the panelled portal swing open again.

In the doorway stood a person of such singular appearance that I should have exclaimed aloud but for the restraints of good breeding. Old, white-bearded, and ragged, my host possessed a countenance and physique which inspired equal wonder and respect. His height could not have been less than six feet, and despite a general air of age and poverty he was stout and powerful in proportion. His face, almost hidden by a long beard which grew high on the cheeks, seemed abnormally ruddy and less wrinkled than one might expect; while over a high forehead fell a shock of white hair little thinned by the years. His blue eyes, though a trifle bloodshot, seemed inexplicably keen and burning. But for his horrible unkemptness the man would have been as distinguished-looking as he was impressive. This unkemptness, however, made him offensive despite his face and figure. Of what his clothing consisted I could hardly tell, for it seemed to me no more than a mass of tatters surmounting a pair of high, heavy boots; and his lack of cleanliness surpassed description.

The appearance of this man, and the instinctive fear he inspired, prepared me for something like enmity; so that I almost shuddered through surprise and a sense of uncanny incongruity when he motioned me to a chair and addressed me in a thin, weak voice full of fawning respect and ingratiating hospitality. His speech was very curious, an extreme form of Yankee dialect I had thought long extinct; and I studied it closely as he sat down opposite me for conversation.

“Ketched in the rain, be ye?” he greeted. “Glad ye was nigh the haouse en’ hed the sense ta come right in. I calc’late I was asleep, else I'd a heerd ye—I ain't as young as I uster be, an' I need a paowerful sight o' naps naowadays. Trav'lin' fur? I hain't seed many folks 'long this rud sence they tuk off the Arkham stage."

I replied that I was going to Arkham, and apologised for my rude entry into his domicile, whereupon he continued.

"Glad ta see ye, young Sir—new faces is scurce arount here, an' I hain't got much ta cheer me up these days. Guess yew hail from Bosting, don't ye? I never ben thar, but I kin tell a taown man when I see 'im—we hed one fer deestrick schoolmaster in 'eighty-four, but he quit suddent an' no one never heerd on 'im sence—" Here the old man lapsed into a kind of chuckle, and made no explanation when I questioned him. He seemed to be in an aboundingly good humour, yet to possess those eccentricities which one might guess from his grooming. For some time he rambled on with an almost feverish geniality, when it struck me to ask him how he came by so rare a book as Pigafetta's *Regnum Congo*. The effect of this volume had not left me, and I felt a certain hesitancy in speaking of it; but curiosity overmastered all the vague fears which had steadily accumulated since my first glimpse of the house. To my relief, the question did not seem an awkward one; for the old man answered freely and volubly.

"Oh, thet Afriky book? Cap'n Ebenezer Holt traded me thet in 'sixty-eight—him as was kilt in the war." Something about the name of Ebenezer Holt caused me to look up sharply. I had encountered it in my genealogical work, but not in any record since the Revolution. I wondered if my host could help me in the task at which I was labouring, and resolved to ask him about it later on. He continued.

"Ebenezer was on a Salem merchantman for years, an' picked up a sight o' queer stuff in every port. He got this in London, I guess—he uster like ter buy things at the shops. I was up ta his haouse onct, on the hill, tradin' hosses, when I see this book. I relished the picters, so he give it in on a swap. 'Tis a queer book—here, leave me git on my spectacles—" The old man fumbled among his rags, producing a pair of dirty and amazingly antique glasses with small octagonal lenses and steel bows. Donning these, he reached for the volume on the table and turned the pages lovingly.

"Ebenezer cud read a leetle o' this—'tis Latin—but I can't. I hed two er three schoolmasters read me a bit, and Passon Clark, him they say got draownded in the pond—kin yew make anything outen it?" I told him that I could, and translated for his benefit a paragraph near the beginning. If I erred, he was not scholar enough to correct me; for he seemed childishly pleased at my English version. His proximity was becoming rather obnoxious, yet I saw no way to escape without offending him. I was amused at the childish fondness of this ignorant old man for the pictures in a book he could not read, and wondered how much better he could read the few books in English which adorned the room. This revelation of simplicity removed much of the ill-defined apprehension I had felt, and I smiled as my host rambled on:

"Queer haow picters kin set a body thinkin.' Take this un here near the front. Hev yew ever seed trees like thet, with big leaves a-floppin' over an' daown? And them men—them can't be niggers—they dew beat all. Kinder like Injuns, I guess, even ef they be in Afriky. Some o' these here critters looks like monkeys, or half monkeys an' half men, but I never heerd o' nothing like this un." Here he pointed to a fabulous creature of the artist, which one might describe as a sort of dragon with the head of an alligator.

"But naow I'll shew ye the best un—over here nigh the middle—" The old man's speech grew a trifle thicker and his eyes assumed a brighter glow; but his fumbling hands, though seemingly clumsier than before, were entirely adequate to their mission. The book fell open, almost of its own accord and as if from frequent consultation at this place, to the repellent twelfth plate shewing a butcher's shop amongst the Anzique cannibals. My sense of restlessness returned, though I did not exhibit it. The especially bizarre thing was that the artist had made his Africans look like white men—the limbs and quarters hanging about the walls of the shop were ghastly, while the butcher with his axe was hideously incongruous. But my host seemed to relish the view as much as I disliked it.

"What d'ye think o' this—ain't never see the like hereabouts, eh? When I see this I telled Eb Holt, 'That's suthin' ta stir ye up an' make yer blood tickle!' When I read in Scripter about slayin'—like them Midianites was slew—I kinder think things, but I ain't got no picter of it. Here a body kin see all they is to it—I s'pose 'tis sinful, but ain't we all born an' livin' in sin?—Thet feller bein' chopped up gives me a tickle every time I look at 'im—I hev ta keep lookin' at 'im—see whar the butcher cut off his feet? Thar's his head on thet bench, with one arm side of it, an' t'other arm's on the graound side o' the meat block."

As the man mumbled on in his shocking ecstasy the expression on his hairy, spectacled face became indescribable, but his voice sank rather than mounted. My own sensations can scarcely be recorded. All the terror I had dimly felt before rushed upon me actively and vividly, and I knew that I loathed the ancient and abhorrent creature so near me with an infinite intensity. His madness, or at least his partial perversion, seemed beyond dispute. He was almost whispering now, with a huskiness more terrible than a scream, and I trembled as I listened.

"As I says, 'tis queer haow picters sets ye thinkin.' D'ye know, young Sir, I'm right sot on this un here. Arter I got the book off Eb I uster look at it a lot, especial when I'd heerd Passon Clark rant o' Sundays in his big wig. Onct I tried suthin' funny–here, young Sir, don't git skeert–all I done was ter look at the picter afore I kilt the sheep for market–killin' sheep was kinder more fun arter lookin' at it–" The tone of the old man now sank very low, sometimes becoming so faint that his words were hardly audible. I listened to the rain, and to the rattling of the bleared, small-paned windows, and marked a rumbling of approaching thunder quite unusual for the season. Once a terrific flash and peal shook the frail house to its foundations, but the whisperer seemed not to notice it.

"Killin' sheep was kinder more fun–but d'ye know, 'twan't quite *satisfyin.'* Queer haow a cravin' gits a holt on ye–As ye love the Almighty, young man, don't tell nobody, but I swar ter Gawd thet picter begun ta make me *hungry fer victuals I couldn't raise nor buy*–here, set still, what's ailin' ye?–I didn't do nothin,' only I wondered haow 'twud be ef I *did*–They say meat makes blood an' flesh, an' gives ye new life, so I wondered ef 'twudn't make a man live longer an' longer ef *'twas more the same*–" But the whisperer never continued. The interruption was not produced by my fright, nor by the rapidly increasing storm amidst whose fury I was presently to open my eyes on a smoky solitude of blackened ruins. It was produced by a very simple though somewhat unusual happening.

The open book lay flat between us, with the picture staring repulsively upward. As the old man whispered the words *"more the same"* a tiny spattering impact was heard, and something shewed on the yellowed paper of the upturned volume. I thought of the rain and of a leaky roof, but rain is not red. On the butcher's shop of the Anzique cannibals a small red spattering glistened picturesquely, lending vividness to the horror of the engraving. The old man saw it, and stopped whispering even before my expression of horror made it necessary; saw it and glanced quickly toward the floor of the room he had left an hour before. I followed his glance, and beheld just above us on the loose plaster of the ancient ceiling a large irregular spot of wet crimson which seemed to spread even as I viewed it. I did not shriek or move, but merely shut my eyes. A moment later came the titanic thunderbolt of thunderbolts; blasting that accursed house of unutterable secrets and bringing the oblivion which alone saved my mind.

Dagon

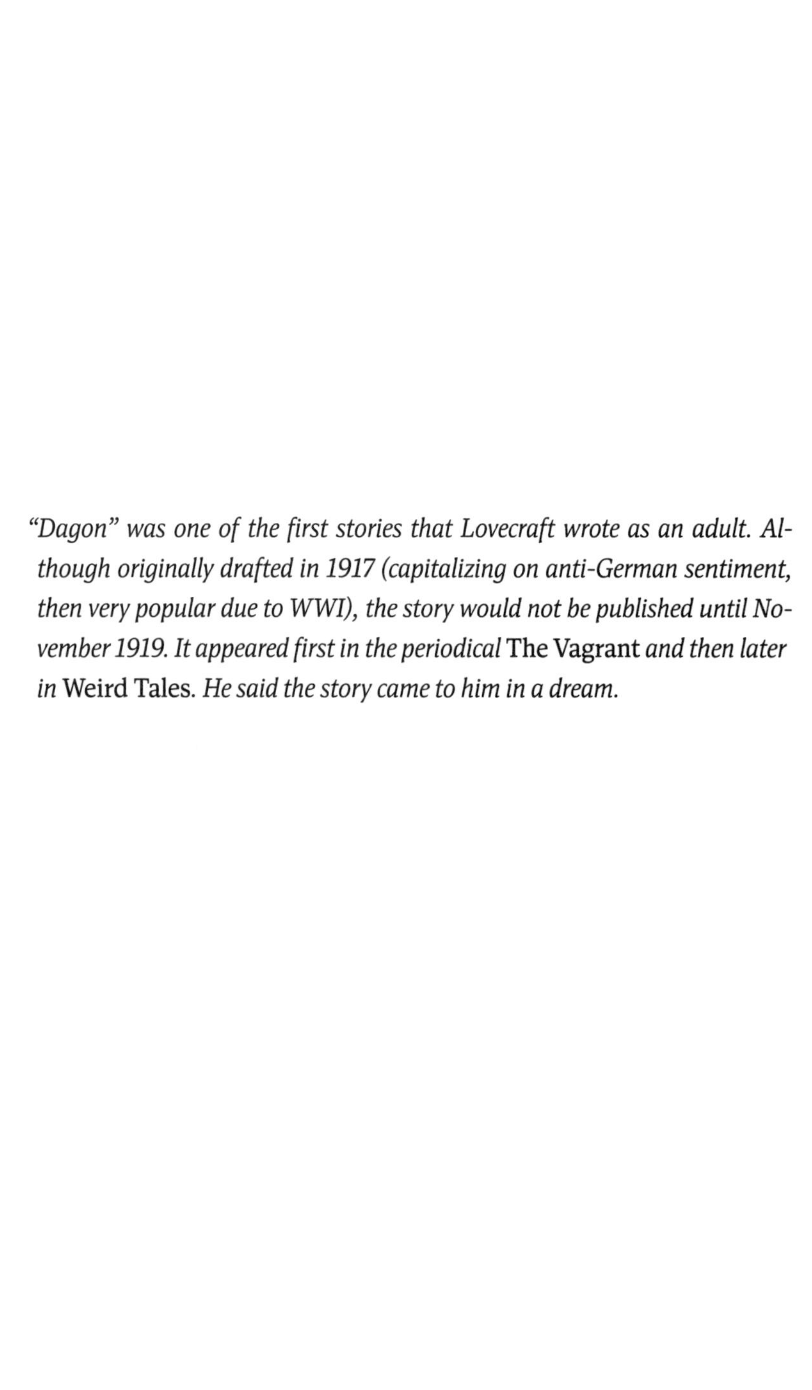

"Dagon" was one of the first stories that Lovecraft wrote as an adult. Although originally drafted in 1917 (capitalizing on anti-German sentiment, then very popular due to WWI), the story would not be published until November 1919. It appeared first in the periodical The Vagrant *and then later in* Weird Tales. *He said the story came to him in a dream.*

I am writing this under an appreciable mental strain, since by tonight I shall be no more. Penniless, and at the end of my supply of the drug which alone makes life endurable, I can bear the torture no longer; and shall cast myself from this garret window into the squalid street below. Do not think from my slavery to morphine that I am a weakling or a degenerate. When you have read these hastily scrawled pages you may guess, though never fully realise, why it is that I must have forgetfulness or death.

It was in one of the most open and least frequented parts of the broad Pacific that the packet of which I was supercargo fell a victim to the German sea-raider. The great war was then at its very beginning, and the ocean forces of the Hun had not completely sunk to their later degradation; so that our vessel was made a legitimate prize, whilst we of her crew were treated with all the fairness and consideration due us as naval prisoners. So liberal, indeed, was the discipline of our captors, that five days after we were taken I managed to escape alone in a small boat with water and provisions for a good length of time.

When I finally found myself adrift and free, I had but little idea of my surroundings. Never a competent navigator, I could only guess vaguely by the sun and stars that I was somewhat south of the equator. Of the longitude I knew nothing, and no island or coast-line was in sight. The weather kept fair, and for uncounted days I drifted aimlessly beneath the scorching sun; waiting either for some passing ship, or to be cast on the shores of some habitable land. But neither ship nor land appeared, and I began to despair in my solitude upon the heaving vastnesses of unbroken blue.

The change happened whilst I slept. Its details I shall never know; for my slumber, though troubled and dream-infested, was continuous. When at last I awaked, it was to discover myself half sucked into a slimy expanse of hellish black mire which extended about me in monotonous undulations as far as I could see, and in which my boat lay grounded some distance away.

Though one might well imagine that my first sensation would be of wonder at so prodigious and unexpected a transformation of scenery, I was in reality more horrified than astonished; for there was in the air and in the rotting soil a sinister quality which chilled me to the very core. The region was putrid with the carcasses of decaying fish, and of other less describable things which I saw protruding from the nasty mud of the unending plain. Perhaps I should not hope to convey in mere words the unutterable hideousness that can dwell in absolute silence and barren immensity. There was nothing within hearing, and nothing in sight save a vast reach of black slime; yet the very completeness of the stillness and the homogeneity of the landscape oppressed me with a nauseating fear.

The sun was blazing down from a sky which seemed to me almost black in its cloudless cruelty; as though reflecting the inky marsh beneath my feet. As I crawled into the stranded boat I realised that only one theory could explain my position. Through some unprecedented volcanic upheaval, a portion of the ocean floor must have been thrown to the surface, exposing regions which for innumerable millions of years had lain hidden under unfathomable watery depths. So great was the extent of the new land which had risen beneath me, that I could not detect the faintest noise of the surging ocean, strain my ears as I might. Nor were there any sea-fowl to prey upon the dead things.

For several hours I sat thinking or brooding in the boat, which lay upon its side and afforded a slight shade as the sun moved across the heavens. As the day progressed, the ground lost some of its stickiness, and seemed likely to dry sufficiently for travelling purposes in a short time. That night I slept but little, and the next day I made for myself a pack containing food and water, preparatory to an overland journey in search of the vanished sea and possible rescue.

On the third morning I found the soil dry enough to walk upon with ease. The odour of the fish was maddening; but I was too much concerned with graver things to mind so slight an evil, and set out boldly for an unknown goal. All day I forged steadily westward, guided by a far-away hummock which rose higher than any other elevation on the rolling desert. That night I encamped, and on the following day still travelled toward the hummock, though that object seemed scarcely nearer than when I had first espied it. By the fourth evening I attained the base of the mound, which turned out to be much higher than it had appeared from a distance; an intervening valley setting it out in sharper relief from the general surface. Too weary to ascend, I slept in the shadow of the hill.

I know not why my dreams were so wild that night; but ere the waning and fantastically gibbous moon had risen far above the eastern plain, I was awake in a cold perspiration, determined to sleep no more. Such visions as I had experienced were too much for me to endure again. And in the glow of the moon I saw how unwise I had been to travel by day. Without the glare of the parching sun, my journey would have cost me less energy; indeed, I now felt quite able to perform the ascent which had deterred me at sunset. Picking up my pack, I started for the crest of the eminence.

I have said that the unbroken monotony of the rolling plain was a source of vague horror to me; but I think my horror was greater when I gained the summit of the mound and looked down the other side into an immeasurable pit or canyon, whose black recesses the moon had not yet soared high enough to illumine. I felt myself on the edge of the world; peering over the rim into a fathomless chaos of eternal night. Through my terror ran curious reminiscences of *Paradise Lost*, and of Satan's hideous climb through the unfashioned realms of darkness.

As the moon climbed higher in the sky, I began to see that the slopes of the valley were not quite so perpendicular as I had imagined. Ledges and outcroppings of rock afforded fairly easy foot-holds for a descent, whilst after a drop of a few hundred feet, the declivity became very gradual. Urged on by an impulse which I cannot definitely analyse, I scrambled with difficulty down the rocks and stood on the gentler slope beneath, gazing into the Stygian deeps where no light had yet penetrated.

All at once my attention was captured by a vast and singular object on the opposite slope, which rose steeply about an hundred yards ahead of me; an object that gleamed whitely in the newly bestowed rays of the ascending moon. That it was merely a gigantic piece of stone, I soon assured myself; but I was conscious of a distinct impression that its contour and position were not altogether the work of Nature. A closer scrutiny filled me with sensations I cannot express; for despite its enormous magnitude, and its position in an abyss which had yawned at the bottom of the sea since the world was young, I perceived beyond a doubt that the strange object was a well-shaped monolith whose massive bulk had known the workmanship and perhaps the worship of living and thinking creatures.

Dazed and frightened, yet not without a certain thrill of the scientist's or archaeologist's delight, I examined my surroundings more closely. The moon, now near the zenith, shone weirdly and vividly above the towering steeps that hemmed in the chasm, and revealed the fact that a far-flung body of water flowed at the bottom, winding out of sight in both directions, and almost lapping my feet as I stood on the slope. Across the chasm, the wavelets washed the base of the Cyclopean monolith; on whose surface I could now trace both inscriptions and crude sculptures. The writing was in a system of hieroglyphics unknown to me, and unlike anything I had ever seen in books; consisting for the most part of conventionalised aquatic symbols such as fishes, eels, octopi, crustaceans, molluscs, whales, and the like. Several characters obviously represented marine things which are unknown to the modern world, but whose decomposing forms I had observed on the ocean-risen plain.

It was the pictorial carving, however, that did most to hold me spellbound. Plainly visible across the intervening water on account of their enormous size, were an array of bas-reliefs whose subjects would have excited the envy of a Doré. I think that these things were supposed to depict men—at least, a certain sort of men; though the creatures were shewn disporting like fishes in the waters of some marine grotto, or paying homage at some monolithic shrine which appeared to be under the waves as well. Of their faces and forms I dare not speak in detail; for the mere remembrance makes me grow faint. Grotesque beyond the imagination of a Poe or a Bulwer, they were damnably human in general outline despite webbed hands and feet, shockingly wide and flabby lips, glassy, bulging eyes, and other features less pleasant to recall. Curiously enough, they seemed to have been chiselled badly out of proportion with their scenic background; for one of the creatures was shewn in the act of killing a whale represented as but little larger than himself. I remarked, as I say, their grotesqueness and strange size; but in a moment decided that they were merely the imaginary gods of some primitive fishing or seafaring tribe; some tribe whose last descendant had perished eras before the first ancestor of the Piltdown or Neanderthal Man was born. Awestruck at this unexpected glimpse into a past beyond the conception of the most daring anthropologist, I stood musing whilst the moon cast queer reflections on the silent channel before me.

Then suddenly I saw it. With only a slight churning to mark its rise to the surface, the thing slid into view above the dark waters. Vast, Polyphemus-like, and loathsome, it darted like a stupendous monster of nightmares to the monolith, about which it flung its gigantic scaly arms, the while it bowed its hideous head and gave vent to certain measured sounds. I think I went mad then.

Of my frantic ascent of the slope and cliff, and of my delirious journey back to the stranded boat, I remember little. I believe I sang a great deal, and laughed oddly when I was unable to sing. I have indistinct recollections of a great storm some time after I reached the boat; at any rate, I know that I heard peals of thunder and other tones which Nature utters only in her wildest moods.

When I came out of the shadows I was in a San Francisco hospital; brought thither by the captain of the American ship which had picked up my boat in mid-ocean. In my delirium I had said much, but found that my words had been given scant attention. Of any land upheaval in the Pacific, my rescuers knew nothing; nor did I deem it necessary to insist upon a thing which I knew they could not believe. Once I sought out a celebrated ethnologist, and amused him with peculiar questions regarding the ancient Philistine legend of Dagon, the Fish-God; but soon perceiving that he was hopelessly conventional, I did not press my inquiries.

It is at night, especially when the moon is gibbous and waning, that I see the thing. I tried morphine; but the drug has given only transient surcease, and has drawn me into its clutches as a hopeless slave. So now I am to end it all, having written a full account for the information or the contemptuous amusement of my fellow-men. Often I ask myself if it could not all have been a pure phantasm—a mere freak of fever as I lay sun-stricken and raving in the open boat after my escape from the German man-of-war. This I ask myself, but ever does there come before me a hideously vivid vision in reply. I cannot think of the deep sea without shuddering at the nameless things that may at this very moment be crawling and floundering on its slimy bed, worshipping their ancient stone idols and carving their own detestable likenesses on submarine obelisks of water-soaked granite. I dream of a day when they may rise above the billows to drag down in their reeking talons the remnants of puny, war-exhausted mankind—of a day when the land shall sink, and the dark ocean floor shall ascend amidst universal pandemonium.

The end is near. I hear a noise at the door, as of some immense slippery body lumbering against it. It shall not find me. God, *that hand!* The window! The window!

The Rats in the Walls

Written in late 1923, this story was first rejected by the pulp magazine Argosy All-Story Weekly *for being (according to Lovecraft) "too horrible for the tender sensibilities of a delicately nurtured publick." Fortunately, it eventually found a home at* Weird Tales *and was published for the first time in October 1924. The publisher of* Weird Tales *J.C. Henneberger, considered it to be the best story Lovecraft had ever written. It was an immediate success, and a later reprint inspired pulp writer Robert E. Howard, author of the famous* Conan the Barbarian *series, to strike up a correspondence and close personal friendship with Lovecraft. Today, all of the story's many finer qualities have been sadly overshadowed by the name of the eldest cat.*

On July 16, 1923, I moved into Exham Priory after the last workman had finished his labours. The restoration had been a stupendous task, for little had remained of the deserted pile but a shell-like ruin; yet because it had been the seat of my ancestors I let no expense deter me. The place had not been inhabited since the reign of James the First, when a tragedy of intensely hideous, though largely unexplained, nature had struck down the master, five of his children, and several servants; and driven forth under a cloud of suspicion and terror the third son, my lineal progenitor and the only survivor of the abhorred line. With this sole heir denounced as a murderer, the estate had reverted to the crown, nor had the accused man made any attempt to exculpate himself or regain his property. Shaken by some horror greater than that of conscience or the law, and expressing only a frantic wish to exclude the ancient edifice from his sight and memory, Walter de la Poer, eleventh Baron Exham, fled to Virginia and there founded the family which by the next century had become known as Delapore.

Exham Priory had remained untenanted, though later allotted to the estates of the Norrys family and much studied because of its peculiarly composite architecture; an architecture involving Gothic towers resting on a Saxon or Romanesque substructure, whose foundation in turn was of a still earlier order or blend of orders–Roman, and even Druidic or native Cymric, if legends speak truly. This foundation was a very singular thing, being merged on one side with the solid limestone of the precipice from whose brink the priory overlooked a desolate valley three miles west of the village of Anchester. Architects and antiquarians loved to examine this strange relic of forgotten centuries, but the country folk hated it. They had hated it hundreds of years before, when my ancestors lived there, and they hated it now, with the moss and mould of abandonment on it. I had not been a day in Anchester before I knew I came of an accursed house. And this week workmen have blown up Exham Priory, and are busy obliterating the traces of its foundations.

The bare statistics of my ancestry I had always known, together with the fact that my first American forbear had come to the colonies under a strange cloud. Of details, however, I had been kept wholly ignorant through the policy of reticence always maintained by the Delapores. Unlike our planter neighbours, we seldom boasted of crusading ancestors or other mediaeval and Renaissance heroes; nor was any kind of tradition handed down except what may have been recorded in the sealed envelope left before the Civil War by every squire to his eldest son for posthumous opening. The glories we cherished were those achieved since the migration; the glories of a proud and honourable, if somewhat reserved and unsocial Virginia line.

During the war our fortunes were extinguished and our whole existence changed by the burning of Carfax, our home on the banks of the James. My grandfather, advanced in years, had perished in that incendiary outrage, and with him the envelope that bound us all to the past. I can recall that fire today as I saw it then at the age of seven, with the Federal soldiers shouting, the women screaming, and the negroes howling and praying. My father was in the army, defending Richmond, and after many formalities my mother and I were passed through the lines to join him. When the war ended we all moved north, whence my mother had come; and I grew to manhood, middle age, and ultimate wealth as a stolid Yankee. Neither my father nor I ever knew what our hereditary envelope had contained, and as I merged into the greyness of Massachusetts business life I lost all interest in the mysteries which evidently lurked far back in my family tree. Had I suspected their nature, how gladly I would have left Exham Priory to its moss, bats, and cobwebs!

My father died in 1904, but without any message to leave me, or to my only child, Alfred, a motherless boy of ten. It was this boy who reversed the order of family information; for although I could give him only jesting conjectures about the past, he wrote me of some very interesting ancestral legends when the late war took him to England in 1917 as an aviation officer. Apparently the Delapores had a colourful and perhaps sinister history, for a friend of my son's, Capt. Edward Norrys of the Royal Flying Corps, dwelt near the family seat at Anchester and related some peasant superstitions which few novelists could equal for wildness and incredibility. Norrys himself, of course, did not take them seriously; but they amused my son and made good material for his letters to me. It was this legendry which definitely turned my attention to my transatlantic heritage, and made me resolve to purchase and restore the family seat which Norrys shewed to Alfred in its picturesque desertion, and offered to get for him at a surprisingly reasonable figure, since his own uncle was the present owner.

I bought Exham Priory in 1918, but was almost immediately distracted from my plans of restoration by the return of my son as a maimed invalid. During the two years that he lived I thought of nothing but his care, having even placed my business under the direction of partners. In 1921, as I found myself bereaved and aimless, a retired manufacturer no longer young, I resolved to divert my remaining years with my new possession. Visiting Anchester in December, I was entertained by Capt. Norrys, a plump, amiable young man who had thought much of my son, and secured his assistance in gathering plans and anecdotes to guide in the coming restoration. Exham Priory itself I saw without emotion, a jumble of tottering mediaeval ruins covered with lichens and honeycombed with rooks' nests, perched perilously upon a precipice, and denuded of floors or other interior features save the stone walls of the separate towers.

As I gradually recovered the image of the edifice as it had been when my ancestor left it over three centuries before, I began to hire workmen for the reconstruction. In every case I was forced to go outside the immediate locality, for the Anchester villagers had an almost unbelievable fear and hatred of the place. This sentiment was so great that it was sometimes communicated to the outside labourers, causing numerous desertions; whilst its scope appeared to include both the priory and its ancient family.

My son had told me that he was somewhat avoided during his visits because he was a de la Poer, and I now found myself subtly ostracised for a like reason until I convinced the peasants how little I knew of my heritage. Even then they sullenly disliked me, so that I had to collect most of the village traditions through the mediation of Norrys. What the people could not forgive, perhaps, was that I had come to restore a symbol so abhorrent to them; for, rationally or not, they viewed Exham Priory as nothing less than a haunt of fiends and werewolves.

Piecing together the tales which Norrys collected for me, and supplementing them with the accounts of several savants who had studied the ruins, I deduced that Exham Priory stood on the site of a prehistoric temple; a Druidical or ante-Druidical thing which must have been contemporary with Stonehenge. That indescribable rites had been celebrated there, few doubted; and there were unpleasant tales of the transference of these rites into the Cybele-worship which the Romans had introduced. Inscriptions still visible in the sub-cellar bore such unmistakable letters as "DIV...OPS...MAGNA. MAT..." sign of the Magna Mater whose dark worship was once vainly forbidden to Roman citizens. Anchester had been the camp of the third Augustan legion, as many remains attest, and it was said that the temple of Cybele was splendid and thronged with worshippers who performed nameless ceremonies at the bidding of a Phrygian priest. Tales added that the fall of the old religion did not end the orgies at the temple, but that the priests lived on in the new faith without real change. Likewise was it said that the rites did not vanish with the Roman power, and that certain among the Saxons added to what remained of the temple, and gave it the essential outline it subsequently preserved, making it the centre of a cult feared through half the heptarchy. About 1000 A.D. the place is mentioned in a chronicle as being a substantial stone priory housing a strange and powerful monastic order and surrounded by extensive gardens which needed no walls to exclude a frightened populace. It was never destroyed by the Danes, though after the Norman Conquest it must have declined tremendously; since there was no impediment when Henry the Third granted the site to my ancestor, Gilbert de la Poer, First Baron Exham, in 1261.

Of my family before this date there is no evil report, but something strange must have happened then. In one chronicle there is a reference to a de la Poer as "cursed of God" in 1307, whilst village legendry had nothing but evil and frantic fear to tell of the castle that went up on the foundations of the old temple and priory. The fireside tales were of the most grisly description, all the ghastlier because of their frightened reticence and cloudy evasiveness. They represented my ancestors as a race of hereditary daemons beside whom Gilles de Retz and the Marquis de Sade would seem the veriest tyros, and hinted whisperingly at their responsibility for the occasional disappearance of villagers through several generations.

The worst characters, apparently, were the barons and their direct heirs; at least, most was whispered about these. If of healthier inclinations, it was said, an heir would early and mysteriously die to make way for another more typical scion. There seemed to be an inner cult in the family, presided over by the head of the house, and sometimes closed except to a few members. Temperament rather than ancestry was evidently the basis of this cult, for it was entered by several who married into the family. Lady Margaret Trevor from Cornwall, wife of Godfrey, the second son of the fifth baron, became a favourite bane of children all over the countryside, and the daemon heroine of a particularly horrible old ballad not yet extinct near the Welsh border. Preserved in balladry, too, though not illustrating the same point, is the hideous tale of Lady Mary de la Poer, who shortly after her marriage to the Earl of Shrewsfield was killed by him and his mother, both of the slayers being absolved and blessed by the priest to whom they confessed what they dared not repeat to the world.

These myths and ballads, typical as they were of crude superstition, repelled me greatly. Their persistence, and their application to so long a line of my ancestors, were especially annoying; whilst the imputations of monstrous habits proved unpleasantly reminiscent of the one known scandal of my immediate forbears—the case of my cousin, young Randolph Delapore of Carfax, who went among the negroes and became a voodoo priest after he returned from the Mexican War.

I was much less disturbed by the vaguer tales of wails and howlings in the barren, windswept valley beneath the limestone cliff; of the graveyard stenches after the spring rains; of the floundering, squealing white thing on which Sir John Clave's horse had trod one night in a lonely field; and of the servant who had gone mad at what he saw in the priory in the full light of day. These things were hackneyed spectral lore, and I was at that time a pronounced sceptic. The accounts of vanished peasants were less to be dismissed, though not especially significant in view of mediaeval custom. Prying curiosity meant death, and more than one severed head had been publicly shewn on the bastions—now effaced—around Exham Priory.

A few of the tales were exceedingly picturesque, and made me wish I had learnt more of comparative mythology in my youth. There was, for instance, the belief that a legion of batwinged devils kept Witches' Sabbath each night at the priory—a legion whose sustenance might explain the disproportionate abundance of coarse vegetables harvested in the vast gardens. And, most vivid of all, there was the dramatic epic of the rats—the scampering army of obscene vermin which had burst forth from the castle three months after the tragedy that doomed it to desertion—the lean, filthy, ravenous army which had swept all before it and devoured fowl, cats, dogs, hogs, sheep, and even two hapless human beings before its fury was spent. Around that unforgettable rodent army a whole separate cycle of myths revolves, for it scattered among the village homes and brought curses and horrors in its train.

Such was the lore that assailed me as I pushed to completion, with an elderly obstinacy, the work of restoring my ancestral home. It must not be imagined for a moment that these tales formed my principal psychological environment. On the other hand, I was constantly praised and encouraged by Capt. Norrys and the antiquarians who surrounded and aided me. When the task was done, over two years after its commencement, I viewed the great rooms, wainscotted walls, vaulted ceilings, mullioned windows, and broad staircases with a pride which fully compensated for the prodigious expense of the restoration. Every attribute of the Middle Ages was cunningly reproduced, and the new parts blended perfectly with the original walls and foundations. The seat of my fathers was complete, and I looked forward to redeeming at last the local fame of the line which ended in me. I would reside here permanently, and prove that a de la Poer (for I had adopted again the original spelling of the name) need not be a fiend. My comfort was perhaps augmented by the fact that, although Exham Priory was mediaevally fitted, its interior was in truth wholly new and free from old vermin and old ghosts alike.

As I have said, I moved in on July 16, 1923. My household consisted of seven servants and nine cats, of which latter species I am particularly fond. My eldest cat, "Nigger-Man," was seven years old and had come with me from my home in Bolton, Massachusetts; the others I had accumulated whilst living with Capt. Norrys' family during the restoration of the priory. For five days our routine proceeded with the utmost placidity, my time being spent mostly in the codification of old family data. I had now obtained some very circumstantial accounts of the final tragedy and flight of Walter de la Poer, which I conceived to be the probable contents of the hereditary paper lost in the fire at Carfax. It appeared that my ancestor was accused with much reason of having killed all the other members of his household, except four servant confederates, in their sleep, about two weeks after a shocking discovery which changed his whole demeanour, but which, except by implication, he disclosed to no one save perhaps the servants who assisted him and afterward fled beyond reach.

This deliberate slaughter, which included a father, three brothers, and two sisters, was largely condoned by the villagers, and so slackly treated by the law that its perpetrator escaped honoured, unharmed, and undisguised to Virginia; the general whispered sentiment being that he had purged the land of an immemorial curse. What discovery had prompted an act so terrible, I could scarcely even conjecture. Walter de la Poer must have known for years the sinister tales about his family, so that this material could have given him no fresh impulse. Had he, then, witnessed some appalling ancient rite, or stumbled upon some frightful and revealing symbol in the priory or its vicinity? He was reputed to have been a shy, gentle youth in England. In Virginia he seemed not so much hard or bitter as harassed and apprehensive. He was spoken of in the diary of another gentleman-adventurer, Francis Harley of Bellview, as a man of unexampled justice, honour, and delicacy.

On July 22 occurred the first incident which, though lightly dismissed at the time, takes on a preternatural significance in relation to later events. It was so simple as to be almost negligible, and could not possibly have been noticed under the circumstances; for it must be recalled that since I was in a building practically fresh and new except for the walls, and surrounded by a well-balanced staff of servitors, apprehension would have been absurd despite the locality. What I afterward remembered is merely this—that my old black cat, whose moods I know so well, was undoubtedly alert and anxious to an extent wholly out of keeping with his natural character. He roved from room to room, restless and disturbed, and sniffed constantly about the walls which formed part of the old Gothic structure. I realise how trite this sounds—like the inevitable dog in the ghost story, which always growls before his master sees the sheeted figure—yet I cannot consistently suppress it.

The following day a servant complained of restlessness among all the cats in the house. He came to me in my study, a lofty west room on the second story, with groined arches, black oak panelling, and a triple Gothic window overlooking the limestone cliff and desolate valley; and even as he spoke I saw the jetty form of Nigger-Man creeping along the west wall and scratching at the new panels which overlaid the ancient stone. I told the man that there must be some singular odour or emanation from the old stonework, imperceptible to human senses, but affecting the delicate organs of cats even through the new woodwork. This I truly believed, and when the fellow suggested the presence of mice or rats, I mentioned that there had been no rats there for three hundred years, and that even the field mice of the surrounding country could hardly be found in these high walls, where they had never been known to stray. That afternoon I called on Capt. Norrys, and he assured me that it would be quite incredible for field mice to infest the priory in such a sudden and unprecedented fashion.

That night, dispensing as usual with a valet, I retired in the west tower chamber which I had chosen as my own, reached from the study by a stone staircase and short gallery—the former partly ancient, the latter entirely restored. This room was circular, very high, and without wainscotting, being hung with arras which I had myself chosen in London. Seeing that Nigger-Man was with me, I shut the heavy Gothic door and retired by the light of the electric bulbs which so cleverly counterfeited candles, finally switching off the light and sinking on the carved and canopied four-poster, with the venerable cat in his accustomed place across my feet. I did not draw the curtains, but gazed out at the narrow north window which I faced. There was a suspicion of aurora in the sky, and the delicate traceries of the window were pleasantly silhouetted.

At some time I must have fallen quietly asleep, for I recall a distinct sense of leaving strange dreams, when the cat started violently from his placid position. I saw him in the faint auroral glow, head strained forward, fore feet on my ankles, and hind feet stretched behind. He was looking intensely at a point on the wall somewhat west of the window, a point which to my eye had nothing to mark it, but toward which all my attention was now directed. And as I watched, I knew that Nigger-Man was not vainly excited. Whether the arras actually moved I cannot say. I think it did, very slightly. But what I can swear to is that behind it I heard a low, distinct scurrying as of rats or mice. In a moment the cat had jumped bodily on the screening tapestry, bringing the affected section to the floor with his weight, and exposing a damp, ancient wall of stone; patched here and there by the restorers, and devoid of any trace of rodent prowlers. Nigger-Man raced up and down the floor by this part of the wall, clawing the fallen arras and seemingly trying at times to insert a paw between the wall and the oaken floor. He found nothing, and after a time returned wearily to his place across my feet. I had not moved, but I did not sleep again that night.

In the morning I questioned all the servants, and found that none of them had noticed anything unusual, save that the cook remembered the actions of a cat which had rested on her windowsill. This cat had howled at some unknown hour of the night, awaking the cook in time for her to see him dart purposefully out of the open door down the stairs. I drowsed away the noontime, and in the afternoon called again on Capt. Norrys, who became exceedingly interested in what I told him. The odd incidents—so slight yet so curious—appealed to his sense of the picturesque, and elicited from him a number of reminiscences of local ghostly lore. We were genuinely perplexed at the presence of rats, and Norrys lent me some traps and Paris green, which I had the servants place in strategic localities when I returned.

I retired early, being very sleepy, but was harassed by dreams of the most horrible sort. I seemed to be looking down from an immense height upon a twilit grotto, knee-deep with filth, where a white-bearded daemon swineherd drove about with his staff a flock of fungous, flabby beasts whose appearance filled me with unutterable loathing. Then, as the swineherd paused and nodded over his task, a mighty swarm of rats rained down on the stinking abyss and fell to devouring beasts and man alike.

From this terrific vision I was abruptly awaked by the motions of Nigger-Man, who had been sleeping as usual across my feet. This time I did not have to question the source of his snarls and hisses, and of the fear which made him sink his claws into my ankle, unconscious of their effect; for on every side of the chamber the walls were alive with nauseous sound—the verminous slithering of ravenous, gigantic rats. There was now no aurora to shew the state of the arras—the fallen section of which had been replaced—but I was not too frightened to switch on the light.

As the bulbs leapt into radiance I saw a hideous shaking all over the tapestry, causing the somewhat peculiar designs to execute a singular dance of death. This motion disappeared almost at once, and the sound with it. Springing out of bed, I poked at the arras with the long handle of a warming-pan that rested near, and lifted one section to see what lay beneath. There was nothing but the patched stone wall, and even the cat had lost his tense realisation of abnormal presences. When I examined the circular trap that had been placed in the room, I found all of the openings sprung, though no trace remained of what had been caught and had escaped.

Further sleep was out of the question, so, lighting a candle, I opened the door and went out in the gallery toward the stairs to my study, Nigger-Man following at my heels. Before we had reached the stone steps, however, the cat darted ahead of me and vanished down the ancient flight. As I descended the stairs myself, I became suddenly aware of sounds in the great room below; sounds of a nature which could not be mistaken. The oak-panelled walls were alive with rats, scampering and milling, whilst Nigger-Man was racing about with the fury of a baffled hunter. Reaching the bottom, I switched on the light, which did not this time cause the noise to subside. The rats continued their riot, stampeding with such force and distinctness that I could finally assign to their motions a definite direction. These creatures, in numbers apparently inexhaustible, were engaged in one stupendous migration from inconceivable heights to some depth conceivably, or inconceivably, below.

I now heard steps in the corridor, and in another moment two servants pushed open the massive door. They were searching the house for some unknown source of disturbance which had thrown all the cats into a snarling panic and caused them to plunge precipitately down several flights of stairs and squat, yowling, before the closed door to the sub-cellar. I asked them if they had heard the rats, but they replied in the negative. And when I turned to call their attention to the sounds in the panels, I realised that the noise had ceased. With the two men, I went down to the door of the sub-cellar, but found the cats already dispersed. Later I resolved to explore the crypt below, but for the present I merely made a round of the traps. All were sprung, yet all were tenantless. Satisfying myself that no one had heard the rats save the felines and me, I sat in my study till morning; thinking profoundly, and recalling every scrap of legend I had unearthed concerning the building I inhabited.

I slept some in the forenoon, leaning back in the one comfortable library chair which my mediaeval plan of furnishing could not banish. Later I telephoned to Capt. Norrys, who came over and helped me explore the sub-cellar. Absolutely nothing untoward was found, although we could not repress a thrill at the knowledge that this vault was built by Roman hands. Every low arch and massive pillar was Roman—not the debased Romanesque of the bungling Saxons, but the severe and harmonious classicism of the age of the Caesars; indeed, the walls abounded with inscriptions familiar to the antiquarians who had repeatedly explored the place—things like "P. GETAE. PROP...TEMP...DONA..." and "L. PRAEC...VS...PONTIFI...ATYS..."

The reference to Atys made me shiver, for I had read Catullus and knew something of the hideous rites of the Eastern god, whose worship was so mixed with that of Cybele. Norrys and I, by the light of lanterns, tried to interpret the odd and nearly effaced designs on certain irregularly rectangular blocks of stone generally held to be altars, but could make nothing of them. We remembered that one pattern, a sort of rayed sun, was held by students to imply a non-Roman origin, suggesting that these altars had merely been adopted by the Roman priests from some older and perhaps aboriginal temple on the same site. On one of these blocks were some brown stains which made me wonder. The largest, in the centre of the room, had certain features on the upper surface which indicated its connexion with fire—probably burnt offerings.

Such were the sights in that crypt before whose door the cats had howled, and where Norrys and I now determined to pass the night. Couches were brought down by the servants, who were told not to mind any nocturnal actions of the cats, and Nigger-Man was admitted as much for help as for companionship. We decided to keep the great oak door—a modern replica with slits for ventilation—tightly closed; and, with this attended to, we retired with lanterns still burning to await whatever might occur.

The vault was very deep in the foundations of the priory, and undoubtedly far down on the face of the beetling limestone cliff overlooking the waste valley. That it had been the goal of the scuffling and unexplainable rats I could not doubt, though why, I could not tell. As we lay there expectantly, I found my vigil occasionally mixed with half-formed dreams from which the uneasy motions of the cat across my feet would rouse me. These dreams were not wholesome, but horribly like the one I had had the night before. I saw again the twilit grotto, and the swineherd with his unmentionable fungous beasts wallowing in filth, and as I looked at these things they seemed nearer and more distinct—so distinct that I could almost observe their features. Then I did observe the flabby features of one of them—and awaked with such a scream that Nigger-Man started up, whilst Capt. Norrys, who had not slept, laughed considerably. Norrys might have laughed more—or perhaps less—had he known what it was that made me scream. But I did not remember myself till later. Ultimate horror often paralyses memory in a merciful way.

Norrys waked me when the phenomena began. Out of the same frightful dream I was called by his gentle shaking and his urging to listen to the cats. Indeed, there was much to listen to, for beyond the closed door at the head of the stone steps was a veritable nightmare of feline yelling and clawing, whilst Nigger-Man, unmindful of his kindred outside, was running excitedly around the bare stone walls, in which I heard the same babel of scurrying rats that had troubled me the night before.

An acute terror now rose within me, for here were anomalies which nothing normal could well explain. These rats, if not the creatures of a madness which I shared with the cats alone, must be burrowing and sliding in Roman walls I had thought to be of solid limestone blocks...unless perhaps the action of water through more than seventeen centuries had eaten winding tunnels which rodent bodies had worn clear and ample... But even so, the spectral horror was no less; for if these were living vermin why did not Norrys hear their disgusting commotion? Why did he urge me to watch Nigger-Man and listen to the cats outside, and why did he guess wildly and vaguely at what could have aroused them?

By the time I had managed to tell him, as rationally as I could, what I thought I was hearing, my ears gave me the last fading impression of the scurrying; which had retreated still downward, far underneath this deepest of sub-cellars till it seemed as if the whole cliff below were riddled with questing rats. Norrys was not as sceptical as I had anticipated, but instead seemed profoundly moved. He motioned to me to notice that the cats at the door had ceased their clamour, as if giving up the rats for lost; whilst Nigger-Man had a burst of renewed restlessness, and was clawing frantically around the bottom of the large stone altar in the centre of the room, which was nearer Norrys' couch than mine.

My fear of the unknown was at this point very great. Something astounding had occurred, and I saw that Capt. Norrys, a younger, stouter, and presumably more naturally materialistic man, was affected fully as much as myself—perhaps because of his lifelong and intimate familiarity with local legend. We could for the moment do nothing but watch the old black cat as he pawed with decreasing fervour at the base of the altar, occasionally looking up and mewing to me in that persuasive manner which he used when he wished me to perform some favour for him.

Norrys now took a lantern close to the altar and examined the place where Nigger-Man was pawing; silently kneeling and scraping away the lichens of centuries which joined the massive pre-Roman block to the tessellated floor. He did not find anything, and was about to abandon his effort when I noticed a trivial circumstance which made me shudder, even though it implied nothing more than I had already imagined. I told him of it, and we both looked at its almost imperceptible manifestation with the fixedness of fascinated discovery and acknowledgment. It was only this—that the flame of the lantern set down near the altar was slightly but certainly flickering from a draught of air which it had not before received, and which came indubitably from the crevice between floor and altar where Norrys was scraping away the lichens.

We spent the rest of the night in the brilliantly lighted study, nervously discussing what we should do next. The discovery that some vault deeper than the deepest known masonry of the Romans underlay this accursed pile—some vault unsuspected by the curious antiquarians of three centuries—would have been sufficient to excite us without any background of the sinister. As it was, the fascination became twofold; and we paused in doubt whether to abandon our search and quit the priory forever in superstitious caution, or to gratify our sense of adventure and brave whatever horrors might await us in the unknown depths. By morning we had compromised, and decided to go to London to gather a group of archaeologists and scientific men fit to cope with the mystery. It should be mentioned that before leaving the sub-cellar we had vainly tried to move the central altar which we now recognised as the gate to a new pit of nameless fear. What secret would open the gate, wiser men than we would have to find.

During many days in London Capt. Norrys and I presented our facts, conjectures, and legendary anecdotes to five eminent authorities, all men who could be trusted to respect any family disclosures which future explorations might develop. We found most of them little disposed to scoff, but instead intensely interested and sincerely sympathetic. It is hardly necessary to name them all, but I may say that they included Sir William Brinton, whose excavations in the Troad excited most of the world in their day. As we all took the train for Anchester I felt myself poised on the brink of frightful revelations, a sensation symbolised by the air of mourning among the many Americans at the unexpected death of the President on the other side of the world.

On the evening of August 7th we reached Exham Priory, where the servants assured me that nothing unusual had occurred. The cats, even old Nigger-Man, had been perfectly placid; and not a trap in the house had been sprung. We were to begin exploring on the following day, awaiting which I assigned well-appointed rooms to all my guests. I myself retired in my own tower chamber, with Nigger-Man across my feet. Sleep came quickly, but hideous dreams assailed me. There was a vision of a Roman feast like that of Trimalchio, with a horror in a covered platter. Then came that damnable, recurrent thing about the swineherd and his filthy drove in the twilit grotto. Yet when I awoke it was full daylight, with normal sounds in the house below. The rats, living or spectral, had not troubled me; and Nigger-Man was quietly asleep. On going down, I found that the same tranquillity had prevailed elsewhere; a condition which one of the assembled savants—a fellow named Thornton, devoted to the psychic—rather absurdly laid to the fact that I had now been shewn the thing which certain forces had wished to shew me.

All was now ready, and at 11 a.m. our entire group of seven men, bearing powerful electric searchlights and implements of excavation, went down to the sub-cellar and bolted the door behind us. Nigger-Man was with us, for the investigators found no occasion to despise his excitability, and were indeed anxious that he be present in case of obscure rodent manifestations. We noted the Roman inscriptions and unknown altar designs only briefly, for three of the savants had already seen them, and all knew their characteristics. Prime attention was paid to the momentous central altar, and within an hour Sir William Brinton had caused it to tilt backward, balanced by some unknown species of counterweight.

There now lay revealed such a horror as would have overwhelmed us had we not been prepared. Through a nearly square opening in the tiled floor, sprawling on a flight of stone steps so prodigiously worn that it was little more than an inclined plane at the centre, was a ghastly array of human or semi-human bones. Those which retained their collocation as skeletons shewed attitudes of panic fear, and over all were the marks of rodent gnawing. The skulls denoted nothing short of utter idiocy, cretinism, or primitive semi-apedom. Above the hellishly littered steps arched a descending passage seemingly chiselled from the solid rock, and conducting a current of air. This current was not a sudden and noxious rush as from a closed vault, but a cool breeze with something of freshness in it. We did not pause long, but shiveringly began to clear a passage down the steps. It was then that Sir William, examining the hewn walls, made the odd observation that the passage, according to the direction of the strokes, must have been chiselled *from beneath.*

I must be very deliberate now, and choose my words.

After ploughing down a few steps amidst the gnawed bones we saw that there was light ahead; not any mystic phosphorescence, but a filtered daylight which could not come except from unknown fissures in the cliff that overlooked the waste valley. That such fissures had escaped notice from outside was hardly remarkable, for not only is the valley wholly uninhabited, but the cliff is so high and beetling that only an aëronaut could study its face in detail. A few steps more, and our breaths were literally snatched from us by what we saw; so literally that Thornton, the psychic investigator, actually fainted in the arms of the dazed man who stood behind him. Norrys, his plump face utterly white and flabby, simply cried out inarticulately; whilst I think that what I did was to gasp or hiss, and cover my eyes. The man behind me—the only one of the party older than I—croaked the hackneyed "My God!" in the most cracked voice I ever heard. Of seven cultivated men, only Sir William Brinton retained his composure; a thing more to his credit because he led the party and must have seen the sight first.

It was a twilit grotto of enormous height, stretching away farther than any eye could see; a subterraneous world of limitless mystery and horrible suggestion. There were buildings and other architectural remains—in one terrified glance I saw a weird pattern of tumuli, a savage circle of monoliths, a low-domed Roman ruin, a sprawling Saxon pile, and an early English edifice of wood—but all these were dwarfed by the ghoulish spectacle presented by the general surface of the ground. For yards about the steps extended an insane tangle of human bones, or bones at least as human as those on the steps. Like a foamy sea they stretched, some fallen apart, but others wholly or partly articulated as skeletons; these latter invariably in postures of daemoniac frenzy, either fighting off some menace or clutching other forms with cannibal intent.

When Dr. Trask, the anthropologist, stooped to classify the skulls, he found a degraded mixture which utterly baffled him. They were mostly lower than the Piltdown man in the scale of evolution, but in every case definitely human. Many were of higher grade, and a very few were the skulls of supremely and sensitively developed types. All the bones were gnawed, mostly by rats, but somewhat by others of the half-human drove. Mixed with them were many tiny bones of rats—fallen members of the lethal army which closed the ancient epic.

I wonder that any man among us lived and kept his sanity through that hideous day of discovery. Not Hoffmann or Huysmans could conceive a scene more wildly incredible, more frenetically repellent, or more Gothically grotesque than the twilit grotto through which we seven staggered; each stumbling on revelation after revelation, and trying to keep for the nonce from thinking of the events which must have taken place there three hundred years, or a thousand, or two thousand, or ten thousand years ago. It was the antechamber of hell, and poor Thornton fainted again when Trask told him that some of the skeleton things must have descended as quadrupeds through the last twenty or more generations.

Horror piled on horror as we began to interpret the architectural remains. The quadruped things—with their occasional recruits from the biped class—had been kept in stone pens, out of which they must have broken in their last delirium of hunger or rat-fear. There had been great herds of them, evidently fattened on the coarse vegetables whose remains could be found as a sort of poisonous ensilage at the bottom of huge stone bins older than Rome. I knew now why my ancestors had had such excessive gardens—would to heaven I could forget! The purpose of the herds I did not have to ask.

Sir William, standing with his searchlight in the Roman ruin, translated aloud the most shocking ritual I have ever known; and told of the diet of the antediluvian cult which the priests of Cybele found and mingled with their own. Norrys, used as he was to the trenches, could not walk straight when he came out of the English building. It was a butcher shop and kitchen—he had expected that—but it was too much to see familiar English implements in such a place, and to read familiar English graffiti there, some as recent as 1610. I could not go in that building—that building whose daemon activities were stopped only by the dagger of my ancestor Walter de la Poer.

What I did venture to enter was the low Saxon building, whose oaken door had fallen, and there I found a terrible row of ten stone cells with rusty bars. Three had tenants, all skeletons of high grade, and on the bony forefinger of one I found a seal ring with my own coat-of-arms. Sir William found a vault with far older cells below the Roman chapel, but these cells were empty. Below them was a low crypt with cases of formally arranged bones, some of them bearing terrible parallel inscriptions carved in Latin, Greek, and the tongue of Phrygia. Meanwhile, Dr. Trask had opened one of the prehistoric tumuli, and brought to light skulls which were slightly more human than a gorilla's, and which bore indescribable ideographic carvings. Through all this horror my cat stalked unperturbed. Once I saw him monstrously perched atop a mountain of bones, and wondered at the secrets that might lie behind his yellow eyes.

Having grasped to some slight degree the frightful revelations of this twilit area—an area so hideously foreshadowed by my recurrent dream—we turned to that apparently boundless depth of midnight cavern where no ray of light from the cliff could penetrate. We shall never know what sightless Stygian worlds yawn beyond the little distance we went, for it was decided that such secrets are not good for mankind. But there was plenty to engross us close at hand, for we had not gone far before the searchlights shewed that accursed infinity of pits in which the rats had feasted, and whose sudden lack of replenishment had driven the ravenous rodent army first to turn on the living herds of starving things, and then to burst forth from the priory in that historic orgy of devastation which the peasants will never forget.

God! those carrion black pits of sawed, picked bones and opened skulls! Those nightmare chasms choked with the pithecanthropoid, Celtic, Roman, and English bones of countless unhallowed centuries! Some of them were full, and none can say how deep they had once been. Others were still bottomless to our searchlights, and peopled by unnamable fancies. What, I thought, of the hapless rats that stumbled into such traps amidst the blackness of their quests in this grisly Tartarus?

Once my foot slipped near a horribly yawning brink, and I had a moment of ecstatic fear. I must have been musing a long time, for I could not see any of the party but the plump Capt. Norrys. Then there came a sound from that inky, boundless, farther distance that I thought I knew; and I saw my old black cat dart past me like a winged Egyptian god, straight into the illimitable gulf of the unknown. But I was not far behind, for there was no doubt after another second. It was the eldritch scurrying of those fiend-born rats, always questing for new horrors, and determined to lead me on even unto those grinning caverns of earth's centre where Nyarlathotep, the mad faceless god, howls blindly to the piping of two amorphous idiot flute-players.

My searchlight expired, but still I ran. I heard voices, and yowls, and echoes, but above all there gently rose that impious, insidious scurrying; gently rising, rising, as a stiff bloated corpse gently rises above an oily river that flows under endless onyx bridges to a black, putrid sea. Something bumped into me—something soft and plump. It must have been the rats; the viscous, gelatinous, ravenous army that feast on the dead and the living...Why shouldn't rats eat a de la Poer as a de la Poer eats forbidden things?...The war ate my boy, damn them all... and the Yanks ate Carfax with flames and burnt Grandsire Delapore and the secret...No, no, I tell you, I am not that daemon swineherd in the twilit grotto! It was not Edward Norrys' fat face on that flabby, fungous thing! Who says I am a de la Poer? He lived, but my boy died!...Shall a Norrys hold the lands of a de la Poer?...It's voodoo, I tell you...that spotted snake... Curse you, Thornton, I'll teach you to faint at what my family do!...'Sblood, thou stinkard, I'll learn ye how to gust...wolde ye swynke me thilke wys?...*Magna Mater! Magna Mater!...Atys... Dia ad aghaidh 's ad aodann...agus bas dunach ort! Dhonas's dholas ort, agus leat-sa!...Ungl...ungl...rrrlh...chchch...*

That is what they say I said when they found me in the blackness after three hours; found me crouching in the blackness over the plump, half-eaten body of Capt. Norrys, with my own cat leaping and tearing at my throat. Now they have blown up Exham Priory, taken my Nigger-Man away from me, and shut me into this barred room at Hanwell with fearful whispers about my heredity and experiences. Thornton is in the next room, but they prevent me from talking to him. They are trying, too, to suppress most of the facts concerning the priory. When I speak of poor Norrys they accuse me of a hideous thing, but they must know that I did not do it. They must know it was the rats; the slithering, scurrying rats whose scampering will never let me sleep; the daemon rats that race behind the padding in this room and beckon me down to greater horrors than I have ever known; the rats they can never hear; the rats, the rats in the walls.

The Street

"The Street" was written after the infamous and largely forgotten 1919 Boston Police strike, after city officials blocked the officers' attempt to unionize. Several days of mass looting and violence ensued, which many likened to the then-recent Bolshevik Revolution in Russia. The violence ended when thousands of Massachusetts State Guardsmen and other volunteers surged into the city and broke up the mob by force. This story reflects concerns Americans had over the growing influence of foreigners and radical political movements during the period. First published in the pulp magazine Wolverine *in December 1920, although regarded by critics as Lovecraft's worst and by far his most racist story, it nonetheless demonstrates his many literary talents.*

There be those who say that things and places have souls, and there be those who say they have not; I dare not say, myself, but I will tell of The Street.

Men of strength and honour fashioned that Street; good, valiant men of our blood who had come from the Blessed Isles across the sea. At first it was but a path trodden by bearers of water from the woodland spring to the cluster of houses by the beach. Then, as more men came to the growing cluster of houses and looked about for places to dwell, they built cabins along the north side; cabins of stout oaken logs with masonry on the side toward the forest, for many Indians lurked there with fire-arrows. And in a few years more, men built cabins on the south side of The Street.

Up and down The Street walked grave men in conical hats, who most of the time carried muskets or fowling pieces. And there were also their bonneted wives and sober children. In the evening these men with their wives and children would sit about gigantic hearths and read and speak. Very simple were the things of which they read and spoke, yet things which gave them courage and goodness and helped them by day to subdue the forest and till the fields. And the children would listen, and learn of the laws and deeds of old, and of that dear England which they had never seen, or could not remember.

There was war, and thereafter no more Indians troubled The Street. The men, busy with labour, waxed prosperous and as happy as they knew how to be. And the children grew up comfortably, and more families came from the Mother Land to dwell on The Street. And the children's children, and the newcomers' children, grew up. The town was now a city, and one by one the cabins gave place to houses; simple, beautiful houses of brick and wood, with stone steps and iron railings and fanlights over the doors. No flimsy creations were these houses, for they were made to serve many a generation. Within there were carven mantels and graceful stairs, and sensible, pleasing furniture, china, and silver, brought from the Mother Land.

So The Street drank in the dreams of a young people, and rejoiced as its dwellers became more graceful and happy. Where once had been only strength and honour, taste and learning now abode as well. Books and paintings and music came to the houses, and the young men went to the university which rose above the plain to the north. In the place of conical hats and muskets there were three-cornered hats and small-swords, and lace and snowy periwigs. And there were cobblestones over which clattered many a blooded horse and rumbled many a gilded coach; and brick sidewalks with horse blocks and hitching-posts.

There were in that Street many trees; elms and oaks and maples of dignity; so that in the summer the scene was all soft verdure and twittering bird-song. And behind the houses were walled rose-gardens with hedged paths and sundials, where at evening the moon and stars would shine bewitchingly while fragrant blossoms glistened with dew.

So The Street dreamed on, past wars, calamities, and changes. Once most of the young men went away, and some never came back. That was when they furled the Old Flag and put up a new Banner of Stripes and Stars. But though men talked of great changes, The Street felt them not; for its folk were still the same, speaking of the old familiar things in the old familiar accents. And the trees still sheltered singing birds, and at evening the moon and stars looked down upon dewy blossoms in the walled rose-gardens.

In time there were no more swords, three-cornered hats, or periwigs in The Street. How strange seemed the denizens with their walking-sticks, tall beavers, and cropped heads! New sounds came from the distance–first strange puffings and shrieks from the river a mile away, and then, many years later, strange puffings and shrieks and rumblings from other directions. The air was not quite so pure as before, but the spirit of the place had not changed. The blood and soul of the people were as the blood and soul of their ancestors who had fashioned The Street. Nor did the spirit change when they tore open the earth to lay down strange pipes, or when they set up tall posts bearing weird wires. There was so much ancient lore in that Street, that the past could not easily be forgotten.

Then came days of evil, when many who had known The Street of old knew it no more; and many knew it, who had not known it before. And those who came were never as those who went away; for their accents were coarse and strident, and their mien and faces unpleasing. Their thoughts, too, fought with the wise, just spirit of The Street, so that The Street pined silently as its houses fell into decay, and its trees died one by one, and its rose-gardens grew rank with weeds and waste. But it felt a stir of pride one day when again marched forth young men, some of whom never came back. These young men were clad in blue.

With the years worse fortune came to The Street. Its trees were all gone now, and its rose-gardens were displaced by the backs of cheap, ugly new buildings on parallel streets. Yet the houses remained, despite the ravages of the years and the storms and worms, for they had been made to serve many a generation. New kinds of faces appeared in The Street; swarthy, sinister faces with furtive eyes and odd features, whose owners spoke unfamiliar words and placed signs in known and unknown characters upon most of the musty houses. Push-carts crowded the gutters. A sordid, undefinable stench settled over the place, and the ancient spirit slept.

Great excitement once came to The Street. War and revolution were raging across the seas; a dynasty had collapsed, and its degenerate subjects were flocking with dubious intent to the Western Land. Many of these took lodgings in the battered houses that had once known the songs of birds and the scent of roses. Then the Western Land itself awoke, and joined the Mother Land in her titanic struggle for civilisation. Over the cities once more floated the Old Flag, companioned by the New Flag and by a plainer yet glorious Tri-colour. But not many flags floated over The Street, for therein brooded only fear and hatred and ignorance. Again young men went forth, but not quite as did the young men of those other days. Something was lacking. And the sons of those young men of other days, who did indeed go forth in olive-drab with the true spirit of their ancestors, went from distant places and knew not The Street and its ancient spirit.

Over the seas there was a great victory, and in triumph most of the young men returned. Those who had lacked something lacked it no longer, yet did fear and hatred and ignorance still brood over The Street; for many had stayed behind, and many strangers had come from distant places to the ancient houses. And the young men who had returned dwelt there no longer. Swarthy and sinister were most of the strangers, yet among them one might find a few faces like those who fashioned The Street and moulded its spirit. Like and yet unlike, for there was in the eyes of all a weird, unhealthy glitter as of greed, ambition, vindictiveness, or misguided zeal. Unrest and treason were abroad amongst an evil few who plotted to strike the Western Land its death-blow, that they might mount to power over its ruins; even as assassins had mounted in that unhappy, frozen land from whence most of them had come. And the heart of that plotting was in The Street, whose crumbling houses teemed with alien makers of discord and echoed with the plans and speeches of those who yearned for the appointed day of blood, flame, and crime.

Of the various odd assemblages in The Street, the law said much but could prove little. With great diligence did men of hidden badges linger and listen about such places as Petrovitch's Bakery, the squalid Rifkin School of Modern Economics, the Circle Social Club, and the Liberty Café. There congregated sinister men in great numbers, yet always was their speech guarded or in a foreign tongue. And still the old houses stood, with their forgotten lore of nobler, departed centuries; of sturdy colonial tenants and dewy rose-gardens in the moonlight. Sometimes a lone poet or traveller would come to view them, and would try to picture them in their vanished glory; yet of such travellers and poets there were not many.

The rumour now spread widely that these houses contained the leaders of a vast band of terrorists, who on a designated day were to launch an orgy of slaughter for the extermination of America and of all the fine old traditions which The Street had loved. Handbills and papers fluttered about filthy gutters; handbills and papers printed in many tongues and in many characters, yet all bearing messages of crime and rebellion. In these writings the people were urged to tear down the laws and virtues that our fathers had exalted; to stamp out the soul of the old America—the soul that was bequeathed through a thousand and a half years of Anglo-Saxon freedom, justice, and moderation. It was said that the swart men who dwelt in The Street and congregated in its rotting edifices were the brains of a hideous revolution; that at their word of command many millions of brainless, besotted beasts would stretch forth their noisome talons from the slums of a thousand cities, burning, slaying, and destroying till the land of our fathers should be no more. All this was said and repeated, and many looked forward in dread to the fourth day of July, about which the strange writings hinted much; yet could nothing be found to place the guilt. None could tell just whose arrest might cut off the damnable plotting at its source. Many times came bands of blue-coated police to search the shaky houses, though at last they ceased to come; for they too had grown tired of law and order, and had abandoned all the city to its fate. Then men in olive-drab came, bearing muskets; till it seemed as if in its sad sleep The Street must have some haunting dreams of those other days, when musket-bearing men in conical hats walked along it from the woodland spring to the cluster of houses by the beach. Yet could no act be performed to check the impending cataclysm; for the swart, sinister men were old in cunning.

So The Street slept uneasily on, till one night there gathered in Petrovitch's Bakery and the Rifkin School of Modern

Economics, and the Circle Social Club, and Liberty Café, and in other places as well, vast hordes of men whose eyes were big with horrible triumph and expectation. Over hidden wires strange messages travelled, and much was said of still stranger messages yet to travel; but most of this was not guessed till afterward, when the Western Land was safe from the peril. The men in olive-drab could not tell what was happening, or what they ought to do; for the swart, sinister men were skilled in subtlety and concealment.

And yet the men in olive-drab will always remember that night, and will speak of The Street as they tell of it to their grandchildren; for many of them were sent there toward morning on a mission unlike that which they had expected. It was known that this nest of anarchy was old, and that the houses were tottering from the ravages of the years and the storms and the worms; yet was the happening of that summer night a surprise because of its very queer uniformity. It was, indeed, an exceedingly singular happening; though after all a simple one. For without warning, in one of the small hours beyond midnight, all the ravages of the years and the storms and the worms came to a tremendous climax; and after the crash there was nothing left standing in The Street save two ancient chimneys and part of a stout brick wall. Nor did anything that had been alive come alive from the ruins.

A poet and a traveller, who came with the mighty crowd that sought the scene, tell odd stories. The poet says that all through the hours before dawn he beheld sordid ruins but indistinctly in the glare of the arc-lights; that there loomed above the wreckage another picture wherein he could descry moonlight and fair houses and elms and oaks and maples of dignity. And the traveller declares that instead of the place's wonted stench there lingered a delicate fragrance as of roses in full bloom. But are not the dreams of poets and the tales of travellers notoriously false?

There be those who say that things and places have souls, and there be those who say they have not; I dare not say, myself, but I have told you of The Street.

The Temple

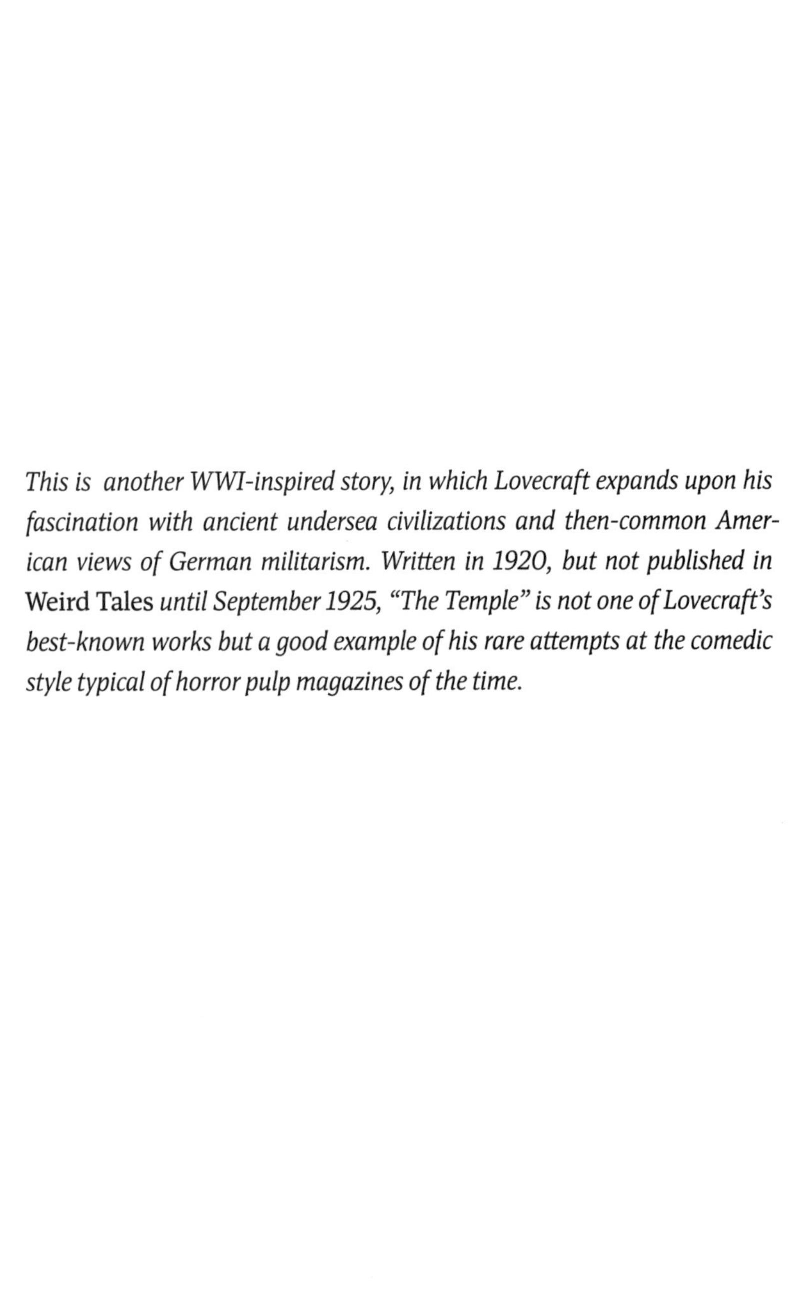

This is another WWI-inspired story, in which Lovecraft expands upon his fascination with ancient undersea civilizations and then-common American views of German militarism. Written in 1920, but not published in Weird Tales *until September 1925, "The Temple" is not one of Lovecraft's best-known works but a good example of his rare attempts at the comedic style typical of horror pulp magazines of the time.*

Manuscript found on the coast of Yucatan.

On August 20, 1917, I, Karl Heinrich, Graf von Altberg-Ehrenstein, Lieutenant-Commander in the Imperial German Navy and in charge of the submarine U-29, deposit this bottle and record in the Atlantic Ocean at a point to me unknown but probably about N. Latitude 20°, W. Longitude 35°, where my ship lies disabled on the ocean floor. I do so because of my desire to set certain unusual facts before the public; a thing I shall not in all probability survive to accomplish in person, since the circumstances surrounding me are as menacing as they are extraordinary, and involve not only the hopeless crippling of the U-29, but the impairment of my iron German will in a manner most disastrous.

On the afternoon of June 18, as reported by wireless to the U-61, bound for Kiel, we torpedoed the British freighter *Victory*, New York to Liverpool, in N. Latitude 45° 16', W. Longitude 28° 34'; permitting the crew to leave in boats in order to obtain a good cinema view for the admiralty records. The ship sank quite picturesquely, bow first, the stern rising high out of the water whilst the hull shot down perpendicularly to the bottom of the sea. Our camera missed nothing, and I regret that so fine a reel of film should never reach Berlin. After that we sank the lifeboats with our guns and submerged.

When we rose to the surface about sunset a seaman's body was found on the deck, hands gripping the railing in curious fashion. The poor fellow was young, rather dark, and very handsome; probably an Italian or Greek, and undoubtedly of the *Victory*'s crew. He had evidently sought refuge on the very ship which had been forced to destroy his own—one more victim of the unjust war of aggression which the English pig-dogs are waging upon the Fatherland. Our men searched him for souvenirs, and found in his coat pocket a very odd bit of ivory carved to represent a youth's head crowned with laurel. My fellow-officer, Lieut. Klenze, believed that the thing was of great age and artistic value, so took it from the men for himself. How it had ever come into the possession of a common sailor, neither he nor I could imagine.

As the dead man was thrown overboard there occurred two incidents which created much disturbance amongst the crew. The fellow's eyes had been closed; but in the dragging of his body to the rail they were jarred open, and many seemed to entertain a queer delusion that they gazed steadily and mockingly at Schmidt and Zimmer, who were bent over the corpse. The Boatswain Müller, an elderly man who would have known better had he not been a superstitious Alsatian swine, became so excited by this impression that he watched the body in the water; and swore that after it sank a little it drew its limbs into a swimming position and sped away to the south under the waves. Klenze and I did not like these displays of peasant ignorance, and severely reprimanded the men, particularly Müller.

The next day a very troublesome situation was created by the indisposition of some of the crew. They were evidently suffering from the nervous strain of our long voyage, and had had bad dreams. Several seemed quite dazed and stupid; and after satisfying myself that they were not feigning their weakness, I excused them from their duties. The sea was rather rough, so we descended to a depth where the waves were less troublesome. Here we were comparatively calm, despite a somewhat puzzling southward current which we could not identify from our oceanographic charts. The moans of the sick men were decidedly annoying; but since they did not appear to demoralise the rest of the crew, we did not resort to extreme measures. It was our plan to remain where we were and intercept the liner *Dacia*, mentioned in information from agents in New York.

In the early evening we rose to the surface, and found the sea less heavy. The smoke of a battleship was on the northern horizon, but our distance and ability to submerge made us safe. What worried us more was the talk of Boatswain Müller, which grew wilder as night came on. He was in a detestably childish state, and babbled of some illusion of dead bodies drifting past the undersea portholes; bodies which looked at him intensely, and which he recognised in spite of bloating as having seen dying during some of our victorious German exploits. And he said that the young man we had found and tossed overboard was their leader. This was very gruesome and abnormal, so we confined Müller in irons and had him soundly whipped. The men were not pleased at his punishment, but discipline was necessary. We also denied the request of a delegation headed by Seaman Zimmer, that the curious carved ivory head be cast into the sea.

On June 20, Seamen Bohm and Schmidt, who had been ill the day before, became violently insane. I regretted that no physician was included in our complement of officers, since German lives are precious; but the constant ravings of the two concerning a terrible curse were most subversive of discipline, so drastic steps were taken. The crew accepted the event in a sullen fashion, but it seemed to quiet Müller; who thereafter gave us no trouble. In the evening we released him, and he went about his duties silently.

In the week that followed we were all very nervous, watching for the *Dacia*. The tension was aggravated by the disappearance of Müller and Zimmer, who undoubtedly committed suicide as a result of the fears which had seemed to harass them, though they were not observed in the act of jumping overboard. I was rather glad to be rid of Müller, for even his silence had unfavourably affected the crew. Everyone seemed inclined to be silent now, as though holding a secret fear. Many were ill, but none made a disturbance. Lieut. Klenze chafed under the strain, and was annoyed by the merest trifles—such as the school of dolphins which gathered about the U-29 in increasing numbers, and the growing intensity of that southward current which was not on our chart.

It at length became apparent that we had missed the Dacia altogether. Such failures are not uncommon, and we were more pleased than disappointed; since our return to Wilhelmshaven was now in order. At noon June 28 we turned northeastward, and despite some rather comical entanglements with the unusual masses of dolphins were soon under way.

The explosion in the engine room at 2 p.m. was wholly a surprise. No defect in the machinery or carelessness in the men had been noticed, yet without warning the ship was racked from end to end with a colossal shock. Lieut. Klenze hurried to the engine room, finding the fuel-tank and most of the mechanism shattered, and Engineers Raabe and Schneider instantly killed. Our situation had suddenly become grave indeed; for though the chemical air regenerators were intact, and though we could use the devices for raising and submerging the ship and opening the hatches as long as compressed air and storage batteries might hold out, we were powerless to propel or guide the submarine. To seek rescue in the lifeboats would be to deliver ourselves into the hands of enemies unreasonably embittered against our great German nation, and our wireless had failed ever since the Victory affair to put us in touch with a fellow U-boat of the Imperial Navy.

From the hour of the accident till July 2 we drifted constantly to the south, almost without plans and encountering no vessel. Dolphins still encircled the U-29, a somewhat remarkable circumstance considering the distance we had covered. On the morning of July 2 we sighted a warship flying American colours, and the men became very restless in their desire to surrender. Finally Lieut. Klenze had to shoot a seaman named Traube, who urged this un-German act with especial violence. This quieted the crew for the time, and we submerged unseen.

The next afternoon a dense flock of sea-birds appeared from the south, and the ocean began to heave ominously. Closing our hatches, we awaited developments until we realised that we must either submerge or be swamped in the mounting waves. Our air pressure and electricity were diminishing, and we wished to avoid all unnecessary use of our slender mechanical resources; but in this case there was no choice. We did not descend far, and when after several hours the sea was calmer, we decided to return to the surface. Here, however, a new trouble developed; for the ship failed to respond to our direction in spite of all that the mechanics could do. As the men grew more frightened at this undersea imprisonment, some of them began to mutter again about Lieut. Klenze's ivory image, but the sight of an automatic pistol calmed them. We kept the poor devils as busy as we could, tinkering at the machinery even when we knew it was useless.

Klenze and I usually slept at different times; and it was during my sleep, about 5 a.m., July 4, that the general mutiny broke loose. The six remaining pigs of seamen, suspecting that we were lost, had suddenly burst into a mad fury at our refusal to surrender to the Yankee battleship two days before; and were in a delirium of cursing and destruction. They roared like the animals they were, and broke instruments and furniture indiscriminately; screaming about such nonsense as the curse of the ivory image and the dark dead youth who looked at them and swam away. Lieut. Klenze seemed paralysed and inefficient, as one might expect of a soft, womanish Rhinelander. I shot all six men, for it was necessary, and made sure that none remained alive.

We expelled the bodies through the double hatches and were alone in the U-29. Klenze seemed very nervous, and drank heavily. It was decided that we remain alive as long as possible, using the large stock of provisions and chemical supply of oxygen, none of which had suffered from the crazy antics of those swine-hound seamen. Our compasses, depth gauges, and other delicate instruments were ruined; so that henceforth our only reckoning would be guesswork, based on our watches, the calendar, and our apparent drift as judged by any objects we might spy through the portholes or from the conning tower. Fortunately we had storage batteries still capable of long use, both for interior lighting and for the searchlight. We often cast a beam around the ship, but saw only dolphins, swimming parallel to our own drifting course. I was scientifically interested in those dolphins; for though the ordinary *Delphinus delphis* is a cetacean mammal, unable to subsist without air, I watched one of the swimmers closely for two hours, and did not see him alter his submerged condition.

With the passage of time Klenze and I decided that we were still drifting south, meanwhile sinking deeper and deeper. We noted the marine fauna and flora, and read much on the subject in the books I had carried with me for spare moments. I could not help observing, however, the inferior scientific knowledge of my companion. His mind was not Prussian, but given to imaginings and speculations which have no value. The fact of our coming death affected him curiously, and he would frequently pray in remorse over the men, women, and children we had sent to the bottom; forgetting that all things are noble which serve the German state. After a time he became noticeably unbalanced, gazing for hours at his ivory image and weaving fanciful stories of the lost and forgotten things under the sea. Sometimes, as a psychological experiment, I would lead him on in these wanderings, and listen to his endless poetical quotations and tales of sunken ships. I was very sorry for him, for I dislike to see a German suffer; but he was not a good man to die with. For myself I was proud, knowing how the Fatherland would revere my memory and how my sons would be taught to be men like me.

On August 9, we espied the ocean floor, and sent a powerful beam from the searchlight over it. It was a vast undulating plain, mostly covered with seaweed, and strown with the shells of small molluscs. Here and there were slimy objects of puzzling contour, draped with weeds and encrusted with barnacles, which Klenze declared must be ancient ships lying in their graves. He was puzzled by one thing, a peak of solid matter, protruding above the ocean bed nearly four feet at its apex; about two feet thick, with flat sides and smooth upper surfaces which met at a very obtuse angle. I called the peak a bit of outcropping rock, but Klenze thought he saw carvings on it. After a while he began to shudder, and turned away from the scene as if frightened; yet could give no explanation save that he was overcome with the vastness, darkness, remoteness, antiquity, and mystery of the oceanic abysses. His mind was tired, but I am always a German, and was quick to notice two things; that the U-29 was standing the deep-sea pressure splendidly, and that the peculiar dolphins were still about us, even at a depth where the existence of high organisms is considered impossible by most naturalists. That I had previously overestimated our depth, I was sure; but none the less we must still be deep enough to make these phenomena remarkable. Our southward speed, as gauged by the ocean floor, was about as I had estimated from the organisms passed at higher levels.

It was at 3:15 p.m., August 12, that poor Klenze went wholly mad. He had been in the conning tower using the searchlight when I saw him bound into the library compartment where I sat reading, and his face at once betrayed him. I will repeat here what he said, underlining the words he emphasised: "He is calling! He is calling! I hear him! We must go!" As he spoke he took his ivory image from the table, pocketed it, and seized my arm in an effort to drag me up the companionway to the deck. In a moment I understood that he meant to open the hatch and plunge with me into the water outside, a vagary of suicidal and homicidal mania for which I was scarcely prepared. As I hung back and attempted to soothe him he grew more violent, saying: "Come now—do not wait until later; it is better to repent and be forgiven than to defy and be condemned." Then I tried the opposite of the soothing plan, and told him he was mad—pitifully demented. But he was unmoved, and cried: "If I am mad, it is mercy! May the gods pity the man who in his callousness can remain sane to the hideous end! Come and be mad whilst *he* still calls with mercy!"

This outburst seemed to relieve a pressure in his brain; for as he finished he grew much milder, asking me to let him depart alone if I would not accompany him. My course at once became clear. He was a German, but only a Rhinelander and a commoner; and he was now a potentially dangerous madman. By complying with his suicidal request I could immediately free myself from one who was no longer a companion but a menace. I asked him to give me the ivory image before he went, but this request brought from him such uncanny laughter that I did not repeat it. Then I asked him if he wished to leave any keepsake or lock of hair for his family in Germany in case I should be rescued, but again he gave me that strange laugh. So as he climbed the ladder I went to the levers, and allowing proper time-intervals operated the machinery which sent him to his death. After I saw that he was no longer in the boat I threw the searchlight around the water in an effort to obtain a last glimpse of him; since I wished to ascertain whether the water-pressure would flatten him as it theoretically should, or whether the body would be unaffected, like those extraordinary dolphins. I did not, however, succeed in finding my late companion, for the dolphins were massed thickly and obscuringly about the conning tower.

That evening I regretted that I had not taken the ivory image surreptitiously from poor Klenze's pocket as he left, for the memory of it fascinated me. I could not forget the youthful, beautiful head with its leafy crown, though I am not by nature an artist. I was also sorry that I had no one with whom to converse. Klenze, though not my mental equal, was much better than no one. I did not sleep well that night, and wondered exactly when the end would come. Surely, I had little enough chance of rescue.

The next day I ascended to the conning tower and commenced the customary searchlight explorations. Northward the view was much the same as it had been all the four days since we had sighted the bottom, but I perceived that the drifting of the U-29 was less rapid. As I swung the beam around to the south, I noticed that the ocean floor ahead fell away in a marked declivity, and bore curiously regular blocks of stone in certain places, disposed as if in accordance with definite patterns. The boat did not at once descend to match the greater ocean depth, so I was soon forced to adjust the searchlight to cast a sharply downward beam. Owing to the abruptness of the change a wire was disconnected, which necessitated a delay of many minutes for repairs; but at length the light streamed on again, flooding the marine valley below me.

I am not given to emotion of any kind, but my amazement was very great when I saw what lay revealed in that electrical glow. And yet as one reared in the best Kultur of Prussia I should not have been amazed, for geology and tradition alike tell us of great transpositions in oceanic and continental areas. What I saw was an extended and elaborate array of ruined edifices; all of magnificent though unclassified architecture, and in various stages of preservation. Most appeared to be of marble, gleaming whitely in the rays of the searchlight, and the general plan was of a large city at the bottom of a narrow valley, with numerous isolated temples and villas on the steep slopes above. Roofs were fallen and columns were broken, but there still remained an air of immemorially ancient splendour which nothing could efface.

Confronted at last with the Atlantis I had formerly deemed largely a myth, I was the most eager of explorers. At the bottom of that valley a river once had flowed; for as I examined the scene more closely I beheld the remains of stone and marble bridges and sea-walls, and terraces and embankments once verdant and beautiful. In my enthusiasm I became nearly as idiotic and sentimental as poor Klenze, and was very tardy in noticing that the southward current had ceased at last, allowing the U-29 to settle slowly down upon the sunken city as an aëroplane settles upon a town of the upper earth. I was slow, too, in realising that the school of unusual dolphins had vanished.

In about two hours the boat rested in a paved plaza close to the rocky wall of the valley. On one side I could view the entire city as it sloped from the plaza down to the old river-bank; on the other side, in startling proximity, I was confronted by the richly ornate and perfectly preserved facade of a great building, evidently a temple, hollowed from the solid rock. Of the original workmanship of this titanic thing I can only make conjectures. The facade, of immense magnitude, apparently covers a continuous hollow recess; for its windows are many and widely distributed. In the centre yawns a great open door, reached by an impressive flight of steps, and surrounded by exquisite carvings like the figures of Bacchanals in relief. Foremost of all are the great columns and frieze, both decorated with sculptures of inexpressible beauty; obviously portraying idealised pastoral scenes and processions of priests and priestesses bearing strange ceremonial devices in adoration of a radiant god. The art is of the most phenomenal perfection, largely Hellenic in idea, yet strangely individual. It imparts an impression of terrible antiquity, as though it were the remotest rather than the immediate ancestor of Greek art. Nor can I doubt that every detail of this massive product was fashioned from the virgin hillside rock of our planet. It is palpably a part of the valley wall, though how the vast interior was ever excavated I cannot imagine. Perhaps a cavern or series of caverns furnished the nucleus. Neither age nor submersion has corroded the pristine grandeur of this awful fane—for fane indeed it must be—and today after thousands of years it rests untarnished and inviolate in the endless night and silence of an ocean chasm.

I cannot reckon the number of hours I spent in gazing at the sunken city with its buildings, arches, statues, and bridges, and the colossal temple with its beauty and mystery. Though I knew that death was near, my curiosity was consuming; and I threw the searchlight's beam about in eager quest. The shaft of light permitted me to learn many details, but refused to shew anything within the gaping door of the rock-hewn temple; and after a time I turned off the current, conscious of the need of conserving power. The rays were now perceptibly dimmer than they had been during the weeks of drifting. And as if sharpened by the coming deprivation of light, my desire to explore the watery secrets grew. I, a German, should be the first to tread those aeon-forgotten ways!

I produced and examined a deep-sea diving suit of joined metal, and experimented with the portable light and air regenerator. Though I should have trouble in managing the double hatches alone, I believed I could overcome all obstacles with my scientific skill and actually walk about the dead city in person.

On August 16 I effected an exit from the U-29, and laboriously made my way through the ruined and mud-choked streets to the ancient river. I found no skeletons or other human remains, but gleaned a wealth of archaeological lore from sculptures and coins. Of this I cannot now speak save to utter my awe at a culture in the full noon of glory when cave-dwellers roamed Europe and the Nile flowed unwatched to the sea. Others, guided by this manuscript if it shall ever be found, must unfold the mysteries at which I can only hint. I returned to the boat as my electric batteries grew feeble, resolved to explore the rock temple on the following day.

On the 17th, as my impulse to search out the mystery of the temple waxed still more insistent, a great disappointment befell me; for I found that the materials needed to replenish the portable light had perished in the mutiny of those pigs in July. My rage was unbounded, yet my German sense forbade me to venture unprepared into an utterly black interior which might prove the lair of some indescribable marine monster or a labyrinth of passages from whose windings I could never extricate myself. All I could do was to turn on the waning searchlight of the U-29, and with its aid walk up the temple steps and study the exterior carvings. The shaft of light entered the door at an upward angle, and I peered in to see if I could glimpse anything, but all in vain. Not even the roof was visible; and though I took a step or two inside after testing the floor with a staff, I dared not go farther. Moreover, for the first time in my life I experienced the emotion of dread. I began to realise how some of poor Klenze's moods had arisen, for as the temple drew me more and more, I feared its aqueous abysses with a blind and mounting terror. Returning to the submarine, I turned off the lights and sat thinking in the dark. Electricity must now be saved for emergencies.

Saturday the 18th I spent in total darkness, tormented by thoughts and memories that threatened to overcome my German will. Klenze had gone mad and perished before reaching this sinister remnant of a past unwholesomely remote, and had advised me to go with him. Was, indeed, Fate preserving my reason only to draw me irresistibly to an end more horrible and unthinkable than any man has dreamed of? Clearly, my nerves were sorely taxed, and I must cast off these impressions of weaker men.

I could not sleep Saturday night, and turned on the lights regardless of the future. It was annoying that the electricity should not last out the air and provisions. I revived my thoughts of euthanasia, and examined my automatic pistol. Toward morning I must have dropped asleep with the lights on, for I awoke in darkness yesterday afternoon to find the batteries dead. I struck several matches in succession, and desperately regretted the improvidence which had caused us long ago to use up the few candles we carried.

After the fading of the last match I dared to waste, I sat very quietly without a light. As I considered the inevitable end my mind ran over preceding events, and developed a hitherto dormant impression which would have caused a weaker and more superstitious man to shudder. *The head of the radiant god in the sculptures on the rock temple is the same as that carven bit of ivory which the dead sailor brought from the sea and which poor Klenze carried back into the sea.*

I was a little dazed by this coincidence, but did not become terrified. It is only the inferior thinker who hastens to explain the singular and the complex by the primitive short cut of supernaturalism. The coincidence was strange, but I was too sound a reasoner to connect circumstances which admit of no logical connexion, or to associate in any uncanny fashion the disastrous events which had led from the *Victory* affair to my present plight. Feeling the need of more rest, I took a sedative and secured some more sleep. My nervous condition was reflected in my dreams, for I seemed to hear the cries of drowning persons, and to see dead faces pressing against the portholes of the boat. And among the dead faces was the living, mocking face of the youth with the ivory image.

I must be careful how I record my awaking today, for I am unstrung, and much hallucination is necessarily mixed with fact. Psychologically my case is most interesting, and I regret that it cannot be observed scientifically by a competent German authority. Upon opening my eyes my first sensation was an overmastering desire to visit the rock temple; a desire which grew every instant, yet which I automatically sought to resist through some emotion of fear which operated in the reverse direction. Next there came to me the impression of *light* amidst the darkness of dead batteries, and I seemed to see a sort of phosphorescent glow in the water through the porthole which opened toward the temple. This aroused my curiosity, for I knew of no deep-sea organism capable of emitting such luminosity. But before I could investigate there came a third impression which because of its irrationality caused me to doubt the objectivity of anything my senses might record. It was an aural delusion; a sensation of rhythmic, melodic sound as of some wild yet beautiful chant or choral hymn, coming from the outside through the absolutely sound-proof hull of the U-29. Convinced of my psychological and nervous abnormality, I lighted some matches and poured a stiff dose of sodium bromide solution, which seemed to calm me to the extent of dispelling the illusion of sound. But the phosphorescence remained, and I had difficulty in repressing a childish impulse to go to the porthole and seek its source. It was horribly realistic, and I could soon distinguish by its aid the familiar objects around me, as well as the empty sodium bromide glass of which I had had no former visual impression in its present location. The last circumstance made me ponder, and I crossed the room and touched the glass. It was indeed in the place where I had seemed to see it. Now I knew that the light was either real or part of a hallucination so fixed and consistent that I could not hope to dispel it, so abandoning all resistance I ascended to the conning tower to look for the luminous agency. Might it not actually be another U-boat, offering possibilities of rescue?

It is well that the reader accept nothing which follows as objective truth, for since the events transcend natural law, they are necessarily the subjective and unreal creations of my overtaxed mind. When I attained the conning tower I found the sea in general far less luminous than I had expected. There was no animal or vegetable phosphorescence about, and the city that sloped down to the river was invisible in blackness. What I did see was not spectacular, not grotesque or terrifying, yet it removed my last vestige of trust in my consciousness. *For the door and windows of the undersea temple hewn from the rocky hill were vividly aglow with a flickering radiance, as from a mighty altar-flame far within.*

Later incidents are chaotic. As I stared at the uncannily lighted door and windows, I became subject to the most extravagant visions—visions so extravagant that I cannot even relate them. I fancied that I discerned objects in the temple—objects both stationary and moving—and seemed to hear again the unreal chant that had floated to me when first I awaked. And over all rose thoughts and fears which centred in the youth from the sea and the ivory image whose carving was duplicated on the frieze and columns of the temple before me. I thought of poor Klenze, and wondered where his body rested with the image he had carried back into the sea. He had warned me of something, and I had not heeded—but he was a soft-headed Rhinelander who went mad at troubles a Prussian could bear with ease.

The rest is very simple. My impulse to visit and enter the temple has now become an inexplicable and imperious command which ultimately cannot be denied. My own German will no longer controls my acts, and volition is henceforward possible only in minor matters. Such madness it was which drove Klenze to his death, bareheaded and unprotected in the ocean; but I am a Prussian and a man of sense, and will use to the last what little will I have. When first I saw that I must go, I prepared my diving suit, helmet, and air regenerator for instant donning; and immediately commenced to write this hurried chronicle in the hope that it may some day reach the world. I shall seal the manuscript in a bottle and entrust it to the sea as I leave the U-29 forever.

I have no fear, not even from the prophecies of the madman Klenze. What I have seen cannot be true, and I know that this madness of my own will at most lead only to suffocation when my air is gone. The light in the temple is a sheer delusion, and I shall die calmly, like a German, in the black and forgotten depths. This daemoniac laughter which I hear as I write comes only from my own weakening brain. So I will carefully don my diving suit and walk boldly up the steps into that primal shrine; that silent secret of unfathomed waters and uncounted years.

The Horror at Red Hook

This story represents a transition for Lovecraft into his "mature" period, though it lacks most of the mythological elements common in his later works. At the time of its writing, Lovecraft badly needed money and was hoping to expand his audience outside of horror and science fiction and capitalize on the popularity of detective stories. The attempt to court this new audience failed, and Lovecraft had to resort to publishing the story in his old standby of Weird Tales *in January 1927. Lovecraft was living in Red Hook while he crafted the story, and his unflattering descriptions of the place and its people were a reflection of his time there.*

"There are sacraments of evil as well as of good about us, and we live and move to my belief in an unknown world, a place where there are caves and shadows and dwellers in twilight. It is possible that man may sometimes return on the track of evolution, and it is my belief that an awful lore is not yet dead."

-Arthur Machen

Not many weeks ago, on a street corner in the village of Pascoag, Rhode Island, a tall, heavily built, and wholesome-looking pedestrian furnished much speculation by a singular lapse of behaviour. He had, it appears, been descending the hill by the road from Chepachet; and encountering the compact section, had turned to his left into the main thoroughfare where several modest business blocks convey a touch of the urban. At this point, without visible provocation, he committed his astonishing lapse; staring queerly for a second at the tallest of the buildings before him, and then, with a series of terrified, hysterical shrieks, breaking into a frantic run which ended in a stumble and fall at the next crossing. Picked up and dusted off by ready hands, he was found to be conscious, organically unhurt, and evidently cured of his sudden nervous attack. He muttered some shamefaced explanations involving a strain he had undergone, and with downcast glance turned back up the Chepachet road, trudging out of sight without once looking behind him. It was a strange incident to befall so large, robust, normal-featured, and capable-looking a man, and the strangeness was not lessened by the remarks of a bystander who had recognised him as the boarder of a well-known dairyman on the outskirts of Chepachet.

He was, it developed, a New York police detective named Thomas F. Malone, now on a long leave of absence under medical treatment after some disproportionately arduous work on a gruesome local case which accident had made dramatic. There had been a collapse of several old brick buildings during a raid in which he had shared, and something about the wholesale loss of life, both of prisoners and of his companions, had peculiarly appalled him. As a result, he had acquired an acute and anomalous horror of any buildings even remotely suggesting the ones which had fallen in, so that in the end mental specialists forbade him the sight of such things for an indefinite period. A police surgeon with relatives in Chepachet had put forward that quaint hamlet of wooden colonial houses as an ideal spot for the psychological convalescence; and thither the sufferer had gone, promising never to venture among the brick-lined streets of larger villages till duly advised by the Woonsocket specialist with whom he was put in touch. This walk to Pascoag for magazines had been a mistake, and the patient had paid in fright, bruises, and humiliation for his disobedience.

So much the gossips of Chepachet and Pascoag knew; and so much, also, the most learned specialists believed. But Malone had at first told the specialists much more, ceasing only when he saw that utter incredulity was his portion. Thereafter he held his peace, protesting not at all when it was generally agreed that the collapse of certain squalid brick houses in the Red Hook section of Brooklyn, and the consequent death of many brave officers, had unseated his nervous equilibrium. He had worked too hard, all said, in trying to clean up those nests of disorder and violence; certain features were shocking enough, in all conscience, and the unexpected tragedy was the last straw. This was a simple explanation which everyone could understand, and because Malone was not a simple person he perceived that he had better let it suffice. To hint to unimaginative people of a horror beyond all human conception—a horror of houses and blocks and cities leprous and cancerous with evil dragged from elder worlds—would be merely to invite a padded cell instead of restful rustication, and Malone was a man of sense despite his mysticism. He had the Celt's far vision of weird and hidden things, but the logician's quick eye for the outwardly unconvincing; an amalgam which had led him far afield in the forty-two years of his life, and set him in strange places for a Dublin University man born in a Georgian villa near Phoenix Park.

And now, as he reviewed the things he had seen and felt and apprehended, Malone was content to keep unshared the secret of what could reduce a dauntless fighter to a quivering neurotic; what could make old brick slums and seas of dark, subtle faces a thing of nightmare and eldritch portent. It would not be the first time his sensations had been forced to bide uninterpreted—for was not his very act of plunging into the polyglot abyss of New York's underworld a freak beyond sensible explanation? What could he tell the prosaic of the antique witcheries and grotesque marvels discernible to sensitive eyes amidst the poison cauldron where all the varied dregs of unwholesome ages mix their venom and perpetuate their obscene terrors? He had seen the hellish green flame of secret wonder in this blatant, evasive welter of outward greed and inward blasphemy, and had smiled gently when all the New-Yorkers he knew scoffed at his experiment in police work. They had been very witty and cynical, deriding his fantastic pursuit of unknowable mysteries and assuring him that in these days New York held nothing but cheapness and vulgarity. One of them had wagered him a heavy sum that he could not—despite many poignant things to his credit in the *Dublin Review*—even write a truly interesting story of New York low life; and now, looking back, he perceived that cosmic irony had justified the prophet's words while secretly confuting their flippant meaning. The horror, as glimpsed at last, could not make a story—for like the book cited by Poe's German authority, *es lässt sich nicht lesen*—it does not permit itself to be read."

II.

To Malone the sense of latent mystery in existence was always present. In youth he had felt the hidden beauty and ecstasy of things, and had been a poet; but poverty and sorrow and exile had turned his gaze in darker directions, and he had thrilled at the imputations of evil in the world around. Daily life had for him come to be a phantasmagoria of macabre shadow-studies; now glittering and leering with concealed rottenness as in Beardsley's best manner, now hinting terrors behind the commonest shapes and objects as in the subtler and less obvious work of Gustave Doré. He would often regard it as merciful that most persons of high intelligence jeer at the inmost mysteries; for, he argued, if superior minds were ever placed in fullest contact with the secrets preserved by ancient and lowly cults, the resultant abnormalities would soon not only wreck the world, but threaten the very integrity of the universe. All this reflection was no doubt morbid, but keen logic and a deep sense of humour ably offset it. Malone was satisfied to let his notions remain as half-spied and forbidden visions to be lightly played with; and hysteria came only when duty flung him into a hell of revelation too sudden and insidious to escape.

He had for some time been detailed to the Butler Street station in Brooklyn when the Red Hook matter came to his notice. Red Hook is a maze of hybrid squalor near the ancient waterfront opposite Governor's Island, with dirty highways climbing the hill from the wharves to that higher ground where the decayed lengths of Clinton and Court Streets lead off toward the Borough Hall. Its houses are mostly of brick, dating from the first quarter to the middle of the nineteenth century, and some of the obscurer alleys and byways have that alluring antique flavour which conventional reading leads us to call "Dickensian." The population is a hopeless tangle and enigma; Syrian, Spanish, Italian, and negro elements impinging upon one another, and fragments of Scandinavian and American belts lying not far distant. It is a babel of sound and filth, and sends out strange cries to answer the lapping of oily waves at its grimy piers and the monstrous organ litanies of the harbour whistles. Here long ago a brighter picture dwelt, with clear-eyed mariners on the lower streets and homes of taste and substance where the larger houses line the hill. One can trace the relics of this former happiness in the trim shapes of the buildings, the occasional graceful churches, and the evidences of original art and background in bits of detail here and there—a worn flight of steps, a battered doorway, a wormy pair of decorative columns or pilasters, or a fragment of once green space with bent and rusted iron railing. The houses are generally in solid blocks, and now and then a many-windowed cupola arises to tell of days when the households of captains and ship-owners watched the sea.

From this tangle of material and spiritual putrescence the blasphemies of a hundred dialects assail the sky. Hordes of prowlers reel shouting and singing along the lanes and thoroughfares, occasional furtive hands suddenly extinguish lights and pull down curtains, and swarthy, sin-pitted faces disappear from windows when visitors pick their way through. Policemen despair of order or reform, and seek rather to erect barriers protecting the outside world from the contagion. The clang of the patrol is answered by a kind of spectral silence, and such prisoners as are taken are never communicative. Visible offences are as varied as the local dialects, and run the gamut from the smuggling of rum and prohibited aliens through diverse stages of lawlessness and obscure vice to murder and mutilation in their most abhorrent guises. That these visible affairs are not more frequent is not to the neighbourhood's credit, unless the power of concealment be an art demanding credit. More people enter Red Hook than leave it—or at least, than leave it by the landward side—and those who are not loquacious are the likeliest to leave.

Malone found in this state of things a faint stench of secrets more terrible than any of the sins denounced by citizens and bemoaned by priests and philanthropists. He was conscious, as one who united imagination with scientific knowledge, that modern people under lawless conditions tend uncannily to repeat the darkest instinctive patterns of primitive half-ape savagery in their daily life and ritual observances; and he had often viewed with an anthropologist's shudder the chanting, cursing processions of blear-eyed and pockmarked young men which wound their way along in the dark small hours of morning. One saw groups of these youths incessantly; sometimes in leering vigils on street corners, sometimes in doorways playing eerily on cheap instruments of music, sometimes in stupefied dozes or indecent dialogues around cafeteria tables near Borough Hall, and sometimes in whispering converse around dingy taxicabs drawn up at the high stoops of crumbling and closely shuttered old houses. They chilled and fascinated him more than he dared confess to his associates on the force, for he seemed to see in them some monstrous thread of secret continuity; some fiendish, cryptical, and ancient pattern utterly beyond and below the sordid mass of facts and habits and haunts listed with such conscientious technical care by the police. They must be, he felt inwardly, the heirs of some shocking and primordial tradition; the sharers of debased and broken scraps from cults and ceremonies older than mankind. Their coherence and definiteness suggested it, and it shewed in the singular suspicion of order which lurked beneath their squalid disorder. He had not read in vain such treatises as Miss Murray's *Witch-Cult in Western Europe*; and knew that up to recent years there had certainly survived among peasants and furtive folk a frightful and clandestine system of assemblies and orgies descended from dark religions antedating the Aryan world, and appearing in popular legends as Black Masses and Witches' Sabbaths. That these hellish vestiges of old Turanian-Asiatic magic and fertility-cults were even now wholly dead he could not for a moment suppose, and he frequently wondered how much older and how much blacker than the very worst of the muttered tales some of them might really be.

III.

It was the case of Robert Suydam which took Malone to the heart of things in Red Hook. Suydam was a lettered recluse of ancient Dutch family, possessed originally of barely independent means, and inhabiting the spacious but ill-preserved mansion which his grandfather had built in Flatbush when that village was little more than a pleasant group of colonial cottages surrounding the steepled and ivy-clad Reformed Church with its iron-railed yard of Netherlandish gravestones. In his lonely house, set back from Martense Street amidst a yard of venerable trees, Suydam had read and brooded for some six decades except for a period a generation before, when he had sailed for the old world and remained there out of sight for eight years. He could afford no servants, and would admit but few visitors to his absolute solitude; eschewing close friendships and receiving his rare acquaintances in one of the three ground-floor rooms which he kept in order—a vast, high-ceiled library whose walls were solidly packed with tattered books of ponderous, archaic, and vaguely repellent aspect. The growth of the town and its final absorption in the Brooklyn district had meant nothing to Suydam, and he had come to mean less and less to the town. Elderly people still pointed him out on the streets, but to most of the recent population he was merely a queer, corpulent old fellow whose unkempt white hair, stubbly beard, shiny black clothes, and gold-headed cane earned him an amused glance and nothing more. Malone did not know him by sight till duty called him to the case, but had heard of him indirectly as a really profound authority on mediaeval superstition, and had once idly meant to look up an out-of-print pamphlet of his on the Kabbalah and the Faustus legend, which a friend had quoted from memory.

Suydam became a "case" when his distant and only relatives sought court pronouncements on his sanity. Their action seemed sudden to the outside world, but was really undertaken only after prolonged observation and sorrowful debate. It was based on certain odd changes in his speech and habits; wild references to impending wonders, and unaccountable hauntings of disreputable Brooklyn neighbourhoods. He had been growing shabbier and shabbier with the years, and now prowled about like a veritable mendicant; seen occasionally by humiliated friends in subway stations, or loitering on the benches around Borough Hall in conversation with groups of swarthy, evil-looking strangers. When he spoke it was to babble of unlimited powers almost within his grasp, and to repeat with knowing leers such mystical words or names as "Sephiroth," "Ashmodai," and "Samaël." The court action revealed that he was using up his income and wasting his principal in the purchase of curious tomes imported from London and Paris, and in the maintenance of a squalid basement flat in the Red Hook district where he spent nearly every night, receiving odd delegations of mixed rowdies and foreigners, and apparently conducting some kind of ceremonial service behind the green blinds of secretive windows. Detectives assigned to follow him reported strange cries and chants and prancing of feet filtering out from these nocturnal rites, and shuddered at their peculiar ecstasy and abandon despite the commonness of weird orgies in that sodden section. When, however, the matter came to a hearing, Suydam managed to preserve his liberty. Before the judge his manner grew urbane and reasonable, and he freely admitted the queerness of demeanour and extravagant cast of language into which he had fallen through excessive devotion to study and research. He was, he said, engaged in the investigation of certain details of European tradition which required the closest contact with foreign groups and their songs and folk dances. The notion that any low secret society was preying upon him, as hinted by his relatives, was obviously absurd; and shewed how sadly limited was their understanding of him and his work. Triumphing with his calm explanations, he was suffered to depart unhindered; and the paid detectives of the Suydams, Corlears, and Van Brunts were withdrawn in resigned disgust.

It was here that an alliance of Federal inspectors and police, Malone with them, entered the case. The law had watched the Suydam action with interest, and had in many instances been called upon to aid the private detectives. In this work it developed that Suydam's new associates were among the blackest and most vicious criminals of Red Hook's devious lanes, and that at least a third of them were known and repeated offenders in the matter of thievery, disorder, and the importation of illegal immigrants. Indeed, it would not have been too much to say that the old scholar's particular circle coincided almost perfectly with the worst of the organised cliques which smuggled ashore certain nameless and unclassified Asian dregs wisely turned back by Ellis Island. In the teeming rookeries of Parker Place—since renamed—where Suydam had his basement flat, there had grown up a very unusual colony of unclassified slant-eyed folk who used the Arabic alphabet but were eloquently repudiated by the great mass of Syrians in and around Atlantic Avenue. They could all have been deported for lack of credentials, but legalism is slow-moving, and one does not disturb Red Hook unless publicity forces one to.

These creatures attended a tumbledown stone church, used Wednesdays as a dance-hall, which reared its Gothic buttresses near the vilest part of the waterfront. It was nominally Catholic; but priests throughout Brooklyn denied the place all standing and authenticity, and policemen agreed with them when they listened to the noises it emitted at night. Malone used to fancy he heard terrible cracked bass notes from a hidden organ far underground when the church stood empty and unlighted, whilst all observers dreaded the shrieking and drumming which accompanied the visible services. Suydam, when questioned, said he thought the ritual was some remnant of Nestorian Christianity tinctured with the Shamanism of Thibet. Most of the people, he conjectured, were of Mongoloid stock, originating somewhere in or near Kurdistan—and Malone could not help recalling that Kurdistan is the land of the Yezidis, last survivors of the Persian devil-worshippers. However this may have been, the stir of the Suydam investigation made it certain that these unauthorised newcomers were flooding Red Hook in increasing numbers; entering through some marine conspiracy unreached by revenue officers and harbour police, overrunning Parker Place and rapidly spreading up the hill, and welcomed with curious fraternalism by the other assorted denizens of the region. Their squat figures and characteristic squinting physiognomies, grotesquely combined with flashy American clothing, appeared more and more numerously among the loafers and nomad gangsters of the Borough Hall section; till at length it was deemed necessary to compute their numbers, ascertain their sources and occupations, and find if possible a way to round them up and deliver them to the proper immigration authorities. To this task Malone was assigned by agreement of Federal and city forces, and as he commenced his canvass of Red Hook he felt poised upon the brink of nameless terrors, with the shabby, unkempt figure of Robert Suydam as arch-fiend and adversary.

IV.

Police methods are varied and ingenious. Malone, through unostentatious rambles, carefully casual conversations, well-timed offers of hip-pocket liquor, and judicious dialogues with frightened prisoners, learned many isolated facts about the movement whose aspect had become so menacing. The newcomers were indeed Kurds, but of a dialect obscure and puzzling to exact philology. Such of them as worked lived mostly as dock-hands and unlicenced pedlars, though frequently serving in Greek restaurants and tending corner news stands. Most of them, however, had no visible means of support; and were obviously connected with underworld pursuits, of which smuggling and "bootlegging" were the least indescribable. They had come in steamships, apparently tramp freighters, and had been unloaded by stealth on moonless nights in rowboats which stole under a certain wharf and followed a hidden canal to a secret subterranean pool beneath a house. This wharf, canal, and house Malone could not locate, for the memories of his informants were exceedingly confused, while their speech was to a great extent beyond even the ablest interpreters; nor could he gain any real data on the reasons for their systematic importation. They were reticent about the exact spot from which they had come, and were never sufficiently off guard to reveal the agencies which had sought them out and directed their course. Indeed, they developed something like acute fright when asked the reasons for their presence. Gangsters of other breeds were equally taciturn, and the most that could be gathered was that some god or great priesthood had promised them unheard-of powers and supernatural glories and rulerships in a strange land.

The attendance of both newcomers and old gangsters at Suydam's closely guarded nocturnal meetings was very regular, and the police soon learned that the erstwhile recluse had leased additional flats to accommodate such guests as knew his password; at last occupying three entire houses and permanently harbouring many of his queer companions. He spent but little time now at his Flatbush home, apparently going and coming only to obtain and return books; and his face and manner had attained an appalling pitch of wildness. Malone twice interviewed him, but was each time brusquely repulsed. He knew nothing, he said, of any mysterious plots or movements; and had no idea how the Kurds could have entered or what they wanted. His business was to study undisturbed the folklore of all the immigrants of the district; a business with which policemen had no legitimate concern. Malone mentioned his admiration for Suydam's old brochure on the Kabbalah and other myths, but the old man's softening was only momentary. He sensed an intrusion, and rebuffed his visitor in no uncertain way; till Malone withdrew disgusted, and turned to other channels of information.

What Malone would have unearthed could he have worked continuously on the case, we shall never know. As it was, a stupid conflict between city and Federal authority suspended the investigations for several months, during which the detective was busy with other assignments. But at no time did he lose interest, or fail to stand amazed at what began to happen to Robert Suydam. Just at the time when a wave of kidnappings and disappearances spread its excitement over New York, the unkempt scholar embarked upon a metamorphosis as startling as it was absurd. One day he was seen near Borough Hall with clean-shaved face, well-trimmed hair, and tastefully immaculate attire, and on every day thereafter some obscure improvement was noticed in him. He maintained his new fastidiousness without interruption, added to it an unwonted sparkle of eye and crispness of speech, and began little by little to shed the corpulence which had so long deformed him. Now frequently taken for less than his age, he acquired an elasticity of step and buoyancy of demeanour to match the new tradition, and shewed a curious darkening of the hair which somehow did not suggest dye. As the months passed, he commenced to dress less and less conservatively, and finally astonished his new friends by renovating and redecorating his Flatbush mansion, which he threw open in a series of receptions, summoning all the acquaintances he could remember, and extending a special welcome to the fully forgiven relatives who had so lately sought his restraint. Some attended through curiosity, others through duty; but all were suddenly charmed by the dawning grace and urbanity of the former hermit. He had, he asserted, accomplished most of his allotted work; and having just inherited some property from a half-forgotten European friend, was about to spend his remaining years in a brighter second youth which ease, care, and diet had made possible to him. Less and less was he seen at Red Hook, and more and more did he move in the society to which he was born. Policemen noted a tendency of the gangsters to congregate at the old stone church and dance-hall instead of at the basement flat in Parker Place, though the latter and its recent annexes still overflowed with noxious life.

Then two incidents occurred—wide enough apart, but both of intense interest in the case as Malone envisaged it. One was a quiet announcement in the *Eagle* of Robert Suydam's engagement to Miss Cornelia Gerritsen of Bayside, a young woman of excellent position, and distantly related to the elderly bridegroom-elect; whilst the other was a raid on the dance-hall church by city police, after a report that the face of a kidnapped child had been seen for a second at one of the basement windows. Malone had participated in this raid, and studied the place with much care when inside. Nothing was found—in fact, the building was entirely deserted when visited—but the sensitive Celt was vaguely disturbed by many things about the interior. There were crudely painted panels he did not like—panels which depicted sacred faces with peculiarly worldly and sardonic expressions, and which occasionally took liberties that even a layman's sense of decorum could scarcely countenance. Then, too, he did not relish the Greek inscription on the wall above the pulpit; an ancient incantation which he had once stumbled upon in Dublin college days, and which read, literally translated:

> "O friend and companion of night, thou who rejoicest in the baying of dogs and spilt blood, who wanderest in the midst of shades among the tombs, who longest for blood and bringest terror to mortals, Gorgo, Mormo, thousand-faced moon, look favourably on our sacrifices!"

When he read this he shuddered, and thought vaguely of the cracked bass organ notes he fancied he had heard beneath the church on certain nights. He shuddered again at the rust around the rim of a metal basin which stood on the altar, and paused nervously when his nostrils seemed to detect a curious and ghastly stench from somewhere in the neighbourhood. That organ memory haunted him, and he explored the basement with particular assiduity before he left. The place was very hateful to him; yet after all, were the blasphemous panels and inscriptions more than mere crudities perpetrated by the ignorant?

By the time of Suydam's wedding the kidnapping epidemic had become a popular newspaper scandal. Most of the victims were young children of the lowest classes, but the increasing number of disappearances had worked up a sentiment of the strongest fury. Journals clamoured for action from the police, and once more the Butler Street station sent its men over Red Hook for clues, discoveries, and criminals. Malone was glad to be on the trail again, and took pride in a raid on one of Suydam's Parker Place houses. There, indeed, no stolen child was found, despite the tales of screams and the red sash picked up in the areaway; but the paintings and rough inscriptions on the peeling walls of most of the rooms, and the primitive chemical laboratory in the attic, all helped to convince the detective that he was on the track of something tremendous. The paintings were appalling—hideous monsters of every shape and size, and parodies on human outlines which cannot be described. The writing was in red, and varied from Arabic to Greek, Roman, and Hebrew letters. Malone could not read much of it, but what he did decipher was portentous and cabbalistic enough. One frequently repeated motto was in a sort of Hebraised Hellenistic Greek, and suggested the most terrible daemon-evocations of the Alexandrian decadence:

> "HEL · HELOYM · SOTHER · EMMANVEL · SABAOTH · AGLA · TETRAGRAMMATON · AGYROS · OTHEOS · ISCHYROS · ATHANATOS · IEHOVA · VA · ADONAI · SADAY · HOMOVSION · MESSIAS · ESCHEREHEYE."

Circles and pentagrams loomed on every hand, and told indubitably of the strange beliefs and aspirations of those who dwelt so squalidly here. In the cellar, however, the strangest thing was found—a pile of genuine gold ingots covered carelessly with a piece of burlap, and bearing upon their shining surfaces the same weird hieroglyphics which also adorned the walls. During the raid the police encountered only a passive resistance from the squinting Orientals that swarmed from every door. Finding nothing relevant, they had to leave all as it was; but the precinct captain wrote Suydam a note advising him to look closely to the character of his tenants and protégés in view of the growing public clamour.

V.

Then came the June wedding and the great sensation. Flatbush was gay for the hour about high noon, and pennanted motors thronged the streets near the old Dutch church where an awning stretched from door to highway. No local event ever surpassed the Suydam-Gerritsen nuptials in tone and scale, and the party which escorted bride and groom to the Cunard Pier was, if not exactly the smartest, at least a solid page from the Social Register. At five o'clock adieux were waved, and the ponderous liner edged away from the long pier, slowly turned its nose seaward, discarded its tug, and headed for the widening water spaces that led to old world wonders. By night the outer harbour was cleared, and late passengers watched the stars twinkling above an unpolluted ocean.

Whether the tramp steamer or the scream was first to gain attention, no one can say. Probably they were simultaneous, but it is of no use to calculate. The scream came from the Suydam stateroom, and the sailor who broke down the door could perhaps have told frightful things if he had not forthwith gone completely mad—as it is, he shrieked more loudly than the first victims, and thereafter ran simpering about the vessel till caught and put in irons. The ship's doctor who entered the stateroom and turned on the lights a moment later did not go mad, but told nobody what he saw till afterward, when he corresponded with Malone in Chepachet. It was murder—strangulation—but one need not say that the claw-mark on Mrs. Suydam's throat could not have come from her husband's or any other human hand, or that upon the white wall there flickered for an instant in hateful red a legend which, later copied from memory, seems to have been nothing less than the fearsome Chaldee letters of the word "LILITH." One need not mention these things because they vanished so quickly—as for Suydam, one could at least bar others from the room until one knew what to think oneself. The doctor has distinctly assured Malone that he did not see *IT*. The open porthole, just before he turned on the lights, was clouded for a second with a certain phosphorescence, and for a moment there seemed to echo in the night outside the suggestion of a faint and hellish tittering; but no real outline met the eye. As proof, the doctor points to his continued sanity.

Then the tramp steamer claimed all attention. A boat put off, and a horde of swart, insolent ruffians in officers' dress swarmed aboard the temporarily halted Cunarder. They wanted Suydam or his body—they had known of his trip, and for certain reasons were sure he would die. The captain's deck was almost a pandemonium; for at the instant, between the doctor's report from the stateroom and the demands of the men from the tramp, not even the wisest and gravest seaman could think what to do. Suddenly the leader of the visiting mariners, an Arab with a hatefully negroid mouth, pulled forth a dirty, crumpled paper and handed it to the captain. It was signed by Robert Suydam, and bore the following odd message:

> "In case of sudden or unexplained accident or death on my part, please deliver me or my body unquestioningly into the hands of the bearer and his associates. Everything, for me, and perhaps for you, depends on absolute compliance. Explanations can come later—do not fail me now.
>
> ROBERT SUYDAM."

Captain and doctor looked at each other, and the latter whispered something to the former. Finally they nodded rather helplessly and led the way to the Suydam stateroom. The doctor directed the captain's glance away as he unlocked the door and admitted the strange seamen, nor did he breathe easily till they filed out with their burden after an unaccountably long period of preparation. It was wrapped in bedding from the berths, and the doctor was glad that the outlines were not very revealing. Somehow the men got the thing over the side and away to their tramp steamer without uncovering it. The Cunarder started again, and the doctor and a ship's undertaker sought out the Suydam stateroom to perform what last services they could. Once more the physician was forced to reticence and even to mendacity, for a hellish thing had happened. When the undertaker asked him why he had drained off all of Mrs. Suydam's blood, he neglected to affirm that he had not done so; nor did he point to the vacant bottle-spaces on the rack, or to the odour in the sink which shewed the hasty disposition of the bottles' original contents. The pockets of those men—if men they were—had bulged damnably when they left the ship. Two hours later, and the world knew by radio all that it ought to know of the horrible affair.

VI.

That same June evening, without having heard a word from the sea, Malone was desperately busy among the alleys of Red Hook. A sudden stir seemed to permeate the place, and as if apprised by "grapevine telegraph" of something singular, the denizens clustered expectantly around the dance-hall church and the houses in Parker Place. Three children had just disappeared—blue-eyed Norwegians from the streets toward Gowanus—and there were rumours of a mob forming among the sturdy Vikings of that section. Malone had for weeks been urging his colleagues to attempt a general cleanup; and at last, moved by conditions more obvious to their common sense than the conjectures of a Dublin dreamer, they had agreed upon a final stroke. The unrest and menace of this evening had been the deciding factor, and just about midnight a raiding party recruited from three stations descended upon Parker Place and its environs. Doors were battered in, stragglers arrested, and candlelighted rooms forced to disgorge unbelievable throngs of mixed foreigners in figured robes, mitres, and other inexplicable devices. Much was lost in the melee, for objects were thrown hastily down unexpected shafts, and betraying odours deadened by the sudden kindling of pungent incense. But spattered blood was everywhere, and Malone shuddered whenever he saw a brazier or altar from which the smoke was still rising.

He wanted to be in several places at once, and decided on Suydam's basement flat only after a messenger had reported the complete emptiness of the dilapidated dance-hall church. The flat, he thought, must hold some clue to a cult of which the occult scholar had so obviously become the centre and leader; and it was with real expectancy that he ransacked the musty rooms, noted their vaguely charnel odour, and examined the curious books, instruments, gold ingots, and glass-stoppered bottles scattered carelessly here and there. Once a lean, black-and-white cat edged between his feet and tripped him, overturning at the same time a beaker half full of a red liquid. The shock was severe, and to this day Malone is not certain of what he saw; but in dreams he still pictures that cat as it scuttled away with certain monstrous alterations and peculiarities. Then came the locked cellar door, and the search for something to break it down. A heavy stool stood near, and its tough seat was more than enough for the antique panels. A crack formed and enlarged, and the whole door gave way—but from the *other* side; whence poured a howling tumult of ice-cold wind with all the stenches of the bottomless pit, and whence reached a sucking force not of earth or heaven, which, coiling sentiently about the paralysed detective, dragged him through the aperture and down unmeasured spaces filled with whispers and wails, and gusts of mocking laughter.

Of course it was a dream. All the specialists have told him so, and he has nothing to prove the contrary. Indeed, he would rather have it thus; for then the sight of old brick slums and dark foreign faces would not eat so deeply into his soul. But at the time it was all horribly real, and nothing can ever efface the memory of those nighted crypts, those titan arcades, and those half-formed shapes of hell that strode gigantically in silence holding half-eaten things whose still surviving portions screamed for mercy or laughed with madness. Odours of incense and corruption joined in sickening concert, and the black air was alive with the cloudy, semi-visible bulk of shapeless elemental things with eyes. Somewhere dark sticky water was lapping at onyx piers, and once the shivery tinkle of raucous little bells pealed out to greet the insane titter of a naked phosphorescent thing which swam into sight, scrambled ashore, and climbed up to squat leeringly on a carved golden pedestal in the background.

Avenues of limitless night seemed to radiate in every direction, till one might fancy that here lay the root of a contagion destined to sicken and swallow cities, and engulf nations in the foetor of hybrid pestilence. Here cosmic sin had entered, and festered by unhallowed rites had commenced the grinning march of death that was to rot us all to fungous abnormalities too hideous for the grave's holding. Satan here held his Babylonish court, and in the blood of stainless childhood the leprous limbs of phosphorescent Lilith were laved. Incubi and succubae howled praise to Hecate, and headless mooncalves bleated to the Magna Mater. Goats leaped to the sound of thin accursed flutes, and aegipans chased endlessly after misshapen fauns over rocks twisted like swollen toads. Moloch and Ashtaroth were not absent; for in this quintessence of all damnation the bounds of consciousness were let down, and man's fancy lay open to vistas of every realm of horror and every forbidden dimension that evil had power to mould. The world and Nature were helpless against such assaults from unsealed wells of night, nor could any sign or prayer check the Walpurgis-riot of horror which had come when a sage with the hateful key had stumbled on a horde with the locked and brimming coffer of transmitted daemon-lore.

Suddenly a ray of physical light shot through these phantasms, and Malone heard the sound of oars amidst the blasphemies of things that should be dead. A boat with a lantern in its prow darted into sight, made fast to an iron ring in the slimy stone pier, and vomited forth several dark men bearing a long burden swathed in bedding. They took it to the naked phosphorescent thing on the carved golden pedestal, and the thing tittered and pawed at the bedding. Then they unswathed it, and propped upright before the pedestal the gangrenous corpse of a corpulent old man with stubbly beard and unkempt white hair. The phosphorescent thing tittered again, and the men produced bottles from their pockets and anointed its feet with red, whilst they afterward gave the bottles to the thing to drink from.

All at once, from an arcaded avenue leading endlessly away, there came the daemoniac rattle and wheeze of a blasphemous organ, choking and rumbling out the mockeries of hell in a cracked, sardonic bass. In an instant every moving entity was electrified; and forming at once into a ceremonial procession, the nightmare horde slithered away in quest of the sound—goat, satyr, and aegipan, incubus, succuba, and lemur, twisted toad and shapeless elemental, dog-faced howler and silent strutter in darkness—all led by the abominable naked phosphorescent thing that had squatted on the carved golden throne, and that now strode insolently bearing in its arms the glassy-eyed corpse of the corpulent old man. The strange dark men danced in the rear, and the whole column skipped and leaped with Dionysiac fury. Malone staggered after them a few steps, delirious and hazy, and doubtful of his place in this or in any world. Then he turned, faltered, and sank down on the cold damp stone, gasping and shivering as the daemon organ croaked on, and the howling and drumming and tinkling of the mad procession grew fainter and fainter.

Vaguely he was conscious of chanted horrors and shocking croakings afar off. Now and then a wail or whine of ceremonial devotion would float to him through the black arcade, whilst eventually there rose the dreadful Greek incantation whose text he had read above the pulpit of that dance-hall church.

"O friend and companion of night, thou who rejoicest in the baying of dogs *(here a hideous howl burst forth)* and spilt blood *(here nameless sounds vied with morbid shriekings)*, who wanderest in the midst of shades among the tombs *(here a whistling sigh occurred)*, who longest for blood and bringest terror to mortals *(short, sharp cries from myriad throats)*, Gorgo *(repeated as response)*, Mormo *(repeated with ecstasy)*, thousand-faced moon *(sighs and flute notes)*, look favourably on our sacrifices!"

As the chant closed, a general shout went up, and hissing sounds nearly drowned the croaking of the cracked bass organ. Then a gasp as from many throats, and a babel of barked and bleated words—"Lilith, Great Lilith, behold the Bridegroom!" More cries, a clamour of rioting, and the sharp, clicking footfalls of a running figure. The footfalls approached, and Malone raised himself to his elbow to look.

The luminosity of the crypt, lately diminished, had now slightly increased; and in that devil-light there appeared the fleeing form of that which should not flee or feel or breathe—the glassy-eyed, gangrenous corpse of the corpulent old man, now needing no support, but animated by some infernal sorcery of the rite just closed. After it raced the naked, tittering, phosphorescent thing that belonged on the carven pedestal, and still farther behind panted the dark men, and all the dread crew of sentient loathsomenesses. The corpse was gaining on its pursuers, and seemed bent on a definite object, straining with every rotting muscle toward the carved golden pedestal, whose necromantic importance was evidently so great. Another moment and it had reached its goal, whilst the trailing throng laboured on with more frantic speed. But they were too late, for in one final spurt of strength which ripped tendon from tendon and sent its noisome bulk floundering to the floor in a state of jellyish dissolution, the staring corpse which had been Robert Suydam achieved its object and its triumph. The push had been tremendous, but the force had held out; and as the pusher collapsed to a muddy blotch of corruption the pedestal he had pushed tottered, tipped, and finally careened from its onyx base into the thick waters below, sending up a parting gleam of carven gold as it sank heavily to undreamable gulfs of lower Tartarus. In that instant, too, the whole scene of horror faded to nothingness before Malone's eyes; and he fainted amidst a thunderous crash which seemed to blot out all the evil universe.

VII.

Malone's dream, experienced in full before he knew of Suydam's death and transfer at sea, was curiously supplemented by some odd realities of the case; though that is no reason why anyone should believe it. The three old houses in Parker Place, doubtless long rotten with decay in its most insidious form, collapsed without visible cause while half the raiders and most of the prisoners were inside; and of both the greater number were instantly killed. Only in the basements and cellars was there much saving of life, and Malone was lucky to have been deep below the house of Robert Suydam. For he really was there, as no one is disposed to deny. They found him unconscious by the edge of a night-black pool, with a grotesquely horrible jumble of decay and bone, identifiable through dental work as the body of Suydam, a few feet away. The case was plain, for it was hither that the smugglers' underground canal led; and the men who took Suydam from the ship had brought him home. They themselves were never found, or at least never identified; and the ship's doctor is not yet satisfied with the simple certitudes of the police.

Suydam was evidently a leader in extensive man-smuggling operations, for the canal to his house was but one of several subterranean channels and tunnels in the neighbourhood. There was a tunnel from this house to a crypt beneath the dance-hall church; a crypt accessible from the church only through a narrow secret passage in the north wall, and in whose chambers some singular and terrible things were discovered. The croaking organ was there, as well as a vast arched chapel with wooden benches and a strangely figured altar. The walls were lined with small cells, in seventeen of which—hideous to relate–solitary prisoners in a state of complete idiocy were found chained, including four mothers with infants of disturbingly strange appearance. These infants died soon after exposure to the light; a circumstance which the doctors thought rather merciful. Nobody but Malone, among those who inspected them, remembered the sombre question of old Delrio: *"An sint unquam daemones incubi et succubae, et an ex tali congressu proles nasci queat?"*

Before the canals were filled up they were thoroughly dredged, and yielded forth a sensational array of sawed and split bones of all sizes. The kidnapping epidemic, very clearly, had been traced home; though only two of the surviving prisoners could by any legal thread be connected with it. These men are now in prison, since they failed of conviction as accessories in the actual murders. The carved golden pedestal or throne so often mentioned by Malone as of primary occult importance was never brought to light, though at one place under the Suydam house the canal was observed to sink into a well too deep for dredging. It was choked up at the mouth and cemented over when the cellars of the new houses were made, but Malone often speculates on what lies beneath. The police, satisfied that they had shattered a dangerous gang of maniacs and man-smugglers, turned over to the Federal authorities the unconvicted Kurds, who before their deportation were conclusively found to belong to the Yezidi clan of devil-worshippers. The tramp ship and its crew remain an elusive mystery, though cynical detectives are once more ready to combat its smuggling and rum-running ventures. Malone thinks these detectives shew a sadly limited perspective in their lack of wonder at the myriad unexplainable details, and the suggestive obscurity of the whole case; though he is just as critical of the newspapers, which saw only a morbid sensation and gloated over a minor sadist cult which they might have proclaimed a horror from the universe's very heart. But he is content to rest silent in Chepachet, calming his nervous system and praying that time may gradually transfer his terrible experience from the realm of present reality to that of picturesque and semi-mythical remoteness.

Robert Suydam sleeps beside his bride in Greenwood Cemetery. No funeral was held over the strangely released bones, and relatives are grateful for the swift oblivion which overtook the case as a whole. The scholar's connexion with the Red Hook horrors, indeed, was never emblazoned by legal proof; since his death forestalled the inquiry he would otherwise have faced. His own end is not much mentioned, and the Suydams hope that posterity may recall him only as a gentle recluse who dabbled in harmless magic and folklore.

As for Red Hook—it is always the same. Suydam came and went; a terror gathered and faded; but the evil spirit of darkness and squalor broods on amongst the mongrels in the old brick houses, and prowling bands still parade on unknown errands past windows where lights and twisted faces unaccountably appear and disappear. Age-old horror is a hydra with a thousand heads, and the cults of darkness are rooted in blasphemies deeper than the well of Democritus. The soul of the beast is omnipresent and triumphant, and Red Hook's legions of blear-eyed, pockmarked youths still chant and curse and howl as they file from abyss to abyss, none knows whence or whither, pushed on by blind laws of biology which they may never understand. As of old, more people enter Red Hook than leave it on the landward side, and there are already rumours of new canals running underground to certain centres of traffic in liquor and less mentionable things.

The dance-hall church is now mostly a dance-hall, and queer faces have appeared at night at the windows. Lately a policeman expressed the belief that the filled-up crypt has been dug out again, and for no simply explainable purpose. Who are we to combat poisons older than history and mankind? Apes danced in Asia to those horrors, and the cancer lurks secure and spreading where furtiveness hides in rows of decaying brick.

Malone does not shudder without cause—for only the other day an officer overheard a swarthy squinting hag teaching a small child some whispered patois in the shadow of an areaway. He listened, and thought it very strange when he heard her repeat over and over again:

> "O friend and companion of night, thou who rejoicest in the baying of dogs and spilt blood, who wanderest in the midst of shades among the tombs, who longest for blood and bringest terror to mortals, Gorgo, Mormo, thousand-faced moon, look favourably on our sacrifices!"

Herbert West—Reanimator

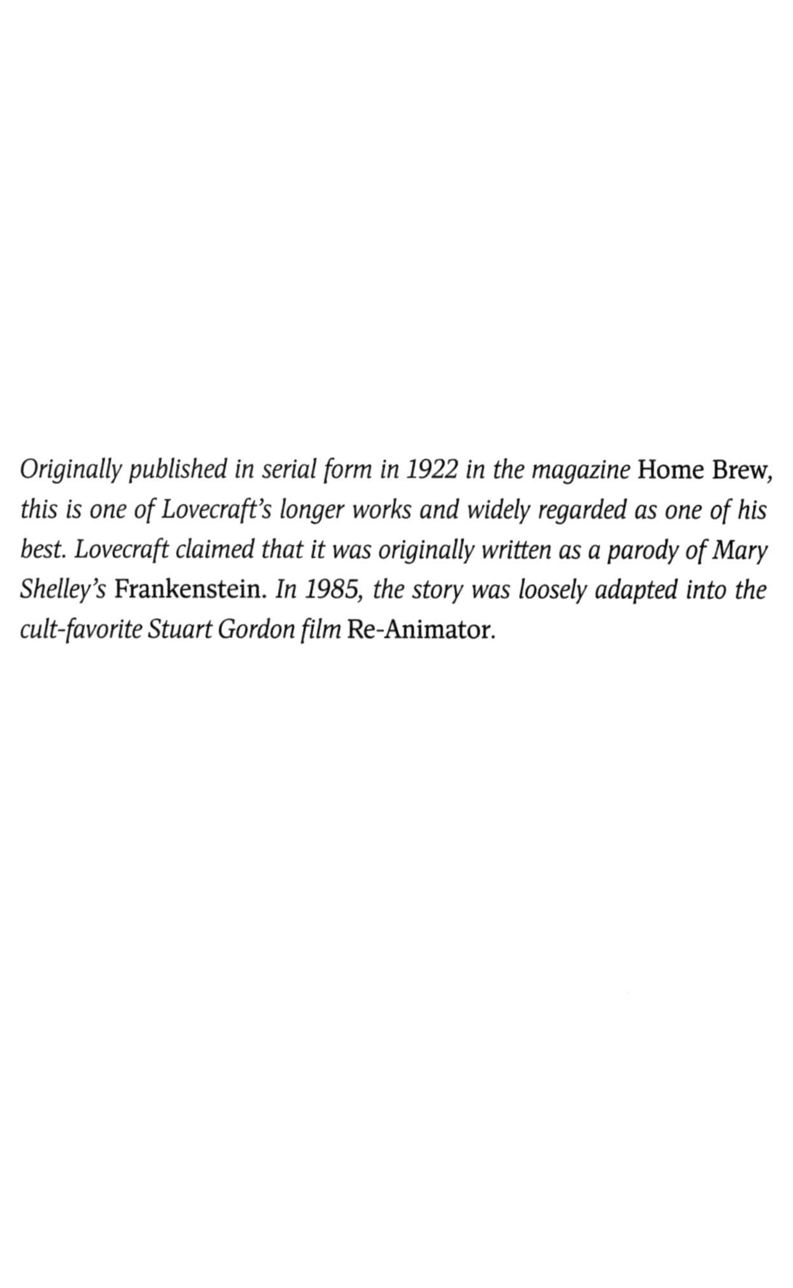

Originally published in serial form in 1922 in the magazine Home Brew, *this is one of Lovecraft's longer works and widely regarded as one of his best. Lovecraft claimed that it was originally written as a parody of Mary Shelley's* Frankenstein. *In 1985, the story was loosely adapted into the cult-favorite Stuart Gordon film* Re-Animator.

I. From the Dark

Of Herbert West, who was my friend in college and in after life, I can speak only with extreme terror. This terror is not due altogether to the sinister manner of his recent disappearance, but was engendered by the whole nature of his life-work, and first gained its acute form more than seventeen years ago, when we were in the third year of our course at the Miskatonic University Medical School in Arkham. While he was with me, the wonder and diabolism of his experiments fascinated me utterly, and I was his closest companion. Now that he is gone and the spell is broken, the actual fear is greater. Memories and possibilities are ever more hideous than realities.

The first horrible incident of our acquaintance was the greatest shock I ever experienced, and it is only with reluctance that I repeat it. As I have said, it happened when we were in the medical school, where West had already made himself notorious through his wild theories on the nature of death and the possibility of overcoming it artificially. His views, which were widely ridiculed by the faculty and his fellow-students, hinged on the essentially mechanistic nature of life; and concerned means for operating the organic machinery of mankind by calculated chemical action after the failure of natural processes. In his experiments with various animating solutions he had killed and treated immense numbers of rabbits, guinea-pigs, cats, dogs, and monkeys, till he had become the prime nuisance of the college. Several times he had actually obtained signs of life in animals supposedly dead; in many cases violent signs; but he soon saw that the perfection of this process, if indeed possible, would necessarily involve a lifetime of research. It likewise became clear that, since the same solution never worked alike on different organic species, he would require human subjects for further and more specialised progress. It was here that he first came into conflict with the college authorities, and was debarred from future experiments by no less a dignitary than the dean of the medical school himself—the learned and benevolent Dr. Allan Halsey, whose work in behalf of the stricken is recalled by every old resident of Arkham.

I had always been exceptionally tolerant of West's pursuits, and we frequently discussed his theories, whose ramifications and corollaries were almost infinite. Holding with Haeckel that all life is a chemical and physical process, and that the so-called "soul" is a myth, my friend believed that artificial reanimation of the dead can depend only on the condition of the tissues; and that unless actual decomposition has set in, a corpse fully equipped with organs may with suitable measures be set going again in the peculiar fashion known as life. That the psychic or intellectual life might be impaired by the slight deterioration of sensitive brain-cells which even a short period of death would be apt to cause, West fully realised. It had at first been his hope to find a reagent which would restore vitality before the actual advent of death, and only repeated failures on animals had shewn him that the natural and artificial life-motions were incompatible. He then sought extreme freshness in his specimens, injecting his solutions into the blood immediately after the extinction of life. It was this circumstance which made the professors so carelessly sceptical, for they felt that true death had not occurred in any case. They did not stop to view the matter closely and reasoningly.

It was not long after the faculty had interdicted his work that West confided to me his resolution to get fresh human bodies in some manner, and continue in secret the experiments he could no longer perform openly. To hear him discussing ways and means was rather ghastly, for at the college we had never procured anatomical specimens ourselves. Whenever the morgue proved inadequate, two local negroes attended to this matter, and they were seldom questioned. West was then a small, slender, spectacled youth with delicate features, yellow hair, pale blue eyes, and a soft voice, and it was uncanny to hear him dwelling on the relative merits of Christchurch Cemetery and the potter's field. We finally decided on the potter's field, because practically every body in Christchurch was embalmed; a thing of course ruinous to West's researches.

I was by this time his active and enthralled assistant, and helped him make all his decisions, not only concerning the source of bodies but concerning a suitable place for our loathsome work. It was I who thought of the deserted Chapman farmhouse beyond Meadow Hill, where we fitted up on the ground floor an operating room and a laboratory, each with dark curtains to conceal our midnight doings. The place was far from any road, and in sight of no other house, yet precautions were none the less necessary; since rumours of strange lights, started by chance nocturnal roamers, would soon bring disaster on our enterprise. It was agreed to call the whole thing a chemical laboratory if discovery should occur. Gradually we equipped our sinister haunt of science with materials either purchased in Boston or quietly borrowed from the college—materials carefully made unrecognisable save to expert eyes—and provided spades and picks for the many burials we should have to make in the cellar. At the college we used an incinerator, but the apparatus was too costly for our unauthorised laboratory. Bodies were always a nuisance—even the small guinea-pig bodies from the slight clandestine experiments in West's room at the boarding-house.

We followed the local death-notices like ghouls, for our specimens demanded particular qualities. What we wanted were corpses interred soon after death and without artificial preservation; preferably free from malforming disease, and certainly with all organs present. Accident victims were our best hope. Not for many weeks did we hear of anything suitable; though we talked with morgue and hospital authorities, ostensibly in the college's interest, as often as we could without exciting suspicion. We found that the college had first choice in every case, so that it might be necessary to remain in Arkham during the summer, when only the limited summer-school classes were held. In the end, though, luck favoured us; for one day we heard of an almost ideal case in the potter's field; a brawny young workman drowned only the morning before in Sumner's Pond, and buried at the town's expense without delay or embalming. That afternoon we found the new grave, and determined to begin work soon after midnight.

It was a repulsive task that we undertook in the black small hours, even though we lacked at that time the special horror of graveyards which later experiences brought to us. We carried spades and oil dark lanterns, for although electric torches were then manufactured, they were not as satisfactory as the tungsten contrivances of today. The process of unearthing was slow and sordid—it might have been gruesomely poetical if we had been artists instead of scientists—and we were glad when our spades struck wood. When the pine box was fully uncovered West scrambled down and removed the lid, dragging out and propping up the contents. I reached down and hauled the contents out of the grave, and then both toiled hard to restore the spot to its former appearance. The affair made us rather nervous, especially the stiff form and vacant face of our first trophy, but we managed to remove all traces of our visit. When we had patted down the last shovelful of earth we put the specimen in a canvas sack and set out for the old Chapman place beyond Meadow Hill.

On an improvised dissecting-table in the old farmhouse, by the light of a powerful acetylene lamp, the specimen was not very spectral looking. It had been a sturdy and apparently unimaginative youth of wholesome plebeian type—large-framed, grey-eyed, and brown-haired—a sound animal without psychological subtleties, and probably having vital processes of the simplest and healthiest sort. Now, with the eyes closed, it looked more asleep than dead; though the expert test of my friend soon left no doubt on that score. We had at last what West had always longed for—a real dead man of the ideal kind, ready for the solution as prepared according to the most careful calculations and theories for human use. The tension on our part became very great. We knew that there was scarcely a chance for anything like complete success, and could not avoid hideous fears at possible grotesque results of partial animation. Especially were we apprehensive concerning the mind and impulses of the creature, since in the space following death some of the more delicate cerebral cells might well have suffered deterioration. I, myself, still held some curious notions about the traditional "soul" of man, and felt an awe at the secrets that might be told by one returning from the dead. I wondered what sights this placid youth might have seen in inaccessible spheres, and what he could relate if fully restored to life. But my wonder was not overwhelming, since for the most part I shared the materialism of my friend. He was calmer than I as he forced a large quantity of his fluid into a vein of the body's arm, immediately binding the incision securely.

The waiting was gruesome, but West never faltered. Every now and then he applied his stethoscope to the specimen, and bore the negative results philosophically. After about three-quarters of an hour without the least sign of life he disappointedly pronounced the solution inadequate, but determined to make the most of his opportunity and try one change in the formula before disposing of his ghastly prize. We had that afternoon dug a grave in the cellar, and would have to fill it by dawn—for although we had fixed a lock on the house we wished to shun even the remotest risk of a ghoulish discovery. Besides, the body would not be even approximately fresh the next night. So taking the solitary acetylene lamp into the adjacent laboratory, we left our silent guest on the slab in the dark, and bent every energy to the mixing of a new solution; the weighing and measuring supervised by West with an almost fanatical care.

The awful event was very sudden, and wholly unexpected. I was pouring something from one test-tube to another, and West was busy over the alcohol blast-lamp which had to answer for a Bunsen burner in this gasless edifice, when from the pitch-black room we had left there burst the most appalling and daemoniac succession of cries that either of us had ever heard. Not more unutterable could have been the chaos of hellish sound if the pit itself had opened to release the agony of the damned, for in one inconceivable cacophony was centred all the supernal terror and unnatural despair of animate nature. Human it could not have been–it is not in man to make such sounds–and without a thought of our late employment or its possible discovery both West and I leaped to the nearest window like stricken animals; overturning tubes, lamp, and retorts, and vaulting madly into the starred abyss of the rural night. I think we screamed ourselves as we stumbled frantically toward the town, though as we reached the outskirts we put on a semblance of restraint–just enough to seem like belated revellers staggering home from a debauch.

We did not separate, but managed to get to West's room, where we whispered with the gas up until dawn. By then we had calmed ourselves a little with rational theories and plans for investigation, so that we could sleep through the day–classes being disregarded. But that evening two items in the paper, wholly unrelated, made it again impossible for us to sleep. The old deserted Chapman house had inexplicably burned to an amorphous heap of ashes; that we could understand because of the upset lamp. Also, an attempt had been made to disturb a new grave in the potter's field, as if by futile and spadeless clawing at the earth. That we could not understand, for we had patted down the mould very carefully.

And for seventeen years after that West would look frequently over his shoulder, and complain of fancied footsteps behind him. Now he has disappeared.

II. The Plague-Daemon

I shall never forget that hideous summer sixteen years ago, when like a noxious afrite from the halls of Eblis typhoid stalked leeringly through Arkham. It is by that satanic scourge that most recall the year, for truly terror brooded with bat-wings over the piles of coffins in the tombs of Christchurch Cemetery; yet for me there is a greater horror in that time—a horror known to me alone now that Herbert West has disappeared.

West and I were doing post-graduate work in summer classes at the medical school of Miskatonic University, and my friend had attained a wide notoriety because of his experiments leading toward the revivification of the dead. After the scientific slaughter of uncounted small animals the freakish work had ostensibly stopped by order of our sceptical dean, Dr. Allan Halsey; though West had continued to perform certain secret tests in his dingy boarding-house room, and had on one terrible and unforgettable occasion taken a human body from its grave in the potter's field to a deserted farmhouse beyond Meadow Hill.

I was with him on that odious occasion, and saw him inject into the still veins the elixir which he thought would to some extent restore life's chemical and physical processes. It had ended horribly—in a delirium of fear which we gradually came to attribute to our own overwrought nerves—and West had never afterward been able to shake off a maddening sensation of being haunted and hunted. The body had not been quite fresh enough; it is obvious that to restore normal mental attributes a body must be very fresh indeed; and a burning of the old house had prevented us from burying the thing. It would have been better if we could have known it was underground.

After that experience West had dropped his researches for some time; but as the zeal of the born scientist slowly returned, he again became importunate with the college faculty, pleading for the use of the dissecting-room and of fresh human specimens for the work he regarded as so overwhelmingly important. His pleas, however, were wholly in vain; for the decision of Dr. Halsey was inflexible, and the other professors all endorsed the verdict of their leader. In the radical theory of reanimation they saw nothing but the immature vagaries of a youthful enthusiast whose slight form, yellow hair, spectacled blue eyes, and soft voice gave no hint of the supernormal–almost diabolical–power of the cold brain within. I can see him now as he was then–and I shiver. He grew sterner of face, but never elderly. And now Sefton Asylum has had the mishap and West has vanished.

West clashed disagreeably with Dr. Halsey near the end of our last undergraduate term in a wordy dispute that did less credit to him than to the kindly dean in point of courtesy. He felt that he was needlessly and irrationally retarded in a supremely great work; a work which he could of course conduct to suit himself in later years, but which he wished to begin while still possessed of the exceptional facilities of the university. That the tradition-bound elders should ignore his singular results on animals, and persist in their denial of the possibility of reanimation, was inexpressibly disgusting and almost incomprehensible to a youth of West's logical temperament. Only greater maturity could help him understand the chronic mental limitations of the "professor-doctor" type–the product of generations of pathetic Puritanism; kindly, conscientious, and sometimes gentle and amiable, yet always narrow, intolerant, custom-ridden, and lacking in perspective. Age has more charity for these incomplete yet high-souled characters, whose worst real vice is timidity, and who are ultimately punished by general ridicule for their intellectual sins—sins like Ptolemaism, Calvinism, anti-Darwinism, anti-Nietzscheism, and every sort of Sabbatarianism and sumptuary legislation. West, young despite his marvellous scientific acquirements, had scant patience with good Dr. Halsey and his erudite colleagues; and nursed an increasing resentment, coupled with a desire to prove his theories to these obtuse worthies in some striking and dramatic fashion. Like most youths, he indulged in elaborate day-dreams of revenge, triumph, and final magnanimous forgiveness.

And then had come the scourge, grinning and lethal, from the nightmare caverns of Tartarus. West and I had graduated about the time of its beginning, but had remained for additional work at the summer school, so that we were in Arkham when it broke with full daemoniac fury upon the town. Though not as yet licenced physicians, we now had our degrees, and were pressed frantically into public service as the numbers of the stricken grew. The situation was almost past management, and deaths ensued too frequently for the local undertakers fully to handle. Burials without embalming were made in rapid succession, and even the Christchurch Cemetery receiving tomb was crammed with coffins of the unembalmed dead. This circumstance was not without effect on West, who thought often of the irony of the situation—so many fresh specimens, yet none for his persecuted researches! We were frightfully overworked, and the terrific mental and nervous strain made my friend brood morbidly.

But West's gentle enemies were no less harassed with prostrating duties. College had all but closed, and every doctor of the medical faculty was helping to fight the typhoid plague. Dr. Halsey in particular had distinguished himself in sacrificing service, applying his extreme skill with whole-hearted energy to cases which many others shunned because of danger or apparent hopelessness. Before a month was over the fearless dean had become a popular hero, though he seemed unconscious of his fame as he struggled to keep from collapsing with physical fatigue and nervous exhaustion. West could not withhold admiration for the fortitude of his foe, but because of this was even more determined to prove to him the truth of his amazing doctrines. Taking advantage of the disorganisation of both college work and municipal health regulations, he managed to get a recently deceased body smuggled into the university dissecting-room one night, and in my presence injected a new modification of his solution. The thing actually opened its eyes, but only stared at the ceiling with a look of soul-petrifying horror before collapsing into an inertness from which nothing could rouse it. West said it was not fresh enough—the hot summer air does not favour corpses. That time we were almost caught before we incinerated the thing, and West doubted the advisability of repeating his daring misuse of the college laboratory.

The peak of the epidemic was reached in August. West and I were almost dead, and Dr. Halsey did die on the 14th. The students all attended the hasty funeral on the 15th, and bought an impressive wreath, though the latter was quite overshadowed by the tributes sent by wealthy Arkham citizens and by the municipality itself. It was almost a public affair, for the dean had surely been a public benefactor. After the entombment we were all somewhat depressed, and spent the afternoon at the bar of the Commercial House; where West, though shaken by the death of his chief opponent, chilled the rest of us with references to his notorious theories. Most of the students went home, or to various duties, as the evening advanced; but West persuaded me to aid him in "making a night of it." West's landlady saw us arrive at his room about two in the morning, with a third man between us; and told her husband that we had all evidently dined and wined rather well.

Apparently this acidulous matron was right; for about 3 a.m. the whole house was aroused by cries coming from West's room, where when they broke down the door they found the two of us unconscious on the blood-stained carpet, beaten, scratched, and mauled, and with the broken remnants of West's bottles and instruments around us. Only an open window told what had become of our assailant, and many wondered how he himself had fared after the terrific leap from the second story to the lawn which he must have made. There were some strange garments in the room, but West upon regaining consciousness said they did not belong to the stranger, but were specimens collected for bacteriological analysis in the course of investigations on the transmission of germ diseases. He ordered them burnt as soon as possible in the capacious fireplace. To the police we both declared ignorance of our late companion's identity. He was, West nervously said, a congenial stranger whom we had met at some downtown bar of uncertain location. We had all been rather jovial, and West and I did not wish to have our pugnacious companion hunted down.

That same night saw the beginning of the second Arkham horror—the horror that to me eclipsed the plague itself. Christchurch Cemetery was the scene of a terrible killing; a watchman having been clawed to death in a manner not only too hideous for description, but raising a doubt as to the human agency of the deed. The victim had been seen alive considerably after midnight—the dawn revealed the unutterable thing. The manager of a circus at the neighbouring town of Bolton was questioned, but he swore that no beast had at any time escaped from its cage. Those who found the body noted a trail of blood leading to the receiving tomb, where a small pool of red lay on the concrete just outside the gate. A fainter trail led away toward the woods, but it soon gave out.

The next night devils danced on the roofs of Arkham, and unnatural madness howled in the wind. Through the fevered town had crept a curse which some said was greater than the plague, and which some whispered was the embodied daemon-soul of the plague itself. Eight houses were entered by a nameless thing which strewed red death in its wake—in all, seventeen maimed and shapeless remnants of bodies were left behind by the voiceless, sadistic monster that crept abroad. A few persons had half seen it in the dark, and said it was white and like a malformed ape or anthropomorphic fiend. It had not left behind quite all that it had attacked, for sometimes it had been hungry. The number it had killed was fourteen; three of the bodies had been in stricken homes and had not been alive.

On the third night frantic bands of searchers, led by the police, captured it in a house on Crane Street near the Miskatonic campus. They had organised the quest with care, keeping in touch by means of volunteer telephone stations, and when someone in the college district had reported hearing a scratching at a shuttered window, the net was quickly spread. On account of the general alarm and precautions, there were only two more victims, and the capture was effected without major casualties. The thing was finally stopped by a bullet, though not a fatal one, and was rushed to the local hospital amidst universal excitement and loathing.

For it had been a man. This much was clear despite the nauseous eyes, the voiceless simianism, and the daemoniac savagery. They dressed its wound and carted it to the asylum at Sefton, where it beat its head against the walls of a padded cell for sixteen years—until the recent mishap, when it escaped under circumstances that few like to mention. What had most disgusted the searchers of Arkham was the thing they noticed when the monster's face was cleaned—the mocking, unbelievable resemblance to a learned and self-sacrificing martyr who had been entombed but three days before—the late Dr. Allan Halsey, public benefactor and dean of the medical school of Miskatonic University.

To the vanished Herbert West and to me the disgust and horror were supreme. I shudder tonight as I think of it; shudder even more than I did that morning when West muttered through his bandages, "Damn it, it wasn't *quite* fresh enough!"

III. Six Shots by Midnight

It is uncommon to fire all six shots of a revolver with great suddenness when one would probably be sufficient, but many things in the life of Herbert West were uncommon. It is, for instance, not often that a young physician leaving college is obliged to conceal the principles which guide his selection of a home and office, yet that was the case with Herbert West. When he and I obtained our degrees at the medical school of Miskatonic University, and sought to relieve our poverty by setting up as general practitioners, we took great care not to say that we chose our house because it was fairly well isolated, and as near as possible to the potter's field.

Reticence such as this is seldom without a cause, nor indeed was ours; for our requirements were those resulting from a life-work distinctly unpopular. Outwardly we were doctors only, but beneath the surface were aims of far greater and more terrible moment—for the essence of Herbert West's existence was a quest amid black and forbidden realms of the unknown, in which he hoped to uncover the secret of life and restore to perpetual animation the graveyard's cold clay. Such a quest demands strange materials, among them fresh human bodies; and in order to keep supplied with these indispensable things one must live quietly and not far from a place of informal interment.

West and I had met in college, and I had been the only one to sympathise with his hideous experiments. Gradually I had come to be his inseparable assistant, and now that we were out of college we had to keep together. It was not easy to find a good opening for two doctors in company, but finally the influence of the university secured us a practice in Bolton—a factory town near Arkham, the seat of the college. The Bolton Worsted Mills are the largest in the Miskatonic Valley, and their polyglot employees are never popular as patients with the local physicians. We chose our house with the greatest care, seizing at last on a rather run-down cottage near the end of Pond Street; five numbers from the closest neighbour, and separated from the local potter's field by only a stretch of meadow land, bisected by a narrow neck of the rather dense forest which lies to the north. The distance was greater than we wished, but we could get no nearer house without going on the other side of the field, wholly out of the factory district. We were not much displeased, however, since there were no people between us and our sinister source of supplies. The walk was a trifle long, but we could haul our silent specimens undisturbed.

Our practice was surprisingly large from the very first—large enough to please most young doctors, and large enough to prove a bore and a burden to students whose real interest lay elsewhere. The mill-hands were of somewhat turbulent inclinations; and besides their many natural needs, their frequent clashes and stabbing affrays gave us plenty to do. But what actually absorbed our minds was the secret laboratory we had fitted up in the cellar—the laboratory with the long table under the electric lights, where in the small hours of the morning we often injected West's various solutions into the veins of the things we dragged from the potter's field. West was experimenting madly to find something which would start man's vital motions anew after they had been stopped by the thing we call death, but had encountered the most ghastly obstacles. The solution had to be differently compounded for different types—what would serve for guinea-pigs would not serve for human beings, and different human specimens required large modifications.

The bodies had to be exceedingly fresh, or the slight decomposition of brain tissue would render perfect reanimation impossible. Indeed, the greatest problem was to get them fresh enough—West had had horrible experiences during his secret college researches with corpses of doubtful vintage. The results of partial or imperfect animation were much more hideous than were the total failures, and we both held fearsome recollections of such things. Ever since our first daemoniac session in the deserted farmhouse on Meadow Hill in Arkham, we had felt a brooding menace; and West, though a calm, blond, blue-eyed scientific automaton in most respects, often confessed to a shuddering sensation of stealthy pursuit. He half felt that he was followed–a psychological delusion of shaken nerves, enhanced by the undeniably disturbing fact that at least one of our reanimated specimens was still alive–a frightful carnivorous thing in a padded cell at Sefton. Then there was another–our first–whose exact fate we had never learned.

We had fair luck with specimens in Bolton–much better than in Arkham. We had not been settled a week before we got an accident victim on the very night of burial, and made it open its eyes with an amazingly rational expression before the solution failed. It had lost an arm–if it had been a perfect body we might have succeeded better. Between then and the next January we secured three more; one total failure, one case of marked muscular motion, and one rather shivery thing–it rose of itself and uttered a sound. Then came a period when luck was poor; interments fell off, and those that did occur were of specimens either too diseased or too maimed for use. We kept track of all the deaths and their circumstances with systematic care.

One March night, however, we unexpectedly obtained a specimen which did not come from the potter's field. In Bolton the prevailing spirit of Puritanism had outlawed the sport of boxing–with the usual result. Surreptitious and ill-conducted bouts among the mill-workers were common, and occasionally professional talent of low grade was imported. This late winter night there had been such a match; evidently with disastrous results, since two timorous Poles had come to us with incoherently whispered entreaties to attend to a very secret and desperate case. We followed them to an abandoned barn, where the remnants of a crowd of frightened foreigners were watching a silent black form on the floor.

The match had been between Kid O'Brien—a lubberly and now quaking youth with a most un-Hibernian hooked nose—and Buck Robinson, "The Harlem Smoke." The negro had been knocked out, and a moment's examination shewed us that he would permanently remain so. He was a loathsome, gorilla-like thing, with abnormally long arms which I could not help calling fore legs, and a face that conjured up thoughts of unspeakable Congo secrets and tom-tom poundings under an eerie moon. The body must have looked even worse in life—but the world holds many ugly things. Fear was upon the whole pitiful crowd, for they did not know what the law would exact of them if the affair were not hushed up; and they were grateful when West, in spite of my involuntary shudders, offered to get rid of the thing quietly—for a purpose I knew too well.

There was bright moonlight over the snowless landscape, but we dressed the thing and carried it home between us through the deserted streets and meadows, as we had carried a similar thing one horrible night in Arkham. We approached the house from the field in the rear, took the specimen in the back door and down the cellar stairs, and prepared it for the usual experiment. Our fear of the police was absurdly great, though we had timed our trip to avoid the solitary patrolman of that section.

The result was wearily anticlimactic. Ghastly as our prize appeared, it was wholly unresponsive to every solution we injected in its black arm; solutions prepared from experience with white specimens only. So as the hour grew dangerously near to dawn, we did as we had done with the others—dragged the thing across the meadows to the neck of the woods near the potter's field, and buried it there in the best sort of grave the frozen ground would furnish. The grave was not very deep, but fully as good as that of the previous specimen—the thing which had risen of itself and uttered a sound. In the light of our dark lanterns we carefully covered it with leaves and dead vines, fairly certain that the police would never find it in a forest so dim and dense.

The next day I was increasingly apprehensive about the police, for a patient brought rumours of a suspected fight and death. West had still another source of worry, for he had been called in the afternoon to a case which ended very threateningly. An Italian woman had become hysterical over her missing child—a lad of five who had strayed off early in the morning and failed to appear for dinner—and had developed symptoms highly alarming in view of an always weak heart. It was a very foolish hysteria, for the boy had often run away before; but Italian peasants are exceedingly superstitious, and this woman seemed as much harassed by omens as by facts. About seven o'clock in the evening she had died, and her frantic husband had made a frightful scene in his efforts to kill West, whom he wildly blamed for not saving her life. Friends had held him when he drew a stiletto, but West departed amidst his inhuman shrieks, curses, and oaths of vengeance. In his latest affliction the fellow seemed to have forgotten his child, who was still missing as the night advanced. There was some talk of searching the woods, but most of the family's friends were busy with the dead woman and the screaming man. Altogether, the nervous strain upon West must have been tremendous. Thoughts of the police and of the mad Italian both weighed heavily.

We retired about eleven, but I did not sleep well. Bolton had a surprisingly good police force for so small a town, and I could not help fearing the mess which would ensue if the affair of the night before were ever tracked down. It might mean the end of all our local work—and perhaps prison for both West and me. I did not like those rumours of a fight which were floating about. After the clock had struck three the moon shone in my eyes, but I turned over without rising to pull down the shade. Then came the steady rattling at the back door.

I lay still and somewhat dazed, but before long heard West's rap on my door. He was clad in dressing-gown and slippers, and had in his hands a revolver and an electric flashlight. From the revolver I knew that he was thinking more of the crazed Italian than of the police.

"We'd better both go," he whispered. "It wouldn't do not to answer it anyway, and it may be a patient—it would be like one of those fools to try the back door."

So we both went down the stairs on tiptoe, with a fear partly justified and partly that which comes only from the soul of the weird small hours. The rattling continued, growing somewhat louder. When we reached the door I cautiously unbolted it and threw it open, and as the moon streamed revealingly down on the form silhouetted there, West did a peculiar thing. Despite the obvious danger of attracting notice and bringing down on our heads the dreaded police investigation—a thing which after all was mercifully averted by the relative isolation of our cottage—my friend suddenly, excitedly, and unnecessarily emptied all six chambers of his revolver into the nocturnal visitor.

For that visitor was neither Italian nor policeman. Looming hideously against the spectral moon was a gigantic misshapen thing not to be imagined save in nightmares—a glassy-eyed, ink-black apparition nearly on all fours, covered with bits of mould, leaves, and vines, foul with caked blood, and having between its glistening teeth a snow-white, terrible, cylindrical object terminating in a tiny hand.

IV. The Scream of the Dead

The scream of a dead man gave to me that acute and added horror of Dr. Herbert West which harassed the latter years of our companionship. It is natural that such a thing as a dead man's scream should give horror, for it is obviously not a pleasing or ordinary occurrence; but I was used to similar experiences, hence suffered on this occasion only because of a particular circumstance. And, as I have implied, it was not of the dead man himself that I became afraid.

Herbert West, whose associate and assistant I was, possessed scientific interests far beyond the usual routine of a village physician. That was why, when establishing his practice in Bolton, he had chosen an isolated house near the potter's field. Briefly and brutally stated, West's sole absorbing interest was a secret study of the phenomena of life and its cessation, leading toward the reanimation of the dead through injections of an excitant solution. For this ghastly experimenting it was necessary to have a constant supply of very fresh human bodies; very fresh because even the least decay hopelessly damaged the brain structure, and human because we found that the solution had to be compounded differently for different types of organisms. Scores of rabbits and guinea-pigs had been killed and treated, but their trail was a blind one. West had never fully succeeded because he had never been able to secure a corpse sufficiently fresh. What he wanted were bodies from which vitality had only just departed; bodies with every cell intact and capable of receiving again the impulse toward that mode of motion called life. There was hope that this second and artificial life might be made perpetual by repetitions of the injection, but we had learned that an ordinary natural life would not respond to the action. To establish the artificial motion, natural life must be extinct—the specimens must be very fresh, but genuinely dead.

The awesome quest had begun when West and I were students at the Miskatonic University Medical School in Arkham, vividly conscious for the first time of the thoroughly mechanical nature of life. That was seven years before, but West looked scarcely a day older now—he was small, blond, clean-shaven, soft-voiced, and spectacled, with only an occasional flash of a cold blue eye to tell of the hardening and growing fanaticism of his character under the pressure of his terrible investigations. Our experiences had often been hideous in the extreme; the results of defective reanimation, when lumps of graveyard clay had been galvanised into morbid, unnatural, and brainless motion by various modifications of the vital solution.

One thing had uttered a nerve-shattering scream; another had risen violently, beaten us both to unconsciousness, and run amuck in a shocking way before it could be placed behind asylum bars; still another, a loathsome African monstrosity, had clawed out of its shallow grave and done a deed—West had had to shoot that object. We could not get bodies fresh enough to shew any trace of reason when reanimated, so had perforce created nameless horrors. It was disturbing to think that one, perhaps two, of our monsters still lived—that thought haunted us shadowingly, till finally West disappeared under frightful circumstances. But at the time of the scream in the cellar laboratory of the isolated Bolton cottage, our fears were subordinate to our anxiety for extremely fresh specimens. West was more avid than I, so that it almost seemed to me that he looked half-covetously at any very healthy living physique.

It was in July, 1910, that the bad luck regarding specimens began to turn. I had been on a long visit to my parents in Illinois, and upon my return found West in a state of singular elation. He had, he told me excitedly, in all likelihood solved the problem of freshness through an approach from an entirely new angle—that of artificial preservation. I had known that he was working on a new and highly unusual embalming compound, and was not surprised that it had turned out well; but until he explained the details I was rather puzzled as to how such a compound could help in our work, since the objectionable staleness of the specimens was largely due to delay occurring before we secured them. This, I now saw, West had clearly recognised; creating his embalming compound for future rather than immediate use, and trusting to fate to supply again some very recent and unburied corpse, as it had years before when we obtained the negro killed in the Bolton prize-fight. At last fate had been kind, so that on this occasion there lay in the secret cellar laboratory a corpse whose decay could not by any possibility have begun. What would happen on re-animation, and whether we could hope for a revival of mind and reason, West did not venture to predict. The experiment would be a landmark in our studies, and he had saved the new body for my return, so that both might share the spectacle in accustomed fashion.

West told me how he had obtained the specimen. It had been a vigorous man; a well-dressed stranger just off the train on his way to transact some business with the Bolton Worsted Mills. The walk through the town had been long, and by the time the traveller paused at our cottage to ask the way to the factories his heart had become greatly overtaxed. He had refused a stimulant, and had suddenly dropped dead only a moment later. The body, as might be expected, seemed to West a heaven-sent gift. In his brief conversation the stranger had made it clear that he was unknown in Bolton, and a search of his pockets subsequently revealed him to be one Robert Leavitt of St. Louis, apparently without a family to make instant inquiries about his disappearance. If this man could not be restored to life, no one would know of our experiment. We buried our materials in a dense strip of woods between the house and the potter's field. If, on the other hand, he could be restored, our fame would be brilliantly and perpetually established. So without delay West had injected into the body's wrist the compound which would hold it fresh for use after my arrival. The matter of the presumably weak heart, which to my mind imperiled the success of our experiment, did not appear to trouble West extensively. He hoped at last to obtain what he had never obtained before—a rekindled spark of reason and perhaps a normal, living creature.

So on the night of July 18, 1910, Herbert West and I stood in the cellar laboratory and gazed at a white, silent figure beneath the dazzling arc-light. The embalming compound had worked uncannily well, for as I stared fascinatedly at the sturdy frame which had lain two weeks without stiffening I was moved to seek West's assurance that the thing was really dead. This assurance he gave readily enough; reminding me that the reanimating solution was never used without careful tests as to life; since it could have no effect if any of the original vitality were present. As West proceeded to take preliminary steps, I was impressed by the vast intricacy of the new experiment; an intricacy so vast that he could trust no hand less delicate than his own. Forbidding me to touch the body, he first injected a drug in the wrist just beside the place his needle had punctured when injecting the embalming compound. This, he said, was to neutralise the compound and release the system to a normal relaxation so that the reanimating solution might freely work when injected. Slightly later, when a change and a gentle tremor seemed to affect the dead limbs, West stuffed a pillow-like object violently over the twitching face, not withdrawing it until the corpse appeared quiet and ready for our attempt at reanimation. The pale enthusiast now applied some last perfunctory tests for absolute lifelessness, withdrew satisfied, and finally injected into the left arm an accurately measured amount of the vital elixir, prepared during the afternoon with a greater care than we had used since college days, when our feats were new and groping. I cannot express the wild, breathless suspense with which we waited for results on this first really fresh specimen—the first we could reasonably expect to open its lips in rational speech, perhaps to tell of what it had seen beyond the unfathomable abyss.

West was a materialist, believing in no soul and attributing all the working of consciousness to bodily phenomena; consequently he looked for no revelation of hideous secrets from gulfs and caverns beyond death's barrier. I did not wholly disagree with him theoretically, yet held vague instinctive remnants of the primitive faith of my forefathers; so that I could not help eyeing the corpse with a certain amount of awe and terrible expectation. Besides—I could not extract from my memory that hideous, inhuman shriek we heard on the night we tried our first experiment in the deserted farmhouse at Arkham.

Very little time had elapsed before I saw the attempt was not to be a total failure. A touch of colour came to cheeks hitherto chalk-white, and spread out under the curiously ample stubble of sandy beard. West, who had his hand on the pulse of the left wrist, suddenly nodded significantly; and almost simultaneously a mist appeared on the mirror inclined above the body's mouth. There followed a few spasmodic muscular motions, and then an audible breathing and visible motion of the chest. I looked at the closed eyelids, and thought I detected a quivering. Then the lids opened, shewing eyes which were grey, calm, and alive, but still unintelligent and not even curious.

In a moment of fantastic whim I whispered questions to the reddening ears; questions of other worlds of which the memory might still be present. Subsequent terror drove them from my mind, but I think the last one, which I repeated, was: "Where have you been?" I do not yet know whether I was answered or not, for no sound came from the well-shaped mouth; but I do know that at that moment I firmly thought the thin lips moved silently, forming syllables I would have vocalised as "only now" if that phrase had possessed any sense or relevancy. At that moment, as I say, I was elated with the conviction that the one great goal had been attained; and that for the first time a reanimated corpse had uttered distinct words impelled by actual reason. In the next moment there was no doubt about the triumph; no doubt that the solution had truly accomplished, at least temporarily, its full mission of restoring rational and articulate life to the dead. But in that triumph there came to me the greatest of all horrors—not horror of the thing that spoke, but of the deed that I had witnessed and of the man with whom my professional fortunes were joined.

For that very fresh body, at last writhing into full and terrifying consciousness with eyes dilated at the memory of its last scene on earth, threw out its frantic hands in a life and death struggle with the air; and suddenly collapsing into a second and final dissolution from which there could be no return, screamed out the cry that will ring eternally in my aching brain:

"Help! Keep off, you cursed little tow-head fiend–keep that damned needle away from me!"

V. The Horror from the Shadows

Many men have related hideous things, not mentioned in print, which happened on the battlefields of the Great War. Some of these things have made me faint, others have convulsed me with devastating nausea, while still others have made me tremble and look behind me in the dark; yet despite the worst of them I believe I can myself relate the most hideous thing of all–the shocking, the unnatural, the unbelievable horror from the shadows.

In 1915 I was a physician with the rank of First Lieutenant in a Canadian regiment in Flanders, one of many Americans to precede the government itself into the gigantic struggle. I had not entered the army on my own initiative, but rather as a natural result of the enlistment of the man whose indispensable assistant I was–the celebrated Boston surgical specialist, Dr. Herbert West. Dr. West had been avid for a chance to serve as surgeon in a great war, and when the chance had come he carried me with him almost against my will. There were reasons why I would have been glad to let the war separate us; reasons why I found the practice of medicine and the companionship of West more and more irritating; but when he had gone to

Ottawa and through a colleague's influence secured a medical commission as Major, I could not resist the imperious persuasion of one determined that I should accompany him in my usual capacity.

When I say that Dr. West was avid to serve in battle, I do not mean to imply that he was either naturally warlike or anxious for the safety of civilisation. Always an ice-cold intellectual machine; slight, blond, blue-eyed, and spectacled; I think he secretly sneered at my occasional martial enthusiasms and censures of supine neutrality. There was, however, something he wanted in embattled Flanders; and in order to secure it he had to assume a military exterior. What he wanted was not a thing which many persons want, but something connected with the peculiar branch of medical science which he had chosen quite clandestinely to follow, and in which he had achieved amazing and occasionally hideous results. It was, in fact, nothing more or less than an abundant supply of freshly killed men in every stage of dismemberment.

Herbert West needed fresh bodies because his life-work was the reanimation of the dead. This work was not known to the fashionable clientele who had so swiftly built up his fame after his arrival in Boston; but was only too well known to me, who had been his closest friend and sole assistant since the old days in Miskatonic University Medical School at Arkham. It was in those college days that he had begun his terrible experiments, first on small animals and then on human bodies shockingly obtained. There was a solution which he injected into the veins of dead things, and if they were fresh enough they responded in strange ways. He had had much trouble in discovering the proper formula, for each type of organism was found to need a stimulus especially adapted to it. Terror stalked him when he reflected on his partial failures; nameless things resulting from imperfect solutions or from bodies insufficiently fresh. A certain number of these failures had remained alive—one was in an asylum while others had vanished—and as he thought of conceivable yet virtually impossible eventualities he often shivered beneath his usual stolidity.

West had soon learned that absolute freshness was the prime requisite for useful specimens, and had accordingly resorted to frightful and unnatural expedients in body-snatching. In college, and during our early practice together in the factory town of Bolton, my attitude toward him had been largely one of fascinated admiration; but as his boldness in methods grew, I began to develop a gnawing fear. I did not like the way he looked at healthy living bodies; and then there came a nightmarish session in the cellar laboratory when I learned that a certain specimen had been a living body when he secured it. That was the first time he had ever been able to revive the quality of rational thought in a corpse; and his success, obtained at such a loathsome cost, had completely hardened him.

Of his methods in the intervening five years I dare not speak. I was held to him by sheer force of fear, and witnessed sights that no human tongue could repeat. Gradually I came to find Herbert West himself more horrible than anything he did—that was when it dawned on me that his once normal scientific zeal for prolonging life had subtly degenerated into a mere morbid and ghoulish curiosity and secret sense of charnel picturesqueness. His interest became a hellish and perverse addiction to the repellently and fiendishly abnormal; he gloated calmly over artificial monstrosities which would make most healthy men drop dead from fright and disgust; he became, behind his pallid intellectuality, a fastidious Baudelaire of physical experiment—a languid Elagabalus of the tombs.

Dangers he met unflinchingly; crimes he committed unmoved. I think the climax came when he had proved his point that rational life can be restored, and had sought new worlds to conquer by experimenting on the reanimation of detached parts of bodies. He had wild and original ideas on the independent vital properties of organic cells and nerve-tissue separated from natural physiological systems; and achieved some hideous preliminary results in the form of never-dying, artificially nourished tissue obtained from the nearly hatched eggs of an indescribable tropical reptile. Two biological points he was exceedingly anxious to settle—first, whether any amount of consciousness and rational action be possible without the brain, proceeding from the spinal cord and various nerve-centres; and second, whether any kind of ethereal, intangible relation distinct from the material cells may exist to link the surgically separated parts of what has previously been a single living organism. All this research work required a prodigious supply of freshly slaughtered human flesh—and that was why Herbert West had entered the Great War.

The phantasmal, unmentionable thing occurred one midnight late in March, 1915, in a field hospital behind the lines at St. Eloi. I wonder even now if it could have been other than a daemoniac dream of delirium. West had a private laboratory in an east room of the barn-like temporary edifice, assigned him on his plea that he was devising new and radical methods for the treatment of hitherto hopeless cases of maiming. There he worked like a butcher in the midst of his gory wares—I could never get used to the levity with which he handled and classified certain things. At times he actually did perform marvels of surgery for the soldiers; but his chief delights were of a less public and philanthropic kind, requiring many explanations of sounds which seemed peculiar even amidst that babel of the damned. Among these sounds were frequent revolver-shots—surely not uncommon on a battlefield, but distinctly uncommon in an hospital. Dr. West's reanimated specimens were not meant for long existence or a large audience. Besides human tissue, West employed much of the reptile embryo tissue which he had cultivated with such singular results. It was better than human material for maintaining life in organless fragments, and that was now my friend's chief activity. In a dark corner of the laboratory, over a queer incubating burner, he kept a large covered vat full of this reptilian cell-matter; which multiplied and grew puffily and hideously.

On the night of which I speak we had a splendid new specimen—a man at once physically powerful and of such high mentality that a sensitive nervous system was assured. It was rather ironic, for he was the officer who had helped West to his commission, and who was now to have been our associate. Moreover, he had in the past secretly studied the theory of re-animation to some extent under West. Major Sir Eric Moreland Clapham-Lee, D.S.O., was the greatest surgeon in our division, and had been hastily assigned to the St. Eloi sector when news of the heavy fighting reached headquarters. He had come in an aëroplane piloted by the intrepid Lieut. Ronald Hill, only to be shot down when directly over his destination. The fall had been spectacular and awful; Hill was unrecognisable afterward, but the wreck yielded up the great surgeon in a nearly decapitated but otherwise intact condition. West had greedily seized the lifeless thing which had once been his friend and fellow-scholar; and I shuddered when he finished severing the head, placed it in his hellish vat of pulpy reptile-tissue to preserve it for future experiments, and proceeded to treat the decapitated body on the operating table. He injected new blood, joined certain veins, arteries, and nerves at the headless neck, and closed the ghastly aperture with engrafted skin from an unidentified specimen which had borne an officer's uniform. I knew what he wanted—to see if this highly organised body could exhibit, without its head, any of the signs of mental life which had distinguished Sir Eric Moreland Clapham-Lee. Once a student of reanimation, this silent trunk was now gruesomely called upon to exemplify it.

I can still see Herbert West under the sinister electric light as he injected his reanimating solution into the arm of the headless body. The scene I cannot describe—I should faint if I tried it, for there is madness in a room full of classified charnel things, with blood and lesser human debris almost ankle-deep on the slimy floor, and with hideous reptilian abnormalities sprouting, bubbling, and baking over a winking bluish-green spectre of dim flame in a far corner of black shadows.

The specimen, as West repeatedly observed, had a splendid nervous system. Much was expected of it; and as a few twitching motions began to appear, I could see the feverish interest on West's face. He was ready, I think, to see proof of his increasingly strong opinion that consciousness, reason, and personality can exist independently of the brain—that man has no central connective spirit, but is merely a machine of nervous matter, each section more or less complete in itself. In one triumphant demonstration West was about to relegate the mystery of life to the category of myth. The body now twitched more vigorously, and beneath our avid eyes commenced to heave in a frightful way. The arms stirred disquietingly, the legs drew up, and various muscles contracted in a repulsive kind of writhing. Then the headless thing threw out its arms in a gesture which was unmistakably one of desperation—an intelligent desperation apparently sufficient to prove every theory of Herbert West. Certainly, the nerves were recalling the man's last act in life; the struggle to get free of the falling aëroplane.

What followed, I shall never positively know. It may have been wholly an hallucination from the shock caused at that instant by the sudden and complete destruction of the building in a cataclysm of German shell-fire—who can gainsay it, since West and I were the only proved survivors? West liked to think that before his recent disappearance, but there were times when he could not; for it was queer that we both had the same hallucination. The hideous occurrence itself was very simple, notable only for what it implied.

The body on the table had risen with a blind and terrible groping, and we had heard a sound. I should not call that sound a voice, for it was too awful. And yet its timbre was not the most awful thing about it. Neither was its message—it had merely screamed, "Jump, Ronald, for God's sake, jump!" The awful thing was its source.

For it had come from the large covered vat in that ghoulish corner of crawling black shadows.

VI. The Tomb-Legions

When Dr. Herbert West disappeared a year ago, the Boston police questioned me closely. They suspected that I was holding something back, and perhaps suspected graver things; but I could not tell them the truth because they would not have believed it. They knew, indeed, that West had been connected with activities beyond the credence of ordinary men; for his hideous experiments in the reanimation of dead bodies had long been too extensive to admit of perfect secrecy; but the final soul-shattering catastrophe held elements of daemoniac phantasy which make even me doubt the reality of what I saw.

I was West's closest friend and only confidential assistant. We had met years before, in medical school, and from the first I had shared his terrible researches. He had slowly tried to perfect a solution which, injected into the veins of the newly deceased, would restore life; a labour demanding an abundance of fresh corpses and therefore involving the most unnatural actions. Still more shocking were the products of some of the experiments—grisly masses of flesh that had been dead, but that West waked to a blind, brainless, nauseous animation. These were the usual results, for in order to reawaken the mind it was necessary to have specimens so absolutely fresh that no decay could possibly affect the delicate brain-cells.

This need for very fresh corpses had been West's moral undoing. They were hard to get, and one awful day he had secured his specimen while it was still alive and vigorous. A struggle, a needle, and a powerful alkaloid had transformed it to a very fresh corpse, and the experiment had succeeded for a brief and memorable moment; but West had emerged with a soul calloused and seared, and a hardened eye which sometimes glanced with a kind of hideous and calculating appraisal at men of especially sensitive brain and especially vigorous physique. Toward the last I became acutely afraid of West, for he began to look at me that way. People did not seem to notice his glances, but they noticed my fear; and after his disappearance used that as a basis for some absurd suspicions.

West, in reality, was more afraid than I; for his abominable pursuits entailed a life of furtiveness and dread of every shadow. Partly it was the police he feared; but sometimes his nervousness was deeper and more nebulous, touching on certain indescribable things into which he had injected a morbid life, and from which he had not seen that life depart. He usually finished his experiments with a revolver, but a few times he had not been quick enough. There was that first specimen on whose rifled grave marks of clawing were later seen. There was also that Arkham professor's body which had done cannibal things before it had been captured and thrust unidentified into a madhouse cell at Sefton, where it beat the walls for sixteen years. Most of the other possibly surviving results were things less easy to speak of—for in later years West's scientific zeal had degenerated to an unhealthy and fantastic mania, and he had spent his chief skill in vitalising not entire human bodies but isolated parts of bodies, or parts joined to organic matter other than human. It had become fiendishly disgusting by the time he disappeared; many of the experiments could not even be hinted at in print. The Great War, through which both of us served as surgeons, had intensified this side of West.

In saying that West's fear of his specimens was nebulous, I have in mind particularly its complex nature. Part of it came merely from knowing of the existence of such nameless monsters, while another part arose from apprehension of the bodily harm they might under certain circumstances do him. Their disappearance added horror to the situation—of them all West knew the whereabouts of only one, the pitiful asylum thing. Then there was a more subtle fear—a very fantastic sensation resulting from a curious experiment in the Canadian army in 1915. West, in the midst of a severe battle, had reanimated Major Sir Eric Moreland Clapham-Lee, D.S.O., a fellow-physician who knew about his experiments and could have duplicated them. The head had been removed, so that the possibilities of quasi-intelligent life in the trunk might be investigated. Just as the building was wiped out by a German shell, there had been a success. The trunk had moved intelligently; and, unbelievable to relate, we were both sickeningly sure that articulate sounds had come from the detached head as it lay in a shadowy corner of the laboratory. The shell had been merciful, in a way–but West could never feel as certain as he wished, that we two were the only survivors. He used to make shuddering conjectures about the possible actions of a headless physician with the power of reanimating the dead.

West's last quarters were in a venerable house of much elegance, overlooking one of the oldest burying-grounds in Boston. He had chosen the place for purely symbolic and fantastically aesthetic reasons, since most of the interments were of the colonial period and therefore of little use to a scientist seeking very fresh bodies. The laboratory was in a sub-cellar secretly constructed by imported workmen, and contained a huge incinerator for the quiet and complete disposal of such bodies, or fragments and synthetic mockeries of bodies, as might remain from the morbid experiments and unhallowed amusements of the owner. During the excavation of this cellar the workmen had struck some exceedingly ancient masonry; undoubtedly connected with the old burying-ground, yet far too deep to correspond with any known sepulchre therein. After a number of calculations West decided that it represented some secret chamber beneath the tomb of the Averills, where the last interment had been made in 1768. I was with him when he studied the nitrous, dripping walls laid bare by the spades and mattocks of the men, and was prepared for the gruesome thrill which would attend the uncovering of centuried grave-secrets; but for the first time West's new timidity conquered his natural curiosity, and he betrayed his degenerating fibre by ordering the masonry left intact and plastered over. Thus it remained till that final hellish night; part of the walls of the secret laboratory. I speak of West's decadence, but must add that it was a purely mental and intangible thing. Outwardly he was the same to the last—calm, cold, slight, and yellow-haired, with spectacled blue eyes and a general aspect of youth which years and fears seemed never to change. He seemed calm even when he thought of that clawed grave and looked over his shoulder; even when he thought of the carnivorous thing that gnawed and pawed at Sefton bars.

The end of Herbert West began one evening in our joint study when he was dividing his curious glance between the newspaper and me. A strange headline item had struck at him from the crumpled pages, and a nameless titan claw had seemed to reach down through sixteen years. Something fearsome and incredible had happened at Sefton Asylum fifty miles away, stunning the neighbourhood and baffling the police. In the small hours of the morning a body of silent men had entered the grounds and their leader had aroused the attendants. He was a menacing military figure who talked without moving his lips and whose voice seemed almost ventriloquially connected with an immense black case he carried. His expressionless face was handsome to the point of radiant beauty, but had shocked the superintendent when the hall light fell on it—for it was a wax face with eyes of painted glass. Some nameless accident had befallen this man. A larger man guided his steps; a repellent hulk whose bluish face seemed half eaten away by some unknown malady. The speaker had asked for the custody of the cannibal monster committed from Arkham sixteen years before; and upon being refused, gave a signal which precipitated a shocking riot. The fiends had beaten, trampled, and bitten every attendant who did not flee; killing four and finally succeeding in the liberation of the monster. Those victims who could recall the event without hysteria swore that the creatures had acted less like men than like unthinkable automata guided by the wax-faced leader. By the time help could be summoned, every trace of the men and of their mad charge had vanished.

From the hour of reading this item until midnight, West sat almost paralysed. At midnight the doorbell rang, startling him fearfully. All the servants were asleep in the attic, so I answered the bell. As I have told the police, there was no wagon in the street; but only a group of strange-looking figures bearing a large square box which they deposited in the hallway after one of them had grunted in a highly unnatural voice, "Express—prepaid." They filed out of the house with a jerky tread, and as I watched them go I had an odd idea that they were turning toward the ancient cemetery on which the back of the house abutted. When I slammed the door after them West came downstairs and looked at the box. It was about two feet square, and bore West's correct name and present address. It also bore the inscription, "From Eric Moreland Clapham-Lee, St. Eloi, Flanders." Six years before, in Flanders, a shelled hospital had fallen upon the headless reanimated trunk of Dr. Clapham-Lee, and upon the detached head which—perhaps—had uttered articulate sounds.

West was not even excited now. His condition was more ghastly. Quickly he said, "It's the finish–but let's incinerate–this." We carried the thing down to the laboratory–listening. I do not remember many particulars–you can imagine my state of mind–but it is a vicious lie to say it was Herbert West's body which I put into the incinerator. We both inserted the whole unopened wooden box, closed the door, and started the electricity. Nor did any sound come from the box, after all.

It was West who first noticed the falling plaster on that part of the wall where the ancient tomb masonry had been covered up. I was going to run, but he stopped me. Then I saw a small black aperture, felt a ghoulish wind of ice, and smelled the charnel bowels of a putrescent earth. There was no sound, but just then the electric lights went out and I saw outlined against some phosphorescence of the nether world a horde of silent toiling things which only insanity–or worse–could create. Their outlines were human, semi-human, fractionally human, and not human at all–the horde was grotesquely heterogeneous. They were removing the stones quietly, one by one, from the centuried wall. And then, as the breach became large enough, they came out into the laboratory in single file; led by a stalking thing with a beautiful head made of wax. A sort of mad-eyed monstrosity behind the leader seized on Herbert West. West did not resist or utter a sound. Then they all sprang at him and tore him to pieces before my eyes, bearing the fragments away into that subterranean vault of fabulous abominations. West's head was carried off by the wax-headed leader, who wore a Canadian officer's uniform. As it disappeared I saw that the blue eyes behind the spectacles were hideously blazing with their first touch of frantic, visible emotion.

Servants found me unconscious in the morning. West was gone. The incinerator contained only unidentifiable ashes. Detectives have questioned me, but what can I say? The Sefton tragedy they will not connect with West; not that, nor the men with the box, whose existence they deny. I told them of the vault, and they pointed to the unbroken plaster wall and laughed. So I told them no more. They imply that I am a madman or a murderer—probably I am mad. But I might not be mad if those accursed tomb-legions had not been so silent.

GILMAN
HOTEL

The Shadow over Innsmouth

“The Shadow over Innsmouth” is Lovecraft’s second most well-known work, and widely regarded as his best detective-themed story. Written in late 1931, the narrative revolves around two of Lovecraft’s most pressing concerns: his fear of inherited mental illness and his great dislike of miscegenation. As with “The Call of Cthulhu,” Lovecraft was dismissive of the quality of “The Shadow over Innsmouth,” as was the editor of Weird Tales *who refused its publication in 1933. It was eventually published as a standalone novella in 1936, but the first edition was riddled with errors and the publisher soon went bankrupt, selling less than 200 copies of the title before folding. Despite its initial commercial failure, “The Shadow over Innsmouth” generated an enormous following after Lovecraft’s death a year later, owing both to Lovecraft’s brilliance and a renewed critical interest in his life's work. “The Shadow over Innsmouth” has inspired several loose adaptations, perhaps most faithfully in the 2005 survival horror video game* The Call of Cthulhu: Dark Corners of the Earth.

During the winter of 1927–28 officials of the Federal government made a strange and secret investigation of certain conditions in the ancient Massachusetts seaport of Innsmouth. The public first learned of it in February, when a vast series of raids and arrests occurred, followed by the deliberate burning and dynamiting—under suitable precautions—of an enormous number of crumbling, worm-eaten, and supposedly empty houses along the abandoned waterfront. Uninquiring souls let this occurrence pass as one of the major clashes in a spasmodic war on liquor.

Keener news-followers, however, wondered at the prodigious number of arrests, the abnormally large force of men used in making them, and the secrecy surrounding the disposal of the prisoners. No trials, or even definite charges, were reported; nor were any of the captives seen thereafter in the regular gaols of the nation. There were vague statements about disease and concentration camps, and later about dispersal in various naval and military prisons, but nothing positive ever developed. Innsmouth itself was left almost depopulated, and is even now only beginning to shew signs of a sluggishly revived existence.

Complaints from many liberal organisations were met with long confidential discussions, and representatives were taken on trips to certain camps and prisons. As a result, these societies became surprisingly passive and reticent. Newspaper men were harder to manage, but seemed largely to cooperate with the government in the end. Only one paper—a tabloid always discounted because of its wild policy—mentioned the deep-diving submarine that discharged torpedoes downward in the marine abyss just beyond Devil Reef. That item, gathered by chance in a haunt of sailors, seemed indeed rather far-fetched; since the low, black reef lies a full mile and a half out from Innsmouth Harbour.

People around the country and in the nearby towns muttered a great deal among themselves, but said very little to the outer world. They had talked about dying and half-deserted Innsmouth for nearly a century, and nothing new could be wilder or more hideous than what they had whispered and hinted years before. Many things had taught them secretiveness, and there was now no need to exert pressure on them. Besides, they really knew very little; for wide salt marshes, desolate and unpeopled, keep neighbours off from Innsmouth on the landward side.

But at last I am going to defy the ban on speech about this thing. Results, I am certain, are so thorough that no public harm save a shock of repulsion could ever accrue from a hinting of what was found by those horrified raiders at Innsmouth. Besides, what was found might possibly have more than one explanation. I do not know just how much of the whole tale has been told even to me, and I have many reasons for not wishing to probe deeper. For my contact with this affair has been closer than that of any other layman, and I have carried away impressions which are yet to drive me to drastic measures.

It was I who fled frantically out of Innsmouth in the early morning hours of July 16, 1927, and whose frightened appeals for government inquiry and action brought on the whole reported episode. I was willing enough to stay mute while the affair was fresh and uncertain; but now that it is an old story, with public interest and curiosity gone, I have an odd craving to whisper about those few frightful hours in that ill-rumoured and evilly shadowed seaport of death and blasphemous abnormality. The mere telling helps me to restore confidence in my own faculties; to reassure myself that I was not simply the first to succumb to a contagious nightmare hallucination. It helps me, too, in making up my mind regarding a certain terrible step which lies ahead of me.

I never heard of Innsmouth till the day before I saw it for the first and—so far—last time. I was celebrating my coming of age by a tour of New England—sightseeing, antiquarian, and genealogical—and had planned to go directly from ancient Newburyport to Arkham, whence my mother's family was derived. I had no car, but was travelling by train, trolley, and motor-coach, always seeking the cheapest possible route. In Newburyport they told me that the steam train was the thing to take to Arkham; and it was only at the station ticket-office, when I demurred at the high fare, that I learned about Innsmouth. The stout, shrewd-faced agent, whose speech shewed him to be no local man, seemed sympathetic toward my efforts at economy, and made a suggestion that none of my other informants had offered.

"You *could* take that old bus, I suppose," he said with a certain hesitation, "but it ain't thought much of hereabouts. It goes through Innsmouth—you may have heard about that—and so the people don't like it. Run by an Innsmouth fellow—Joe Sargent—but never gets any custom from here, or Arkham either, I guess. Wonder it keeps running at all. I s'pose it's cheap enough, but I never see more'n two or three people in it—nobody but those Innsmouth folks. Leaves the Square—front of Hammond's Drug Store—at 10 a.m. and 7 p.m. unless they've changed lately. Looks like a terrible rattletrap—I've never ben on it."

That was the first I ever heard of shadowed Innsmouth. Any reference to a town not shewn on common maps or listed in recent guide-books would have interested me, and the agent's odd manner of allusion roused something like real curiosity. A town able to inspire such dislike in its neighbours, I thought, must be at least rather unusual, and worthy of a tourist's attention. If it came before Arkham I would stop off there—and so I asked the agent to tell me something about it. He was very deliberate, and spoke with an air of feeling slightly superior to what he said.

"Innsmouth? Well, it's a queer kind of a town down at the mouth of the Manuxet. Used to be almost a city—quite a port before the War of 1812—but all gone to pieces in the last hundred years or so. No railroad now—B. & M. never went through, and the branch line from Rowley was given up years ago.

"More empty houses than there are people, I guess, and no business to speak of except fishing and lobstering. Everybody trades mostly here or in Arkham or Ipswich. Once they had quite a few mills, but nothing's left now except one gold refinery running on the leanest kind of part time.

"That refinery, though, used to be a big thing, and Old Man Marsh, who owns it, must be richer'n Croesus. Queer old duck, though, and sticks mighty close in his home. He's supposed to have developed some skin disease or deformity late in life that makes him keep out of sight. Grandson of Captain Obed Marsh, who founded the business. His mother seems to've ben some kind of foreigner—they say a South Sea islander—so everybody raised Cain when he married an Ipswich girl fifty years ago. They always do that about Innsmouth people, and folks here and hereabouts always try to cover up any Innsmouth blood they have in 'em. But Marsh's children and grandchildren look just like anyone else so far's I can see. I've had 'em pointed out to me here—though, come to think of it, the elder children don't seem to be around lately. Never saw the old man.

"And why is everybody so down on Innsmouth? Well, young fellow, you mustn't take too much stock in what people around here say. They're hard to get started, but once they do get started they never let up. They've ben telling things about Innsmouth—whispering 'em, mostly—for the last hundred years, I guess, and I gather they're more scared than anything else. Some of the stories would make you laugh—about old Captain Marsh driving bargains with the devil and bringing imps out of hell to live in Innsmouth, or about some kind of devil-worship and awful sacrifices in some place near the wharves that people stumbled on around 1845 or thereabouts—but I come from Panton, Vermont, and that kind of story don't go down with me.

"You ought to hear, though, what some of the old-timers tell about the black reef off the coast—Devil Reef, they call it. It's well above water a good part of the time, and never much below it, but at that you could hardly call it an island. The story is that there's a whole legion of devils seen sometimes on that reef—sprawled about, or darting in and out of some kind of caves near the top. It's a rugged, uneven thing, a good bit over a mile out, and toward the end of shipping days sailors used to make big detours just to avoid it.

"That is, sailors that didn't hail from Innsmouth. One of the things they had against old Captain Marsh was that he was supposed to land on it sometimes at night when the tide was right. Maybe he did, for I dare say the rock formation was interesting, and it's just barely possible he was looking for pirate loot and maybe finding it; but there was talk of his dealing with daemons there. Fact is, I guess on the whole it was really the Captain that gave the bad reputation to the reef.

"That was before the big epidemic of 1846, when over half the folks in Innsmouth was carried off. They never did quite figure out what the trouble was, but it was probably some foreign kind of disease brought from China or somewhere by the shipping. It surely was bad enough—there was riots over it, and all sorts of ghastly doings that I don't believe ever got outside of town—and it left the place in awful shape. Never came back—there can't be more'n 300 or 400 people living there now.

"But the real thing behind the way folks feel is simply race prejudice—and I don't say I'm blaming those that hold it. I hate those Innsmouth folks myself, and I wouldn't care to go to their town. I s'pose you know—though I can see you're a Westerner by your talk—what a lot our New England ships used to have to do with queer ports in Africa, Asia, the South Seas, and everywhere else, and what queer kinds of people they sometimes brought back with 'em. You've probably heard about the Salem man that came home with a Chinese wife, and maybe you know there's still a bunch of Fiji Islanders somewhere around Cape Cod.

"Well, there must be something like that back of the Innsmouth people. The place always was badly cut off from the rest of the country by marshes and creeks, and we can't be sure about the ins and outs of the matter; but it's pretty clear that old Captain Marsh must have brought home some odd specimens when he had all three of his ships in commission back in the twenties and thirties. There certainly is a strange kind of streak in the Innsmouth folks today—I don't know how to explain it, but it sort of makes you crawl. You'll notice a little in Sargent if you take his bus. Some of 'em have queer narrow heads with flat noses and bulgy, stary eyes that never seem to shut, and their skin ain't quite right. Rough and scabby, and the sides of their necks are all shrivelled or creased up. Get bald, too, very young. The older fellows look the worst—fact is, I don't believe I've ever seen a very old chap of that kind. Guess they must die of looking in the glass! Animals hate 'em —they used to have lots of horse trouble before autos came in.

"Nobody around here or in Arkham or Ipswich will have anything to do with 'em, and they act kind of offish themselves when they come to town or when anyone tries to fish on their grounds. Queer how fish are always thick off Innsmouth Harbour when there ain't any anywhere else around—but just try to fish there yourself and see how the folks chase you off! Those people used to come here on the railroad—walking and taking the train at Rowley after the branch was dropped—but now they use that bus.

"Yes, there's a hotel in Innsmouth—called the Gilman House—but I don't believe it can amount to much. I wouldn't advise you to try it. Better stay over here and take the ten o'clock bus tomorrow morning; then you can get an evening bus there for Arkham at eight o'clock. There was a factory inspector who stopped at the Gilman a couple of years ago, and he had a lot of unpleasant hints about the place. Seems they get a queer crowd there, for this fellow heard voices in other rooms—though most of 'em was empty—that gave him the shivers. It was foreign talk, he thought, but he said the bad thing about it was the kind of voice that sometimes spoke. It sounded so unnatural—slopping-like, he said—that he didn't dare undress and go to sleep. Just waited up and lit out the first thing in the morning. The talk went on most all night.

"This fellow—Casey, his name was—had a lot to say about how the Innsmouth folks watched him and seemed kind of on guard. He found the Marsh refinery a queer place—it's in an old mill on the lower falls of the Manuxet. What he said tallied up with what I'd heard. Books in bad shape, and no clear account of any kind of dealings. You know it's always ben a kind of mystery where the Marshes get the gold they refine. They've never seemed to do much buying in that line, but years ago they shipped out an enormous lot of ingots.

"Used to be talk of a queer foreign kind of jewellery that the sailors and refinery men sometimes sold on the sly, or that was seen once or twice on some of the Marsh womenfolks. People allowed maybe old Captain Obed traded for it in some heathen port, especially since he was always ordering stacks of glass beads and trinkets such as seafaring men used to get for native trade. Others thought and still think he'd found an old pirate cache out on Devil Reef. But here's a funny thing. The old Captain's ben dead these sixty years, and there ain't ben a good-sized ship out of the place since the Civil War; but just the same the Marshes still keep on buying a few of those native trade things—mostly glass and rubber gewgaws, they tell me. Maybe the Innsmouth folks like 'em to look at themselves—

Gawd knows they've gotten to be about as bad as South Sea cannibals and Guinea savages.

"That plague of '46 must have taken off the best blood in the place. Anyway, they're a doubtful lot now, and the Marshes and the other rich folks are as bad as any. As I told you, there probably ain't more'n 400 people in the whole town in spite of all the streets they say there are. I guess they're what they call 'white trash' down South—lawless and sly, and full of secret doings. They get a lot of fish and lobsters and do exporting by truck. Queer how the fish swarm right there and nowhere else.

"Nobody can ever keep track of these people, and state school officials and census men have a devil of a time. You can bet that prying strangers ain't welcome around Innsmouth. I've heard personally of more'n one business or government man that's disappeared there, and there's loose talk of one who went crazy and is out at Danvers now. They must have fixed up some awful scare for that fellow.

"That's why I wouldn't go at night if I was you. I've never ben there and have no wish to go, but I guess a daytime trip couldn't hurt you—even though the people hereabouts will advise you not to make it. If you're just sightseeing, and looking for old-time stuff, Innsmouth ought to be quite a place for you."

And so I spent part of that evening at the Newburyport Public Library looking up data about Innsmouth. When I had tried to question the natives in the shops, the lunch room, the garages, and the fire station, I had found them even harder to get started than the ticket-agent had predicted; and realised that I could not spare the time to overcome their first instinctive reticences. They had a kind of obscure suspiciousness, as if there were something amiss with anyone too much interested in Innsmouth. At the Y.M.C.A., where I was stopping, the clerk merely discouraged my going to such a dismal, decadent place; and the people at the library shewed much the same attitude. Clearly, in the eyes of the educated, Innsmouth was merely an exaggerated case of civic degeneration.

The Essex County histories on the library shelves had very little to say, except that the town was founded in 1643, noted for shipbuilding before the Revolution, a seat of great marine prosperity in the early nineteenth century, and later a minor factory centre using the Manuxet as power. The epidemic and riots of 1846 were very sparsely treated, as if they formed a discredit to the county.

References to decline were few, though the significance of the later record was unmistakable. After the Civil War all industrial life was confined to the Marsh Refining Company, and the marketing of gold ingots formed the only remaining bit of major commerce aside from the eternal fishing. That fishing paid less and less as the price of the commodity fell and large-scale corporations offered competition, but there was never a dearth of fish around Innsmouth Harbour. Foreigners seldom settled there, and there was some discreetly veiled evidence that a number of Poles and Portuguese who had tried it had been scattered in a peculiarly drastic fashion.

Most interesting of all was a glancing reference to the strange jewellery vaguely associated with Innsmouth. It had evidently impressed the whole countryside more than a little, for mention was made of specimens in the museum of Miskatonic University at Arkham, and in the display room of the Newburyport Historical Society. The fragmentary descriptions of these things were bald and prosaic, but they hinted to me an undercurrent of persistent strangeness. Something about them seemed so odd and provocative that I could not put them out of my mind, and despite the relative lateness of the hour I resolved to see the local sample—said to be a large, queerly proportioned thing evidently meant for a tiara—if it could possibly be arranged.

The librarian gave me a note of introduction to the curator of the Society, a Miss Anna Tilton, who lived nearby, and after a brief explanation that ancient gentlewoman was kind enough to pilot me into the closed building, since the hour was not outrageously late. The collection was a notable one indeed, but in my present mood I had eyes for nothing but the bizarre object which glistened in a corner cupboard under the electric lights.

It took no excessive sensitiveness to beauty to make me literally gasp at the strange, unearthly splendour of the alien, opulent phantasy that rested there on a purple velvet cushion. Even now I can hardly describe what I saw, though it was clearly enough a sort of tiara, as the description had said. It was tall in front, and with a very large and curiously irregular periphery, as if designed for a head of almost freakishly elliptical outline. The material seemed to be predominantly gold, though a weird lighter lustrousness hinted at some strange alloy with an equally beautiful and scarcely identifiable metal. Its condition was almost perfect, and one could have spent hours in studying the striking and puzzlingly untraditional designs—some simply geometrical, and some plainly marine—chased or moulded in high relief on its surface with a craftsmanship of incredible skill and grace.

The longer I looked, the more the thing fascinated me; and in this fascination there was a curiously disturbing element hardly to be classified or accounted for. At first I decided that it was the queer other-worldly quality of the art which made me uneasy. All other art objects I had ever seen either belonged to some known racial or national stream, or else were consciously modernistic defiances of every recognised stream. This tiara was neither. It clearly belonged to some settled technique of infinite maturity and perfection, yet that technique was utterly remote from any—Eastern or Western, ancient or modern—which I had ever heard of or seen exemplified. It was as if the workmanship were that of another planet.

However, I soon saw that my uneasiness had a second and perhaps equally potent source residing in the pictorial and mathematical suggestions of the strange designs. The patterns all hinted of remote secrets and unimaginable abysses in time and space, and the monotonously aquatic nature of the reliefs became almost sinister. Among these reliefs were fabulous monsters of abhorrent grotesqueness and malignity—half ichthyic and half batrachian in suggestion—which one could not dissociate from a certain haunting and uncomfortable sense of pseudo-memory, as if they called up some image from deep cells and tissues whose retentive functions are wholly primal and awesomely ancestral. At times I fancied that every contour of these blasphemous fish-frogs was overflowing with the ultimate quintessence of unknown and inhuman evil.

In odd contrast to the tiara's aspect was its brief and prosy history as related by Miss Tilton. It had been pawned for a ridiculous sum at a shop in State Street in 1873, by a drunken Innsmouth man shortly afterward killed in a brawl. The Society had acquired it directly from the pawnbroker, at once giving it a display worthy of its quality. It was labelled as of probable East-Indian or Indo-Chinese provenance, though the attribution was frankly tentative.

Miss Tilton, comparing all possible hypotheses regarding its origin and its presence in New England, was inclined to believe that it formed part of some exotic pirate hoard discovered by old Captain Obed Marsh. This view was surely not weakened by the insistent offers of purchase at a high price which the Marshes began to make as soon as they knew of its presence, and which they repeated to this day despite the Society's unvarying determination not to sell.

As the good lady shewed me out of the building she made it clear that the pirate theory of the Marsh fortune was a popular one among the intelligent people of the region. Her own attitude toward shadowed Innsmouth—which she had never seen—was one of disgust at a community slipping far down the cultural scale, and she assured me that the rumours of devil-worship were partly justified by a peculiar secret cult which had gained force there and engulfed all the orthodox churches.

It was called, she said, "The Esoteric Order of Dagon," and was undoubtedly a debased, quasi-pagan thing imported from the East a century before, at a time when the Innsmouth fisheries seemed to be going barren. Its persistence among a simple people was quite natural in view of the sudden and permanent return of abundantly fine fishing, and it soon came to be the greatest influence on the town, replacing Freemasonry altogether and taking up headquarters in the old Masonic Hall on New Church Green.

All this, to the pious Miss Tilton, formed an excellent reason for shunning the ancient town of decay and desolation; but to me it was merely a fresh incentive. To my architectural and historical anticipations was now added an acute anthropological zeal, and I could scarcely sleep in my small room at the "Y" as the night wore away.

II.

Shortly before ten the next morning I stood with one small valise in front of Hammond's Drug Store in old Market Square waiting for the Innsmouth bus. As the hour for its arrival drew near I noticed a general drift of the loungers to other places up the street, or to the Ideal Lunch across the square. Evidently the ticket-agent had not exaggerated the dislike which local people bore toward Innsmouth and its denizens. In a few moments a small motor-coach of extreme decrepitude and dirty grey colour rattled down State Street, made a turn, and drew up at the curb beside me. I felt immediately that it was the right one; a guess which the half-illegible sign on the windshield—*"Arkham-Innsmouth-Newb'port"*—soon verified.

There were only three passengers—dark, unkempt men of sullen visage and somewhat youthful cast—and when the vehicle stopped they clumsily shambled out and began walking up State Street in a silent, almost furtive fashion. The driver also alighted, and I watched him as he went into the drug store to make some purchase. This, I reflected, must be the Joe Sargent mentioned by the ticket-agent; and even before I noticed any details there spread over me a wave of spontaneous aversion which could be neither checked nor explained. It suddenly struck me as very natural that the local people should not wish to ride on a bus owned and driven by this man, or to visit any oftener than possible the habitat of such a man and his kinsfolk.

When the driver came out of the store I looked at him more carefully and tried to determine the source of my evil impression. He was a thin, stoop-shouldered man not much under six feet tall, dressed in shabby blue civilian clothes and wearing a frayed grey golf cap. His age was perhaps thirty-five, but the odd, deep creases in the sides of his neck made him seem older when one did not study his dull, expressionless face. He had a narrow head, bulging, watery blue eyes that seemed never to wink, a flat nose, a receding forehead and chin, and singularly undeveloped ears. His long, thick lip and coarse-pored, greyish cheeks seemed almost beardless except for some sparse yellow hairs that straggled and curled in irregular patches; and in places the surface seemed queerly irregular, as if peeling from some cutaneous disease. His hands were large and heavily veined, and had a very unusual greyish-blue tinge. The fingers were strikingly short in proportion to the rest of the structure, and seemed to have a tendency to curl closely into the huge palm. As he walked toward the bus I observed his peculiarly shambling gait and saw that his feet were inordinately immense. The more I studied them the more I wondered how he could buy any shoes to fit them.

A certain greasiness about the fellow increased my dislike. He was evidently given to working or lounging around the fish docks, and carried with him much of their characteristic smell. Just what foreign blood was in him I could not even guess. His oddities certainly did not look Asiatic, Polynesian, Levantine, or negroid, yet I could see why the people found him alien. I myself would have thought of biological degeneration rather than alienage.

I was sorry when I saw that there would be no other passengers on the bus. Somehow I did not like the idea of riding alone with this driver. But as leaving time obviously approached I conquered my qualms and followed the man aboard, extending him a dollar bill and murmuring the single word "Innsmouth."

He looked curiously at me for a second as he returned forty cents change without speaking. I took a seat far behind him, but on the same side of the bus, since I wished to watch the shore during the journey.

At length the decrepit vehicle started with a jerk, and rattled noisily past the old brick buildings of State Street amidst a cloud of vapour from the exhaust. Glancing at the people on the sidewalks, I thought I detected in them a curious wish to avoid looking at the bus—or at least a wish to avoid seeming to look at it. Then we turned to the left into High Street, where the going was smoother; flying by stately old mansions of the early republic and still older colonial farmhouses, passing the Lower Green and Parker River, and finally emerging into a long, monotonous stretch of open shore country.

The day was warm and sunny, but the landscape of sand, sedge-grass, and stunted shrubbery became more and more desolate as we proceeded. Out the window I could see the blue water and the sandy line of Plum Island, and we presently drew very near the beach as our narrow road veered off from the main highway to Rowley and Ipswich. There were no visible houses, and I could tell by the state of the road that traffic was very light hereabouts. The small, weather-worn telephone poles carried only two wires. Now and then we crossed crude wooden bridges over tidal creeks that wound far inland and promoted the general isolation of the region.

Once in a while I noticed dead stumps and crumbling foundation-walls above the drifting sand, and recalled the old tradition quoted in one of the histories I had read, that this was once a fertile and thickly settled countryside. The change, it was said, came simultaneously with the Innsmouth epidemic of 1846, and was thought by simple folk to have a dark connexion with hidden forces of evil. Actually, it was caused by the unwise cutting of woodlands near the shore, which robbed the soil of its best protection and opened the way for waves of wind-blown sand.

At last we lost sight of Plum Island and saw the vast expanse of the open Atlantic on our left. Our narrow course began to climb steeply, and I felt a singular sense of disquiet in looking at the lonely crest ahead where the rutted roadway met the sky. It was as if the bus were about to keep on in its ascent, leaving the sane earth altogether and merging with the unknown arcana of upper air and cryptical sky. The smell of the sea took on ominous implications, and the silent driver's bent, rigid back and narrow head became more and more hateful. As I looked at him I saw that the back of his head was almost as hairless as his face, having only a few straggling yellow strands upon a grey scabrous surface.

Then we reached the crest and beheld the outspread valley beyond, where the Manuxet joins the sea just north of the long line of cliffs that culminate in Kingsport Head and veer off toward Cape Ann. On the far, misty horizon I could just make out the dizzy profile of the Head, topped by the queer ancient house of which so many legends are told; but for the moment all my attention was captured by the nearer panorama just below me. I had, I realised, come face to face with rumour-shadowed Innsmouth.

It was a town of wide extent and dense construction, yet one with a portentous dearth of visible life. From the tangle of chimney-pots scarcely a wisp of smoke came, and the three tall steeples loomed stark and unpainted against the seaward horizon. One of them was crumbling down at the top, and in that and another there were only black gaping holes where clock-dials should have been. The vast huddle of sagging gambrel roofs and peaked gables conveyed with offensive clearness the idea of wormy decay, and as we approached along the now descending road I could see that many roofs had wholly caved in. There were some large square Georgian houses, too, with hipped roofs, cupolas, and railed "widow's walks." These were mostly well back from the water, and one or two seemed to be in moderately sound condition. Stretching inland from among them I saw the rusted, grass-grown line of the abandoned railway, with leaning telegraph-poles now devoid of wires, and the half-obscured lines of the old carriage roads to Rowley and Ipswich.

The decay was worst close to the waterfront, though in its very midst I could spy the white belfry of a fairly well-preserved brick structure which looked like a small factory. The harbour, long clogged with sand, was enclosed by an ancient stone breakwater; on which I could begin to discern the minute forms of a few seated fishermen, and at whose end were what looked like the foundations of a bygone lighthouse. A sandy tongue had formed inside this barrier, and upon it I saw a few decrepit cabins, moored dories, and scattered lobster-pots. The only deep water seemed to be where the river poured out past the belfried structure and turned southward to join the ocean at the breakwater's end.

Here and there the ruins of wharves jutted out from the shore to end in indeterminate rottenness, those farthest south seeming the most decayed. And far out at sea, despite a high tide, I glimpsed a long, black line scarcely rising above the water yet carrying a suggestion of odd latent malignancy. This, I knew, must be Devil Reef. As I looked, a subtle, curious sense of beckoning seemed superadded to the grim repulsion; and oddly enough, I found this overtone more disturbing than the primary impression.

We met no one on the road, but presently began to pass deserted farms in varying stages of ruin. Then I noticed a few inhabited houses with rags stuffed in the broken windows and shells and dead fish lying about the littered yards. Once or twice I saw listless-looking people working in barren gardens or digging clams on the fishy-smelling beach below, and groups of dirty, simian-visaged children playing around weed-grown doorsteps. Somehow these people seemed more disquieting than the dismal buildings, for almost every one had certain peculiarities of face and motions which I instinctively disliked without being able to define or comprehend them. For a second I thought this typical physique suggested some picture I had seen, perhaps in a book, under circumstances of particular horror or melancholy; but this pseudo-recollection passed very quickly.

As the bus reached a lower level I began to catch the steady note of a waterfall through the unnatural stillness. The leaning, unpainted houses grew thicker, lined both sides of the road, and displayed more urban tendencies than did those we were leaving behind. The panorama ahead had contracted to a street scene, and in spots I could see where a cobblestone pavement and stretches of brick sidewalk had formerly existed. All the houses were apparently deserted, and there were occasional gaps where tumbledown chimneys and cellar walls told of buildings that had collapsed. Pervading everything was the most nauseous fishy odour imaginable.

Soon cross streets and junctions began to appear; those on the left leading to shoreward realms of unpaved squalor and decay, while those on the right shewed vistas of departed grandeur. So far I had seen no people in the town, but there now came signs of a sparse habitation—curtained windows here and there, and an occasional battered motor-car at the curb. Pavement and sidewalks were increasingly well defined, and though most of the houses were quite old—wood and brick structures of the early nineteenth century—they were obviously kept fit for habitation. As an amateur antiquarian I almost lost my olfactory disgust and my feeling of menace and repulsion amidst this rich, unaltered survival from the past.

But I was not to reach my destination without one very strong impression of poignantly disagreeable quality. The bus had come to a sort of open concourse or radial point with churches on two sides and the bedraggled remains of a circular green in the centre, and I was looking at a large pillared hall on the right-hand junction ahead. The structure's once white paint was now grey and peeling, and the black and gold sign on the pediment was so faded that I could only with difficulty make out the words "Esoteric Order of Dagon." This, then, was the former Masonic Hall now given over to a degraded cult. As I strained to decipher this inscription my notice was distracted by the raucous tones of a cracked bell across the street, and I quickly turned to look out the window on my side of the coach.

The sound came from a squat-towered stone church of manifestly later date than most of the houses, built in a clumsy Gothic fashion and having a disproportionately high basement with shuttered windows. Though the hands of its clock were missing on the side I glimpsed, I knew that those hoarse strokes were telling the hour of eleven. Then suddenly all thoughts of time were blotted out by an onrushing image of sharp intensity and unaccountable horror which had seized me before I knew what it really was. The door of the church basement was open, revealing a rectangle of blackness inside. And as I looked, a certain object crossed or seemed to cross that dark rectangle; burning into my brain a momentary conception of nightmare which was all the more maddening because analysis could not shew a single nightmarish quality in it.

It was a living object—the first except the driver that I had seen since entering the compact part of the town—and had I been in a steadier mood I would have found nothing whatever of terror in it. Clearly, as I realised a moment later, it was the pastor; clad in some peculiar vestments doubtless introduced since the Order of Dagon had modified the ritual of the local churches. The thing which had probably caught my first subconscious glance and supplied the touch of bizarre horror was the tall tiara he wore; an almost exact duplicate of the one Miss Tilton had shewn me the previous evening. This, acting on my imagination, had supplied namelessly sinister qualities to the indeterminate face and robed, shambling form beneath it. There was not, I soon decided, any reason why I should have felt that shuddering touch of evil pseudo-memory. Was it not natural that a local mystery cult should adopt among its regimentals an unique type of head-dress made familiar to the community in some strange way—perhaps as treasure-trove?

A very thin sprinkling of repellent-looking youngish people now became visible on the sidewalks—lone individuals, and silent knots of two or three. The lower floors of the crumbling houses sometimes harboured small shops with dingy signs, and I noticed a parked truck or two as we rattled along. The sound of waterfalls became more and more distinct, and presently I saw a fairly deep river-gorge ahead, spanned by a wide, iron-railed highway bridge beyond which a large square opened out. As we clanked over the bridge I looked out on both sides and observed some factory buildings on the edge of the grassy bluff or part way down. The water far below was very abundant, and I could see two vigorous sets of falls upstream on my right and at least one downstream on my left. From this point the noise was quite deafening. Then we rolled into the large semicircular square across the river and drew up on the right-hand side in front of a tall, cupola-crowned building with remnants of yellow paint and with a half-effaced sign proclaiming it to be the Gilman House.

I was glad to get out of that bus, and at once proceeded to check my valise in the shabby hotel lobby. There was only one person in sight—an elderly man without what I had come to call the "Innsmouth look"—and I decided not to ask him any of the questions which bothered me; remembering that odd things had been noticed in this hotel. Instead, I strolled out on the square, from which the bus had already gone, and studied the scene minutely and appraisingly.

One side of the cobblestoned open space was the straight line of the river; the other was a semicircle of slant-roofed brick buildings of about the 1800 period, from which several streets radiated away to the southeast, south, and southwest. Lamps were depressingly few and small—all low-powered incandescents—and I was glad that my plans called for departure before dark, even though I knew the moon would be bright. The buildings were all in fair condition, and included perhaps a dozen shops in current operation; of which one was a grocery of the First National chain, others a dismal restaurant, a drug store, and a wholesale fish-dealer's office, and still another, at the eastern extremity of the square near the river, an office of the town's only industry—the Marsh Refining Company. There were perhaps ten people visible, and four or five automobiles and motor trucks stood scattered about. I did not need to be told that this was the civic centre of Innsmouth. Eastward I could catch blue glimpses of the harbour, against which rose the decaying remains of three once beautiful Georgian steeples. And toward the shore on the opposite bank of the river I saw the white belfry surmounting what I took to be the Marsh refinery.

For some reason or other I chose to make my first inquiries at the chain grocery, whose personnel was not likely to be native to Innsmouth. I found a solitary boy of about seventeen in charge, and was pleased to note the brightness and affability which promised cheerful information. He seemed exceptionally eager to talk, and I soon gathered that he did not like the place, its fishy smell, or its furtive people. A word with any outsider was a relief to him. He hailed from Arkham, boarded with a family who came from Ipswich, and went back home whenever he got a moment off. His family did not like him to work in Innsmouth, but the chain had transferred him there and he did not wish to give up his job.

There was, he said, no public library or chamber of commerce in Innsmouth, but I could probably find my way about. The street I had come down was Federal. West of that were the fine old residence streets—Broad, Washington, Lafayette, and Adams—and east of it were the shoreward slums. It was in these slums—along Main Street—that I would find the old Georgian churches, but they were all long abandoned. It would be well not to make oneself too conspicuous in such neighbourhoods—especially north of the river—since the people were sullen and hostile. Some strangers had even disappeared.

Certain spots were almost forbidden territory, as he had learned at considerable cost. One must not, for example, linger much around the Marsh refinery, or around any of the still used churches, or around the pillared Order of Dagon Hall at New Church Green. Those churches were very odd—all violently disavowed by their respective denominations elsewhere, and apparently using the queerest kind of ceremonials and clerical vestments. Their creeds were heterodox and mysterious, involving hints of certain marvellous transformations leading to bodily immortality—of a sort—on this earth. The youth's own pastor—Dr. Wallace of Asbury M.E. Church in Arkham—had gravely urged him not to join any church in Innsmouth.

As for the Innsmouth people—the youth hardly knew what to make of them. They were as furtive and seldom seen as animals that live in burrows, and one could hardly imagine how they passed the time apart from their desultory fishing. Perhaps—judging from the quantities of bootleg liquor they consumed—they lay for most of the daylight hours in an alcoholic stupor. They seemed sullenly banded together in some sort of fellowship and understanding—despising the world as if they had access to other and preferable spheres of entity. Their appearance—especially those staring, unwinking eyes which one never saw shut—was certainly shocking enough; and their voices were disgusting. It was awful to hear them chanting in their churches at night, and especially during their main festivals or revivals, which fell twice a year on April 30th and October 31st.

They were very fond of the water, and swam a great deal in both river and harbour. Swimming races out to Devil Reef were very common, and everyone in sight seemed well able to share in this arduous sport. When one came to think of it, it was generally only rather young people who were seen about in public, and of these the oldest were apt to be the most tainted-looking. When exceptions did occur, they were mostly persons with no trace of aberrancy, like the old clerk at the hotel. One wondered what became of the bulk of the older folk, and whether the "Innsmouth look" were not a strange and insidious disease-phenomenon which increased its hold as years advanced.

Only a very rare affliction, of course, could bring about such vast and radical anatomical changes in a single individual after maturity—changes involving osseous factors as basic as the shape of the skull—but then, even this aspect was no more baffling and unheard-of than the visible features of the malady as a whole. It would be hard, the youth implied, to form any real conclusions regarding such a matter; since one never came to know the natives personally no matter how long one might live in Innsmouth.

The youth was certain that many specimens even worse than the worst visible ones were kept locked indoors in some places. People sometimes heard the queerest kind of sounds. The tottering waterfront hovels north of the river were reputedly connected by hidden tunnels, being thus a veritable warren of unseen abnormalities. What kind of foreign blood—if any—these beings had, it was impossible to tell. They sometimes kept certain especially repulsive characters out of sight when government agents and others from the outside world came to town.

It would be of no use, my informant said, to ask the natives anything about the place. The only one who would talk was a very aged but normal-looking man who lived at the poorhouse on the north rim of the town and spent his time walking about or lounging around the fire station. This hoary character, Zadok Allen, was ninety-six years old and somewhat touched in the head, besides being the town drunkard. He was a strange, furtive creature who constantly looked over his shoulder as if afraid of something, and when sober could not be persuaded to talk at all with strangers. He was, however, unable to resist any offer of his favourite poison; and once drunk would furnish the most astonishing fragments of whispered reminiscence.

After all, though, little useful data could be gained from him; since his stories were all insane, incomplete hints of impossible marvels and horrors which could have no source save in his own disordered fancy. Nobody ever believed him, but the natives did not like him to drink and talk with strangers; and it was not always safe to be seen questioning him. It was probably from him that some of the wildest popular whispers and delusions were derived.

Several non-native residents had reported monstrous glimpses from time to time, but between old Zadok's tales and the malformed denizens it was no wonder such illusions were current. None of the non-natives ever stayed out late at night, there being a widespread impression that it was not wise to do so. Besides, the streets were loathsomely dark.

As for business—the abundance of fish was certainly almost uncanny, but the natives were taking less and less advantage of it. Moreover, prices were falling and competition was growing. Of course the town's real business was the refinery, whose commercial office was on the square only a few doors east of where we stood. Old Man Marsh was never seen, but sometimes went to the works in a closed, curtained car.

There were all sorts of rumours about how Marsh had come to look. He had once been a great dandy, and people said he still wore the frock-coated finery of the Edwardian age, curiously adapted to certain deformities. His sons had formerly conducted the office in the square, but latterly they had been keeping out of sight a good deal and leaving the brunt of affairs to the younger generation. The sons and their sisters had come to look very queer, especially the elder ones; and it was said that their health was failing.

One of the Marsh daughters was a repellent, reptilian-looking woman who wore an excess of weird jewellery clearly of the same exotic tradition as that to which the strange tiara belonged. My informant had noticed it many times, and had heard it spoken of as coming from some secret hoard, either of pirates or of daemons. The clergymen—or priests, or whatever they were called nowadays—also wore this kind of ornament as a head-dress; but one seldom caught glimpses of them. Other specimens the youth had not seen, though many were rumoured to exist around Innsmouth.

The Marshes, together with the other three gently bred families of the town—the Waites, the Gilmans, and the Eliots—were all very retiring. They lived in immense houses along Washington Street, and several were reputed to harbour in concealment certain living kinsfolk whose personal aspect forbade public view, and whose deaths had been reported and recorded.

Warning me that many of the street signs were down, the youth drew for my benefit a rough but ample and painstaking sketch map of the town's salient features. After a moment's study I felt sure that it would be of great help, and pocketed it with profuse thanks. Disliking the dinginess of the single restaurant I had seen, I bought a fair supply of cheese crackers and ginger wafers to serve as a lunch later on. My programme, I decided, would be to thread the principal streets, talk with any non-natives I might encounter, and catch the eight o'clock coach for Arkham. The town, I could see, formed a significant and exaggerated example of communal decay; but being no sociologist I would limit my serious observations to the field of architecture.

Thus I began my systematic though half-bewildered tour of Innsmouth's narrow, shadow-blighted ways. Crossing the bridge and turning toward the roar of the lower falls, I passed close to the Marsh refinery, which seemed oddly free from the noise of industry. This building stood on the steep river bluff near a bridge and an open confluence of streets which I took to be the earliest civic centre, displaced after the Revolution by the present Town Square.

Re-crossing the gorge on the Main Street bridge, I struck a region of utter desertion which somehow made me shudder. Collapsing huddles of gambrel roofs formed a jagged and fantastic skyline, above which rose the ghoulish, decapitated steeple of an ancient church. Some houses along Main Street were tenanted, but most were tightly boarded up. Down unpaved side streets I saw the black, gaping windows of deserted hovels, many of which leaned at perilous and incredible angles through the sinking of part of the foundations. Those windows stared so spectrally that it took courage to turn eastward toward the waterfront. Certainly, the terror of a deserted house swells in geometrical rather than arithmetical progression as houses multiply to form a city of stark desolation. The sight of such endless avenues of fishy-eyed vacancy and death, and the thought of such linked infinities of black, brooding compartments given over to cobwebs and memories and the conqueror worm, start up vestigial fears and aversions that not even the stoutest philosophy can disperse.

Fish Street was as deserted as Main, though it differed in having many brick and stone warehouses still in excellent shape. Water Street was almost its duplicate, save that there were great seaward gaps where wharves had been. Not a living thing did I see, except for the scattered fishermen on the distant breakwater, and not a sound did I hear save the lapping of the harbour tides and the roar of the falls in the Manuxet. The town was getting more and more on my nerves, and I looked behind me furtively as I picked my way back over the tottering Water Street bridge. The Fish Street bridge, according to the sketch, was in ruins.

North of the river there were traces of squalid life—active fish-packing houses in Water Street, smoking chimneys and patched roofs here and there, occasional sounds from indeterminate sources, and infrequent shambling forms in the dismal streets and unpaved lanes—but I seemed to find this even more oppressive than the southerly desertion. For one thing, the people were more hideous and abnormal than those near the centre of the town; so that I was several times evilly reminded of something utterly fantastic which I could not quite place. Undoubtedly the alien strain in the Innsmouth folk was stronger here than farther inland—unless, indeed, the "Innsmouth look" were a disease rather than a blood strain, in which case this district might be held to harbour the more advanced cases.

One detail that annoyed me was the distribution of the few faint sounds I heard. They ought naturally to have come wholly from the visibly inhabited houses, yet in reality were often strongest inside the most rigidly boarded-up facades. There were creakings, scurryings, and hoarse doubtful noises; and I thought uncomfortably about the hidden tunnels suggested by the grocery boy. Suddenly I found myself wondering what the voices of those denizens would be like. I had heard no speech so far in this quarter, and was unaccountably anxious not to do so.

Pausing only long enough to look at two fine but ruinous old churches at Main and Church Streets, I hastened out of that vile waterfront slum. My next logical goal was New Church Green, but somehow or other I could not bear to repass the church in whose basement I had glimpsed the inexplicably frightening form of that strangely diademed priest or pastor. Besides, the grocery youth had told me that the churches, as well as the Order of Dagon Hall, were not advisable neighbourhoods for strangers.

Accordingly I kept north along Main to Martin, then turning inland, crossing Federal Street safely north of the Green, and entering the decayed patrician neighbourhood of northern Broad, Washington, Lafayette, and Adams Streets. Though these stately old avenues were ill-surfaced and unkempt, their elm-shaded dignity had not entirely departed. Mansion after mansion claimed my gaze, most of them decrepit and boarded up amidst neglected grounds, but one or two in each street shewing signs of occupancy. In Washington Street there was a row of four or five in excellent repair and with finely tended lawns and gardens. The most sumptuous of these—with wide terraced parterres extending back the whole way to Lafayette Street—I took to be the home of Old Man Marsh, the afflicted refinery owner.

In all these streets no living thing was visible, and I wondered at the complete absense of cats and dogs from Innsmouth. Another thing which puzzled and disturbed me, even in some of the best-preserved mansions, was the tightly shuttered condition of many third-story and attic windows. Furtiveness and secretiveness seemed universal in this hushed city of alienage and death, and I could not escape the sensation of being watched from ambush on every hand by sly, staring eyes that never shut.

I shivered as the cracked stroke of three sounded from a belfry on my left. Too well did I recall the squat church from which those notes came. Following Washington Street toward the river, I now faced a new zone of former industry and commerce; noting the ruins of a factory ahead, and seeing others, with the traces of an old railway station and covered railway bridge beyond, up the gorge on my right.

The uncertain bridge now before me was posted with a warning sign, but I took the risk and crossed again to the south bank where traces of life reappeared. Furtive, shambling creatures stared cryptically in my direction, and more normal faces eyed me coldly and curiously. Innsmouth was rapidly becoming intolerable, and I turned down Paine Street toward the Square in the hope of getting some vehicle to take me to Arkham before the still-distant starting-time of that sinister bus.

It was then that I saw the tumbledown fire station on my left, and noticed the red-faced, bushy-bearded, watery-eyed old man in nondescript rags who sat on a bench in front of it talking with a pair of unkempt but not abnormal-looking firemen. This, of course, must be Zadok Allen, the half-crazed, liquorish nonagenarian whose tales of old Innsmouth and its shadow were so hideous and incredible.

III.

It must have been some imp of the perverse—or some sardonic pull from dark, hidden sources—which made me change my plans as I did. I had long before resolved to limit my observations to architecture alone, and I was even then hurrying toward the Square in an effort to get quick transportation out of this festering city of death and decay; but the sight of old Zadok Allen set up new currents in my mind and made me slacken my pace uncertainly.

I had been assured that the old man could do nothing but hint at wild, disjointed, and incredible legends, and I had been warned that the natives made it unsafe to be seen talking to him; yet the thought of this aged witness to the town's decay, with memories going back to the early days of ships and factories, was a lure that no amount of reason could make me resist. After all, the strangest and maddest of myths are often merely symbols or allegories based upon truth—and old Zadok must have seen everything which went on around Innsmouth for the last ninety years. Curiosity flared up beyond sense and caution, and in my youthful egotism I fancied I might be able to sift a nucleus of real history from the confused, extravagant outpouring I would probably extract with the aid of raw whiskey.

I knew that I could not accost him then and there, for the firemen would surely notice and object. Instead, I reflected, I would prepare by getting some bootleg liquor at a place where the grocery boy had told me it was plentiful. Then I would loaf near the fire station in apparent casualness, and fall in with old Zadok after he had started on one of his frequent rambles. The youth said that he was very restless, seldom sitting around the station for more than an hour or two at a time.

A quart bottle of whiskey was easily, though not cheaply, obtained in the rear of a dingy variety-store just off the Square in Eliot Street. The dirty-looking fellow who waited on me had a touch of the staring "Innsmouth look," but was quite civil in his way; being perhaps used to the custom of such convivial strangers—truckmen, gold-buyers, and the like—as were occasionally in town.

Reentering the Square I saw that luck was with me; for—shuffling out of Paine Street around the corner of the Gilman House—I glimpsed nothing less than the tall, lean, tattered form of old Zadok Allen himself. In accordance with my plan, I attracted his attention by brandishing my newly purchased bottle; and soon realised that he had begun to shuffle wistfully after me as I turned into Waite Street on my way to the most deserted region I could think of.

I was steering my course by the map the grocery boy had prepared, and was aiming for the wholly abandoned stretch of southern waterfront which I had previously visited. The only people in sight there had been the fishermen on the distant breakwater; and by going a few squares south I could get beyond the range of these, finding a pair of seats on some abandoned wharf and being free to question old Zadok unobserved for an indefinite time. Before I reached Main Street I could hear a faint and wheezy "Hey, Mister!" behind me, and I presently allowed the old man to catch up and take copious pulls from the quart bottle.

I began putting out feelers as we walked along to Water Street and turned southward amidst the omnipresent desolation and crazily tilted ruins, but found that the aged tongue did not loosen as quickly as I had expected. At length I saw a grass-grown opening toward the sea between crumbling brick walls, with the weedy length of an earth-and-masonry wharf projecting beyond. Piles of moss-covered stones near the water promised tolerable seats, and the scene was sheltered from all possible view by a ruined warehouse on the north. Here, I thought, was the ideal place for a long secret colloquy; so I guided my companion down the lane and picked out spots to sit in among the mossy stones. The air of death and desertion was ghoulish, and the smell of fish almost insufferable; but I was resolved to let nothing deter me.

About four hours remained for conversation if I were to catch the eight o'clock coach for Arkham, and I began to dole out more liquor to the ancient tippler; meanwhile eating my own frugal lunch. In my donations I was careful not to overshoot the mark, for I did not wish Zadok's vinous garrulousness to pass into a stupor. After an hour his furtive taciturnity shewed signs of disappearing, but much to my disappointment he still sidetracked my questions about Innsmouth and its shadow-haunted past. He would babble of current topics, revealing a wide acquaintance with newspapers and a great tendency to philosophise in a sententious village fashion.

Toward the end of the second hour I feared my quart of whiskey would not be enough to produce results, and was wondering whether I had better leave old Zadok and go back for more. Just then, however, chance made the opening which my questions had been unable to make; and the wheezing ancient's rambling took a turn that caused me to lean forward and listen alertly. My back was toward the fishy-smelling sea, but he was facing it, and something or other had caused his wandering gaze to light on the low, distant line of Devil Reef, then shewing plainly and almost fascinatingly above the waves. The sight seemed to displease him, for he began a series of weak curses which ended in a confidential whisper and a knowing leer. He bent toward me, took hold of my coat lapel, and hissed out some hints that could not be mistaken.

"Thar's whar it all begun—that cursed place of all wickedness whar the deep water starts. Gate o' hell—sheer drop daown to a bottom no saoundin'-line kin tech. Ol' Cap'n Obed done it—him that faound aout more'n was good fer him in the Saouth Sea islands.

"Everybody was in a bad way them days. Trade fallin' off, mills losin' business—even the new ones—an' the best of our menfolks kilt a-privateerin' in the War of 1812 or lost with the *Elizy* brig an' the *Ranger* snow—both of 'em Gilman venters. Obed Marsh he had three ships afloat—brigantine *Columby*, brig *Hetty*, an' barque *Sumatry Queen*. He was the only one as kep' on with the East-Injy an' Pacific trade, though Esdras Martin's barkentine *Malay Pride* made a venter as late as 'twenty-eight.

"Never was nobody like Cap'n Obed—old limb o' Satan! Heh, heh! I kin mind him a-tellin' abaout furren parts, an' callin' all the folks stupid fer goin' to Christian meetin' an' bearin' their burdens meek an' lowly. Says they'd orter git better gods like some o' the folks in the Injies—gods as ud bring 'em good fishin' in return for their sacrifices, an' ud reely answer folks's prayers.

"Matt Eliot, his fust mate, talked a lot, too, only he was agin' folks's doin' any heathen things. Told abaout an island east of Otaheité whar they was a lot o' stone ruins older'n anybody knew anything abaout, kind o' like them on Ponape, in the Carolines, but with carvin's of faces that looked like the big statues on Easter Island. They was a little volcanic island near thar, too, whar they was other ruins with diff'rent carvin's—ruins all wore away like they'd ben under the sea onct, an' with picters of awful monsters all over 'em.

"Wal, Sir, Matt he says the natives araound thar had all the fish they cud ketch, an' sported bracelets an' armlets an' head rigs made aout of a queer kind o' gold an' covered with picters o' monsters jest like the ones carved over the ruins on the little island—sorter fish-like frogs or frog-like fishes that was drawed in all kinds o' positions like they was human bein's. Nobody cud git aout o' them whar they got all the stuff, an' all the other natives wondered haow they managed to find fish in plenty even when the very next islands had lean pickin's. Matt he got to wonderin' too, an' so did Cap'n Obed. Obed he notices, besides, that lots of the han'some young folks ud drop aout o' sight fer good from year to year, an' that they wa'n't many old folks araound. Also, he thinks some of the folks looks durned queer even fer Kanakys.

"It took Obed to git the truth aout o' them heathen. I dun't know haow he done it, but he begun by tradin' fer the gold-like things they wore. Ast 'em whar they come from, an' ef they cud git more, an' finally wormed the story aout o' the old chief—Walakea, they called him. Nobody but Obed ud ever a believed the old yeller devil, but the Cap'n cud read folks like they was books. Heh, heh! Nobody never believes me naow when I tell 'em, an' I dun't s'pose you will, young feller—though come to look at ye, ye hev kind o' got them sharp-readin' eyes like Obed had."

The old man's whisper grew fainter, and I found myself shuddering at the terrible and sincere portentousness of his intonation, even though I knew his tale could be nothing but drunken phantasy.

"Wal, Sir, Obed he larnt that they's things on this arth as most folks never heerd abaout—an' wouldn't believe ef they did hear. It seems these Kanakys was sacrificin' heaps o' their young men an' maidens to some kind o' god-things that lived under the sea, an' gittin' all kinds o' favour in return. They met the things on the little islet with the queer ruins, an' it seems them awful picters o' frog-fish monsters was supposed to be picters o' these things. Mebbe they was the kind o' critters as got all the mermaid stories an' sech started. They had all kinds o' cities on the sea-bottom, an' this island was heaved up from thar. Seems they was some of the things alive in the stone buildin's when the island come up sudden to the surface. That's haow the Kanakys got wind they was daown thar. Made sign-talk as soon as they got over bein' skeert, an' pieced up a bargain afore long.

"Them things liked human sacrifices. Had had 'em ages afore, but lost track o' the upper world arter a time. What they done to the victims it ain't fer me to say, an' I guess Obed wa'n't none too sharp abaout askin.' But it was all right with the heathens, because they'd ben havin' a hard time an' was desp'rate abaout everything. They give a sarten number o' young folks to the sea-things twict every year—May-Eve an' Hallowe'en—reg'lar as cud be. Also give some o' the carved knick-knacks they made. What the things agreed to give in return was plenty o' fish—they druv 'em in from all over the sea—an' a few gold-like things naow an' then.

"Wal, as I says, the natives met the things on the little volcanic islet—goin' thar in canoes with the sacrifices et cet'ry, and bringin' back any of the gold-like jools as was comin' to 'em. At fust the things didn't never go onto the main island, but arter a time they come to want to. Seems they hankered arter mixin' with the folks, an' havin' j'int ceremonies on the big days—May-Eve an' Hallowe'en. Ye see, they was able to live both in an' aout o' water—what they call amphibians, I guess. The Kanakys told 'em as haow folks from the other islands might wanta wipe 'em aout ef they got wind o' their bein' thar, but they says they dun't keer much, because they cud wipe aout the hull brood o' humans ef they was willin' to bother—that is, any as didn't hev sarten signs sech as was used onct by the lost Old Ones, who-ever they was. But not wantin' to bother, they'd lay low when anybody visited the island.

"When it come to matin' with them toad-lookin' fishes, the Kanakys kind o' balked, but finally they larnt something as put a new face on the matter. Seems that human folks has got a kind o' relation to sech water-beasts—that everything alive come aout o' the water onct, an' only needs a little change to go back agin. Them things told the Kanakys that ef they mixed bloods there'd be children as ud look human at fust, but later turn more'n more like the things, till finally they'd take to the water an' jine the main lot o' things daown thar. An' this is the important part, young feller—them as turned into fish things an' went into the water *wouldn't never die*. Them things never died excep' they was kilt violent.

"Wal, Sir, it seems by the time Obed knowed them island-ers they was all full o' fish blood from them deep-water things. When they got old an' begun to shew it, they was kep' hid until they felt like takin' to the water an' quittin' the place. Some was more teched than others, an' some never did change quite enough to take to the water; but mostly they turned aout jest the way them things said. Them as was born more like the things changed arly, but them as was nearly human sometimes stayed on the island till they was past seventy, though they'd usually go daown under fer trial trips afore that. Folks as had took to the water gen'rally come back a good deal to visit, so's a man ud often be a-talkin' to his own five-times-great-grandfather, who'd left the dry land a couple o' hundred years or so afore.

"Everybody got aout o' the idee o' dyin'—excep' in canoe wars with the other islanders, or as sacrifices to the sea-gods daown below, or from snake-bite or plague or sharp gallopin' ailments or somethin' afore they cud take to the water—but simply looked forrad to a kind o' change that wa'n't a bit horrible arter a while. They thought what they'd got was well wuth all they'd had to give up—an' I guess Obed kind o' come to think the same hisself when he'd chewed over old Walakea's story a bit. Walakea, though, was one of the few as hadn't got none of the fish blood—bein' of a royal line that intermarried with royal lines on other islands.

"Walakea he shewed Obed a lot o' rites an' incantations as had to do with the sea-things, an' let him see some o' the folks in the village as had changed a lot from human shape. Somehaow or other, though, he never would let him see one of the reg'lar things from right aout o' the water. In the end he give him a funny kind o' thingumajig made aout o' lead or something, that he said ud bring up the fish things from any place in the water whar they might be a nest of 'em. The idee was to drop it daown with the right kind o' prayers an' sech. Walakea allaowed as the things was scattered all over the world, so's anybody that looked abaout cud find a nest an' bring 'em up ef they was wanted.

"Matt he didn't like this business at all, an' wanted Obed shud keep away from the island; but the Cap'n was sharp fer gain, an' faound he cud git them gold-like things so cheap it ud pay him to make a specialty of 'em. Things went on that way fer years, an' Obed got enough o' that gold-like stuff to make him start the refinery in Waite's old run-daown fullin' mill. He didn't dass sell the pieces like they was, fer folks ud be all the time askin' questions. All the same his crews ud git a piece an' dispose of it naow and then, even though they was swore to keep quiet; an' he let his women-folks wear some o' the pieces as was more human-like than most.

"Wal, come abaout 'thutty-eight—when I was seven year' old—Obed he faound the island people all wiped aout between v'yages. Seems the other islanders had got wind o' what was goin' on, an' had took matters into their own hands. S'pose they musta had, arter all, them old magic signs as the sea-things says was the only things they was afeard of. No tellin' what any o' them Kanakys will chance to git a holt of when the sea-bottom throws up some island with ruins older'n the deluge. Pious cusses, these was—they didn't leave nothin' standin' on either the main island or the little volcanic islet excep' what parts of the ruins was too big to knock daown. In some places they was little stones strewed abaout—like charms—with somethin' on 'em like what ye call a swastika naowadays. Prob'ly them was the Old Ones' signs. Folks all wiped aout, no trace o' no gold-like things, an' none o' the nearby Kanakys ud breathe a word abaout the matter. Wouldn't even admit they'd ever ben any people on that island.

"That naturally hit Obed pretty hard, seein' as his normal trade was doin' very poor. It hit the whole of Innsmouth, too, because in seafarin' days what profited the master of a ship gen'lly profited the crew proportionate. Most o' the folks araound the taown took the hard times kind o' sheep-like an' resigned, but they was in bad shape because the fishin' was peterin' aout an' the mills wa'n't doin' none too well.

"Then's the time Obed he begun a-cursin' at the folks fer bein' dull sheep an' prayin' to a Christian heaven as didn't help 'em none. He told 'em he'd knowed of folks as prayed to gods that give somethin' ye reely need, an' says ef a good bunch o' men ud stand by him, he cud mebbe git a holt o' sarten paowers as ud bring plenty o' fish an' quite a bit o' gold. O' course them as sarved on the *Sumatry Queen* an' seed the island knowed what he meant, an' wa'n't none too anxious to git clost to sea-things like they'd heerd tell on, but them as didn't know what 'twas all abaout got kind o' swayed by what Obed had to say, an' begun to ast him what he cud do to set 'em on the way to the faith as ud bring 'em results."

Here the old man faltered, mumbled, and lapsed into a moody and apprehensive silence; glancing nervously over his shoulder and then turning back to stare fascinatedly at the distant black reef. When I spoke to him he did not answer, so I knew I would have to let him finish the bottle. The insane yarn I was hearing interested me profoundly, for I fancied there was contained within it a sort of crude allegory based upon the strangenesses of Innsmouth and elaborated by an imagination at once creative and full of scraps of exotic legend. Not for a moment did I believe that the tale had any really substantial foundation; but none the less the account held a hint of genuine terror, if only because it brought in references to strange jewels clearly akin to the malign tiara I had seen at Newburyport. Perhaps the ornaments had, after all, come from some strange island; and possibly the wild stories were lies of the bygone Obed himself rather than of this antique toper.

I handed Zadok the bottle, and he drained it to the last drop. It was curious how he could stand so much whiskey, for not even a trace of thickness had come into his high, wheezy voice. He licked the nose of the bottle and slipped it into his pocket, then beginning to nod and whisper softly to himself. I bent close to catch any articulate words he might utter, and thought I saw a sardonic smile behind the stained, bushy whiskers. Yes—he was really forming words, and I could grasp a fair proportion of them.

"Poor Matt—Matt he allus was agin' it—tried to line up the folks on his side, an' had long talks with the preachers—no use—they run the Congregational parson aout o' taown, an' the Methodist feller quit—never did see Resolved Babcock, the Baptist parson, agin—Wrath o' Jehovy—I was a mighty little critter, but I heerd what I heerd an' seen what I seen—Dagon an' Ashtoreth—Belial an' Beëlzebub—Golden Caff an' the idols o' Canaan an' the Philistines—Babylonish abominations—*Mene, mene, tekel, upharsin*—"

He stopped again, and from the look in his watery blue eyes I feared he was close to a stupor after all. But when I gently shook his shoulder he turned on me with astonishing alertness and snapped out some more obscure phrases.

"Dun't believe me, hey? Heh, heh, heh—then jest tell me, young feller, why Cap'n Obed an' twenty odd other folks used to row aout to Devil Reef in the dead o' night an' chant things so laoud ye cud hear 'em all over taown when the wind was right? Tell me that, hey? An' tell me why Obed was allus droppin' heavy things daown into the deep water t'other side o' the reef whar the bottom shoots daown like a cliff lower'n ye kin saound? Tell me what he done with that funny-shaped lead thingumajig as Walakea give him? Hey, boy? An' what did they all haowl on May-Eve, an' agin the next Hallowe'en? An' why'd the new church parsons—fellers as used to be sailors—wear them queer robes an' cover theirselves with them gold-like things Obed brung? Hey?"

The watery blue eyes were almost savage and maniacal now, and the dirty white beard bristled electrically. Old Zadok probably saw me shrink back, for he had begun to cackle evilly.

"Heh, heh, heh, heh! Beginnin' to see, hey? Mebbe ye'd like to a ben me in them days, when I seed things at night aout to sea from the cupalo top o' my haouse. Oh, I kin tell ye, little pitchers hev big ears, an' I wa'n't missin' nothin' o' what was gossiped abaout Cap'n Obed an' the folks aout to the reef! Heh, heh, heh! Haow abaout the night I took my pa's ship's glass up to the cupalo an' seed the reef a-bristlin' thick with shapes that dove off quick soon's the moon riz? Obed an' the folks was in a dory, but them shapes dove off the far side into the deep water an' never come up...Haow'd ye like to be a little shaver alone up in a cupalo a-watchin' shapes *as wa'n't human shapes?*...Hey?... Heh, heh, heh, heh..."

The old man was getting hysterical, and I began to shiver with a nameless alarm. He laid a gnarled claw on my shoulder, and it seemed to me that its shaking was not altogether that of mirth.

"S'pose one night ye seed somethin' heavy heaved offen Obed's dory beyond the reef, an' then larned nex' day a young feller was missin' from home? Hey? Did anybody ever see hide or hair o' Hiram Gilman agin? Did they? An' Nick Pierce, an' Luelly Waite, an' Adoniram Saouthwick, an' Henry Garrison? Hey? Heh, heh, heh, heh...Shapes talkin' sign language with their hands...them as had reel hands...

"Wal, Sir, that was the time Obed begun to git on his feet agin. Folks see his three darters a-wearin' gold-like things as nobody'd never see on 'em afore, an' smoke started comin' aout o' the refin'ry chimbly. Other folks were prosp'rin,' too—fish begun to swarm into the harbour fit to kill, an' heaven knows what sized cargoes we begun to ship aout to Newb'ry-port, Arkham, an' Boston. 'Twas then Obed got the ol' branch railrud put through. Some Kingsport fishermen heerd abaout the ketch an' come up in sloops, but they was all lost. Nobody never see 'em agin. An' jest then our folks organised the Esoteric Order o' Dagon, an' bought Masonic Hall offen Calvary Commandery for it...heh, heh, heh! Matt Eliot was a Mason an' agin' the sellin,' but he dropped aout o' sight jest then.

"Remember, I ain't sayin' Obed was set on hevin' things jest like they was on that Kanaky isle. I dun't think he aimed at fust to do no mixin,' nor raise no younguns to take to the water an' turn into fishes with eternal life. He wanted them gold things, an' was willin' to pay heavy, an' I guess the others was satisfied fer a while...

"Come in 'forty-six the taown done some lookin' an' thinkin' fer itself. Too many folks missin'—too much wild preachin' at meetin' of a Sunday—too much talk abaout that reef. I guess I done a bit by tellin' Selectman Mowry what I see from the cupa-lo. They was a party one night as follered Obed's craowd aout to the reef, an' I heerd shots betwixt the dories. Nex' day Obed an' thutty-two others was in gaol, with everbody a-wonderin' jest what was afoot an' jest what charge agin' 'em cud be got to holt. God, ef anybody'd look'd ahead...a couple o' weeks later, when nothin' had ben throwed into the sea fer that long..."

Zadok was shewing signs of fright and exhaustion, and I let him keep silence for a while, though glancing apprehensively at my watch. The tide had turned and was coming in now, and the sound of the waves seemed to arouse him. I was glad of that tide, for at high water the fishy smell might not be so bad. Again I strained to catch his whispers.

"That awful night...I seed 'em...I was up in the cupalo... hordes of 'em...swarms of 'em...all over the reef an' swimmin' up the harbour into the Manuxet...God, what happened in the streets of Innsmouth that night...they rattled our door, but pa wouldn't open...then he clumb aout the kitchen winder with his musket to find Selectman Mowry an' see what he cud do... Maounds o' the dead an' the dyin'...shots an' screams...shaoutin' in Ol' Squar an' Taown Squar an' New Church Green...gaol throwed open...proclamation...treason...called it the plague when folks come in an' faound haff our people missin.'..nobody left but them as ud jine in with Obed an' them things or else keep quiet...never heerd o' my pa no more..."

The old man was panting, and perspiring profusely. His grip on my shoulder tightened.

"Everything cleaned up in the mornin'—but they was *traces*...Obed he kinder takes charge an' says things is goin' to be changed...*others'll* worship with us at meetin'-time, an' sarten haouses hez got to entertain *guests*...they wanted to mix like they done with the Kanakys, an' he fer one didn't feel baound to stop 'em. Far gone, was Obed...jest like a crazy man on the subjeck. He says they brung us fish an' treasure, an' shud hev what they hankered arter...

"Nothin' was to be diff'runt on the aoutside, only we was to keep shy o' strangers ef we knowed what was good fer us. We all hed to take the Oath o' Dagon, an' later on they was secon' an' third Oaths that some on us took. Them as ud help special, ud git special rewards—gold an' sech—No use balkin,' fer they was millions of 'em daown thar. They'd ruther not start risin' an' wipin' aout humankind, but ef they was gave away an' forced to, they cud do a lot toward jest that. We didn't hev them old charms to cut 'em off like folks in the Saouth Sea did, an' them Kanakys wudn't never give away their secrets.

"Yield up enough sacrifices an' savage knick-knacks an' harbourage in the taown when they wanted it, an' they'd let well enough alone. Wudn't bother no strangers as might bear tales aoutside–that is, withaout they got pryin.' All in the band of the faithful–Order o' Dagon–an' the children shud never die, but go back to the Mother Hydra an' Father Dagon what we all come from onct–*Iä! Iä! Cthulhu fhtagn! Ph'nglui mglw'nafh Cthulhu R'lyeh wgah-nagl fhtagn–*"

Old Zadok was fast lapsing into stark raving, and I held my breath. Poor old soul–to what pitiful depths of hallucination had his liquor, plus his hatred of the decay, alienage, and disease around him, brought that fertile, imaginative brain! He began to moan now, and tears were coursing down his channelled cheeks into the depths of his beard.

"God, what I seen senct I was fifteen year' old–*Mene, mene, tekel, upharsin!*–the folks as was missin,' an' them as kilt theirselves–them as told things in Arkham or Ipswich or sech places was all called crazy, like you're a-callin' me right naow–but God, what I seen–They'd a kilt me long ago fer what I know, only I'd took the fust an' secon' Oaths o' Dagon offen Obed, so was pertected unlessen a jury of 'em proved I told things knowin' an' delib'rit...but I wudn't take the third Oath–I'd a died ruther'n take that–

"It got wuss araound Civil War time, *when children born senct 'forty-six begun to grow up*–some of 'em, that is. I was afeard–never did no pryin' arter that awful night, an' never see one of—*them*—clost to in all my life. That is, never no full-blooded one. I went to the war, an' ef I'd a had any guts or sense I'd a never come back, but settled away from here. But folks wrote me things wa'n't so bad. That, I s'pose, was because gov'munt draft men was in taown arter 'sixty-three. Arter the war it was jest as bad agin. People begun to fall off—mills an' shops shet daown—shippin' stopped an' the harbour choked up—railrud give up—but *they*...they never stopped swimmin' in an' aout o' the river from that cursed reef o' Satan—an' more an' more attic winders got a-boarded up, an' more an' more noises was heerd in haouses as wa'n't s'posed to hev nobody in 'em...

"Folks aoutside hev their stories abaout us—s'pose you've heerd a plenty on 'em, seein' what questions ye ast—stories abaout things they've seed naow an' then, an' abaout that queer joolry as still comes in from somewhars an' ain't quite all melted up—but nothin' never gits def'nite. Nobody'll believe nothin.' They call them gold-like things pirate loot, an' allaow the Innsmouth folks hez furren blood or is distempered or somethin.' Besides, them that lives here shoo off as many strangers as they kin, an' encourage the rest not to git very cur'ous, specially raound night time. Beasts balk at the critters—hosses wuss'n mules—but when they got autos that was all right.

"In 'forty-six Cap'n Obed took a second wife *that nobody in the taown never see*—some says he didn't want to, but was made to by them as he'd called in—had three children by her—two as disappeared young, but one gal as looked like anybody else an' was eddicated in Europe. Obed finally got her married off by a trick to an Arkham feller as didn't suspect nothin.' But nobody aoutside'll hev nothin' to do with Innsmouth folks naow. Barnabas Marsh that runs the refin'ry naow is Obed's grandson by his fust wife—son of Onesiphorus, his eldest son, *but his mother was another o' them as wa'n't never seed aoutdoors.*

"Right naow Barnabas is abaout changed. Can't shet his eyes no more, an' is all aout o' shape. They say he still wears clothes, but he'll take to the water soon. Mebbe he's tried it already—they do sometimes go daown fer little spells afore they go fer good. Ain't ben seed abaout in public fer nigh on ten year.' Dun't know haow his poor wife kin feel—she come from Ipswich, an' they nigh lynched Barnabas when he courted her fifty odd year' ago. Obed he died in 'seventy-eight, an' all the next gen'ration is gone naow—the fust wife's children dead, an' the rest...God knows..."

The sound of the incoming tide was now very insistent, and little by little it seemed to change the old man's mood from maudlin tearfulness to watchful fear. He would pause now and then to renew those nervous glances over his shoulder or out toward the reef, and despite the wild absurdity of his tale, I could not help beginning to share his vague apprehensiveness. Zadok now grew shriller, and seemed to be trying to whip up his courage with louder speech.

"Hey, yew, why dun't ye say somethin'? Haow'd ye like to be livin' in a taown like this, with everything a-rottin' an' a-dyin,' an' boarded-up monsters crawlin' an' bleatin' an' barkin' an' hoppin' araoun' black cellars an' attics every way ye turn? Hey? Haow'd ye like to hear the haowlin' night arter night from the churches an' Order o' Dagon Hall, *an' know what's doin' part o' the haowlin'?* Haow'd ye like to hear what comes from that awful reef every May-Eve an' Hallowmass? Hey? Think the old man's crazy, eh? Wal, Sir, *let me tell ye that ain't the wust!*"

Zadok was really screaming now, and the mad frenzy of his voice disturbed me more than I care to own.

"Curse ye, dun't set thar a-starin' at me with them eyes—I tell Obed Marsh he's in hell, an' hez got to stay thar! Heh, heh...in hell, I says! Can't git me—I hain't done nothin' nor told nobody nothin'—

"Oh, you, young feller? Wal, even ef I hain't told nobody nothin' yet, I'm a-goin' to naow! You jest set still an' listen to me, boy—this is what I ain't never told nobody...I says I didn't do no pryin' arter that night—*but I faound things aout jest the same!*

"Yew want to know what the reel horror is, hey? Wal, it's this—it ain't what them fish devils *hez done, but what they're a-goin' to do!* They're a-bringin' things up aout o' whar they come from into the taown—ben doin' it fer years, an' slackenin' up lately. Them haouses north o' the river betwixt Water an' Main Streets is full of 'em—them devils an' *what they brung*—an' when they git ready...I say, when they git ready...ever hear tell of a *shoggoth?...*

"Hey, d'ye hear me? I tell ye *I know what them things be—I seen 'em one night when*...EH—AHHHH—AH! E'YAAHHHH..."

The hideous suddenness and inhuman frightfulness of the old man's shriek almost made me faint. His eyes, looking past me toward the malodorous sea, were positively starting from his head; while his face was a mask of fear worthy of Greek tragedy. His bony claw dug monstrously into my shoulder, and he made no motion as I turned my head to look at whatever he had glimpsed.

There was nothing that I could see. Only the incoming tide, with perhaps one set of ripples more local than the long-flung line of breakers. But now Zadok was shaking me, and I turned back to watch the melting of that fear-frozen face into a chaos of twitching eyelids and mumbling gums. Presently his voice came back—albeit as a trembling whisper.

"*Git aout o' here!* Git aout o' here! *They seen us*—git aout fer your life! Dun't wait fer nothin'—*they know naow*—Run fer it—quick—*aout o' this taown*—"

Another heavy wave dashed against the loosening masonry of the bygone wharf, and changed the mad ancient's whisper to another inhuman and blood-curdling scream.

"E—YAAHHHH!...YHAAAAAAA!..."

Before I could recover my scattered wits he had relaxed his clutch on my shoulder and dashed wildly inland toward the street, reeling northward around the ruined warehouse wall.

I glanced back at the sea, but there was nothing there. And when I reached Water Street and looked along it toward the north there was no remaining trace of Zadok Allen.

IV.

I can hardly describe the mood in which I was left by this harrowing episode—an episode at once mad and pitiful, grotesque and terrifying. The grocery boy had prepared me for it, yet the reality left me none the less bewildered and disturbed. Puerile though the story was, old Zadok's insane earnestness and horror had communicated to me a mounting unrest which joined with my earlier sense of loathing for the town and its blight of intangible shadow.

Later I might sift the tale and extract some nucleus of historic allegory; just now I wished to put it out of my head. The hour had grown perilously late—my watch said 7:15, and the Arkham bus left Town Square at eight—so I tried to give my thoughts as neutral and practical a cast as possible, meanwhile walking rapidly through the deserted streets of gaping roofs and leaning houses toward the hotel where I had checked my valise and would find my bus.

Though the golden light of late afternoon gave the ancient roofs and decrepit chimneys an air of mystic loveliness and peace, I could not help glancing over my shoulder now and then. I would surely be very glad to get out of malodorous and fear-shadowed Innsmouth, and wished there were some other vehicle than the bus driven by that sinister-looking fellow Sargent. Yet I did not hurry too precipitately, for there were architectural details worth viewing at every silent corner; and I could easily, I calculated, cover the necessary distance in a half-hour.

Studying the grocery youth's map and seeking a route I had not traversed before, I chose Marsh Street instead of State for my approach to Town Square. Near the corner of Fall Street I began to see scattered groups of furtive whisperers, and when I finally reached the Square I saw that almost all the loiterers were congregated around the door of the Gilman House. It seemed as if many bulging, watery, unwinking eyes looked oddly at me as I claimed my valise in the lobby, and I hoped that none of these unpleasant creatures would be my fellow-passengers on the coach.

The bus, rather early, rattled in with three passengers somewhat before eight, and an evil-looking fellow on the sidewalk muttered a few indistinguishable words to the driver. Sargent threw out a mail-bag and a roll of newspapers, and entered the hotel; while the passengers—the same men whom I had seen arriving in Newburyport that morning—shambled to the sidewalk and exchanged some faint guttural words with a loafer in a language I could have sworn was not English. I boarded the empty coach and took the same seat I had taken before, but was hardly settled before Sargent reappeared and began mumbling in a throaty voice of peculiar repulsiveness.

I was, it appeared, in very bad luck. There had been something wrong with the engine, despite the excellent time made from Newburyport, and the bus could not complete the journey to Arkham. No, it could not possibly be repaired that night, nor was there any other way of getting transportation out of Innsmouth, either to Arkham or elsewhere. Sargent was sorry, but I would have to stop over at the Gilman. Probably the clerk would make the price easy for me, but there was nothing else to do. Almost dazed by this sudden obstacle, and violently dreading the fall of night in this decaying and half-unlighted town, I left the bus and reëntered the hotel lobby; where the sullen, queer-looking night clerk told me I could have Room 428 on next the top floor—large, but without running water—for a dollar.

Despite what I had heard of this hotel in Newburyport, I signed the register, paid my dollar, let the clerk take my valise, and followed that sour, solitary attendant up three creaking flights of stairs past dusty corridors which seemed wholly devoid of life. My room, a dismal rear one with two windows and bare, cheap furnishings, overlooked a dingy courtyard otherwise hemmed in by low, deserted brick blocks, and commanded a view of decrepit westward-stretching roofs with a marshy countryside beyond. At the end of the corridor was a bathroom—a discouraging relique with ancient marble bowl, tin tub, faint electric light, and musty wooden panelling around all the plumbing fixtures.

It being still daylight, I descended to the Square and looked around for a dinner of some sort; noticing as I did so the strange glances I received from the unwholesome loafers. Since the grocery was closed, I was forced to patronise the restaurant I had shunned before; a stooped, narrow-headed man with staring, unwinking eyes, and a flat-nosed wench with unbelievably thick, clumsy hands being in attendance. The service was of the counter type, and it relieved me to find that much was evidently served from cans and packages. A bowl of vegetable soup with crackers was enough for me, and I soon headed back for my cheerless room at the Gilman; getting an evening paper and a flyspecked magazine from the evil-visaged clerk at the rickety stand beside his desk.

As twilight deepened I turned on the one feeble electric bulb over the cheap, iron-framed bed, and tried as best I could to continue the reading I had begun. I felt it advisable to keep my mind wholesomely occupied, for it would not do to brood over the abnormalities of this ancient, blight-shadowed town while I was still within its borders. The insane yarn I had heard from the aged drunkard did not promise very pleasant dreams, and I felt I must keep the image of his wild, watery eyes as far as possible from my imagination.

Also, I must not dwell on what that factory inspector had told the Newburyport ticket-agent about the Gilman House and the voices of its nocturnal tenants—not on that, nor on the face beneath the tiara in the black church doorway; the face for whose horror my conscious mind could not account. It would perhaps have been easier to keep my thoughts from disturbing topics had the room not been so gruesomely musty. As it was, the lethal mustiness blended hideously with the town's general fishy odour and persistently focussed one's fancy on death and decay.

Another thing that disturbed me was the absence of a bolt on the door of my room. One had been there, as marks clearly shewed, but there were signs of recent removal. No doubt it had become out of order, like so many other things in this decrepit edifice. In my nervousness I looked around and discovered a bolt on the clothes-press which seemed to be of the same size, judging from the marks, as the one formerly on the door. To gain a partial relief from the general tension I busied myself by transferring this hardware to the vacant place with the aid of a handy three-in-one device including a screw-driver which I kept on my key-ring. The bolt fitted perfectly, and I was somewhat relieved when I knew that I could shoot it firmly upon retiring. Not that I had any real apprehension of its need, but that any symbol of security was welcome in an environment of this kind. There were adequate bolts on the two lateral doors to connecting rooms, and these I proceeded to fasten.

I did not undress, but decided to read till I was sleepy and then lie down with only my coat, collar, and shoes off. Taking a pocket flashlight from my valise, I placed it in my trousers, so that I could read my watch if I woke up later in the dark. Drowsiness, however, did not come; and when I stopped to analyse my thoughts I found to my disquiet that I was really unconsciously listening for something–listening for something which I dreaded but could not name. That inspector's story must have worked on my imagination more deeply than I had suspected. Again I tried to read, but found that I made no progress.

After a time I seemed to hear the stairs and corridors creak at intervals as if with footsteps, and wondered if the other rooms were beginning to fill up. There were no voices, however, and it struck me that there was something subtly furtive about the creaking. I did not like it, and debated whether I had better try to sleep at all. This town had some queer people, and there had undoubtedly been several disappearances. Was this one of those inns where travellers were slain for their money? Surely I had no look of excessive prosperity. Or were the townsfolk really so resentful about curious visitors? Had my obvious sightseeing, with its frequent map-consultations, aroused unfavourable notice? It occurred to me that I must be in a highly nervous state to let a few random creakings set me off speculating in this fashion—but I regretted none the less that I was unarmed.

At length, feeling a fatigue which had nothing of drowsiness in it, I bolted the newly outfitted hall door, turned off the light, and threw myself down on the hard, uneven bed—coat, collar, shoes, and all. In the darkness every faint noise of the night seemed magnified, and a flood of doubly unpleasant thoughts swept over me. I was sorry I had put out the light, yet was too tired to rise and turn it on again. Then, after a long, dreary interval, and prefaced by a fresh creaking of stairs and corridor, there came that soft, damnably unmistakable sound which seemed like a malign fulfilment of all my apprehensions. Without the least shadow of a doubt, the lock on my hall door was being tried—cautiously, furtively, tentatively—with a key.

My sensations upon recognising this sign of actual peril were perhaps less rather than more tumultuous because of my previous vague fears. I had been, albeit without definite reason, instinctively on my guard—and that was to my advantage in the new and real crisis, whatever it might turn out to be. Nevertheless the change in the menace from vague premonition to immediate reality was a profound shock, and fell upon me with the force of a genuine blow. It never once occurred to me that the fumbling might be a mere mistake. Malign purpose was all I could think of, and I kept deathly quiet, awaiting the would-be intruder's next move.

After a time the cautious rattling ceased, and I heard the room to the north entered with a pass-key. Then the lock of the connecting door to my room was softly tried. The bolt held, of course, and I heard the floor creak as the prowler left the room. After a moment there came another soft rattling, and I knew that the room to the south of me was being entered. Again a furtive trying of a bolted connecting door, and again a receding creaking. This time the creaking went along the hall and down the stairs, so I knew that the prowler had realised the bolted condition of my doors and was giving up his attempt for a greater or lesser time, as the future would shew.

The readiness with which I fell into a plan of action proves that I must have been subconsciously fearing some menace and considering possible avenues of escape for hours. From the first I felt that the unseen fumbler meant a danger not to be met or dealt with, but only to be fled from as precipitately as possible. The one thing to do was to get out of that hotel alive as quickly as I could, and through some channel other than the front stairs and lobby.

Rising softly and throwing my flashlight on the switch, I sought to light the bulb over my bed in order to choose and pocket some belongings for a swift, valiseless flight. Nothing, however, happened; and I saw that the power had been cut off. Clearly, some cryptic, evil movement was afoot on a large scale—just what, I could not say. As I stood pondering with my hand on the now useless switch I heard a muffled creaking on the floor below, and thought I could barely distinguish voices in conversation. A moment later I felt less sure that the deeper sounds were voices, since the apparent hoarse barkings and loose-syllabled croakings bore so little resemblance to recognised human speech. Then I thought with renewed force of what the factory inspector had heard in the night in this mouldering and pestilential building.

Having filled my pockets with the flashlight's aid, I put on my hat and tiptoed to the windows to consider chances of descent. Despite the state's safety regulations there was no fire escape on this side of the hotel, and I saw that my windows commanded only a sheer three-story drop to the cobbled courtyard. On the right and left, however, some ancient brick business blocks abutted on the hotel; their slant roofs coming up to a reasonable jumping distance from my fourth-story level. To reach either of these lines of buildings I would have to be in a room two doors from my own—in one case on the north and in the other case on the south—and my mind instantly set to work calculating what chances I had of making the transfer.

I could not, I decided, risk an emergence into the corridor; where my footsteps would surely be heard, and where the difficulties of entering the desired room would be insuperable. My progress, if it was to be made at all, would have to be through the less solidly built connecting doors of the rooms; the locks and bolts of which I would have to force violently, using my shoulder as a battering-ram whenever they were set against me. This, I thought, would be possible owing to the rickety nature of the house and its fixtures; but I realised I could not do it noiselessly. I would have to count on sheer speed, and the chance of getting to a window before any hostile forces became coordinated enough to open the right door toward me with a pass-key. My own outer door I reinforced by pushing the bureau against it—little by little, in order to make a minimum of sound.

I perceived that my chances were very slender, and was fully prepared for any calamity. Even getting to another roof would not solve the problem, for there would then remain the task of reaching the ground and escaping from the town. One thing in my favour was the deserted and ruinous state of the abutting buildings, and the number of skylights gaping blackly open in each row.

Gathering from the grocery boy's map that the best route out of town was southward, I glanced first at the connecting door on the south side of the room. It was designed to open in my direction, hence I saw—after drawing the bolt and finding other fastenings in place—it was not a favourable one for forcing. Accordingly abandoning it as a route, I cautiously moved the bedstead against it to hamper any attack which might be made on it later from the next room. The door on the north was hung to open away from me, and this—though a test proved it to be locked or bolted from the other side—I knew must be my route. If I could gain the roofs of the buildings in Paine Street and descend successfully to the ground level, I might perhaps dart through the courtyard and the adjacent or opposite buildings to Washington or Bates—or else emerge in Paine and edge around southward into Washington. In any case, I would aim to strike Washington somehow and get quickly out of the Town Square region. My preference would be to avoid Paine, since the fire station there might be open all night.

As I thought of these things I looked out over the squalid sea of decaying roofs below me, now brightened by the beams of a moon not much past full. On the right the black gash of the river-gorge clove the panorama; abandoned factories and railway station clinging barnacle-like to its sides. Beyond it the rusted railway and the Rowley road led off through a flat, marshy terrain dotted with islets of higher and dryer scrub-grown land. On the left the creek-threaded countryside was nearer, the narrow road to Ipswich gleaming white in the moonlight. I could not see from my side of the hotel the southward route toward Arkham which I had determined to take.

I was irresolutely speculating on when I had better attack the northward door, and on how I could least audibly manage it, when I noticed that the vague noises underfoot had given place to a fresh and heavier creaking of the stairs. A wavering flicker of light shewed through my transom, and the boards of the corridor began to groan with a ponderous load. Muffled sounds of possible vocal origin approached, and at length a firm knock came at my outer door.

For a moment I simply held my breath and waited. Eternities seemed to elapse, and the nauseous fishy odour of my environment seemed to mount suddenly and spectacularly. Then the knocking was repeated–continuously, and with growing insistence. I knew that the time for action had come, and forthwith drew the bolt of the northward connecting door, bracing myself for the task of battering it open. The knocking waxed louder, and I hoped that its volume would cover the sound of my efforts. At last beginning my attempt, I lunged again and again at the thin panelling with my left shoulder, heedless of shock or pain. The door resisted even more than I had expected, but I did not give in. And all the while the clamour at the outer door increased.

Finally the connecting door gave, but with such a crash that I knew those outside must have heard. Instantly the outside knocking became a violent battering, while keys sounded ominously in the hall doors of the rooms on both sides of me. Rushing through the newly opened connexion, I succeeded in bolting the northerly hall door before the lock could be turned; but even as I did so I heard the hall door of the third room—the one from whose window I had hoped to reach the roof below—being tried with a pass-key.

For an instant I felt absolute despair, since my trapping in a chamber with no window egress seemed complete. A wave of almost abnormal horror swept over me, and invested with a terrible but unexplainable singularity the flashlight-glimpsed dust prints made by the intruder who had lately tried my door from this room. Then, with a dazed automatism which persisted despite hopelessness, I made for the next connecting door and performed the blind motion of pushing at it in an effort to get through and—granting that fastenings might be as providentially intact as in this second room—bolt the hall door beyond before the lock could be turned from outside.

Sheer fortunate chance gave me my reprieve—for the connecting door before me was not only unlocked but actually ajar. In a second I was through, and had my right knee and shoulder against a hall door which was visibly opening inward. My pressure took the opener off guard, for the thing shut as I pushed, so that I could slip the well-conditioned bolt as I had done with the other door. As I gained this respite I heard the battering at the two other doors abate, while a confused clatter came from the connecting door I had shielded with the bedstead. Evidently the bulk of my assailants had entered the southerly room and were massing in a lateral attack. But at the same moment a pass-key sounded in the next door to the north, and I knew that a nearer peril was at hand.

The northward connecting door was wide open, but there was no time to think about checking the already turning lock in the hall. All I could do was to shut and bolt the open connecting door, as well as its mate on the opposite side—pushing a bedstead against the one and a bureau against the other, and moving a washstand in front of the hall door. I must, I saw, trust to such makeshift barriers to shield me till I could get out the window and on the roof of the Paine Street block. But even in this acute moment my chief horror was something apart from the immediate weakness of my defences. I was shuddering because not one of my pursuers, despite some hideous pantings, gruntings, and subdued barkings at odd intervals, was uttering an unmuffled or intelligible vocal sound.

As I moved the furniture and rushed toward the windows I heard a frightful scurrying along the corridor toward the room north of me, and perceived that the southward battering had ceased. Plainly, most of my opponents were about to concentrate against the feeble connecting door which they knew must open directly on me. Outside, the moon played on the ridgepole of the block below, and I saw that the jump would be desperately hazardous because of the steep surface on which I must land.

Surveying the conditions, I chose the more southerly of the two windows as my avenue of escape; planning to land on the inner slope of the roof and make for the nearest skylight. Once inside one of the decrepit brick structures I would have to reckon with pursuit; but I hoped to descend and dodge in and out of yawning doorways along the shadowed courtyard, eventually getting to Washington Street and slipping out of town toward the south.

The clatter at the northerly connecting door was now terrific, and I saw that the weak panelling was beginning to splinter. Obviously, the besiegers had brought some ponderous object into play as a battering-ram. The bedstead, however, still held firm; so that I had at least a faint chance of making good my escape. As I opened the window I noticed that it was flanked by heavy velour draperies suspended from a pole by brass rings, and also that there was a large projecting catch for the shutters on the exterior. Seeing a possible means of avoiding the dangerous jump, I yanked at the hangings and brought them down, pole and all; then quickly hooking two of the rings in the shutter catch and flinging the drapery outside. The heavy folds reached fully to the abutting roof, and I saw that the rings and catch would be likely to bear my weight. So, climbing out of the window and down the improvised rope ladder, I left behind me forever the morbid and horror-infested fabric of the Gilman House.

I landed safely on the loose slates of the steep roof, and succeeded in gaining the gaping black skylight without a slip. Glancing up at the window I had left, I observed it was still dark, though far across the crumbling chimneys to the north I could see lights ominously blazing in the Order of Dagon Hall, the Baptist church, and the Congregational church which I recalled so shiveringly. There had seemed to be no one in the courtyard below, and I hoped there would be a chance to get away before the spreading of a general alarm. Flashing my pocket lamp into the skylight, I saw that there were no steps down. The distance was slight, however, so I clambered over the brink and dropped; striking a dusty floor littered with crumbling boxes and barrels.

The place was ghoulish-looking, but I was past minding such impressions and made at once for the staircase revealed by my flashlight—after a hasty glance at my watch, which shewed the hour to be 2 a.m. The steps creaked, but seemed tolerably sound; and I raced down past a barn like second story to the ground floor. The desolation was complete, and only echoes answered my footfalls. At length I reached the lower hall, at one end of which I saw a faint luminous rectangle marking the ruined Paine Street doorway. Heading the other way, I found the back door also open; and darted out and down five stone steps to the grass-grown cobblestones of the courtyard.

The moonbeams did not reach down here, but I could just see my way about without using the flashlight. Some of the windows on the Gilman House side were faintly glowing, and I thought I heard confused sounds within. Walking softly over to the Washington Street side I perceived several open doorways, and chose the nearest as my route out. The hallway inside was black, and when I reached the opposite end I saw that the street door was wedged immovably shut. Resolved to try another building, I groped my way back toward the courtyard, but stopped short when close to the doorway.

For out of an opened door in the Gilman House a large crowd of doubtful shapes was pouring–lanterns bobbing in the darkness, and horrible croaking voices exchanging low cries in what was certainly not English. The figures moved uncertainly, and I realised to my relief that they did not know where I had gone; but for all that they sent a shiver of horror through my frame. Their features were indistinguishable, but their crouching, shambling gait was abominably repellent. And worst of all, I perceived that one figure was strangely robed, and unmistakably surmounted by a tall tiara of a design altogether too familiar. As the figures spread throughout the courtyard, I felt my fears increase. Suppose I could find no egress from this building on the street side? The fishy odour was detestable, and I wondered I could stand it without fainting. Again groping toward the street, I opened a door off the hall and came upon an empty room with closely shuttered but sashless windows. Fumbling in the rays of my flashlight, I found I could open the shutters; and in another moment had climbed outside and was carefully closing the aperture in its original manner.

I was now in Washington Street, and for the moment saw no living thing nor any light save that of the moon. From several directions in the distance, however, I could hear the sound of hoarse voices, of footsteps, and of a curious kind of pattering which did not sound quite like footsteps. Plainly I had no time to lose. The points of the compass were clear to me, and I was glad that all the street-lights were turned off, as is often the custom on strongly moonlit nights in unprosperous rural regions. Some of the sounds came from the south, yet I retained my design of escaping in that direction. There would, I knew, be plenty of deserted doorways to shelter me in case I met any person or group who looked like pursuers.

I walked rapidly, softly, and close to the ruined houses. While hatless and dishevelled after my arduous climb, I did not look especially noticeable; and stood a good chance of passing unheeded if forced to encounter any casual wayfarer. At Bates Street I drew into a yawning vestibule while two shambling figures crossed in front of me, but was soon on my way again and approaching the open space where Eliot Street obliquely crosses Washington at the intersection of South. Though I had never seen this space, it had looked dangerous to me on the grocery youth's map; since the moonlight would have free play there. There was no use trying to evade it, for any alternative course would involve detours of possibly disastrous visibility and delaying effect. The only thing to do was to cross it boldly and openly; imitating the typical shamble of the Innsmouth folk as best I could, and trusting that no one—or at least no pursuer of mine—would be there.

Just how fully the pursuit was organised—and indeed, just what its purpose might be—I could form no idea. There seemed to be unusual activity in the town, but I judged that the news of my escape from the Gilman had not yet spread. I would, of course, soon have to shift from Washington to some other southward street; for that party from the hotel would doubtless be after me. I must have left dust prints in that last old building, revealing how I had gained the street.

The open space was, as I had expected, strongly moonlit; and I saw the remains of a park-like, iron-railed green in its centre. Fortunately no one was about, though a curious sort of buzz or roar seemed to be increasing in the direction of Town Square. South Street was very wide, leading directly down a slight declivity to the waterfront and commanding a long view out at sea; and I hoped that no one would be glancing up it from afar as I crossed in the bright moonlight.

My progress was unimpeded, and no fresh sound arose to hint that I had been spied. Glancing about me, I involuntarily let my pace slacken for a second to take in the sight of the sea, gorgeous in the burning moonlight at the street's end. Far out beyond the breakwater was the dim, dark line of Devil Reef, and as I glimpsed it I could not help thinking of all the hideous legends I had heard in the last thirty-four hours—legends which portrayed this ragged rock as a veritable gateway to realms of unfathomed horror and inconceivable abnormality.

Then, without warning, I saw the intermittent flashes of light on the distant reef. They were definite and unmistakable, and awaked in my mind a blind horror beyond all rational proportion. My muscles tightened for panic flight, held in only by a certain unconscious caution and half-hypnotic fascination. And to make matters worse, there now flashed forth from the lofty cupola of the Gilman House, which loomed up to the northeast behind me, a series of analogous though differently spaced gleams which could be nothing less than an answering signal.

Controlling my muscles, and realising afresh how plainly visible I was, I resumed my brisker and feignedly shambling pace; though keeping my eyes on that hellish and ominous reef as long as the opening of South Street gave me a seaward view. What the whole proceeding meant, I could not imagine; unless it involved some strange rite connected with Devil Reef, or unless some party had landed from a ship on that sinister rock. I now bent to the left around the ruinous green; still gazing toward the ocean as it blazed in the spectral summer moonlight, and watching the cryptical flashing of those nameless, unexplainable beacons.

It was then that the most horrible impression of all was borne in upon me—the impression which destroyed my last vestige of self-control and set me running frantically southward past the yawning black doorways and fishily staring windows of that deserted nightmare street. For at a closer glance I saw that the moonlit waters between the reef and the shore were far from empty. They were alive with a teeming horde of shapes swimming inward toward the town; and even at my vast distance and in my single moment of perception I could tell that the bobbing heads and flailing arms were alien and aberrant in a way scarcely to be expressed or consciously formulated.

My frantic running ceased before I had covered a block, for at my left I began to hear something like the hue and cry of organised pursuit. There were footsteps and guttural sounds, and a rattling motor wheezed south along Federal Street. In a second all my plans were utterly changed—for if the southward highway were blocked ahead of me, I must clearly find another egress from Innsmouth. I paused and drew into a gaping doorway, reflecting how lucky I was to have left the moonlit open space before these pursuers came down the parallel street.

A second reflection was less comforting. Since the pursuit was down another street, it was plain that the party was not following me directly. It had not seen me, but was simply obeying a general plan of cutting off my escape. This, however, implied that all roads leading out of Innsmouth were similarly patrolled; for the denizens could not have known what route I intended to take. If this were so, I would have to make my retreat across country away from any road; but how could I do that in view of the marshy and creek-riddled nature of all the surrounding region? For a moment my brain reeled—both from sheer hopelessness and from a rapid increase in the omnipresent fishy odour.

Then I thought of the abandoned railway to Rowley, whose solid line of ballasted, weed-grown earth still stretched off to the northwest from the crumbling station on the edge of the river-gorge. There was just a chance that the townsfolk would not think of that; since its brier-choked desertion made it half-impassable, and the unlikeliest of all avenues for a fugitive to choose. I had seen it clearly from my hotel window, and knew about how it lay. Most of its earlier length was uncomfortably visible from the Rowley road, and from high places in the town itself; but one could perhaps crawl inconspicuously through the undergrowth. At any rate, it would form my only chance of deliverance, and there was nothing to do but try it.

Drawing inside the hall of my deserted shelter, I once more consulted the grocery boy's map with the aid of the flashlight. The immediate problem was how to reach the ancient railway; and I now saw that the safest course was ahead to Babson Street, then west to Lafayette—there edging around but not crossing an open space homologous to the one I had traversed—and subsequently back northward and westward in a zigzagging line through Lafayette, Bates, Adams, and Bank Streets—the latter skirting the river-gorge—to the abandoned and dilapidated station I had seen from my window. My reason for going ahead to Babson was that I wished neither to re-cross the earlier open space nor to begin my westward course along a cross street as broad as South.

Starting once more, I crossed the street to the right-hand side in order to edge around into Babson as inconspicuously as possible. Noises still continued in Federal Street, and as I glanced behind me I thought I saw a gleam of light near the building through which I had escaped. Anxious to leave Washington Street, I broke into a quiet dog-trot, trusting to luck not to encounter any observing eye. Next the corner of Babson Street I saw to my alarm that one of the houses was still inhabited, as attested by curtains at the window; but there were no lights within, and I passed it without disaster.

In Babson Street, which crossed Federal and might thus reveal me to the searchers, I clung as closely as possible to the sagging, uneven buildings; twice pausing in a doorway as the noises behind me momentarily increased. The open space ahead shone wide and desolate under the moon, but my route would not force me to cross it. During my second pause I began to detect a fresh distribution of the vague sounds; and upon looking cautiously out from cover beheld a motor-car darting across the open space, bound outward along Eliot Street, which there intersects both Babson and Lafayette.

As I watched—choked by a sudden rise in the fishy odour after a short abatement—I saw a band of uncouth, crouching shapes loping and shambling in the same direction; and knew that this must be the party guarding the Ipswich road, since that highway forms an extension of Eliot Street. Two of the figures I glimpsed were in voluminous robes, and one wore a peaked diadem which glistened whitely in the moonlight. The gait of this figure was so odd that it sent a chill through me—for it seemed to me the creature was almost hopping.

When the last of the band was out of sight I resumed my progress; darting around the corner into Lafayette Street, and crossing Eliot very hurriedly lest stragglers of the party be still advancing along that thoroughfare. I did hear some croaking and clattering sounds far off toward Town Square, but accomplished the passage without disaster. My greatest dread was in re-crossing broad and moonlit South Street—with its seaward view—and I had to nerve myself for the ordeal. Someone might easily be looking, and possible Eliot Street stragglers could not fail to glimpse me from either of two points. At the last moment I decided I had better slacken my trot and make the crossing as before in the shambling gait of an average Innsmouth native.

When the view of the water again opened out—this time on my right—I was half-determined not to look at it at all. I could not, however, resist; but cast a sidelong glance as I carefully and imitatively shambled toward the protecting shadows ahead. There was no ship visible, as I had half expected there would be. Instead, the first thing which caught my eye was a small rowboat pulling in toward the abandoned wharves and laden with some bulky, tarpaulin-covered object. Its rowers, though distantly and indistinctly seen, were of an especially repellent aspect. Several swimmers were still discernible; while on the far black reef I could see a faint, steady glow unlike the winking beacon visible before, and of a curious colour which I could not precisely identify. Above the slant roofs ahead and to the right there loomed the tall cupola of the Gilman House, but it was completely dark. The fishy odour, dispelled for a moment by some merciful breeze, now closed in again with maddening intensity.

I had not quite crossed the street when I heard a muttering band advancing along Washington from the north. As they reached the broad open space where I had had my first disquieting glimpse of the moonlit water I could see them plainly only a block away—and was horrified by the bestial abnormality of their faces and the dog-like sub-humanness of their crouching gait. One man moved in a positively simian way, with long arms frequently touching the ground; while another figure—robed and tiaraed—seemed to progress in an almost hopping fashion. I judged this party to be the one I had seen in the Gilman's courtyard—the one, therefore, most closely on my trail. As some of the figures turned to look in my direction I was transfixed with fright, yet managed to preserve the casual, shambling gait I had assumed. To this day I do not know whether they saw me or not. If they did, my stratagem must have deceived them, for they passed on across the moonlit space without varying their course—meanwhile croaking and jabbering in some hateful guttural patois I could not identify.

Once more in shadow, I resumed my former dog-trot past the leaning and decrepit houses that stared blankly into the night. Having crossed to the western sidewalk I rounded the nearest corner into Bates Street, where I kept close to the buildings on the southern side. I passed two houses shewing signs of habitation, one of which had faint lights in upper rooms, yet met with no obstacle. As I turned into Adams Street I felt measurably safer, but received a shock when a man reeled out of a black doorway directly in front of me. He proved, however, too hopelessly drunk to be a menace; so that I reached the dismal ruins of the Bank Street warehouses in safety.

No one was stirring in that dead street beside the river-gorge, and the roar of the waterfalls quite drowned my footsteps. It was a long dog-trot to the ruined station, and the great brick warehouse walls around me seemed somehow more terrifying than the fronts of private houses. At last I saw the ancient arcaded station—or what was left of it—and made directly for the tracks that started from its farther end.

The rails were rusty but mainly intact, and not more than half the ties had rotted away. Walking or running on such a surface was very difficult; but I did my best, and on the whole made very fair time. For some distance the line kept on along the gorge's brink, but at length I reached the long covered bridge where it crossed the chasm at a dizzy height. The condition of this bridge would determine my next step. If humanly possible, I would use it; if not, I would have to risk more street wandering and take the nearest intact highway bridge.

The vast, barn-like length of the old bridge gleamed spectrally in the moonlight, and I saw that the ties were safe for at least a few feet within. Entering, I began to use my flashlight, and was almost knocked down by the cloud of bats that flapped past me. About half way across there was a perilous gap in the ties which I feared for a moment would halt me; but in the end I risked a desperate jump which fortunately succeeded.

I was glad to see the moonlight again when I emerged from that macabre tunnel. The old tracks crossed River Street at grade, and at once veered off into a region increasingly rural and with less and less of Innsmouth's abhorrent fishy odour. Here the dense growth of weeds and briers hindered me and cruelly tore my clothes, but I was none the less glad that they were there to give me concealment in case of peril. I knew that much of my route must be visible from the Rowley road.

The marshy region began very shortly, with the single track on a low, grassy embankment where the weedy growth was somewhat thinner. Then came a sort of island of higher ground, where the line passed through a shallow open cut choked with bushes and brambles. I was very glad of this partial shelter, since at this point the Rowley road was uncomfortably near according to my window view. At the end of the cut it would cross the track and swerve off to a safer distance; but meanwhile I must be exceedingly careful. I was by this time thankfully certain that the railway itself was not patrolled.

Just before entering the cut I glanced behind me, but saw no pursuer. The ancient spires and roofs of decaying Innsmouth gleamed lovely and ethereal in the magic yellow moonlight, and I thought of how they must have looked in the old days before the shadow fell. Then, as my gaze circled inland from the town, something less tranquil arrested my notice and held me immobile for a second.

What I saw—or fancied I saw—was a disturbing suggestion of undulant motion far to the south; a suggestion which made me conclude that a very large horde must be pouring out of the city along the level Ipswich road. The distance was great, and

I could distinguish nothing in detail; but I did not at all like the look of that moving column. It undulated too much, and glistened too brightly in the rays of the now westering moon. There was a suggestion of sound, too, though the wind was blowing the other way—a suggestion of bestial scraping and bellowing even worse than the muttering of the parties I had lately overheard.

All sorts of unpleasant conjectures crossed my mind. I thought of those very extreme Innsmouth types said to be hidden in crumbling, centuried warrens near the waterfront. I thought, too, of those nameless swimmers I had seen. Counting the parties so far glimpsed, as well as those presumably covering other roads, the number of my pursuers must be strangely large for a town as depopulated as Innsmouth.

Whence could come the dense personnel of such a column as I now beheld? Did those ancient, unplumbed warrens teem with a twisted, uncatalogued, and unsuspected life? Or had some unseen ship indeed landed a legion of unknown outsiders on that hellish reef? Who were they? Why were they there? And if such a column of them was scouring the Ipswich road, would the patrols on the other roads be likewise augmented?

I had entered the brush-grown cut and was struggling along at a very slow pace when that damnable fishy odour again waxed dominant. Had the wind suddenly changed eastward, so that it blew in from the sea and over the town? It must have, I concluded, since I now began to hear shocking guttural murmurs from that hitherto silent direction. There was another sound, too—a kind of wholesale, colossal flopping or pattering which somehow called up images of the most detestable sort. It made me think illogically of that unpleasantly undulating column on the far-off Ipswich road.

And then both stench and sounds grew stronger, so that I paused shivering and grateful for the cut's protection. It was here, I recalled, that the Rowley road drew so close to the old railway before crossing westward and diverging. Something was coming along that road, and I must lie low till its passage and vanishment in the distance. Thank heaven these creatures employed no dogs for tracking—though perhaps that would have been impossible amidst the omnipresent regional odour. Crouched in the bushes of that sandy cleft I felt reasonably safe, even though I knew the searchers would have to cross the track in front of me not much more than a hundred yards away. I would be able to see them, but they could not, except by a malign miracle, see me.

All at once I began dreading to look at them as they passed. I saw the close moonlit space where they would surge by, and had curious thoughts about the irredeemable pollution of that space. They would perhaps be the worst of all Innsmouth types—something one would not care to remember.

The stench waxed overpowering, and the noises swelled to a bestial babel of croaking, baying, and barking without the least suggestion of human speech. Were these indeed the voices of my pursuers? Did they have dogs after all? So far I had seen none of the lower animals in Innsmouth. That flopping or pattering was monstrous—I could not look upon the degenerate creatures responsible for it. I would keep my eyes shut till the sounds receded toward the west. The horde was very close now—the air foul with their hoarse snarlings, and the ground almost shaking with their alien-rhythmed footfalls. My breath nearly ceased to come, and I put every ounce of will power into the task of holding my eyelids down.

I am not even yet willing to say whether what followed was a hideous actuality or only a nightmare hallucination. The later action of the government, after my frantic appeals, would tend to confirm it as a monstrous truth; but could not an hallucination have been repeated under the quasi-hypnotic spell of that ancient, haunted, and shadowed town? Such places have strange properties, and the legacy of insane legend might well have acted on more than one human imagination amidst those dead, stench-cursed streets and huddles of rotting roofs and crumbling steeples. Is it not possible that the germ of an actual contagious madness lurks in the depths of that shadow over Innsmouth? Who can be sure of reality after hearing things like the tale of old Zadok Allen? The government men never found poor Zadok, and have no conjectures to make as to what became of him. Where does madness leave off and reality begin? Is it possible that even my latest fear is sheer delusion?

But I must try to tell what I thought I saw that night under the mocking yellow moon—saw surging and hopping down the Rowley road in plain sight in front of me as I crouched among the wild brambles of that desolate railway cut. Of course my resolution to keep my eyes shut had failed. It was foredoomed to failure—for who could crouch blindly while a legion of croaking, baying entities of unknown source flopped noisomely past, scarcely more than a hundred yards away?

I thought I was prepared for the worst, and I really ought to have been prepared considering what I had seen before. My other pursuers had been accursedly abnormal—so should I not have been ready to face a *strengthening* of the abnormal element; to look upon forms in which there was no mixture of the normal at all? I did not open my eyes until the raucous clamour came loudly from a point obviously straight ahead. Then

I knew that a long section of them must be plainly in sight where the sides of the cut flattened out and the road crossed the track—and I could no longer keep myself from sampling whatever horror that leering yellow moon might have to shew.

It was the end, for whatever remains to me of life on the surface of this earth, of every vestige of mental peace and confidence in the integrity of Nature and of the human mind. Nothing that I could have imagined—nothing, even, that I could have gathered had I credited old Zadok's crazy tale in the most literal way—would be in any way comparable to the daemoniac, blasphemous reality that I saw—or believe I saw. I have tried to hint what it was in order to postpone the horror of writing it down baldly. Can it be possible that this planet has actually spawned such things; that human eyes have truly seen, as objective flesh, what man has hitherto known only in febrile phantasy and tenuous legend?

And yet I saw them in a limitless stream—flopping, hopping, croaking, bleating—surging inhumanly through the spectral moonlight in a grotesque, malignant saraband of fantastic nightmare. And some of them had tall tiaras of that nameless whitish-gold metal...and some were strangely robed...and one, who led the way, was clad in a ghoulishly humped black coat and striped trousers, and had a man's felt hat perched on the shapeless thing that answered for a head...

I think their predominant colour was a greyish-green, though they had white bellies. They were mostly shiny and slippery, but the ridges of their backs were scaly. Their forms vaguely suggested the anthropoid, while their heads were the heads of fish, with prodigious bulging eyes that never closed. At the sides of their necks were palpitating gills, and their long paws were webbed. They hopped irregularly, sometimes on two legs and sometimes on four. I was somehow glad that they had no more than four limbs. Their croaking, baying voices, clearly used for articulate speech, held all the dark shades of expression which their staring faces lacked.

But for all of their monstrousness they were not unfamiliar to me. I knew too well what they must be—for was not the memory of that evil tiara at Newburyport still fresh? They were the blasphemous fish-frogs of the nameless design—living and horrible—and as I saw them I knew also of what that humped, tiaraed priest in the black church basement had so fearsomely reminded me. Their number was past guessing. It seemed to me that there were limitless swarms of them—and certainly my momentary glimpse could have shewn only the least fraction. In another instant everything was blotted out by a merciful fit of fainting; the first I had ever had.

V.

It was a gentle daylight rain that awaked me from my stupor in the brush-grown railway cut, and when I staggered out to the roadway ahead I saw no trace of any prints in the fresh mud. The fishy odour, too, was gone. Innsmouth's ruined roofs and toppling steeples loomed up greyly toward the southeast, but not a living creature did I spy in all the desolate salt marshes around. My watch was still going, and told me that the hour was past noon.

The reality of what I had been through was highly uncertain in my mind, but I felt that something hideous lay in the background. I must get away from evil-shadowed Innsmouth—and accordingly I began to test my cramped, wearied powers of locomotion. Despite weakness, hunger, horror, and bewilderment I found myself after a long time able to walk; so started slowly along the muddy road to Rowley. Before evening I was in the village, getting a meal and providing myself with presentable clothes. I caught the night train to Arkham, and the next day talked long and earnestly with government officials there; a process I later repeated in Boston. With the main result of these colloquies the public is now familiar—and I wish, for normality's sake, there were nothing more to tell. Perhaps it is madness that is overtaking me—yet perhaps a greater horror—or a greater marvel—is reaching out.

As may well be imagined, I gave up most of the foreplanned features of the rest of my tour—the scenic, architectural, and antiquarian diversions on which I had counted so heavily. Nor did I dare look for that piece of strange jewellery said to be in the Miskatonic University Museum. I did, however, improve my stay in Arkham by collecting some genealogical notes I had long wished to possess; very rough and hasty data, it is true, but capable of good use later on when I might have time to collate and codify them. The curator of the historical society there—Mr. E. Lapham Peabody—was very courteous about assisting me, and expressed unusual interest when I told him I was a grandson of Eliza Orne of Arkham, who was born in 1867 and had married James Williamson of Ohio at the age of seventeen.

It seemed that a maternal uncle of mine had been there many years before on a quest much like my own; and that my grandmother's family was a topic of some local curiosity. There had, Mr. Peabody said, been considerable discussion about the marriage of her father, Benjamin Orne, just after the Civil War; since the ancestry of the bride was peculiarly puzzling. That bride was understood to have been an orphaned

Marsh of New Hampshire—a cousin of the Essex County Marshes—but her education had been in France and she knew very little of her family. A guardian had deposited funds in a Boston bank to maintain her and her French governess; but that guardian's name was unfamiliar to Arkham people, and in time he dropped out of sight, so that the governess assumed his role by court appointment. The Frenchwoman—now long dead—was very taciturn, and there were those who said she could have told more than she did.

But the most baffling thing was the inability of anyone to place the recorded parents of the young woman—Enoch and Lydia (Meserve) Marsh—among the known families of New Hampshire. Possibly, many suggested, she was the natural daughter of some Marsh of prominence—she certainly had the true Marsh eyes. Most of the puzzling was done after her early death, which took place at the birth of my grandmother—her only child. Having formed some disagreeable impressions connected with the name of Marsh, I did not welcome the news that it belonged on my own ancestral tree; nor was I pleased by Mr. Peabody's suggestion that I had the true Marsh eyes myself. However, I was grateful for data which I knew would prove valuable; and took copious notes and lists of book references regarding the well-documented Orne family.

I went directly home to Toledo from Boston, and later spent a month at Maumee recuperating from my ordeal. In September I entered Oberlin for my final year, and from then till the next June was busy with studies and other wholesome activities—reminded of the bygone terror only by occasional official visits from government men in connexion with the campaign which my pleas and evidence had started. Around the middle of July—just a year after the Innsmouth experience—I spent a week with my late mother's family in Cleveland; checking some of my new genealogical data with the various notes, traditions, and bits of heirloom material in existence there, and seeing what kind of connected chart I could construct.

I did not exactly relish the task, for the atmosphere of the Williamson home had always depressed me. There was a strain of morbidity there, and my mother had never encouraged my visiting her parents as a child, although she always welcomed her father when he came to Toledo. My Arkham-born grandmother had seemed strange and almost terrifying to me, and I do not think I grieved when she disappeared. I was eight years old then, and it was said that she had wandered off in grief after the suicide of my uncle Douglas, her eldest son. He had shot himself after a trip to New England—the same trip, no doubt, which had caused him to be recalled at the Arkham Historical Society.

This uncle had resembled her, and I had never liked him either. Something about the staring, unwinking expression of both of them had given me a vague, unaccountable uneasiness. My mother and uncle Walter had not looked like that. They were like their father, though poor little cousin Lawrence—Walter's son—had been an almost perfect duplicate of his grandmother before his condition took him to the permanent seclusion of a sanitarium at Canton. I had not seen him in four years, but my uncle once implied that his state, both mental and physical, was very bad. This worry had probably been a major cause of his mother's death two years before.

My grandfather and his widowed son Walter now comprised the Cleveland household, but the memory of older times hung thickly over it. I still disliked the place, and tried to get my researches done as quickly as possible. Williamson records and traditions were supplied in abundance by my grandfather; though for Orne material I had to depend on my uncle Walter, who put at my disposal the contents of all his files, including notes, letters, cuttings, heirlooms, photographs, and miniatures.

It was in going over the letters and pictures on the Orne side that I began to acquire a kind of terror of my own ancestry. As I have said, my grandmother and uncle Douglas had always disturbed me. Now, years after their passing, I gazed at their pictured faces with a measurably heightened feeling of repulsion and alienation. I could not at first understand the change, but gradually a horrible *sort of comparison* began to obtrude itself on my unconscious mind despite the steady refusal of my consciousness to admit even the least suspicion of it. It was clear that the typical expression of these faces now suggested something it had not suggested before—something which would bring stark panic if too openly thought of.

But the worst shock came when my uncle shewed me the Orne jewellery in a downtown safe-deposit vault. Some of the items were delicate and inspiring enough, but there was one box of strange old pieces descended from my mysterious great-grandmother which my uncle was almost reluctant to produce. They were, he said, of very grotesque and almost repulsive design, and had never to his knowledge been publicly worn; though my grandmother used to enjoy looking at them. Vague legends of bad luck clustered around them, and my great-grandmother's French governess had said they ought not to be worn in New England, though it would be quite safe to wear them in Europe.

As my uncle began slowly and grudgingly to unwrap the things he urged me not to be shocked by the strangeness and frequent hideousness of the designs. Artists and archaeologists who had seen them pronounced the workmanship superlatively and exotically exquisite, though no one seemed able to define their exact material or assign them to any specific art tradition. There were two armlets, a tiara, and a kind of pectoral; the latter having in high relief certain figures of almost unbearable extravagance.

During this description I had kept a tight rein on my emotions, but my face must have betrayed my mounting fears. My uncle looked concerned, and paused in his unwrapping to study my countenance. I motioned to him to continue, which he did with renewed signs of reluctance. He seemed to expect some demonstration when the first piece—the tiara—became visible, but I doubt if he expected quite what actually happened. I did not expect it, either, for I thought I was thoroughly forewarned regarding what the jewellery would turn out to be. What I did was to faint silently away, just as I had done in that brier-choked railway cut a year before.

From that day on my life has been a nightmare of brooding and apprehension, nor do I know how much is hideous truth and how much madness. My great-grandmother had been a Marsh of unknown source whose husband lived in Arkham—and did not old Zadok say that the daughter of Obed Marsh by a monstrous mother was married to an Arkham man through a trick? What was it the ancient toper had muttered about the likeness of my eyes to Captain Obed's? In Arkham, too, the curator had told me I had the true Marsh eyes. Was Obed Marsh my own great-great-grandfather? Who—or what—then, was my great-great-grandmother? But perhaps this was all madness. Those whitish-gold ornaments might easily have been bought from some Innsmouth sailor by the father of my great-grandmother, whoever he was. And that look in the staring-eyed faces of my grandmother and self-slain uncle might be sheer fancy on my part—sheer fancy, bolstered up by the Innsmouth shadow which had so darkly coloured my imagination. But why had my uncle killed himself after an ancestral quest in New England?

For more than two years I fought off these reflections with partial success. My father secured me a place in an insurance office, and I buried myself in routine as deeply as possible. In the winter of 1930–31, however, the dreams began. They were very sparse and insidious at first, but increased in frequency and vividness as the weeks went by. Great watery spaces opened out before me, and I seemed to wander through titanic sunken porticos and labyrinths of weedy Cyclopean walls with grotesque fishes as my companions. Then the other shapes began to appear, filling me with nameless horror the moment I awoke. But during the dreams they did not horrify me at all—I was one with them; wearing their unhuman trappings, treading their aqueous ways, and praying monstrously at their evil sea-bottom temples.

There was much more than I could remember, but even what I did remember each morning would be enough to stamp me as a madman or a genius if ever I dared write it down. Some frightful influence, I felt, was seeking gradually to drag me out of the sane world of wholesome life into unnamable abysses of blackness and alienage; and the process told heavily on me. My health and appearance grew steadily worse, till finally I was forced to give up my position and adopt the static, secluded life of an invalid. Some odd nervous affliction had me in its grip, and I found myself at times almost unable to shut my eyes.

It was then that I began to study the mirror with mounting alarm. The slow ravages of disease are not pleasant to watch, but in my case there was something subtler and more puzzling in the background. My father seemed to notice it, too, for he began looking at me curiously and almost affrightedly. What was taking place in me? Could it be that I was coming to resemble my grandmother and uncle Douglas?

One night I had a frightful dream in which I met my grandmother under the sea. She lived in a phosphorescent palace of many terraces, with gardens of strange leprous corals and grotesque brachiate efflorescences, and welcomed me with a warmth that may have been sardonic. She had changed—as those who take to the water change—and told me she had never died. Instead, she had gone to a spot her dead son had learned about, and had leaped to a realm whose wonders—destined for him as well—he had spurned with a smoking pistol. This was to be my realm, too—I could not escape it. I would never die, but would live with those who had lived since before man ever walked the earth.

I met also that which had been her grandmother. For eighty thousand years Pth'thya-l'yi had lived in Y'ha-nthlei, and thither she had gone back after Obed Marsh was dead. Y'ha-nthlei was not destroyed when the upper-earth men shot death into the sea. It was hurt, but not destroyed. The Deep Ones could never be destroyed, even though the palaeogean magic of the forgotten Old Ones might sometimes check them. For the present they would rest; but some day, if they remembered, they would rise again for the tribute Great Cthulhu craved. It would be a city greater than Innsmouth next time. They had planned to spread, and had brought up that which would help them, but now they must wait once more. For bringing the upper-earth men's death I must do a penance, but that would not be heavy. This was the dream in which I saw a shoggoth for the first time, and the sight set me awake in a frenzy of screaming. That morning the mirror definitely told me I had acquired the Innsmouth look.

So far I have not shot myself as my uncle Douglas did. I bought an automatic and almost took the step, but certain dreams deterred me. The tense extremes of horror are lessening, and I feel queerly drawn toward the unknown sea-deeps instead of fearing them. I hear and do strange things in sleep, and awake with a kind of exaltation instead of terror. I do not believe I need to wait for the full change as most have waited. If I did, my father would probably shut me up in a sanitarium as my poor little cousin is shut up. Stupendous and unheard-of splendours await me below, and I shall seek them soon. *Iä-R'lyeh! Cthulhu fhtagn! Iä! Iä!* No, I shall not shoot myself—I cannot be made to shoot myself!

I shall plan my cousin's escape from that Canton madhouse, and together we shall go to marvel-shadowed Innsmouth. We shall swim out to that brooding reef in the sea and dive down through black abysses to Cyclopean and many-columned Y'ha-nthlei, and in that lair of the Deep Ones we shall dwell amidst wonder and glory for ever.

The Call of Cthulhu

"The Call of Cthulhu" has become synonymous with the name H.P. Lovecraft, though the story came from inauspicious beginnings. As with many of Lovecraft's works, it was first conceived in 1919 in a series of strange dreams. These haunting visions would gestate until 1925 when Lovecraft began sketching out a full-length narrative. Finally finishing the story in 1926, and despite the half-decade he devoted to writing it, Lovecraft considered "The Call of Cthulhu" to be one of his "middling" works. The editor of Weird Tales *shared this low opinion and refused to buy the story until one of Lovecraft's friends lied, claiming that Lovecraft was shopping it to another magazine. Only Robert E. Howard, Lovecraft's friend and confidant, was initially optimistic about the story, proclaiming it to be a masterpiece. Eventually published in the February 1928 issue of* Weird Tales, *"The Call of Cthulhu" would go on to become Lovecraft's most recognizable work, an archetype of American horror, though the story itself has been directly adapted on only a few occassions.*

Found among the papers of the late
Francis Wayland Thurston, of Boston.

"Of such great powers or beings there may be conceivably a survival...a survival of a hugely remote period when...consciousness was manifested, perhaps, in shapes and forms long since withdrawn before the tide of advancing humanity...forms of which poetry and legend alone have caught a flying memory and called them gods, monsters, mythical beings of all sorts and kinds..."

-Algernon Blackwood

I. The Horror in Clay

The most merciful thing in the world, I think, is the inability of the human mind to correlate all its contents. We live on a placid island of ignorance in the midst of black seas of infinity, and it was not meant that we should voyage far. The sciences, each straining in its own direction, have hitherto harmed us little; but some day the piecing together of dissociated knowledge will open up such terrifying vistas of reality, and of our frightful position therein, that we shall either go mad from the revelation or flee from the deadly light into the peace and safety of a new dark age.

Theosophists have guessed at the awesome grandeur of the cosmic cycle wherein our world and human race form transient incidents. They have hinted at strange survivals in terms which would freeze the blood if not masked by a bland optimism. But it is not from them that there came the single glimpse of forbidden aeons which chills me when I think of it and maddens me when I dream of it. That glimpse, like all dread glimpses of truth, flashed out from an accidental piecing together of separated things—in this case an old newspaper item and the notes of a dead professor. I hope that no one else will accomplish this piecing out; certainly, if I live, I shall never knowingly supply a link in so hideous a chain. I think that the professor, too, intended to keep silent regarding the part he knew, and that he would have destroyed his notes had not sudden death seized him.

My knowledge of the thing began in the winter of 1926–27 with the death of my grand-uncle George Gammell Angell, Professor Emeritus of Semitic Languages in Brown University, Providence, Rhode Island. Professor Angell was widely known as an authority on ancient inscriptions, and had frequently been resorted to by the heads of prominent museums; so that his passing at the age of ninety-two may be recalled by many. Locally, interest was intensified by the obscurity of the cause of death. The professor had been stricken whilst returning from the Newport boat; falling suddenly, as witnesses said, after having been jostled by a nautical-looking negro who had come from one of the queer dark courts on the precipitous hillside which formed a short cut from the waterfront to the deceased's home in Williams Street. Physicians were unable to find any visible disorder, but concluded after perplexed debate that some obscure lesion of the heart, induced by the brisk ascent of so steep a hill by so elderly a man, was responsible for the end. At the time I saw no reason to dissent from this dictum, but latterly I am inclined to wonder—and more than wonder.

As my grand-uncle's heir and executor, for he died a childless widower, I was expected to go over his papers with some thoroughness; and for that purpose moved his entire set of files and boxes to my quarters in Boston. Much of the material which I correlated will be later published by the American Archaeological Society, but there was one box which I found exceedingly puzzling, and which I felt much averse from shewing to other eyes. It had been locked, and I did not find the key till it occurred to me to examine the personal ring which the professor carried always in his pocket. Then indeed I succeeded in opening it, but when I did so seemed only to be confronted by a greater and more closely locked barrier. For what could be the meaning of the queer clay bas-relief and the disjointed jottings, ramblings, and cuttings which I found? Had my uncle, in his latter years, become credulous of the most superficial impostures? I resolved to search out the eccentric sculptor responsible for this apparent disturbance of an old man's peace of mind.

The bas-relief was a rough rectangle less than an inch thick and about five by six inches in area; obviously of modern origin. Its designs, however, were far from modern in atmosphere and suggestion; for although the vagaries of cubism and futurism are many and wild, they do not often reproduce that cryptic regularity which lurks in prehistoric writing. And writing of some kind the bulk of these designs seemed certainly to be;

though my memory, despite much familiarity with the papers and collections of my uncle, failed in any way to identify this particular species, or even to hint at its remotest affiliations.

Above these apparent hieroglyphics was a figure of evidently pictorial intent, though its impressionistic execution forbade a very clear idea of its nature. It seemed to be a sort of monster, or symbol representing a monster, of a form which only a diseased fancy could conceive. If I say that my somewhat extravagant imagination yielded simultaneous pictures of an octopus, a dragon, and a human caricature, I shall not be unfaithful to the spirit of the thing. A pulpy, tentacled head surmounted a grotesque and scaly body with rudimentary wings; but it was the general outline of the whole which made it most shockingly frightful. Behind the figure was a vague suggestion of a Cyclopean architectural background.

The writing accompanying this oddity was, aside from a stack of press cuttings, in Professor Angell's most recent hand; and made no pretence to literary style. What seemed to be the main document was headed "CTHULHU CULT" in characters painstakingly printed to avoid the erroneous reading of a word so unheard-of. The manuscript was divided into two sections, the first of which was headed "1925–Dream and Dream Work of H.A. Wilcox, 7 Thomas St., Providence, R.I.," and the second, "Narrative of Inspector John R. Legrasse, 121 Bienville St., New Orleans, La., at 1908 A.A.S. Mtg.–Notes on Same, & Prof. Webb's Acct." The other manuscript papers were all brief notes, some of them accounts of the queer dreams of different persons, some of them citations from theosophical books and magazines (notably W. Scott-Elliot's *Atlantis and the Lost Lemuria*), and the rest comments on long-surviving secret societies and hidden cults, with references to passages in such mythological and anthropological source-books as Frazer's *Golden Bough* and Miss Murray's *Witch-Cult in Western Europe*. The cuttings largely alluded to outré mental illnesses and outbreaks of group folly or mania in the spring of 1925.

The first half of the principal manuscript told a very peculiar tale. It appears that on March 1st, 1925, a thin, dark young man of neurotic and excited aspect had called upon Professor Angell bearing the singular clay bas-relief, which was then exceedingly damp and fresh. His card bore the name of Henry Anthony Wilcox, and my uncle had recognised him as the youngest son of an excellent family slightly known to him, who had latterly been studying sculpture at the Rhode Island School of Design and living alone at the Fleur-de-Lys Building near that institution. Wilcox was a precocious youth of known genius but great eccentricity, and had from childhood excited attention through the strange stories and odd dreams he was in the habit of relating. He called himself "psychically hypersensitive," but the staid folk of the ancient commercial city dismissed him as merely "queer." Never mingling much with his kind, he had dropped gradually from social visibility, and was now known only to a small group of aesthetes from other towns. Even the Providence Art Club, anxious to preserve its conservatism, had found him quite hopeless.

On the occasion of the visit, ran the professor's manuscript, the sculptor abruptly asked for the benefit of his host's archaeological knowledge in identifying the hieroglyphics on the bas-relief. He spoke in a dreamy, stilted manner which suggested pose and alienated sympathy; and my uncle shewed some sharpness in replying, for the conspicuous freshness of the tablet implied kinship with anything but archaeology. Young Wilcox's rejoinder, which impressed my uncle enough to make him recall and record it verbatim, was of a fantastically poetic cast which must have typified his whole conversation, and which I have since found highly characteristic of him. He said, "It is new, indeed, for I made it last night in a dream of strange cities; and dreams are older than brooding Tyre, or the contemplative Sphinx, or garden-girdled Babylon."

It was then that he began that rambling tale which suddenly played upon a sleeping memory and won the fevered interest of my uncle. There had been a slight earthquake tremor the night before, the most considerable felt in New England for some years; and Wilcox's imagination had been keenly affected. Upon retiring, he had had an unprecedented dream of great Cyclopean cities of titan blocks and sky-flung monoliths, all dripping with green ooze and sinister with latent horror. Hieroglyphics had covered the walls and pillars, and from some undetermined point below had come a voice that was not a voice; a chaotic sensation which only fancy could transmute into sound, but which he attempted to render by the almost unpronounceable jumble of letters, *"Cthulhu fhtagn."*

This verbal jumble was the key to the recollection which excited and disturbed Professor Angell. He questioned the sculptor with scientific minuteness; and studied with almost frantic intensity the bas-relief on which the youth had found himself working, chilled and clad only in his night-clothes, when waking had stolen bewilderingly over him. My uncle blamed his old age, Wilcox afterward said, for his slowness in recognising both hieroglyphics and pictorial design. Many of his questions seemed highly out-of-place to his visitor, especially those which tried to connect the latter with strange cults or societies; and Wilcox could not understand the repeated promises of silence which he was offered in exchange for an admission of membership in some widespread mystical or paganly religious body. When Professor Angell became convinced that the sculptor was indeed ignorant of any cult or system of cryptic lore, he besieged his visitor with demands for future reports of dreams. This bore regular fruit, for after the first interview the manuscript records daily calls of the young man, during which he related startling fragments of nocturnal imagery whose burden was always some terrible Cyclopean vista of dark and dripping stone, with a subterrene voice or intelligence shouting monotonously in enigmatical sense-impacts uninscribable save as gibberish. The two sounds most frequently repeated are those rendered by the letters *"Cthulhu"* and *"R'lyeh."*

On March 23rd, the manuscript continued, Wilcox failed to appear; and inquiries at his quarters revealed that he had been stricken with an obscure sort of fever and taken to the home of his family in Waterman Street. He had cried out in the night, arousing several other artists in the building, and had manifested since then only alternations of unconsciousness and delirium. My uncle at once telephoned the family, and from that time forward kept close watch of the case; calling often at the Thayer Street office of Dr. Tobey, whom he learned to be in charge. The youth's febrile mind, apparently, was dwelling on strange things; and the doctor shuddered now and then as he spoke of them. They included not only a repetition of what he had formerly dreamed, but touched wildly on a gigantic thing "miles high" which walked or lumbered about. He at no time fully described this object, but occasional frantic words, as repeated by Dr. Tobey, convinced the professor that it must be identical with the nameless monstrosity he had sought to depict in his dream-sculpture. Reference to this object, the doctor added, was invariably a prelude to the young man's subsidence into lethargy. His temperature, oddly enough, was not greatly above normal; but his whole condition was otherwise such as to suggest true fever rather than mental disorder.

On April 2nd at about 3 p.m. every trace of Wilcox's malady suddenly ceased. He sat upright in bed, astonished to find himself at home and completely ignorant of what had happened in dream or reality since the night of March 22nd. Pronounced well by his physician, he returned to his quarters in three days; but to Professor Angell he was of no further assistance. All traces of strange dreaming had vanished with his recovery, and my uncle kept no record of his night-thoughts after a week of pointless and irrelevant accounts of thoroughly usual visions.

Here the first part of the manuscript ended, but references to certain of the scattered notes gave me much material for thought—so much, in fact, that only the ingrained scepticism then forming my philosophy can account for my continued distrust of the artist. The notes in question were those descriptive of the dreams of various persons covering the same period as that in which young Wilcox had had his strange visitations. My uncle, it seems, had quickly instituted a prodigiously far-flung body of inquiries amongst nearly all the friends whom he could question without impertinence, asking for nightly reports of their dreams, and the dates of any notable visions for some time past. The reception of his request seems to have been varied; but he must, at the very least, have received more responses than any ordinary man could have handled without a secretary. This original correspondence was not preserved, but his notes formed a thorough and really significant digest. Average people in society and business—New England's traditional "salt of the earth"—gave an almost completely negative result, though scattered cases of uneasy but formless nocturnal impressions appear here and there, always between March 23rd and April 2nd—the period of young Wilcox's delirium. Scientific men were little more affected, though four cases of vague description suggest fugitive glimpses of strange landscapes, and in one case there is mentioned a dread of something abnormal.

It was from the artists and poets that the pertinent answers came, and I know that panic would have broken loose had they been able to compare notes. As it was, lacking their original letters, I half suspected the compiler of having asked leading questions, or of having edited the correspondence in corroboration of what he had latently resolved to see. That is why I continued to feel that Wilcox, somehow cognisant of the old data which my uncle had possessed, had been imposing on the veteran scientist. These responses from aesthetes told a disturbing tale. From February 28th to April 2nd a large proportion of them had dreamed very bizarre things, the intensity of the dreams being immeasurably the stronger during the period of the sculptor's delirium. Over a fourth of those who reported anything, reported scenes and half-sounds not unlike those which Wilcox had described; and some of the dreamers confessed acute fear of the gigantic nameless thing visible toward the last. One case, which the note describes with emphasis, was very sad. The subject, a widely known architect with leanings toward theosophy and occultism, went violently insane on the date of young Wilcox's seizure, and expired several months later after incessant screamings to be saved from some escaped denizen of hell. Had my uncle referred to these cases by name instead of merely by number, I should have attempted some corroboration and personal investigation; but as it was, I succeeded in tracing down only a few. All of these, however, bore out the notes in full. I have often wondered if all the objects of the professor's questioning felt as puzzled as did this fraction. It is well that no explanation shall ever reach them.

The press cuttings, as I have intimated, touched on cases of panic, mania, and eccentricity during the given period. Professor Angell must have employed a cutting bureau, for the number of extracts was tremendous and the sources scattered throughout the globe. Here was a nocturnal suicide in London, where a lone sleeper had leaped from a window after a shocking cry. Here likewise a rambling letter to the editor of a paper in South America, where a fanatic deduces a dire future from visions he has seen. A despatch from California describes a theosophist colony as donning white robes en masse for some "glorious fulfilment" which never arrives, whilst items from India speak guardedly of serious native unrest toward the end of March. Voodoo orgies multiply in Hayti, and African outposts report ominous mutterings. American officers in the Philippines find certain tribes bothersome about this time, and New York policemen are mobbed by hysterical Levantines on the night of March 22nd–23rd. The west of Ireland, too, is full of wild rumour and legendry, and a fantastic painter named Ardois-Bonnot hangs a blasphemous "Dream Landscape" in the Paris spring salon of 1926. And so numerous are the recorded troubles in insane asylums, that only a miracle can have stopped the medical fraternity from noting strange parallelisms and drawing mystified conclusions. A weird bunch of cuttings, all told; and I can at this date scarcely envisage the callous rationalism with which I set them aside. But I was then convinced that young Wilcox had known of the older matters mentioned by the professor.

II. The Tale of Inspector Legrasse

The older matters which had made the sculptor's dream and bas-relief so significant to my uncle formed the subject of the second half of his long manuscript. Once before, it appears, Professor Angell had seen the hellish outlines of the nameless monstrosity, puzzled over the unknown hieroglyphics, and heard the ominous syllables which can be rendered only as "Cthulhu;" and all this in so stirring and horrible a connexion that it is small wonder he pursued young Wilcox with queries and demands for data.

The earlier experience had come in 1908, seventeen years before, when the American Archaeological Society held its annual meeting in St. Louis. Professor Angell, as befitted one of his authority and attainments, had had a prominent part in all the deliberations; and was one of the first to be approached by the several outsiders who took advantage of the convocation to offer questions for correct answering and problems for expert solution.

The chief of these outsiders, and in a short time the focus of interest for the entire meeting, was a commonplace-looking middle-aged man who had travelled all the way from New Orleans for certain special information unobtainable from any local source. His name was John Raymond Legrasse, and he was by profession an Inspector of Police. With him he bore the subject of his visit, a grotesque, repulsive, and apparently very ancient stone statuette whose origin he was at a loss to determine. It must not be fancied that Inspector Legrasse had the least interest in archaeology. On the contrary, his wish for enlightenment was prompted by purely professional considerations. The statuette, idol, fetish, or whatever it was, had been captured some months before in the wooded swamps south of New Orleans during a raid on a supposed voodoo meeting; and so singular and hideous were the rites connected with it, that the police could not but realise that they had stumbled on a dark cult totally unknown to them, and infinitely more diabolic than even the blackest of the African voodoo circles. Of its origin, apart from the erratic and unbelievable tales extorted from the captured members, absolutely nothing was to be discovered; hence the anxiety of the police for any antiquarian lore which might help them to place the frightful symbol, and through it track down the cult to its fountain-head.

Inspector Legrasse was scarcely prepared for the sensation which his offering created. One sight of the thing had been enough to throw the assembled men of science into a state of tense excitement, and they lost no time in crowding around him to gaze at the diminutive figure whose utter strangeness and air of genuinely abysmal antiquity hinted so potently at unopened and archaic vistas. No recognised school of sculpture had animated this terrible object, yet centuries and even thousands of years seemed recorded in its dim and greenish surface of unplaceable stone.

The figure, which was finally passed slowly from man to man for close and careful study, was between seven and eight inches in height, and of exquisitely artistic workmanship. It represented a monster of vaguely anthropoid outline, but with an octopus-like head whose face was a mass of feelers, a scaly, rubbery-looking body, prodigious claws on hind and fore feet, and long, narrow wings behind. This thing, which seemed instinct with a fearsome and unnatural malignancy, was of a somewhat bloated corpulence, and squatted evilly on a rectangular block or pedestal covered with undecipherable characters. The tips of the wings touched the back edge of the block, the seat occupied the centre, whilst the long, curved claws of the doubled-up, crouching hind legs gripped the front edge and extended a quarter of the way down toward the bottom of the pedestal. The cephalopod head was bent forward, so that the ends of the facial feelers brushed the backs of huge fore paws which clasped the croucher's elevated knees. The aspect of the whole was abnormally life-like, and the more subtly fearful because its source was so totally unknown. Its vast, awesome, and incalculable age was unmistakable; yet not one link did it shew with any known type of art belonging to civilisation's youth—or indeed to any other time. Totally separate and apart, its very material was a mystery; for the soapy, greenish-black stone with its golden or iridescent flecks and striations resembled nothing familiar to geology or mineralogy. The characters along the base were equally baffling; and no member present, despite a representation of half the world's expert learning in this field, could form the least notion of even their remotest linguistic kinship. They, like the subject and material, belonged to something horribly remote and distinct from mankind as we know it; something frightfully suggestive of old and unhallowed cycles of life in which our world and our conceptions have no part.

And yet, as the members severally shook their heads and confessed defeat at the Inspector's problem, there was one man in that gathering who suspected a touch of bizarre familiarity in the monstrous shape and writing, and who presently told with some diffidence of the odd trifle he knew. This person was the late William Channing Webb, Professor of Anthropology in Princeton University, and an explorer of no slight note. Professor Webb had been engaged, forty-eight years before, in a tour of Greenland and Iceland in search of some Runic inscriptions which he failed to unearth; and whilst high up on the West Greenland coast had encountered a singular tribe or cult of degenerate Esquimaux whose religion, a curious form of devil-worship, chilled him with its deliberate bloodthirstiness and repulsiveness. It was a faith of which other Esquimaux knew little, and which they mentioned only with shudders, saying that it had come down from horribly ancient aeons before ever the world was made. Besides nameless rites and human sacrifices there were certain queer hereditary rituals addressed to a supreme elder devil or *tornasuk*; and of this Professor Webb had taken a careful phonetic copy from an aged *angekok* or wizard-priest, expressing the sounds in Roman letters as best he knew how. But just now of prime significance was the fetish which this cult had cherished, and around which they danced when the aurora leaped high over the ice cliffs. It was, the professor stated, a very crude bas-relief of stone, comprising a hideous picture and some cryptic writing. And so far as he could tell, it was a rough parallel in all essential features of the bestial thing now lying before the meeting.

This data, received with suspense and astonishment by the assembled members, proved doubly exciting to Inspector Legrasse; and he began at once to ply his informant with questions. Having noted and copied an oral ritual among the swamp cult-worshippers his men had arrested, he besought the professor to remember as best he might the syllables taken down amongst the diabolist Esquimaux. There then followed an exhaustive comparison of details, and a moment of really awed silence when both detective and scientist agreed on the virtual identity of the phrase common to two hellish rituals so many worlds of distance apart. What, in substance, both the Esquimau wizards and the Louisiana swamp-priests had chanted to their kindred idols was something very like this—the word-divisions being guessed at from traditional breaks in the phrase as chanted aloud:

"*Ph'nglui mglw'nafh Cthulhu R'lyeh wgah'nagl fhtagn.*"

Legrasse had one point in advance of Professor Webb, for several among his mongrel prisoners had repeated to him what older celebrants had told them the words meant. This text, as given, ran something like this:

"*In his house at R'lyeh dead Cthulhu waits dreaming.*"

And now, in response to a general and urgent demand, Inspector Legrasse related as fully as possible his experience with the swamp worshippers; telling a story to which I could see my uncle attached profound significance. It savoured of the wildest dreams of myth-maker and theosophist, and disclosed an astonishing degree of cosmic imagination among such half-castes and pariahs as might be least expected to possess it.

On November 1st, 1907, there had come to the New Orleans police a frantic summons from the swamp and lagoon country to the south. The squatters there, mostly primitive but good-natured descendants of Lafitte's men, were in the grip of stark terror from an unknown thing which had stolen upon them in the night. It was voodoo, apparently, but voodoo of a more terrible sort than they had ever known; and some of their women and children had disappeared since the malevolent tom-tom had begun its incessant beating far within the black haunted woods where no dweller ventured. There were insane shouts and harrowing screams, soul-chilling chants and dancing devil-flames; and, the frightened messenger added, the people could stand it no more.

So a body of twenty police, filling two carriages and an automobile, had set out in the late afternoon with the shivering squatter as a guide. At the end of the passable road they alighted, and for miles splashed on in silence through the terrible cypress woods where day never came. Ugly roots and malignant hanging nooses of Spanish moss beset them, and now and then a pile of dank stones or fragment of a rotting wall intensified by its hint of morbid habitation a depression which every malformed tree and every fungous islet combined to create. At length the squatter settlement, a miserable huddle of huts, hove in sight; and hysterical dwellers ran out to cluster around the group of bobbing lanterns. The muffled beat of tom-toms was now faintly audible far, far ahead; and a curdling shriek came at infrequent intervals when the wind shifted. A reddish glare, too, seemed to filter through the pale undergrowth beyond endless avenues of forest night. Reluctant even to be left alone again, each one of the cowed squatters refused point-blank to advance another inch toward the scene of unholy worship, so Inspector Legrasse and his nineteen colleagues plunged on unguided into black arcades of horror that none of them had ever trod before.

The region now entered by the police was one of traditionally evil repute, substantially unknown and untraversed by white men. There were legends of a hidden lake unglimpsed by mortal sight, in which dwelt a huge, formless white polypous thing with luminous eyes; and squatters whispered that bat-winged devils flew up out of caverns in inner earth to worship it at midnight. They said it had been there before D'Iberville, before La Salle, before the Indians, and before even the wholesome beasts and birds of the woods. It was nightmare itself, and to see it was to die. But it made men dream, and so they knew enough to keep away. The present voodoo orgy was, indeed, on the merest fringe of this abhorred area, but that location was bad enough; hence perhaps the very place of the worship had terrified the squatters more than the shocking sounds and incidents.

Only poetry or madness could do justice to the noises heard by Legrasse's men as they ploughed on through the black morass toward the red glare and the muffled tom-toms. There are vocal qualities peculiar to men, and vocal qualities peculiar to beasts; and it is terrible to hear the one when the source should yield the other. Animal fury and orgiastic licence here whipped themselves to daemoniac heights by howls and squawking ecstasies that tore and reverberated through those nighted woods like pestilential tempests from the gulfs of hell. Now and then the less organised ululation would cease, and from what seemed a well-drilled chorus of hoarse voices would rise in sing-song chant that hideous phrase or ritual:

"*Ph'nglui mglw'nafh Cthulhu R'lyeh wgah'nagl fhtagn.*"

Then the men, having reached a spot where the trees were thinner, came suddenly in sight of the spectacle itself. Four of them reeled, one fainted, and two were shaken into a frantic cry which the mad cacophony of the orgy fortunately deadened. Legrasse dashed swamp water on the face of the fainting man, and all stood trembling and nearly hypnotised with horror.

In a natural glade of the swamp stood a grassy island of perhaps an acre's extent, clear of trees and tolerably dry. On this now leaped and twisted a more indescribable horde of human abnormality than any but a Sime or an Angarola could paint.

Void of clothing, this hybrid spawn were braying, bellowing, and writhing about a monstrous ring-shaped bonfire; in the centre of which, revealed by occasional rifts in the curtain of flame, stood a great granite monolith some eight feet in height; on top of which, incongruous with its diminutiveness, rested the noxious carven statuette. From a wide circle of ten scaffolds set up at regular intervals with the flame-girt monolith as a centre hung, head downward, the oddly marred bodies of the helpless squatters who had disappeared. It was inside this circle that the ring of worshippers jumped and roared, the general direction of the mass motion being from left to right in endless Bacchanal between the ring of bodies and the ring of fire.

It may have been only imagination and it may have been only echoes which induced one of the men, an excitable Spaniard, to fancy he heard antiphonal responses to the ritual from some far and unillumined spot deeper within the wood of ancient legendry and horror. This man, Joseph D. Galvez, I later met and questioned; and he proved distractingly imaginative. He indeed went so far as to hint of the faint beating of great wings, and of a glimpse of shining eyes and a mountainous white bulk beyond the remotest trees—but I suppose he had been hearing too much native superstition.

Actually, the horrified pause of the men was of comparatively brief duration. Duty came first; and although there must have been nearly a hundred mongrel celebrants in the throng, the police relied on their firearms and plunged determinedly into the nauseous rout. For five minutes the resultant din and chaos were beyond description. Wild blows were struck, shots were fired, and escapes were made; but in the end Legrasse was able to count some forty-seven sullen prisoners, whom he forced to dress in haste and fall into line between two rows of policemen. Five of the worshippers lay dead, and two severely wounded ones were carried away on improvised stretchers by their fellow-prisoners. The image on the monolith, of course, was carefully removed and carried back by Legrasse.

Examined at headquarters after a trip of intense strain and weariness, the prisoners all proved to be men of a very low, mixed-blooded, and mentally aberrant type. Most were seamen, and a sprinkling of negroes and mulattoes, largely West Indians or Brava Portuguese from the Cape Verde Islands, gave a colouring of voodooism to the heterogeneous cult. But before many questions were asked, it became manifest that something far deeper and older than negro fetichism was involved. Degraded and ignorant as they were, the creatures held with surprising consistency to the central idea of their loathsome faith.

They worshipped, so they said, the Great Old Ones who lived ages before there were any men, and who came to the young world out of the sky. Those Old Ones were gone now, inside the earth and under the sea; but their dead bodies had told their secrets in dreams to the first men, who formed a cult which had never died. This was that cult, and the prisoners said it had always existed and always would exist, hidden in distant wastes and dark places all over the world until the time when the great priest Cthulhu, from his dark house in the mighty city of R'lyeh under the waters, should rise and bring the earth again beneath his sway. Some day he would call, when the stars were ready, and the secret cult would always be waiting to liberate him.

Meanwhile no more must be told. There was a secret which even torture could not extract. Mankind was not absolutely alone among the conscious things of earth, for shapes came out of the dark to visit the faithful few. But these were not the Great Old Ones. No man had ever seen the Old Ones. The carven idol was great Cthulhu, but none might say whether or not the others were precisely like him. No one could read the old writing now, but things were told by word of mouth. The chanted ritual was not the secret—that was never spoken aloud, only whispered. The chant meant only this: "In his house at R'lyeh dead Cthulhu waits dreaming."

Only two of the prisoners were found sane enough to be hanged, and the rest were committed to various institutions. All denied a part in the ritual murders, and averred that the killing had been done by Black Winged Ones which had come to them from their immemorial meeting-place in the haunted wood. But of those mysterious allies no coherent account could ever be gained. What the police did extract, came mainly from an immensely aged mestizo named Castro, who claimed to have sailed to strange ports and talked with undying leaders of the cult in the mountains of China.

Old Castro remembered bits of hideous legend that paled the speculations of theosophists and made man and the world seem recent and transient indeed. There had been aeons when other Things ruled on the earth, and They had had great cities. Remains of Them, he said the deathless Chinamen had told him, were still to be found as Cyclopean stones on islands in the Pacific. They all died vast epochs of time before men came, but there were arts which could revive Them when the stars had come round again to the right positions in the cycle of eternity. They had, indeed, come themselves from the stars, and brought Their images with Them.

These Great Old Ones, Castro continued, were not composed altogether of flesh and blood. They had shape—for did not this star-fashioned image prove it?—but that shape was not made of matter. When the stars were right, They could plunge from world to world through the sky; but when the stars were wrong, They could not live. But although They no longer lived, They would never really die. They all lay in stone houses in Their great city of R'lyeh, preserved by the spells of mighty Cthulhu for a glorious resurrection when the stars and the earth might once more be ready for Them. But at that time some force from outside must serve to liberate Their bodies. The spells that preserved Them intact likewise prevented Them from making an initial move, and They could only lie awake in the dark and think whilst uncounted millions of years rolled by. They knew all that was occurring in the universe, but Their mode of speech was transmitted thought. Even now They talked in Their tombs. When, after infinities of chaos, the first men came, the Great Old Ones spoke to the sensitive among them by moulding their dreams; for only thus could Their language reach the fleshly minds of mammals.

Then, whispered Castro, those first men formed the cult around small idols which the Great Ones shewed them; idols brought in dim aeras from dark stars. That cult would never die till the stars came right again, and the secret priests would take great Cthulhu from His tomb to revive His subjects and resume His rule of earth. The time would be easy to know, for then mankind would have become as the Great Old Ones; free and wild and beyond good and evil, with laws and morals thrown aside and all men shouting and killing and revelling in joy. Then the liberated Old Ones would teach them new ways to shout and kill and revel and enjoy themselves, and all the earth would flame with a holocaust of ecstasy and freedom. Meanwhile the cult, by appropriate rites, must keep alive the memory of those ancient ways and shadow forth the prophecy of their return.

In the elder time chosen men had talked with the entombed Old Ones in dreams, but then something had happened. The great stone city R'lyeh, with its monoliths and sepulchres, had sunk beneath the waves; and the deep waters, full of the one primal mystery through which not even thought can pass, had cut off the spectral intercourse. But memory never died, and high-priests said that the city would rise again when the stars were right. Then came out of the earth the black spirits of earth, mouldy and shadowy, and full of dim rumours picked up in caverns beneath forgotten sea-bottoms. But of them old Castro dared not speak much. He cut himself off hurriedly, and no amount of persuasion or subtlety could elicit more in this direction. The *size* of the Old Ones, too, he curiously declined to mention. Of the cult, he said that he thought the centre lay amid the pathless deserts of Arabia, where Irem, the City of Pillars, dreams hidden and untouched. It was not allied to the European witch-cult, and was virtually unknown beyond its members. No book had ever really hinted of it, though the deathless Chinamen said that there were double meanings in the Necronomicon of the mad Arab Abdul Alhazred which the initiated might read as they chose, especially the much-discussed couplet:

"That is not dead which can eternal lie,
And with strange aeons even death may die."

Legrasse, deeply impressed and not a little bewildered, had inquired in vain concerning the historic affiliations of the cult. Castro, apparently, had told the truth when he said that it was wholly secret. The authorities at Tulane University could shed no light upon either cult or image, and now the detective had come to the highest authorities in the country and met with no more than the Greenland tale of Professor Webb.

The feverish interest aroused at the meeting by Legrasse's tale, corroborated as it was by the statuette, is echoed in the subsequent correspondence of those who attended; although scant mention occurs in the formal publications of the society. Caution is the first care of those accustomed to face occasional charlatanry and imposture. Legrasse for some time lent the image to Professor Webb, but at the latter's death it was returned to him and remains in his possession, where I viewed it not long ago. It is truly a terrible thing, and unmistakably akin to the dream-sculpture of young Wilcox.

That my uncle was excited by the tale of the sculptor I did not wonder, for what thoughts must arise upon hearing, after a knowledge of what Legrasse had learned of the cult, of a sensitive young man who had *dreamed* not only the figure and exact hieroglyphics of the swamp-found image and the Greenland devil tablet, but had come *in his dreams* upon at least three of the precise words of the formula uttered alike by Esquimau diabolists and mongrel Louisianans? Professor Angell's instant start on an investigation of the utmost thoroughness was eminently natural; though privately I suspected young Wilcox of having heard of the cult in some indirect way, and of having invented a series of dreams to heighten and continue the mystery at my uncle's expense. The dream-narratives and cuttings collected by the professor were, of course, strong corroboration; but the rationalism of my mind and the extravagance of the whole subject led me to adopt what I thought the most sensible conclusions. So, after thoroughly studying the manuscript again and correlating the theosophical and anthropological notes with the cult narrative of Legrasse, I made a trip to Providence to see the sculptor and give him the rebuke I thought proper for so boldly imposing upon a learned and aged man.

Wilcox still lived alone in the Fleur-de-Lys Building in Thomas Street, a hideous Victorian imitation of seventeenth-century Breton architecture which flaunts its stuccoed front amidst the lovely colonial houses on the ancient hill, and under the very shadow of the finest Georgian steeple in America. I found him at work in his rooms, and at once conceded from the specimens scattered about that his genius is indeed profound and authentic. He will, I believe, some time be heard from as one of the great decadents; for he has crystallised in clay and will one day mirror in marble those nightmares and phantasies which Arthur Machen evokes in prose, and Clark Ashton Smith makes visible in verse and in painting.

Dark, frail, and somewhat unkempt in aspect, he turned languidly at my knock and asked me my business without rising. When I told him who I was, he displayed some interest; for my uncle had excited his curiosity in probing his strange dreams, yet had never explained the reason for the study. I did not enlarge his knowledge in this regard, but sought with some subtlety to draw him out. In a short time I became convinced of his absolute sincerity, for he spoke of the dreams in a manner none could mistake. They and their subconscious residuum had influenced his art profoundly, and he shewed me a morbid statue whose contours almost made me shake with the potency of its black suggestion. He could not recall having seen the original of this thing except in his own dream bas-relief, but the outlines had formed themselves insensibly under his hands. It was, no doubt, the giant shape he had raved of in delirium. That he really knew nothing of the hidden cult, save from what my uncle's relentless catechism had let fall, he soon made clear; and again I strove to think of some way in which he could possibly have received the weird impressions.

He talked of his dreams in a strangely poetic fashion; making me see with terrible vividness the damp Cyclopean city of slimy green stone—whose *geometry*, he oddly said, was *all wrong*—and hear with frightened expectancy the ceaseless, half-mental calling from underground: "*Cthulhu fhtagn,*" "*Cthulhu fhtagn.*" These words had formed part of that dread ritual which told of dead Cthulhu's dream-vigil in his stone vault at R'lyeh, and I felt deeply moved despite my rational beliefs. Wilcox, I was sure, had heard of the cult in some casual way, and had soon forgotten it amidst the mass of his equally weird reading and imagining. Later, by virtue of its sheer impressiveness, it had found subconscious expression in dreams, in the bas-relief, and in the terrible statue I now beheld; so that his imposture upon my uncle had been a very innocent one. The youth was of a type, at once slightly affected and slightly ill-mannered, which I could never like; but I was willing enough now to admit both his genius and his honesty. I took leave of him amicably, and wish him all the success his talent promises.

The matter of the cult still remained to fascinate me, and at times I had visions of personal fame from researches into its origin and connexions. I visited New Orleans, talked with Legrasse and others of that old-time raiding-party, saw the frightful image, and even questioned such of the mongrel prisoners as still survived. Old Castro, unfortunately, had been dead for some years. What I now heard so graphically at first-hand, though it was really no more than a detailed confirmation of what my uncle had written, excited me afresh; for I felt sure that I was on the track of a very real, very secret, and very ancient religion whose discovery would make me an anthropologist of note. My attitude was still one of absolute materialism, *as I wish it still were*, and I discounted with almost inexplicable perversity the coincidence of the dream notes and odd cuttings collected by Professor Angell.

One thing I began to suspect, and which I now fear I know, is that my uncle's death was far from natural. He fell on a narrow hill street leading up from an ancient waterfront swarming with foreign mongrels, after a careless push from a negro sailor. I did not forget the mixed blood and marine pursuits of the cult-members in Louisiana, and would not be surprised to learn of secret methods and poison needles as ruthless and as anciently known as the cryptic rites and beliefs. Legrasse and his men, it is true, have been let alone; but in Norway a certain seaman who saw things is dead. Might not the deeper inquiries of my uncle after encountering the sculptor's data have come to sinister ears? I think Professor Angell died because he knew too much, or because he was likely to learn too much. Whether I shall go as he did remains to be seen, for I have learned much now.

III. The Madness from the Sea

If heaven ever wishes to grant me a boon, it will be a total effacing of the results of a mere chance which fixed my eye on a certain stray piece of shelf-paper. It was nothing on which I would naturally have stumbled in the course of my daily round, for it was an old number of an Australian journal, the *Sydney Bulletin* for April 18, 1925. It had escaped even the cutting bureau which had at the time of its issuance been avidly collecting material for my uncle's research.

I had largely given over my inquiries into what Professor Angell called the "Cthulhu Cult," and was visiting a learned friend in Paterson, New Jersey; the curator of a local museum and a mineralogist of note. Examining one day the reserve specimens roughly set on the storage shelves in a rear room of the museum, my eye was caught by an odd picture in one of the old papers spread beneath the stones. It was the *Sydney Bulletin* I have mentioned, for my friend has wide affiliations in all conceivable foreign parts; and the picture was a half-tone cut of a hideous stone image almost identical with that which Legrasse had found in the swamp.

Eagerly clearing the sheet of its precious contents, I scanned the item in detail; and was disappointed to find it of only moderate length. What it suggested, however, was of portentous significance to my flagging quest; and I carefully tore it out for immediate action. It read as follows:

MYSTERY DERELICT FOUND AT SEA
Vigilant Arrives With Helpless Armed New Zealand Yacht in Tow.
One Survivor and Dead Man Found Aboard. Tale of Desperate Battle and Deaths at Sea.
Rescued Seaman Refuses Particulars of

STRANGE EXPERIENCE.
ODD IDOL FOUND IN HIS POSSESSION.
INQUIRY TO FOLLOW.

THE MORRISON CO.'s freighter *Vigilant,* bound from Valparaiso, arrived this morning at its wharf in Darling Harbour, having in tow the battled and disabled but heavily armed steam yacht *Alert* of Dunedin, N. Z., which was sighted April 12th in S. Latitude 34° 21', W. Longitude 152° 17' with one living and one dead man aboard.

The *Vigilant* left Valparaiso March 25th, and on April 2nd was driven considerably south of her course by exceptionally heavy storms and monster waves. On April 12th the derelict was sighted; and though apparently deserted, was found upon boarding to contain one survivor in a half-delirious condition and one man who had evidently been dead for more than a week. The living man was clutching a horrible stone idol of unknown origin, about a foot in height, regarding whose nature authorities at Sydney University, the Royal Society, and the Museum in College Street all profess complete bafflement, and which the survivor says he found in the cabin of the yacht, in a small carved shrine of common pattern.

This man, after recovering his senses, told an exceedingly strange story of piracy and slaughter. He is Gustaf Johansen, a Norwegian of some intelligence, and had been second mate of the two-masted schooner *Emma* of Auckland, which sailed for Callao February 20th with a complement of eleven men. The

Emma, he says, was delayed and thrown widely south of her course by the great storm of March 1st, and on March 22nd, in S. Latitude 49° 51', W. Longitude 128° 34", encountered the *Alert*, manned by a queer and evil-looking crew of Kanakas and half-castes. Being ordered peremptorily to turn back, Capt. Collins refused; whereupon the strange crew began to fire savagely and without warning upon the schooner with a peculiarly heavy battery of brass cannon forming part of the yacht's equipment. The Emma's men shewed fight, says the survivor, and though the schooner began to sink from shots beneath the waterline they managed to heave alongside their enemy and board her, grappling with the savage crew on the yacht's deck, and being forced to kill them all, the number being slightly superior, because of their particularly abhorrent and desperate though rather clumsy mode of fighting.

Three of the Emma's men, including Capt. Collins and First Mate Green, were killed; and the remaining eight under Second Mate Johansen proceeded to navigate the captured yacht, going ahead in their original direction to see if any reason for their ordering back had existed. The next day, it appears, they raised and landed on a small island, although none is known to exist in that part of the ocean; and six of the men somehow died ashore, though Johansen is queerly reticent about this part of his story, and speaks only of their falling into a rock chasm. Later, it seems, he and one companion boarded the yacht and tried to manage her, but were beaten about by

> the storm of April 2nd. From that time till his rescue on the 12th the man remembers little, and he does not even recall when William Briden, his companion, died. Briden's death reveals no apparent cause, and was probably due to excitement or exposure. Cable advices from Dunedin report that the *Alert* was well known there as an island trader, and bore an evil reputation along the waterfront. It was owned by a curious group of half-castes whose frequent meetings and night trips to the woods attracted no little curiosity; and it had set sail in great haste just after the storm and earth tremors of March 1st. Our Auckland correspondent gives the *Emma* and her crew an excellent reputation, and Johansen is described as a sober and worthy man. The admiralty will institute an inquiry on the whole matter beginning tomorrow, at which every effort will be made to induce Johansen to speak more freely than he has done hitherto.

This was all, together with the picture of the hellish image; but what a train of ideas it started in my mind! Here were new treasuries of data on the Cthulhu Cult, and evidence that it had strange interests at sea as well as on land. What motive prompted the hybrid crew to order back the *Emma* as they sailed about with their hideous idol? What was the unknown island on which six of the *Emma's* crew had died, and about which the mate Johansen was so secretive? What had the vice-admiralty's investigation brought out, and what was known of the noxious cult in Dunedin? And most marvellous of all, what deep and more than natural linkage of dates was this which gave a malign and now undeniable significance to the various turns of events so carefully noted by my uncle?

March 1st—our February 28th according to the International Date Line—the earthquake and storm had come. From Dunedin the *Alert* and her noisome crew had darted eagerly forth as if imperiously summoned, and on the other side of the earth poets and artists had begun to dream of a strange, dank Cyclopean city whilst a young sculptor had moulded in his sleep the form of the dreaded Cthulhu. March 23rd the crew of the *Emma* landed on an unknown island and left six men dead; and on that date the dreams of sensitive men assumed a heightened vividness and darkened with dread of a giant monster's malign pursuit, whilst an architect had gone mad and a sculptor had lapsed suddenly into delirium! And what of this storm of April 2nd—the date on which all dreams of the dank city ceased, and Wilcox emerged unharmed from the bondage of strange fever? What of all this—and of those hints of old Castro about the sunken, star-born Old Ones and their coming reign; their faithful cult *and their mastery of dreams*? Was I tottering on the brink of cosmic horrors beyond man's power to bear? If so, they must be horrors of the mind alone, for in some way the second of April had put a stop to whatever monstrous menace had begun its siege of mankind's soul.

That evening, after a day of hurried cabling and arranging, I bade my host adieu and took a train for San Francisco. In less than a month I was in Dunedin; where, however, I found that little was known of the strange cult-members who had lingered in the old sea-taverns. Waterfront scum was far too common for special mention; though there was vague talk about one inland trip these mongrels had made, during which faint drumming and red flame were noted on the distant hills. In

Auckland I learned that Johansen had returned *with yellow hair turned white* after a perfunctory and inconclusive questioning at Sydney, and had thereafter sold his cottage in West Street and sailed with his wife to his old home in Oslo. Of his stirring experience he would tell his friends no more than he had told the admiralty officials, and all they could do was to give me his Oslo address.

After that I went to Sydney and talked profitlessly with seamen and members of the vice-admiralty court. I saw the *Alert*, now sold and in commercial use, at Circular Quay in Sydney Cove, but gained nothing from its non-committal bulk. The crouching image with its cuttlefish head, dragon body, scaly wings, and hieroglyphed pedestal, was preserved in the Museum at Hyde Park; and I studied it long and well, finding it a thing of balefully exquisite workmanship, and with the same utter mystery, terrible antiquity, and unearthly strangeness of material which I had noted in Legrasse's smaller specimen. Geologists, the curator told me, had found it a monstrous puzzle; for they vowed that the world held no rock like it. Then I thought with a shudder of what old Castro had told Legrasse about the primal Great Ones: "They had come from the stars, and had brought Their images with Them."

Shaken with such a mental revolution as I had never before known, I now resolved to visit Mate Johansen in Oslo. Sailing for London, I reëmbarked at once for the Norwegian capital; and one autumn day landed at the trim wharves in the shadow of the Egeberg. Johansen's address, I discovered, lay in the Old Town of King Harold Haardrada, which kept alive the name of Oslo during all the centuries that the greater city masqueraded as "Christiana." I made the brief trip by taxicab, and knocked with palpitant heart at the door of a neat and ancient building with plastered front. A sad-faced woman in black answered my summons, and I was stung with disappointment when she told me in halting English that Gustaf Johansen was no more.

He had not survived his return, said his wife, for the doings at sea in 1925 had broken him. He had told her no more than he had told the public, but had left a long manuscript—of "technical matters" as he said—written in English, evidently in order to safeguard her from the peril of casual perusal. During a walk through a narrow lane near the Gothenburg dock, a bundle of papers falling from an attic window had knocked him down. Two Lascar sailors at once helped him to his feet, but before the ambulance could reach him he was dead. Physicians found no adequate cause for the end, and laid it to heart trouble and a weakened constitution.

I now felt gnawing at my vitals that dark terror which will never leave me till I, too, am at rest; "accidentally" or otherwise. Persuading the widow that my connexion with her husband's "technical matters" was sufficient to entitle me to his manuscript, I bore the document away and began to read it on the London boat. It was a simple, rambling thing—a naive sailor's effort at a post-facto diary—and strove to recall day by day that last awful voyage. I cannot attempt to transcribe it verbatim in all its cloudiness and redundance, but I will tell its gist enough to shew why the sound of the water against the vessel's sides became so unendurable to me that I stopped my ears with cotton.

Johansen, thank God, did not know quite all, even though he saw the city and the Thing, but I shall never sleep calmly again when I think of the horrors that lurk ceaselessly behind life in time and in space, and of those unhallowed blasphemies from elder stars which dream beneath the sea, known and favoured by a nightmare cult ready and eager to loose them on the world whenever another earthquake shall heave their monstrous stone city again to the sun and air.

Johansen's voyage had begun just as he told it to the vice-admiralty. The *Emma*, in ballast, had cleared Auckland on February 20th, and had felt the full force of that earthquake-born tempest which must have heaved up from the sea-bottom the horrors that filled men's dreams. Once more under control, the ship was making good progress when held up by the *Alert* on March 22nd, and I could feel the mate's regret as he wrote of her bombardment and sinking. Of the swarthy cult-fiends on the *Alert* he speaks with significant horror. There was some peculiarly abominable quality about them which made their destruction seem almost a duty, and Johansen shews ingenuous wonder at the charge of ruthlessness brought against his party during the proceedings of the court of inquiry. Then, driven ahead by curiosity in their captured yacht under Johansen's command, the men sight a great stone pillar sticking out of the sea, and in S. Latitude 47° 9', W. Longitude 126° 43' come upon a coast-line of mingled mud, ooze, and weedy Cyclopean masonry which can be nothing less than the tangible substance of earth's supreme terror—the nightmare corpse-city of R'lyeh, that was built in measureless aeons behind history by the vast, loathsome shapes that seeped down from the dark stars. There lay great Cthulhu and his hordes, hidden in green slimy vaults and sending out at last, after cycles incalculable, the thoughts that spread fear to the dreams of the sensitive and called imperiously to the faithful to come on a pilgrimage of liberation and restoration. All this Johansen did not suspect, but God knows he soon saw enough!

I suppose that only a single mountain-top, the hideous monolith-crowned citadel whereon great Cthulhu was buried, actually emerged from the waters. When I think of the *extent* of all that may be brooding down there I almost wish to kill myself forthwith. Johansen and his men were awed by the cosmic majesty of this dripping Babylon of elder daemons, and must have guessed without guidance that it was nothing of this or of any sane planet. Awe at the unbelievable size of the greenish stone blocks, at the dizzying height of the great carven monolith, and at the stupefying identity of the colossal statues and bas-reliefs with the queer image found in the shrine on the *Alert*, is poignantly visible in every line of the mate's frightened description.

Without knowing what futurism is like, Johansen achieved something very close to it when he spoke of the city; for instead of describing any definite structure or building, he dwells only on broad impressions of vast angles and stone surfaces—surfaces too great to belong to any thing right or proper for this earth, and impious with horrible images and hieroglyphs. I mention his talk about angles because it suggests something Wilcox had told me of his awful dreams. He had said that the geometry of the dream-place he saw was abnormal, non-Euclidean, and loathsomely redolent of spheres and dimensions apart from ours. Now an unlettered seaman felt the same thing whilst gazing at the terrible reality.

Johansen and his men landed at a sloping mud-bank on this monstrous Acropolis, and clambered slipperily up over titan oozy blocks which could have been no mortal staircase. The very sun of heaven seemed distorted when viewed through the polarising miasma welling out from this sea-soaked perversion, and twisted menace and suspense lurked leeringly in those crazily elusive angles of carven rock where a second glance shewed concavity after the first shewed convexity.

Something very like fright had come over all the explorers before anything more definite than rock and ooze and weed was seen. Each would have fled had he not feared the scorn of the others, and it was only half-heartedly that they searched—vainly, as it proved—for some portable souvenir to bear away.

It was Rodriguez the Portuguese who climbed up the foot of the monolith and shouted of what he had found. The rest followed him, and looked curiously at the immense carved door with the now familiar squid-dragon bas-relief. It was, Johansen said, like a great barn-door; and they all felt that it was a door because of the ornate lintel, threshold, and jambs around it, though they could not decide whether it lay flat like a trap-door or slantwise like an outside cellar-door. As Wilcox would have said, the geometry of the place was all wrong. One could not be sure that the sea and the ground were horizontal, hence the relative position of everything else seemed phantasmally variable.

Briden pushed at the stone in several places without result. Then Donovan felt over it delicately around the edge, pressing each point separately as he went. He climbed interminably along the grotesque stone moulding—that is, one would call it climbing if the thing was not after all horizontal—and the men wondered how any door in the universe could be so vast. Then, very softly and slowly, the acre-great panel began to give inward at the top; and they saw that it was balanced. Donovan slid or somehow propelled himself down or along the jamb and rejoined his fellows, and everyone watched the queer recession of the monstrously carven portal. In this phantasy of prismatic distortion it moved anomalously in a diagonal way, so that all the rules of matter and perspective seemed upset.

The aperture was black with a darkness almost material. That tenebrousness was indeed a *positive quality*; for it obscured such parts of the inner walls as ought to have been revealed, and actually burst forth like smoke from its aeon-long imprisonment, visibly darkening the sun as it slunk away into the shrunken and gibbous sky on flapping membraneous wings. The odour arising from the newly opened depths was intolerable, and at length the quick-eared Hawkins thought he heard a nasty, slopping sound down there. Everyone listened, and everyone was listening still when It lumbered slobberingly into sight and gropingly squeezed Its gelatinous green immensity through the black doorway into the tainted outside air of that poison city of madness.

Poor Johansen's handwriting almost gave out when he wrote of this. Of the six men who never reached the ship, he thinks two perished of pure fright in that accursed instant. The Thing cannot be described—there is no language for such abysms of shrieking and immemorial lunacy, such eldritch contradictions of all matter, force, and cosmic order. A mountain walked or stumbled. God! What wonder that across the earth a great architect went mad, and poor Wilcox raved with fever in that telepathic instant? The Thing of the idols, the green, sticky spawn of the stars, had awaked to claim his own. The stars were right again, and what an age-old cult had failed to do by design, a band of innocent sailors had done by accident. After vigintillions of years great Cthulhu was loose again, and ravening for delight.

Three men were swept up by the flabby claws before anybody turned. God rest them, if there be any rest in the universe.

They were Donovan, Guerrera, and Ångstrom. Parker slipped as the other three were plunging frenziedly over endless vistas of green-crusted rock to the boat, and Johansen swears he was swallowed up by an angle of masonry which shouldn't have been there; an angle which was acute, but behaved as if it were obtuse. So only Briden and Johansen reached the boat, and pulled desperately for the *Alert* as the mountainous monstrosity flopped down the slimy stones and hesitated floundering at the edge of the water.

Steam had not been suffered to go down entirely, despite the departure of all hands for the shore; and it was the work of only a few moments of feverish rushing up and down between wheel and engines to get the *Alert* under way. Slowly, amidst the distorted horrors of that indescribable scene, she began to churn the lethal waters; whilst on the masonry of that charnel shore that was not of earth the titan Thing from the stars slavered and gibbered like Polypheme cursing the fleeing ship of Odysseus. Then, bolder than the storied Cyclops, great Cthulhu slid greasily into the water and began to pursue with vast wave-raising strokes of cosmic potency. Briden looked back and went mad, laughing shrilly as he kept on laughing at intervals till death found him one night in the cabin whilst Johansen was wandering deliriously.

But Johansen had not given out yet. Knowing that the Thing could surely overtake the *Alert* until steam was fully up, he resolved on a desperate chance; and, setting the engine for full speed, ran lightning-like on deck and reversed the wheel. There was a mighty eddying and foaming in the noisome brine, and as the steam mounted higher and higher the brave Norwegian drove his vessel head on against the pursuing jelly which rose above the unclean froth like the stern of a daemon galleon. The awful squid-head with writhing feelers came nearly up to the bowsprit of the sturdy yacht, but Johansen drove on relentlessly. There was a bursting as of an exploding bladder, a slushy nastiness as of a cloven sunfish, a stench as of a thousand opened graves, and a sound that the chronicler would not put on paper. For an instant the ship was befouled by an acrid and blinding green cloud, and then there was only a venomous seething astern; where—God in heaven!—the scattered plasticity of that nameless sky-spawn was nebulously *recombining* in its hateful original form, whilst its distance widened every second as the *Alert* gained impetus from its mounting steam.

That was all. After that Johansen only brooded over the idol in the cabin and attended to a few matters of food for himself and the laughing maniac by his side. He did not try to navigate after the first bold flight, for the reaction had taken something out of his soul. Then came the storm of April 2nd, and a gathering of the clouds about his consciousness. There is a sense of spectral whirling through liquid gulfs of infinity, of dizzying rides through reeling universes on a comet's tail, and of hysterical plunges from the pit to the moon and from the moon back again to the pit, all livened by a cachinnating chorus of the distorted, hilarious elder gods and the green, bat-winged mocking imps of Tartarus.

Out of that dream came rescue—the *Vigilant,* the vice-admiralty court, the streets of Dunedin, and the long voyage back home to the old house by the Egeberg. He could not tell—they would think him mad. He would write of what he knew before death came, but his wife must not guess. Death would be a boon if only it could blot out the memories.

That was the document I read, and now I have placed it in the tin box beside the bas-relief and the papers of Professor

Angell. With it shall go this record of mine—this test of my own sanity, wherein is pieced together that which I hope may never be pieced together again. I have looked upon all that the universe has to hold of horror, and even the skies of spring and the flowers of summer must ever afterward be poison to me. But I do not think my life will be long. As my uncle went, as poor Johansen went, so I shall go. I know too much, and the cult still lives.

Cthulhu still lives, too, I suppose, again in that chasm of stone which has shielded him since the sun was young. His accursed city is sunken once more, for the *Vigilant* sailed over the spot after the April storm; but his ministers on earth still bellow and prance and slay around idol-capped monoliths in lonely places. He must have been trapped by the sinking whilst within his black abyss, or else the world would by now be screaming with fright and frenzy. Who knows the end? What has risen may sink, and what has sunk may rise. Loathsomeness waits and dreams in the deep, and decay spreads over the tottering cities of men. A time will come—but I must not and cannot think! Let me pray that, if I do not survive this manuscript, my executors may put caution before audacity and see that it meets no other eye.

MORE FROM PASSAGE CLASSICS

Mine Were of Trouble by Peter Kemp

No Colours or Crest by Peter Kemp

Alms for Oblivion by Peter Kemp

Ten Years at War by Peter Kemp

The Influence of Sea Power upon History by Alfred Thayer Mahan

Storm of Steel by Ernst Jünger

Always With Honor by Pyotr Wrangel

One Man In His Time by Serge Obolensky

The Masterworks of Joseph Conrad: Volumes I, II, and III

My Hunt After the Captain by Oliver Wendell Holmes, Sr.

FORTHCOMING

The Masterworks of H.P. Lovecraft: Volume II

The Masterworks of Robert E. Howard:

Volume I: *Kings of Unchristian Lands*

Volume II: *American Violence*

Volume III: *Grace and Treachery*

Available for purchase at www.passage.press